Housing Elephants
Copyright © 2015 Eleanor Lloyd-Jones

Front cover image and internal graphics:
Shower Of Schmidt Designs
https://www.facebook.com/groups/shower.of.schmidt.d
esigns/

Formatting and internal graphics:
Irish Ink Publishing
http://www.facebook.com/IrishInkPublishing

Editor:
Heather's Red Pen Editing Services
https://www.facebook.com/HeathersRedPen

HOUSING
elephants

FOLLOW YOUR HEART DUET
BOOK ONE

by
Eleanor LLOYD-JONES

A NOTE TO
the reader

Housing Elephants is the debut novel written by Eleanor Lloyd-Jones.
For more information on the author's work, please follow this link:

www.linktr.ee/eleanorlloydjones

HOUSING ELEPHANTS
playlist

Music is such a huge part of my life, so it will come as no surprise that it played an equally huge part in the writing of this book. From the 220-song playlist that I created during the long months of writing, I have picked out some of the more important tracks that meant so much to me during the writing of this story.
For anyone who wishes to hear the full playlist, please follow this Spotify link:

bit.ly/HousingElephants-Playlist

DEDICATED
to...

Granny Smith

We wish you were here to delight in all that we have accomplished.

"Their eyes met, locked and never left. He didn't believe in love at first sight, no. He was too cynical for that. But something in those eyes had struck a deep chord in him. He was bewitched. He willed himself to look away, but nothing could make him do so. This woman had raged a storm in him, just with those eyes…"

~ *Smriti Brar*

prologue

Ivory – Adam French

"DADDY! DADDY! I made you a picture. Look, Daddy."

A torrent of brown hair and tiny limbs tumbled down the hallway as Dave Swallow walked in through the door to his five-bedroomed home. His eyes shone with love and pride as his four-year-old daughter, Eve, flew towards him, wrapping her arms around his neck and smothering him with kisses.

"Hey, princess. Did you miss me?"

"Yes! I made you a picture. Look."

Dave took hold of the crumpled sheet of paper that was being shoved in his face, smoothing it out and absorbing the multi-coloured scene in front of him.

"That's you." Eve impatiently pointed a chubby finger at a suited and booted figure. "And this is me. I've got pink hair."

"So you have. And who is this?" He pointed to another figure in a green dress standing next to the drawing of him.

"Mummy, of course, silly Daddy."

Dave laughed and kissed the side of Eve's cheek. "And what about this person here? Who is this?" Another male figure stood in front of the red brick house.

"That's Uncle Peter. He's wearing his hat that smells funny."

He lingered on the drawing of his older brother for a second or two more before he gently lowered his daughter to the floor, taking hold of her hand and leading her further into the house. "Where's Mummy?"

Eve pulled free and raced ahead of him. "Mummy, Mummy. Daddy is here. Come see." She burst into the large, open-plan kitchen and settled herself back at the table with her crayons, her attention span waning as her busy little mind focused on the next thing.

Dave followed Eve to where his wife stood at the hob, stirring some delicious smelling something-or-other. He circled his arms around her waist from behind and nuzzled into her neck, breathing in the familiar scent of her that still drove him wild after ten years together. "Mmm. Smells good."

Gillian smiled down at the pan. "It will be chicken and bacon hot pot when it's finished. If it gets finished. You need to let me get on with it." She patted his hand and turned her head to kiss the side of his face.

"Yeah, I guess the hotpot smells good, too." He nibbled the skin on Gillian's neck, causing her to swat at his head.

"Let me cook tea. Go and play with Eve."

Her husband retreated woefully, his head bowed in mock rejection. He loosened his tie and walked towards the living area, scooping his daughter up into his arms as he passed the table. Lifting her T-shirt over her face, he blew raspberries on her bare tummy, causing Eve to erupt into fits of screams and giggles.

"No, No. Stop, Daddy. Stop!"

The pair fell onto the sofa, laughing and breathless as Eve attempted to get her own back, her little red mouth blowing as hard as it could onto her father's shirt.

"Okay, okay, you win." Dave pulled her up his body, smoothing her hair down her back. He leaned to the floor and picked up the television remote, flicking on the screen, as they lay snuggled up, Eve flat to his chest. "Who's up for some Rosie and Jim?"

Eve's thumb snuck into her mouth before she nodded, blinking slowly as she listened to his heartbeat and focused on the comforting smell of him.

"You tired, poppet?"

She shook her head and zoned in on the opening credits of her favourite show.

"Don't let her fall asleep, please," Gillian shouted from across the room, the clatter of plates and cutlery indicating that dinner was nearly ready.

***

TUCKING HIS PRIDE and joy into bed after her third story, Dave thanked Jesus, Mary and the baby orphans the same way he did every night. He kissed her cheek and whispered I love yous in her ear as Eve counted them silently until she fell asleep.

Moving stealthily out of her room, he left her night light on and her door open 'just enough'. he smiled to himself again. He was the luckiest son-of-a-bitch on the planet. He'd fallen in love with and married his best friend, and now they had the most perfect little girl. She had her father's deep grey eyes and her mother's thick brown hair, was kind and loving and always full of wonder and excitement. A sociable little thing, Eve would chatter away to anyone, and they couldn't be more proud.

It had been touch and go during Gillian's pregnancy, and there was a scary moment during labour when Dave thought he might lose them both. Thanking whoever was listening had become part of his daily routine, just to be sure they knew exactly how grateful he was for their survival and to be sure they continued to watch over both of them.

Shrugging away the painful memories, he walked into the kitchen and helped Gillian to clear the dishes from dinner. "Wine?"

"Mmm, yes please. There's a Merlot in the pantry."

He tapped his wife's bottom on his way past. As he reached for the bottle, the doorbell rang and he checked his watch, frowning as he registered the time. It would be either a neighbour or his brother—who had taken to calling in more often over the last couple of months—and he would bet on the latter.

"I'll get it." Gillian shuffled in her slippers and opened the front door. "Hi, Pete. Come in." She stepped to the side. "Honey, it's your brother."

Dave rolled his eyes and backed out of the pantry, sighing. Friday nights were always set aside for Gillian and him. Being interrupted was irritating, particularly as it was Pete who was doing the interrupting.

"Hi, bro." Pete walked into the kitchen and slapped him on the back, a huge grin across his face. "Was just passing, so thought I'd pop in. You okay?"

"Yeah good. Thanks. We were just going to settle down for a night in with a bottle of wine, though. It's Friday,

18

yeah?"

"Oh, I won't spoil your evening. Don't you worry. Just thought it would be rude to not call and say hi since I was in the vicinity." He walked towards the fridge, helping himself to a cold beer before twisting the lid off and flicking it into the bin. Sucking on the neck, he winked across the kitchen at Gillian, who stood, her gaze shifting between the two brothers.

"Make yourself at home, why don't you?" Dave mumbled as he moved to collect two wine glasses before heading into the lounge area and slumping onto the couch.

"He always was a grumpy bastard, eh, chick?" Pete threw another wink at Gillian and walked with a swagger to join his little brother. She closed her eyes and shook her head, an exasperated smirk forming on her lips. She'd grown up with the pair of them and knew Pete almost as well as she knew Dave. There wasn't much love lost between the two men. They'd always been at loggerheads with one another, but she had a soft spot for Pete and was always a little easier on him than her husband chose to be.

The three sat together in the living area, Pete commanding their attention and Dave seething on the inside at his brother's inconsiderate behavior. After almost an hour, and his third beer, and after regaling them with story after story, Pete leaned forwards and pushed himself to his feet, stretching his arms above his head. "Right, I guess I will leave you two love birds to your romantic evening then. I'll just nip to the loo." He picked his beanie hat up from the arm of the chair, shoving it on his head, and disappeared through the door to the stairs.

Dave threw his head back against the sofa, huffing out. "Thank fuck for that."

"Give him a break, honey. He's your brother."

"He's my pain in the arse is what he is."

She smiled fondly and leaned into her husband's shoulder.

"Shall we stick a DVD on or see what's on *Sky*?"

"Let's treat ourselves, shall we?" Gillian looked up at him, her nose scrunched up cheekily.

Dave took his arm from around his wife's shoulders and leaned forward, flicking to the movie channel and bringing up the list.

The usual creak of the second-to-last stair indicated Pete's return, and Gillian twisted her head around to smile at him as he walked through the door, booming a loud 'goodbye'.

"Jesus, Peter. Eve's asleep," Dave growled at his brother. He always seemed to be in the wrong place at the wrong time, always the clown. When they were children, he had spoiled family outings because of his impulsive behavior—his uncanny ability to find trouble wherever he went. Dave had begun to see from a very early age that the only explanation for his behaviour was that Pete was just a twat. He was obviously born a twat and was always going to grow up into an adult twat. He wasn't as academically inclined as his younger brother, and he pissed his school years away with twat-ish behaviour. Dave had tried time after time to sit Pete down and talk to him about pulling himself together or getting some qualifications and finding a job he loved. Instead, his brother would laugh it off, cuff him round the head and tell him to stop worrying about him. He preferred to spend as little time as possible thinking about work. Manual labour in any form meant he could work with his shirt off in the summer, often clock off early in the winter due to dark nights and could spend as much or as little of his free time—and his wages—in the pub as he chose. A bad case of blinkered living meant that Pete walked around doing anything and everything to please himself.

"I'll see you out," Gillian offered, collecting Pete's empties as she walked past the coffee table.

"Good to see you, bro. Cheers for the beers." Pete held his hand out over the back of the sofa for Dave to high-five, but the reciprocation was less than half-hearted.

"Yep." Dave didn't even look at him, his concentration remaining firmly on the television.

Pete followed Gillian to the front door and pecked her cheek as she opened it for him. "Thanks, love. See you next time. Maybe you'll have successfully removed the stick from his arse by then, eh?"

Gillian rolled her eyes and moved to close the door. "Night, Pete. Drive safely."

She returned to her position curled up next to her husband and trained her eyes on the television screen.

"Three beers and then driving." Dave shook his head and huffed out of his nose. He scrolled down the list of movies too quickly for her to read them, his mind elsewhere. "How long was he up there for?"

"Whoah. Slow down. I can't read them. Up where?"

"Upstairs. In the toilet."

"God, I don't know. I didn't time him. Ten minutes?"

"I'm off to make sure he cleaned the toilet bowl then." Gillian batted his arm. "Eww!"

CHAPTER
one

Run - Rondé
fourteen years later...

THE WORDS *SUMMER* and *ball* had filled Eve with a skin-crawling dread for the past few weeks. The prospect of spending all evening with a whole host of people she didn't know was all she'd been able to think about. Buying a ticket had been an ordeal in itself—one she had been forced into—but the day had finally arrived when she'd agreed to step out of her bubble of oils and pastels to find a suitable outfit.

Spending the majority of her time in paint-stained, oversized shirts, she was not in the least bit interested in buying a dress. She'd insisted that if she were to be dragged into town, they would go midweek and early morning to avoid any crowds. Eve's inability to grapple with social situations meant that shopping was a huge deal and was usually avoided at all costs. Online delivery was an absolute godsend, and it meant that quite often, other than dashing across campus to the art rooms or visiting the botanical gardens, she never really needed to leave the house.

Recluse was the technical term, she supposed, but it wasn't quite that simple.

She was afraid.

She was mostly afraid of herself and how she might act or react around others.

What if she made herself look stupid? What if she said the wrong thing or didn't understand what was being asked of her and stumbled over her words? What if people didn't think she looked smart enough, or clean enough, or pretty enough? Smart, clean or pretty enough for what, she wasn't sure, but avoiding other people was her best shot at just being able to live a normal life.

She had few recollections of being younger than about eight years old, but running away had always been her coping strategy once she was able to navigate her way around the neighbourhood independently—running to get as much space between her and whatever it was that was closing in on her, be it a person, a room, a feeling... running to the fields, her safe place. The wide-open space, the lack of humans and the vast sky above her gave her the permission she sought to breathe.

No restrictions.

There she would sit, pull out her pencil and her sketchbook and lose herself in the expanse around her. But running, of course, got her into trouble, and on more than one occasion she was delivered back to her seemingly distraught mother by the police or a neighbour, two or three hours later.

Wandering aimlessly around the first shop, Eve felt lost, not really knowing what to look for. She wiped her clammy hands down her thighs and continued to contemplate the dresses that were on offer. Rachel wandered towards her, holding up a nude-coloured dress: fitted and short.

Eve raised her eyebrows and took a hold of the hem, absorbing all the details in complete wonderment. "Really? You seriously think that's the one for me?" She let it fall from her fingers and tucked her hair behind her ears, folding her arms defensively across her chest.

Rachel waved a hand in the air dismissively. "Maybe it's not your colour." She strolled past another rack of dresses, feeling the fabric of items that lined her path. Eve followed dutifully and shook her head as her friend played dress-up.

"We need something blue. Your eyes are grey, and it will bring them out." She was dissecting and examining Eve like a damn science project.

Eve huffed before following her friend towards yet another display of chiffon and silk. "Umm... Do I get a say in this at all? I mean, it is me that has to wear it. What if I don't like blue?"

Rachel turned slowly, looked at Eve with wide eyes and snorted. "Mate, you're a feckin' artist. You like all colours, right?" The look on her face made it clear that this was not up for discussion.

Eve raised her eyebrows and walked towards the shop door, resigning herself to the fact that she really didn't have a say in it at all and could therefore technically bypass the whole shopping experience and spend an hour in Museum Gardens instead.

She looked back over her shoulder and shouted to her friend. "Text me when you've finally chosen, and I'll come and pay for it."

Sitting in the park in the late-June sunshine,

sketchbook on her knees, Eve's mind flicked to hazy memories of her father from when she was very little: the smell of his aftershave, the sound of the front door opening that told her he was home from work and the way he would say 'I love you' over and over until she fell asleep. Whenever she thought of him, emptiness filled her. He had disappeared before Eve turned six, and she hadn't seen him since. Her mother refused to talk about him: he'd become a 'he who must not be named', and any mention of him at all was met with unreasonable annoyance. He no longer existed, and Eve was expected to accept that.

She sighed, sadness washing over her at not being able to share her successes with her daddy.

The antagonistic relationship she had with her mother had grown worse over the years due to Gillian's overprotective nature and constant need to criticise Eve at every opportunity. Nothing she did was ever good enough, and the constant put downs that she received from her had begun to grind her down as she'd entered adolescence.

Gillian Swallow pushed her daughter in all directions with her obsessive behaviour. She expected Eve to be immaculately turned out at all times, and as an artist, it was beyond suffocating. It was not in Eve's nature to conform to straight lines and neatness, so her defiance and non-compliance led to more and more arguments and more distance between the two.

The more her mother pushed, the more Eve retreated.

Her mother's no-holds-barred attitude had been in full swing during discussions about going to university:

"You don't have the strategies in place to be able to cope without me."

Or…

"You're not strong enough, or brave enough, which will only lead to failure."

And finally…

"You will only end up crawling back home."

… where she would undoubtedly receive no sympathy after a harsh 'I told you so'.

Eve had read somewhere that a teenager's brain is wired differently to that of an adult—something to do with it not being fully formed at the end of childhood, instead, continuing to develop throughout the teenage years. Apparently, the greatest changes to the parts of the brain responsible for judgment, decision-making, planning and organisation occur in adolescence. This area of the brain does not reach full maturity until around the age of twenty-five. Well, she was only six years away from being able to rationalise like an adult…

So, at the time, Eve had believed everything her mother told her: she would be unable to hold her own and she would not manage in a strange city. Giving up all hope of ever pursuing her ambitions, she'd withdrawn her application and had begun making plans for a life at home under her mother's rule.

However, Rachel, her best friend, had had different ideas for Eve.

They'd grown up in each other's pockets, living on the same street, despite attending different schools. Rachel's father was incredibly wealthy, so she and her brother had been pushed through private schooling instead of attending the local secondary with Eve. She'd been dead set on studying psychology and spent a long time researching universities that would cater for her and, at the same time, have the facilities that Eve needed to study art.

They would go to the University of York together.

Rachel's father had been instrumental in helping the girls get set up with somewhere to live. A short walk from the university building, the terraced house they noe lived in was a typical student home: shared bathroom, kitchen and living area and two bedrooms. It was perfect.

Eve had been so nervous during the months leading up to the start of university life and had wanted nothing more than support and reassurance. The only person she got that from was Rachel, who was the only human being who completely understood her and accommodated her troubled mind.

But now she could say she had survived her first year.

Eve's plans for life after the three-year degree were still sketchy to say the least, but her affinity for and love of art in all its forms had always been her outlet. It was her joie de vivre, her passion. Her need to pour her head onto paper was as desperate as her need to breathe, and any length of time spent doing other things only gave her head the space to throw panic around and fret about coping in everyday situations. Behind her sketchbook, she was able to hide away from reality, from the hustle and bustle of other people. Drawing and painting were the only things that occupied her thoughts when she wasn't already doing them, and with a brush or a pencil in her hand and her ears plugged with music, Eve was at peace.

At school, she'd been what other kids had called a 'loner', but she'd been so wrapped up in her creative world that she hadn't really taken much notice of what others thought of her. Some kids had been bullied for being too fat, too short, too spotty, but other than confused whispers and a bit of snickering, the bullies hadn't been interested in her. As much as she was reserved and had been unable to interact with them like other people, they'd seemed to 'get' that she needed space and had pretty much left her alone.

She hadn't been a typical teenager by any stretch of the imagination, and she was no more typical at the tender age of nineteen. She wasn't one to be persuaded by the latest fashion, makeup to her was pretty much an alien concept and boys had always been, and still were, a mystery. Boyfriends had never been an option because anything remotely physical, anything that required her to get close to someone, would have had her bolting—and still would.

Billy Taylor had been the biggest mystery to her.

Not the most attractive boy in school, he'd had an air about him that intrigued her. She couldn't put her finger on it, but there was *something* behind the seemingly tough exterior and the confidence he appeared to carry around with him.

He'd had Eve mesmerised from the word go.

Of course, he'd never noticed her—not at first anyway. She'd always been hidden behind her hair, or a sketchbook, and never once deluded herself into thinking he'd take the time to glance her way, never mind talk to her—not that she would have dared to respond if he had.

She hadn't been the type to mope around, pining for any sort of unrequited attention, nor would she have known how to cope with any had she got it, and the fact he was three years older than her had made him even less accessible. So, she'd allowed herself to be intrigued by him from a distance, and that had been enough for her at fourteen.

After an awkward meeting in the corridor at the end of the school year, Eve never saw him again. He'd left town with his family in a cloud of mystery before the start of the next academic year, and no one really knew why.

It was one of those completely clichéd moments.

In a rush to get to her next lesson before the crowds of pupils spilled out from their classrooms, Eve hurried along the corridor towards the science labs. Her arms were full of books, her headphones surgically attached to her ears—as was standard—and her ever-occupied mind was on her latest composition.

It was two weeks before the summer, and it couldn't come fast enough.

As they both rounded the corner from different directions, they collided, Eve's belongings clattering to the floor. Dropping to their knees, they both reached out, picking up books and pencils that were rolling across the corridor. Eve fumbled around, struggling to breathe due to the closeness of their bodies and the fact there was a wall behind her. There was nowhere that she could run to this time. Her path was blocked by Billy Taylor, and she began to panic. Eve avoided being close to anyone, let alone the boy who'd had her in a spin for the best part of a year.

Her eyes connected with his for the briefest of moments, flickering across his face before he broke the spell by speaking, asking her if she was okay. He handed her a pile of her books as she stuffed her pencil case back into her bag, and rabbing them from him, she mumbled an embarrassed 'thank you', stood up and walked away as quickly as she could. Had that been the end of it, she might have been able to brush it off, but he came after her. He ran along the corridor and caught her up, cupping her elbow and spinning her towards him.

Like a rabbit caught in headlights, she stood there and stared at him.

"Eve?"

She swallowed as his bright blue eyes poured all over her face, unable to respond.

"It's Eve, right?" Billy's eyebrows rose in question as he spoke.

She nodded, glued to the spot. How, she was not sure, but he was searching every part of her, and after a few excruciating seconds, she ducked her head and moved away, hurrying back down the corridor. Turning to look over her shoulder, refusing to make eye contact, she whispered to him, to Billy Taylor. "I'm sorry."

It was barely audible, and Billy froze. He'd seen this girl before and knew she was different to the others—her eyes spoke volumes about just how different. Something behind the grey swirls reflected feelings that were inside of him, and he frowned with emptiness and confusion as she walked away.

The memory of Billy never really left her, and for years after, she would often wonder about the boy who she felt had seen straight into her soul.

***

STANDING IN FRONT of Rachel's full-length mirror, Eve turned to point out her exposed bra strap, dropping her arms by her sides and sagging her shoulders. The dress was a beautiful azure blue with a modest neckline and cap sleeves. It pinched in around Eve's waist and then fell down in soft folds of chiffon to her knees. The back of it was a low scoop that stopped at the base of her spine.

She hated it.

"Just go without." Rachel was deadly serious. She got

up from her seat on the bed and walked towards Eve, who raised an eyebrow at her in the mirror.

"Umm… excuse me? Hello! Have you met me?"

Rachel unhooked Eve's bra, laughing.

Completely horrified, Eve spun around, holding onto her chest for dear life. "Okay, okay. Stop right there, you. I have relinquished all control so far, but I draw the line at this. This is my bloody dignity, Rae. Come on."

"Oh, lighten up, woman. For God's sake! No one will be able to tell. If you're that bothered, I'll get my tit tape."

Eve snorted.

"You can't have your bra showing. You'll look ridiculous."

She sighed. "I look ridiculous already." Defeated, she turned back to the mirror and checked herself out, smoothing her hair off her face. "This just isn't me."

Rachel rested her chin on Eve's shoulder, searching the reflection of her friend for something. "It's not about being who we really are tonight, though, bud. It's about letting go—living it up. It's about celebrating and just forgetting that in a couple of years we will have to walk into the huge, scary world of adulthood where we'll need to be responsible and shit. Yeah?"

Eve held her friend's gaze in the mirror for a moment and then breathed in deeply through her nose, exhaling again noisily to make a point. "Yep. Yep. Okay. Okay. Whip it off."

"Atta girl!"

Eve pulled her bra through the sleeve of the dress, holding it by her side. It didn't look as obvious as she'd thought it might, but she was still incredibly uncomfortable with the idea. "What on earth will people think?"

Rachel grinned and spun her around gently by her arm. "They'll think you look hot and that you have amazing wangers!" She winked and handed her a makeup bag. "This you can do yourself. I'll leave you to it." She was out of the door before Eve could protest.

Looking inside the bag and back up at her reflection, Eve rolled her eyes. She'd never worn anything more than a light slick of mascara—even that was infrequent—and she was not about to learn the art of makeup application in the half hour before they were due to leave. She dug around and found the wand, leaning into the mirror so she could see what she was doing. "Maybe I'll go for a couple of extra coats tonight—push the boat out." She rolled her eyes again at herself and applied the thick, black liquid to her already long, dark lashes.

Debbie, who was on Rachel's course, had come around to go to the ball with them, and once they were ready, the girls gathered in the living room. Debbie popped the cork on a cheap bottle of Cava that she'd picked up on her way over. "Here's to us." She handed a glass to the other two and the girls clinked glasses, lifting them to their lips. Lager and lime had always been Eve's tipple, but the cool, bubbly liquid slid easily down the back of her throat and fizzed on her tongue. She took another mouthful. "I think I could get used to this."

After another glass each, Rachel—dressed in bright red—fluffed up her black hair and announced that it was time to leave. As they walked towards the door, she stopped short and spun around. "Oh, my God. We didn't get you any shoes." She stared wide-eyed at Eve for a moment before dropping her eyes to Eve's feet and the *Dr Marten's* that she had slipped into slyly. "Oh no you don't!"

Eve stood staring at the ceiling, feigning innocence, rolling onto the outside of her feet.

Rachel looked at them again, sighed and then lifted her eyes back up to Eve's face. "Nah. You look perfect." Giving her best friend's shoulders a gentle squeeze, she looked determinedly into her eyes. "You ready?"

Eve glanced in the mirror at her hair that was, courtesy of Rachel, piled on top of her head with loose tendrils hanging by her now ridiculously exposed neck. She smiled tightly. "As I'll ever be."

CHAPTER
two

Strange And Beautiful - Aqualung

LIVING LIFE IN a constant state of apprehension meant that Eve's body and mind were persistently at loggerheads with one another. She was sometimes able to trick herself into a mindset that allowed her to push against the fear, depending on the situation she found herself in. Going to the University Summer Ball, however—where there would be hundreds of out of control students in a relatively small space—was not a situation she was finding easy to wrap her mind around. Her fight or flight mechanism was already flashing its blue light.

As the three girls walked through the darkening streets towards the university, Eve hid a heavily beating heart and a dry mouth from the other two. She focused on the dim light from the streetlamps that reflected off the damp pavements and twisted the ties on her hoodie around her fingers until they went numb. The closer they got to the gates, the more effort it took to keep going. Fleeing was quickly becoming the only option visible beyond the thick blackness that fell like a curtain in front of any clarity that might have been trying to wrestle its way to the forefront of her thinking.

The most important person in her world was walking next to her. She didn't need, nor did she want, to spend the evening getting separated from her in crowds of drunken, sweaty people that she didn't know. She couldn't imagine that she'd be able to hear anything Rachel had to say once they arrived anyway, not only because of the noise levels in the place, but for the ringing in her ears, the screaming of her soul to run—to get out.

Fear crawled up her spine, and her defences kicked in. She stopped dead in her tracks, unable to move, unable to break through the shutters that had fallen into place.

It took a few seconds for the girls to realise that she was no longer walking alongside them.

"Eve, what the fuck?" Debbie wasn't ever one to mince her words, impatient at the best of times. Tonight was the biggest night on the social calendar and something she had been preparing for for weeks: haircut, waxing in all the right places, manicures, facials… "You're not wimping out on us now. Get your arse over here." Her bluntness flicked at the wrong switches for Eve, reminiscent of the life she had thankfully left behind her for the time being, and her eyes darted to Rachel for support.

"Hang about, Deb. Give her a minute." Rachel walked back to stand with Eve, making sure she stopped in front of her but just far enough away, wrapping her bare arms around herself in an attempt to stay warm. The sun had been gracious, but the evenings were still chilly, and the unpredictable—or predictable, depending on how you looked at it—British weather had delivered rain most nights over the past few weeks. Coats, of course, were more hassle than they were worth on nights out, and Debbie delighted in causing unnecessary fuss about having to stand around in the cold air by stamping her feet and rubbing her skin while huffing and puffing.

Rachel raised her eyebrows and squinted at her friend. "You okay, dude?"

Dropping her chin, Eve drew patterns on the pavement with the toe of her boot. "Not really." She shoved her hands deep into her pockets and glanced up. "I'm just not into all this, y'know?" She searched Rachel's face for a reaction—she must have heard the same statement a thousand times, yet her resolve remained. She didn't speak. She waited, patience oozing from her expression.

Eve sighed. "I just don't think I can go through with it. We'll end up getting separated anyway, and I'll spend half the night looking for you if we go in there, and you know how I won't cope with that. It's going to be wall-to-wall drunks, Rae. I just can't do it. I thought I could push through, but I can't."

Debbie shouted over, teeth chattering. "I'm not standing here all night. I'll see you in there." She spun on her heel and flounced down the street towards the union bar.

Rachel caught the flicker of guilt that fluttered across Eve's face. "It's okay. I'll catch her up. She knows plenty of people."

"I don't want to ruin your night. You go on ahead. I'll go back and get the kettle on ready for you coming home later, yeah?" Eve smiled feebly.

Rachel sighed, turning her head towards the union and back to Eve, studying her closely. Life with Eve was a delicate balance between leaving her to it and gentle encouragement. Sometimes, she got it wrong and Eve would retreat even further, going for days without surfacing, emotionally and physically. She didn't want to get it wrong this time. They had been riding a whole boatload of luck so far. Persuading her to buy the ticket at all had been a massive deal. Rachel had been convinced it was Eve's way of appeasing her and that she would back out soon enough. But when she'd agreed to look for dresses as well, Rachel had almost choked on her breakfast. She didn't want to push it now, but she was her best friend, and the last thing she wanted was to spend the night without her.

She pulled Eve's hand out of her pocket, taking hold of her little finger, and swung their arms back and forth. Looking towards the ground, she tapped her shoe against Eve's clunky boot, searching for the right words and the right tone of voice. "Just come for an hour?"

Eve scrubbed her other hand down her face, stopping as it rested across her mouth, exhaling deeply through her nose. She looked directly at Rachel, who was squinting off to the side in an attempt to give Eve some thinking time. She loved Rachel to bits and hated that she couldn't be what she wanted to be for her. She didn't know if it was possible to miss something she'd never had, but she missed what she saw others have with their friends. There was no real physical closeness—no hugging, no snuggling up on the sofa together watching movies. There was always the distance, always nothing more than arm's reach or a light touch, and Eve hated that between her and Rachel more than anyone.

She hadn't had closeness with her mother for as long as she could remember. Although the pain caused by that gaping hole would sometimes push through her with such potency that her skin would crawl, their tumultuous relationship was something she had learned to accept, and the need for closeness wasn't there.

"I'll not leave your side. I promise. I'll come with you to the toilet. I'll come with you to the bar. I'll come with you to chat up any hot boys that might catch your eye…"

Eve smiled sheepishly. "Hot boys? I think not. I'm not looking for anything like that. You'll have more fun without me. You'll feel like you have to babysit me all the time. You'll worry when you're not. You'll miss out."

"But you'll come?" Rachel lifted her head up and met Eve's face, her eyes pleading with her to think about it. "You're my best friend, dude. I don't want to do this without you."

Fight or flight.

Flight was winning, as usual, even though fighting was something she was always desperately trying to do. She needed to fight for her own sake. She needed to fight for her friend.

Eve took a deep breath and checked her watch. "I'll come. For one hour." She gave Rachel's finger a little squeeze, a squeeze that had been a secret alternative to a hug between the two of them since they were small.

Rachel beamed and bounced on her toes. "I will not leave you."

The pair walked side by side with their fingers still linked, Rachel being careful to go at just the pace Eve dictated. They joined the growing throng of pedestrians who were walking the same way. Everyone was dressed in their ball outfits: girls in floor length dresses, boys in suits and tuxedos, all relaxed and bronzed from outdoor, weekend drinking. There was a buzz of excitement about the place as students embarked on the biggest night out of the year.

Eve's heart hammered away in her chest as she worked up the courage to continue placing one foot in front of the other and, squeezing Rachel's finger a little tighter, she closed her eyes. Her mother had been right: she wasn't coping very well at all.

As they approached the door to the union bar, Eve remembered what she was wearing and fussed with her dress and hair, tucking the tendrils behind her ears. She fumbled around in her oversized bag for her tub of lip balm for something else to do.

What if I look out of place? What if my hair isn't tidy? What if people laugh at my boots? Why the hell did I wear my boots?

"Here." Rachel pulled out her lip-gloss and came a little closer before slicking the sticky substance across Eve's lips, standing back to admire her. "You really do look gorgeous, y'know. Stop fussing. And leave your hair alone. It suits you off your face like that. I've got your back."

Debbie had settled herself amongst a group of friends from their course and shouted them over when she saw them, indicating that she had bought a round of drinks.

Eve scanned the room. It was fairly early, so the crowds had not yet gathered, and there were only pockets of noise and raucous behaviour. She was already hopeful that it would stay that way until her hour was up and she was able to make her escape. The thought of spending longer there filled her with dread again.

Keeping her distance, she followed Rachel sheepishly and stood on the edge of the group, trying her hardest to look inconspicuous and to not attract any unwanted attention. Being dressed the way she was made her feel even more on show. Had she come dressed in her usual attire, she might have felt like she could take on this challenge a little more easily. As it was, she felt naked, exposed and vulnerable.

Is my dress designer enough? Does my makeup look right?

Rachel pulled up a pair of stools, placing them next to each other, one just slightly further away from the group than the others, and sat down. Eve took her place on the empty one and put her nose in her drink in an attempt to steady her breathing. Feeling incredibly warm, partly due to the atmosphere, partly due to the fear, she removed her hoodie and placed it on the ground on top of her bag.

Without much warning, the night was in full swing. The room had filled up with more and more people, and the drinks were flowing readily around the group of psychology students.

An hour.

She checked the time on her watch again, crossed one leg over the other, allowing it to dangle, and began counting the bounces it made in her head.

Just three thousand six hundred...

...Thirty-five. Thirty-six. Thirty-seven...

Eve had made her leg bounce eight hundred and forty-three times when she felt the mood in the room shift ever so slightly. The temperature dropped and the hairs around her face blew gently with a gust of air that whisked through the room from an open window. She moved her gaze lazily to where the others were sitting, and her concentration was shattered.

She lost count.

Leaning against the wall, a bottle of beer dangling

loosely from his fingers, he looked as out of place in his jeans and T-shirt as Eve felt amongst the ball gowns and tuxedos.

And he was staring directly at her.

A familiarly uncomfortable feeling crept along her forearms and uneasiness settled in her stomach as she fought with herself to look away, but she could not take her eyes off him. The walls seemed to close in around her, and Eve's skin became too much, anxiety clawing at it like a cat, prickles of fear tiptoeing their way up the back of her neck.

Look away. Look away.

Inhaling deeply, she blinked, forcing herself to break eye contact, just as Flight kicked in. She scrabbled around frantically near her legs to gather up her belongings. She shoved her stool with the back of her legs as she pushed to her feet, hitting the unfortunate person behind her. She needed to get out.

"Watch it, love!"

Lifting her face to apologise, she squeezed her eyes closed in a bid to shut out the rest of the room. She pressed the heels of her hands hard against her ears to stop the pounding that distorted the noise from the throng of students, which seemed to have tripled in size now, and started to move towards her escape.

Run. Run away. Run fast.

Her knees buckled, causing her to grab a hold of a nearby table to steady herself, knocking someone's drink into their lap.

"Fuck's sake!"

The growl from the owner of the pint was lost on Eve as she barged her way past a group of stunned girls.

Where the hell was Rachel?

Concerned onlookers tried to catch hold of her as she bustled her way towards the exits, but she yanked herself away, thrashing her arms around her head to block out the cries of 'you alright love?' and 'what's up with 'er?' that ricocheted around the room.

She neared the far side of the room and caught a glimpse of her friend hanging over the bar, shouting something into the barman's ear. A vague recollection of her saying she was going to get drinks clattered around her head, but all that didn't matter now.

As she escaped into the outside, the cold air caught her breath and she stumbled to her knees, grazing them on the concrete. The rain was heavy and soaked into her clothes, but she clambered to her feet, heading towards the campus gates that taunted her—so close but so far away— She ran through puddles of muddy rainwater that splashed around her legs as she pelted the ground clumsily in her boots, and she winced at the piercing whistle of the wind that now replaced the ringing in her ears.

Finally passing through the exit and onto the street that led back to her home, Eve took a left instead of a right, heading towards the main road. The traffic was busy, and pubs were spitting groups of punters out into the cold air, causing her to weave in and out and navigate around them. She continued, her heavy bag slamming against her hips, her hoodie dragging along the floor in the wet.

The nearest open space was the park, two miles out of town, and her head switched into survival mode in order to get her there fast. She ditched her hoodie and slung the strap of her bag over her head, adjusting it around her back. Her stride widened, her heart beat steadied, and her breathing deepened.

HOUSING *elephants*

Swiping her forearm across her eyes to clear the rain, Eve ran.

CHAPTER
three

Every Breath You Take - The Police

RETURNING TO THE seating area, Rachel dumped the drinks on the table. "Jesus, that was a mission. Where's Eve?" She scoured the vicinity, narrowing her eyes as it was clear she wasn't anywhere to be seen. Debbie was wrapped around a blue-eyed, blonde-haired footballer, her tongue down his throat, and she shrugged casually when questioned.

Squeezing her way through clusters of people, Rachel headed to the toilets, where she expected to find her friend huddled in a cubicle. She sighed as she pushed through the door and past the line of drunken girls waiting to pee.

"Oi. There's a queue, you know?"

She ignored the shouts and started banging on the cubicle doors. "Eve? Eve, you in there, babe?" She waited in front of the first cubicle, head down as she listened for a response. Ducking down, she scanned under the door to check for shoes, and realising they weren't Eve's, moved along to the next toilet.

The more cubicles she checked, the more obvious it

was that Eve was not hiding out in the loos, and Rachel became unnerved. She charged back through the line of girls—not caring that she was being met with dirty looks—and ran back out into the bar area. Her eyes scanned the tops of heads and through gaps between bodies to get a glimpse of a blue dress or *Docs*.

She pulled her mobile from her bag and speed dialled Eve's number, pacing the floor impatiently as it rang and rang. The click to indicate she had reached the voicemail had her sinking into the nearest chair.

She shouldn't have left her. She'd promised she wouldn't leave her.

"Fuck." She hit her forehead with the heel of her and squeezed her eyes shut, unsure what to do next, until she felt a warm hand on her shoulder. Looking up into the face of a stranger—a guy she hadn't noticed before—she frowned.

"I'll help you look for her."

Rachel scoured his face for some clue as to who he was and why he even knew Eve was missing. "Excuse me?"

"I'll help you find her, but I think we should go now. She seemed really upset."

Rachel needed no more cajoling. She swiped her bag from the table and headed towards the door, the mystery bloke in tow. As the pair stepped out into the rain, Rachel headed to the gates, assuming Eve would just have headed home.

"Where would she go if she was scared?" the mystery bloke shouted to her, the rain and wind distorting his words. Rachel stopped and turned, teetering back towards him in her heels and trying not to slip on the wet floor. "What?"

"Where would she go if she was scared?" he repeated,

scanning the area, flicking his eyes across the windows on the second floor, pacing back and forth,

"Scared? What do you mean scared? You said upset. She will have gone home, probably."

Scouring the edges of the grounds, he continued to speak absentmindedly. "She was scared," he shouted above the noise of the elements. "Definitely scared."

Her new companion called Eve's name again, looking for any sign of movement.

"For fuck's sake." Rachel threw her arms up in exasperation as despair began to take over. "You said upset!" she screeched at him, ragging her hands through her hair. She watched him as he walked away from her, his chest heaving.

Eve could have been anywhere.

Rachel shouted her name, scanning the university building doorways. She rounded back to the courtyard, watching her new companion do the same from the other side.

"Eve!" His voice was deep and loud. He walked under the arch to the quad where more doors to more corridors stood locked under their porches. Rachel followed him, watching curiously as he hurried into each one of them, peering through windows and then backing out into the middle, his eyes squinted.

How did Eve even know him? And how did he even know she was gone?

He stopped, planting his hands on his hips, squinting up at the sky in thought. His floppy black hair was plastered to his head, rivulets of rainwater chasing each other onto his skin.

"Who are you?" Rachel shouted over to him. "I mean,

what's your name? How do you even know Eve?"

"I don't really... Not yet anyway. Billy." He continued to breathe heavily, his eyes darting around. "Billy Taylor."

"Right, well, Billy Taylor. We kinda need to find my friend now, so if you're still a member of this search party, please can we quit star gazing and just go?"

"Where? Where would she go?" He snapped his head around to look at her.

Rachel cast her eyes to the side as she thought. "Well, as I said, home. But I doubt it if she was scared. A wide-open space. Where is there a wide-open space near here?"

He spun to face her. "Flatlands Park. About two miles from here. Come on." Billy grabbed her hand and pulled her along.

"I have no idea where that is." They ducked their heads down to shield their faces from the biting wind and rain.

"It's okay. I do," he shouted back at her, dragging her faster. "We'll get my car."

"You've been drinking."

"I've had one. I've had one beer. Let's go."

The two of them ran in silence for the next five minutes as Billy guided Rachel through the streets behind the university to what she assumed to be his digs. They rounded the corner of Bright Street and halted outside a beat up *Fiesta*. Running his hands through his hair in an attempt to get it out of his face, Billy dug in his coat pocket and pulled out his car keys. He unlocked the passenger side door and then ran around to climb into the driver's seat. Once inside, he leaned over into the back and pulled a towel from the footwell, throwing it at Rachel. "Here. Dry off. You'll be ill."

She took the towel gratefully, rubbing at the ends of her hair, never once taking her eyes off this strange guy.

***

THE PEDESTRIAN GATES to the park were locked, so Eve skirted around the edge, looking for another way in rather than having to walk the three miles to the main gates at the other end. She found a small gap in the bushes around to the left-hand side and sank to her haunches in an attempt to crawl through. Her lungs burned and her bag weighed heavy on her back. She took it off and tugged it through with her as best she could.

As she moved through the gap, her dress caught on a branch and she fell forwards onto her hands and knees, yanking the material away, ripping it, and swiping at her face with her muddy hands to clear the rainwater that was trickling into her eyes.

Stupid fucking dress. Stupid fucking ball.

Dragging her body through the opening to stand on the other side, she was greeted with the sight of open space. Vast skies and an expanse of grass and trees stood resplendent in front of her, and the hammering in her head immediately begin to subside.

The fact it was dark made it difficult to make out the paths through to the middle, but that was the last thing on Eve's mind. She readjusted her bag and set off to find a spot to sit and breathe and on reaching the centre of the park, slumped down on the wet grass, inhaled deeply through her nose and slowly began counting backwards from thirty to control her still rapid breathing, the rain seeping into her clothes.

Once her heart rate had returned to noral, she pulled her hair out of the intricate up-do that Rachel had insisted on, throwing bobby pins to the floor. Her long brown hair tumbled around her shoulders, some of it still dry from being tucked away under curls and twists, and she ran her hand through it. She rolled her head back on her shoulders, gazing up at the inky blackness to pick out the few constellations that shone brightly between the gaps in the clouds in the smog free skies of the parkland.

The sound of an owl in a nearby tree broke the silence as her calm restored, and she saw the blinding beam of car headlights before she heard the engine. She froze before sitting bolt upright and getting to her feet. With her eyes darting around, she tentatively walked backwards as the sound of a car door being slammed shut echoed towards her.

Spinning on her heel, Eve bolted again.

Eve was a much faster runner, but ditching her heels, Rachel moved quickly through the dark, adrenaline pumping through her body as she cursed her best friend through gritted teeth for making her run barefoot through wet grass. "Eww! *Eve?*"

Billy was at her heels in no time, and she spun around, instructing him to stay at the car. "She won't stop if you're with me. Do not come with me."

Turning back around, she sprinted off, the darkness becoming denser the further into the park she ran. Her chest was tight from exertion and the cold wind, and she stopped to catch her breath, bending at the waist and placing her hands on her thighs. Calling Eve's name again seemed a futile exercise, because she knew she wouldn't answer her.

Behind her, twigs snapped and grass rustled. It was Billy.

"Did you not hear me?" She stood up and held her palms skywards, raising her eyebrows at him. She was not in the mood for stupidity right now. He didn't look at her, instead walking past her slowly, before peering into the darkness. "Yep."

Gob smacked, Rachel followed him, catching him up and grabbing hold of his elbow. "Then you will remember that I said if she sees I'm with someone else, she won't stop. She's…." Rachel sighed, struggling to find a word to describe Eve without sounding unkind. "Fragile. She's fragile. You have to treat her with kid gloves. You charging in like a bull won't work."

Billy still hadn't looked at her, his eyes moving around stealthily, shining in the moonlight. "You mean like you, charging up to her after slamming the car door as hard as you could? You're the one who frightened her off. Now stop talking and let's find her."

Rachel opened her mouth to protest, but he had already taken hold of her hand and was moving forwards. She clamped it shut and found herself compliant, stunned by the straight-forward, no-nonsense approach that he had. She decided, too, that it was also quite good to have a man with her, because creeping around in a dark park with owls, and no doubt bats, was not really her idea of fun, even if it was for the sake of her best friend.

They walked slowly, hand in hand, searching the darkness.

"A torch would be good right now, huh?" Rachel glanced over at him trying to break the painful silence, but Billy ignored her and put his fingers to his lips, shushing her. Suitably chastised, she did as she was told, again, and walked dutifully by his side. He had completely taken over this search now, and Rachel became more intrigued by the second.

Why was he so involved, and why was he so concerned about Eve if he didn't even know her?

As their feet finally connected with one of the paths, Rachel spotted a flash of movement from the corner of her eye and twisted her head slowly to where it had come from. She gently pulled her hand from Billy's, and he nodded once with encouragement, taking the hint this time and staying put.

The sight of Eve caused a lump to form in Rachel's throat. Up against a large oak tree, she sat with her legs tucked in tight to her chest, her arms wrapped around them, shivering from the cold and wet.

Eve pulled in shaky breaths, her bedraggled hair hanging long over her face.

Kneeling down in front of her friend, Rachel took hold of her little finger with her own, squeezing on it gently, her voice quiet and calm. "Eve. Babe, it's me. It's just me."

Eve inhaled deeply and lifted her face to meet Rachel's. She held her eyes for a moment, flicking between the two of them before biting down on her bottom lip. "I'm so sorry."

They hadn't had an episode like this since three months into the university year, and Rachel had allowed herself to think that things were getting better.

She swallowed down in an attempt to find the strength she needed to get through to her friend, and shuffling a little, she picked up Eve's bag and gently reached over to move her hair away from her face. "You don't need to be sorry. But, we're going to go home now, dude. I've got your stuff here. I need you to stand up, okay?"

Eve nodded slowly, untwisting her fingers from around her legs, her white knuckles flexing as she prepared to get to her feet.

"Babe?" Rachel took a deep breath. "Someone else is here, but I need you to try not to freak out."

Eve threw her head up to meet Rachel's gaze, her eyes wide and her heart pounding once more. "Whose car is it? Who have you come with?"

Rachel grimaced and looked at the floor. "Umm, this guy. Just this guy. I don't know. He was worried for you. I think he saw that you were upset in the union and he wanted to help. He just wants to help, Eve, okay?"

Eve's shutters fell back into place as she plucked up the courage to ask her next question. "Wh... What's his name?"

"Billy. Billy Taylor."

She began to move her head from side to side in protestation. "No. No, no, no. I cannot go near that guy, Rae. You have to listen to me. I can't. I just can't. Tell him to go home."

"What do you mean? You don't even know him. Besides, he is going to give us a lift home in his car, if we can even find the damn thing."

"I'll walk home."

"The hell you will! It's after midnight, it's freezing and you look like shit."

"Well there's no other option. I can't do it. You are just going to have to trust me on this one. I'll walk."

Rachel sighed. "Wait here. I'll go speak to him."

Eve nodded and sat back down on the grass, shivering against the cool air.

Being too close to anyone who was not Rachel, or her

mother, could often be an excruciating experience when her anxiety was high, and the need to claw at her skin sometimes became terrifyingly real. The idea of being anywhere near him right now was nauseating. It hadn't been the crowds or the fact that Rachel wasn't there by her side that had caused her to run: it had been that look, and she'd been convinced Billy would come over to her. That look had drawn her in so close that she hadn't been able to look away; she hadn't been able to breathe.

Her breath hitched as she contemplated how the last hour would have played out had he tried to approach her. It didn't bear thinking about. Her spectacular exit from the union had been bad enough. Christ only knew how many people had seen her freak out, and that was not something you could come back from easily. This was why she avoided situations like this. This was why she should never have gone to the fucking ball in the first place.

Her need to get away from him had intensified immediately, but there was something in those blue eyes that gripped her and was refusing to let go. She'd only been fourteen the first time, but those feelings had been real, even if she'd not really been able to define them back then.

What was it about this guy that had her in such a state?

The way he'd looked at her just now was no coincidence. Her memory of that look had her heart beating hard against her rib cage, just as it had that day in the corridor.

She'd barely even spoken to the guy before and look at what he was doing to her.

Who was he, anyway? Billy fucking Taylor… Why the fuck was he there and why had he follow her? Why was he at the university ball? He'd disappeared. He didn't owe her anything; it's wasn't his job to save her.

How dare he get involved in my life like this after all these years? Why? Why did he have to look at me like that?

He'd filled up her thoughts as a teenager, but he wasn't supposed to come back and haunt her—not now. Now she was almost a grown up with a life to build.

Eve's inability to socialise or cope in situations most people wouldn't bat an eye lid at seemed to get worse as she got older and more self-conscious, and she'd been working so damn hard to keep on top of these outbursts of hers this year. How was she supposed to be calm and in control if he was around?

Engulfed by the feelings that were coursing through her after making eye contact with him again after all this time, she was convinced that if it had affected him even half as much as it had affected her, he was going to try and find her again.

She could not let this happen…

A repeat performance of tonight was out of the question.

There was no way she was ever going to put herself in another situation where Billy Taylor got to see what a fuck-up she was.

Rachel sauntered over to where he was leaning up against a tree, a cigarette hanging loosely from his mouth as he stared up at the sky.

"So…"

He pushed himself away quickly, taking a final drag on the cigarette before stubbing it out with the toe of his *Converse*. "Hey. How is she?"

Rachel bounced on her toes and twisted her fingers together behind her back. "Umm. Not great. She's… Hmm.

She's refusing to get in the car with you. Cars and Eve don't mix. Cars and strangers are even more of a trigger for weird behaviour, so…"

Pulling his car keys from his pocket, Billy threw them at Rachel, who caught them, a little stunned. "You take her home. I'll walk. I'll come and pick it up tomorrow."

She stared at him with her mouth open slightly. Seriously, who was this guy? "Umm. Are you sure?"

"Where do you live?"

"Elton Terrace. Number seven. Are you sure?"

Billy tucked his hands into his pockets and turned on his heel, setting off to walk towards the gates. "See you tomorrow."

"Those gates are locked, dufus!" Rachel shouted after him, rolling her eyes. He ignored her and continued to walk, raising his arm by way of a goodbye. She sighed, watching his silhouette disappear into the blackness, and jogged back across to where Eve was still sitting.

She dangled the keys in front of her face and smiled kindly. "He's gone. I'm driving. Can we prepare you for that, do you think?"

Eve frowned and stood, taking the keys from Rachel and turning them over in her hands.

Billy Taylor's car keys…

She gently folded her fingers over the top of them, feeling the warmth of the metal on her skin—Billy's warmth. Her heart beat a little faster, but this time not through fear, and her fingers continued to rub against the smooth surface of the keys, her eyes never leaving them once. She inhaled through her mouth, bent down to pick up her bag again and looked at Rachel, who stared at her intently. "I'll be okay."

Being inside a car could sometimes trigger a panic attack.

The small spaces often felt suffocating, and the fact she couldn't just jump out of a moving vehicle meant that anxiety levels could potentially explode.

"Are you sure? This will require you to be focused, and you will not be able to just run if you freak out. Right? You do know this?"

Eve ignored her and started to retrace her steps.

Rachel caught up with her and took hold of her finger again. "Bud?"

"Yeah. I know. I can do it. You can trust me, right?"

Rachel cleared her throat and screwed her face up. "Of course I can trust you. I just don't know if your trust in yourself is particularly well-informed tonight. So I am, of course, a little apprehensive about this."

Eve rolled her eyes. "I'll be with you, my darling friend. I'll be fine."

CHAPTER
four

Electron Blue – R.E.M

THE CAR HAD been abandoned haphazardly, and Eve approached the passenger side with wariness. Could she do this? She'd convinced herself before, but now she was standing in front of it, the prospect of getting into the vehicle and shutting the door was much more daunting. Perhaps she had been trying harder to convince Rachel than herself.

She looked over the roof at her friend, who was watching cautiously, wondering if she had made the right decision.

"We'll walk, mate. I don't want to put you in this position."

"I put myself in this position. This isn't your fault, okay?" Eve was half in the car before Rachel could interject.

She climbed into the driver's seat and sighed. "I think we need to talk when we get home, buddy." She glanced nervously over at Eve after familiarising herself with the dashboard.

The girls sat in silence for a minute before Eve

glanced across at her and nodded. "Okay. We'll talk."

With a nod and a tight-lipped smile in response, Rachel started the engine. "Ready?"

"Ready." Eve slammed her door shut and gripped hold of the handle, tensing every muscle in her body, her knuckles white and her breath held tight in her chest. It was only a four-mile drive and would take less than ten minutes. She just needed to hold on.

Squeezing her eyes shut, she clenched her jaw as Rachel began manoeuvring the car back onto the narrow road that led out of the park and remained that way for the entire journey.

The car had barely pulled up at the side of the road when Eve opened the door, falling out onto her knees, her stomach heaving and retching.

"Shit." Rachel switched off the engine and was round by the passenger side instantly, watching as her friend emptied her stomach into the gutter outside their house. "What the fuck, Eve? What are you not telling me?"

She bent down and reached for her, but Eve held her arm out, shaking her head as she retched some more. Rachel stood up, raking her hands though her hair. She had sensed for a while now that there was more to her friend's issues than just a controlling mother but, either Eve didn't have an answer, or she was hiding it from her. Really well. She had no idea where to start looking for whatever it was that haunted her friend.

Eve got herself into a sitting position on the edge of the curb, her breathing heavy and her face pale. She wiped the back of her hand across her mouth and let her head fall into the palm of it.

Rachel tentatively moved over towards her and sat

down, assuming a similar position, and the girls sat in silence, the rain beginning to ease off.

It was Eve who spoke first, gently dropping her hand by her side and taking hold of Rachel's little finger. She lifted her head and took a deep breath. "So that was a bit weird, huh?"

Rachel nodded, her elbow on her knee, index finger smoothing across her bottom lip. She swallowed down the tears that were building behind her eyes and gave Eve's finger a squeeze. "I'm worried about you, babe. I don't know how to fix you, and it looks like you still need some fixing."

Eve rested her head on Rachel's shoulder and sighed. "I'm not sure I can be fixed, Rae. I think this is just who I am."

"Bullshit!" She twisted herself round to face her best friend, desperate to grab her into a hug. "Bull. Shit. No one is just this broken. No one is born with demons rattling around in their heads. Something isn't right. Something needs sorting."

Eve searched Rachel's face. "What do I do then?"

Rachel shrugged. "I don't know. Maybe you should go see a doctor or something? A counsellor? I mean, why your mother hasn't organised this for you before now it just—"

"Can we not?" The fear in Eve's eyes indicated that this was not something she was going to agree to easily. Visiting a doctor's surgery was not an enjoyable experience for anyone, but for Eve it was another social activity that didn't bear thinking about. Sitting in a waiting room full of strangers who would watch as you walked in, watch as you sat down, watch to see which magazine you picked up or what you were wearing... No. It was not something she would ever choose to do. "I'm not sure it's all that bad." She smiled, tight-lipped. "I think a visit to the doctors would be a little over the top. I've been feeling a bit under the weather anyway, so maybe I just have a bug and that's why I was sick."

Rachel gave her a nod, understanding exactly what Eve was trying to say, the pair of them standing and walking towards the front door, stepping into their haven and shutting the rest of the world out. "Okay, well, for the time being, we will get you in the bath then into bed, and as your best friend, I reserve all rights to enforce rules that include no more summer balls, no more cars and certainly no more Billy Taylor. Right?"

"Right."

***

HEAD DOWN AND hands deep in his pockets, Billy trudged across the park to the gap in the bushes that he had seen Eve crawling through when he and Rachel sped past earlier to get to the back entrance. He reached into the top pocket of his jacket for his pack of Camel Blues, pulling one out with his teeth as he found his box of matches.

Shielding the lit match against the bitter wind, he held it to the cigarette and took a long drag, inhaling the smoke and the events of the evening into his lungs, holding them for as long as he could before blowing them out to the stars.

It was that first drag he was addicted to, filling his lungs to capacity until they burned—until it was all he could feel or think about.

The sweet release after so much tension had him closing his eyes, rolling his neck from side to side and cracking away the anxieties that were chattering in his ear.

The fact he had not managed to see her again that

night bit at his nerve endings and tugged at his temper, and he took another long drag, attempting to push away the ache that had settled in the pit of his stomach. He squinted his eyes to shield them from the smoke and leaned back against a large silver birch, the flat of his foot resting on the trunk as he picked out the Big Dipper and the North Star.

He sucked on his bottom lip, dragging his teeth over it as he released it, keeping hold of the corner momentarily as he remembered those eyes.

She'd locked onto his gaze so intently he'd been unable to move, captivated by the softness of her skin and the delicate bow of her lips. But it had been the pools of grey he'd been lost in, just like before, only she was no longer a scared young girl: she was a young woman—a beautiful young woman. She was still filled with fear though, and he was desperate to find out just what or who it was that was hurting her.

Throwing his cigarette butt to the floor, he pushed away from the tree and continued his walk home. He had to bend low to get through the gap in the hedge, and as he sunk to his haunches, his attention was caught by a leather-bound book that lay on the ground in front of him. It was wet and muddy, abandoned and out of place in the mush of leaves and soil.

He reached over and pulled it from its nesting place, turning it over. Carefully wiping the top cover with the heel of his hand, he dug around in his pockets for his phone and switched on the built-in torch laying the book on his knee. There were some words etched into the leather in the top right-hand corner and he traced the intricate swirls with his finger: Eve Swallow.

Knowing what he already did of Eve, he had some

expectations about what was inside, and his pulse quickened as he contemplated what it was that he was in possession of. On the odd occasion, he'd seen her dashing down the back streets to the art buildings of the university, head down, headphones in and arms full of books, exactly as he remembered her at school. He assumed she was good at what she did, otherwise why would she dedicate her whole university career to it?

He was not prepared in the slightest, though, for what he found when he began to turn the pages.

Smoothing his palm across the leather, back and forth, back and forth, he built up the nerve to open it up.

It took his breath away.

He swallowed down hard, dragging his hand down his face as he took in the exquisite drawings and sketches that filled every corner. As he turned more pages, he became desirous, drinking in the images with his eyes wide, his heart fluttering in his chest as the enormity of her outrageous talent became clear.

Sitting inside the tiny space under the bramble bushes, Billy was lost in a world of charcoal and pencil, of ballerinas and old men's hands. He gently ran his index finger along the curve of a young woman's neck, absentmindedly touching his lip with the tip of it when he managed to pull it away. It was as if he'd been let in on some sort of secret, a private viewing of her heart and soul, and his own heart was struggling to cope with the way it was making him feel.

He had no idea how she would have reacted if he had ever just approached her in the street, and after tonight, he was pretty sure keeping his distance had been the right decision. However, it was becoming clear that not being able to get close to her was driving him crazy.

What is this girl doing to me?

Going to the summer ball that night had been a last-minute decision. His pal was friends with some of the third-year students and had blagged a couple of tickets for them both. It wasn't really Billy's scene: he usually avoided situations where he might be tempted with alcohol. Dobbo had convinced him that it might be fun for a couple of hours, though, and the prospect of being surrounded by female students was waved in front of his nose like a carrot. As it turned out, the only person he was interested in when he got there was her.

He flicked over a couple more pages and frowned as a pair of bright blue eyes looked up at him. Curls of light pencil strokes created lashes framing the mystery that seemed to cry out from the paper. He flicked to another page. There, in the top corner, was another version of the same eyes—the same bright blue. He continued to turn, and every other page was home to yet another interpretation.

Don't be so fucking stupid.

He shook his head to clear the ridiculousness from his mind and showers of doubt and confusion ran down his spine, but the more sketches he saw, the more he was convinced.

They were his eyes.

"Shit." His heart beat fast in his chest and he fell onto his backside, resting his arms across the top of his knees, the wind knocked out of him. He scrunched his eyes closed and slammed the book shut, bringing it up to touch his mouth, breathing in the scent: leather and lead, vanilla and charcoal.

Crawling out the other side of the small clearing under

63

the hedge, he tucked it inside his jacket, buttoning it up to protect it from the elements. The decisions he was making were happening fast and without much forethought. He was going to go there now. He was going to turn up at their house now and exchange the book for the car keys and hope to God that he got to see her face before he left.

He rose to his feet and began walking—two miles of walking the road that led to her—an urgent need to get there fast making his heart pump hard and the muscles in his jaw tense with nervous energy as he picked up his pace to a light jog.

The rain continued to soak through his clothes, and the water in his hair dripped into his eyes, causing him to squint and wipe his face with the sleeve of his jacket. He rounded the corner near the university twenty minutes later and stopped to catch his breath, crouching down to compose himself, dipping his head and stretching his arms out along the length of his thighs.

As the muscles in his legs twitched and contracted into a more relaxed state, Billy rubbed his chin and ran his hand through his hair to scrape it from his face. Unbuttoning his jacket slowly, he pulled the sketchbook out and held it in front of him again.

Under the streetlamp, everything was much clearer. He flipped open the book to the last used page and a droplet of rainwater fell from his hair onto the paper. He ran the pad of his thumb across it carefully to remove it and exhaled through his nose.

Number seven was at the far end of the street, and it would take him at least three more minutes to get there.

Three minutes.

The pounding in his chest terrified him. The fact that

this person, essentially a stranger, was controlling the way he was acting, the way he was thinking and feeling, scared the shit out of him.

Hiding the sketchbook away once more, he walked towards the house. It was a typical row of terraces—all occupied with students; all with overgrown front paths and rusty gates. The number was hanging loose, and the cream, patterned curtains in the front window were drawn across.

Was that her room?

The gate creaked as he pushed it open slowly, and Billy bit the inside of his cheek as he walked towards the front door, climbing the steps.

Standing in front of it, his knuckles poised to knock, he closed his eyes.

What the hell was he thinking? This girl had run from him tonight. Why the fuck did he think she would be open to a little light conversation at one o'clock in the morning? She'd been petrified, and he would just be adding fuel to an already raging fire. Of course she wouldn't want to see him. He needed to plan this, not go storming in after what had happened tonight.

He exhaled deeply and clenched his teeth, swearing before turning around and heading back the way he had just walked.

It had been a stupid idea, but as he walked away, he realised there was also a part of him that was scared of what he might feel if he looked into her eyes again.

Billy lit another cigarette and headed back down the street, kicking a pebble across the paving stones. He turned the corner and made his way to the gate of number twenty-five Lowther Road. Digging around in his jeans pocket, he pulled out his door key, sliding it into the lock quietly and pausing for a moment before twisting it.

The front door creaked on its hinges and Billy winced.

He used his toes to pull off his Chucks, placing the key inside the left one ready for the morning before heading down the narrow hallway towards the stairs.

Stopping dead in his tracks, he flinched at the familiar slur of words that emanated from the front room. He dropped his head and waited for the string of incoherent abuse that was about to be released.

"Where the fuck've you been 'til this time, you little twat?"

Taking a deep breath, Billy moved towards the living room and stood, unseen, with his ear to the thin opening of the door, his head bowed. "I'm going to bed, Dad. I'll talk to you in the morning."

"I said, where the fuck have you been? I don't fucking need this shit, Bill. Get in here now."

Billy squinted his eyes and stalled as he placed his hand on the doorknob. He was about to walk in when he remembered the sketchbook hidden inside his coat. Undoing his buttons quickly, he pulled out the most precious thing he'd ever been in possession of, leaving a cold feeling near his heart.

"Bill!"

"I'm coming, Dad. I'm coming." He placed the book on the bottom step and braced himself, pushing into the darkened room to see his father sitting with hooded eyes in his favourite armchair, an almost empty bottle of whiskey hanging limply from his hand.

Eyeing it carefully, Billy stared with a certain air of confidence at his old man. Without warning, his father dived out of the chair, launching the bottle at Billy's face.

HOUSING *elephants*

"You little fucker!"

Billy ducked, causing the bottle to smash against the far wall. His dad stumbled forwards and Billy contemplated letting him fall on his fucking face, but instead, he moved towards him and caught him clumsily by his arm, a mistake he regretted very quickly.

"Get your fucking hands off me." His dad swung his huge tattooed arm out, his fist catching Billy across the jaw. "It's not a fucking hotel."

Living with the monster that his father had become had not been his decision to start with, but as he'd got older, it had been a conscious choice he made and one he was continuing to deal with for the time being. After his mother became seriously ill, his father had fallen apart over a long, torturous stretch of time until he was a shell of his former self. The early onset of dementia had been a slow deterioration of a strong, independent woman, and it had ripped the family apart.

He had never hit Billy back then, nor had he hit Jenny—his wife and Billy's mother—choosing instead to take his anger outside, smashing household objects and pummeling his fists against brick walls, his knuckles constantly smattered with scabs and bruises.

Neville's relationship with alcohol was not a new one. He had always found solace in the bottom of a bottle, and it had begun to take its toll on all of them. His outbursts of aggression after a session on the sauce had become more frequent, and as the disease took away the woman he loved, his love of alcohol grew deeper.

These days, his son was the target.

As a young teenager, Billy had been taken aside by his father and the severity of his mother's medical condition explained to him. Of course, being thirteen, he'd been wrapped up in his own dramas. Struggling with changing hormones had been the biggest of Billy's worries.

Neville had found it difficult to get through to him, and this had added to his internal worries. He would be greeted only with shrugs and grunts when he'd ask Billy how he was feeling about it all, and this would infuriate him.

Against professional advice and his own better judgment, he'd spent hours trying to force Billy into opening up. This had only pushed him further away. Billy had become hostile, and outwardly it had seemed as if he hadn't cared. He'd rebelled, spending more and more time away from his mother and father.

When Billy was seventeen, his mother's decline had been so bad, she was moved to York where her parents were from and placed in a convalescent home. The family was uprooted to be near her, moving to a small, two-bedroomed terraced in the back streets—bought for them by Jenny's parents who were extremely wealthy—where Billy and his father had lived ever since.

Billy left his old life and dreams behind him, and with them, the chance to get to know Eve Swallow.

At six feet, three inches and built like a truck, Nev Taylor was not a force to be messed with, and Billy fell backwards to the floor. His hand moved up to his face as he winced with pain, wiping the blood from the corner of his mouth with the back of it. It had been an unlucky and foolish judgment call trying to protect his father from himself, but he had learned the hard way again tonight. He had youth and sobriety on his side, though, and he jumped up to his feet quickly, backing towards the door, ensuring he didn't take his eyes from his father's frame.

Nev turned around and stared menacingly at Billy, his breathing heavy and laboured. "You don't come and go as you fucking please in this house. D'ya hear me, boy?"

Billy's breathing mirrored his father's and he nodded quickly, maintaining contact with eyes that could have been his own.

Nev physically backed down, rubbing his hand across the top of his closely shaved head. He dipped it and turned around, walking into the kitchen.

Billy tentatively moved towards the back of the room and bent down, collecting into the palm of his hand the brown shards of glass that littered the carpet like huge thorns.

CHAPTER
five

Find Her Way To Me – Josh Record

THE FRONT DOOR slammed, the sound of his father's door keys rattling in the lock, as Billy rolled over onto his back. He stretched his arms, linking his fingers and resting them behind his head, his eyes settling on the crack in the ceiling above his bed.

It was Saturday, so he had hours to himself. His dad would be at the pub all day and would be practically comatose by the time he returned home later on.

Reaching over to his bedside table, Billy grabbed Eve's sketchbook and rested it against his legs. He smoothed the flat of his hand across the cover of the book and then spent the next ten minutes poring over the interpretations on each page, just as he had done into the early hours of the night before, unable to tear his eyes away.

His favourite image was a charcoal drawing of a little girl standing in the middle of a field, her hair blowing in the wind and her arms outstretched. There was something innocent and carefree about the look on her face, and it reminded him of simpler times. He closed the book, placing it back down, and returned his gaze to the ceiling. His fingers traced lazy patterns across his chest as he lost himself in the memory of her eyes.

Something inside him awoke, stirring up old urges, and he jumped off the bed, slipped into a pair of joggers and descended the stairs. He stopped and leaned against the doorframe of the dining room, slipping his hands into his pockets and allowing his eyes to take in the contents of the room.

The top of the piano was covered in knick-knacks belonging to his mother and a pile of old bills and letters that his father had discarded. He wandered lazily into the room and halted in front of the beautiful instrument. Taking his hand out of his pocket, he ran it slowly along the lid, his eyes drinking in the familiarity and his skin dancing at the feel of it beneath his fingers.

As a young child, he'd had the standard music tuition. He'd been ferried to and from piano lessons at the opposite side of town where he picked up the basics, but he'd soon become frustrated with the technical side of learning—the step-by-step training that he was required to follow. After the news of his mother's illness, he'd refused to go anymore, choosing instead to lock himself in his room with his keyboard, experimenting and composing. With four years of lessons under his belt, though, he'd been competent enough to continue teaching himself, and it had become clear very quickly that he had a huge talent. His grandparents gave Billy their antique walnut upright for his sixteenth birthday, and he would spend all his spare time at the keys, wallowing in his teenage self-pity and frustrations. When the family relocated, the piano came with them, but it had been untouched and collecting dust for a good three years now.

The emotion running through his veins as he fingered the wood was his soul's way of begging him to rectify that.

He hadn't allowed anyone to see how much the illness had affected him, least of all his father, and he'd shut down inside. His grandparents (his mother's parents) were oblivious to the hurt that the house held. Despite living in the same city, they had gone longer and longer between visits, unsure how to step in and help Neville, and phone calls only seemed to occur at Christmas or on birthdays.

There was a huge elephant, not only in the room, but also in their lives, and every one of them repeatedly side-stepped it, leaving a gaping hole in their communication. Each family member had retreated into a shell of his or her own, and anyone knocking to come in was either shooed away or ignored.

Losing his mother to dementia had been like having his heart ripped out, and without his heart, there was no reason for music.

But here it was stirring again.

It beat faster, it beat louder and the girl behind the grey eyes filled his head.

He couldn't even begin to contemplate how or why she was locked inside of him, so close to him, when they had barely even spoken to each other, but what he did know was that he was drawn to the fact she wasn't perfectly put together—the fact that she ran so fiercely from him.

But what else was she running from? What had her so scared that she couldn't even be near him?

He wanted to reach out and pluck her from whatever hell she was living in, but he had a feeling that would have her running harder, faster and further away.

He lifted the lid, and as his eyes looked upon the ebony and ivory, he realised he had missed them desperately. There was no stool to sit on anymore: it had been taken to the skip after his dad had thrown it at him six months earlier, the legs smashing off against the front door. Billy had been tidying up the top of the piano, and Neville had walked in on him wrapping his wife's ornaments up in tissue paper. Had he not drunk his own body weight in alcohol, the scene may have been a little less antagonistic, but he'd grabbed hold of the piano stool and Billy, throwing him to the ground, screaming at him about how he had no business wrapping the memories of his mother away.

Billy never contemplated going to the police.

This was his father, and he needed to keep him safe. He needed to protect him from his own horrific grief.

Neville hadn't been to the home to see Jenny in months, and Billy had continued to make excuses for him: he was too busy with work, he was ill, he was just… Billy needed to stay strong for all of them. Nev had given up, and Billy needed to continue fighting for him. He needed to do everything in his power to ensure that the family stayed as much a unit as possible, even though it was already broken beyond repair, and if he went to the police, he would lose his dad, too.

Billy breathed in deeply and walked his fingers up the keys, his pulse beating faster as the notes filled the room. The more he heard, the more he played, and before long, he had settled himself into an abridged version of *Beethoven's Moonlight Sonata*. The music wrapped around him, and he lost all control over his fingers as they danced along the keys effortlessly, as if he'd never been away.

As he played the last notes, Billy realised he was

shaking, his back glittering with sweat. An emotion that had been locked away for too long was starting to break free.

He stood up, wiping his face with the back of his hand, and moved to an old box that lay beneath the bay window. It was full of scores that he had borrowed, bought and written himself, just sitting and waiting to be loved again. He dug around and pulled out a wad of them, tucking them under his arm and running up to his room. Discarding them on the bed, he grabbed his towel from the back of the door and locked himself in the bathroom.

Standing in the shower, he dipped his head under the spray and let it wash over him. It ran into his mouth, stinging the cut on his lip as he rested his arm against the wall of the cubicle and allowed himself a few minutes to mentally let go.

He felt so much older than his years, holding the weight of other people's sadness on his shoulders when he should have been the one being supported and held. His father had no interest in reaching out to him, so the only way to keep him close was to be there for whatever he needed, even if that was a punch bag. It never lasted long and was usually nothing more than a backhander across the cheek or a bloody nose—nothing Billy couldn't handle. He'd built up a tough exterior that never faltered, taking the hits in an attempt to absorb the hurt that was behind the power of his father's fists.

He stood up, reaching for the shower gel, and washed his hair and body, wincing as he moved his hand across the side of his rib cage where he'd taken a beating only a couple of days before. Once out of the shower, he dried off and dressed quickly in a clean shirt and jeans and reached for his car keys on his side table.

"Fuck."

Billy's mother's home was a fifteen-minute drive from where he lived, and his plan to see today her was scuppered when he remembered where his keys, and indeed his car was. "Fuck. Fuck. Fuck."

He was not ready to turn up at Eve's house, still, especially now he had spent so long pouring over the sketchbook. He was not ready to give that up. It was almost as if the connection they shared was sealed when he had it in his hands, and he was scared that it might break if he gave it back.

He paced around the bedroom, head down with his hand scratching the back of his neck, while he tried to come up with a means of travel. He walked around the side of his bed, picking up his jacket and fumbling for his wallet. The weight of it in his hand was enough evidence to suggest that there was no loose change in there, so the bus was out of the question.

Billy worked in a record store just outside of the main city, and the money he had left after giving most of it to his dad towards bills and food, was pittance. Anything left was usually spent on gifts for his mother, or, if he was particularly flush, some new threads. On occasion he would go drinking with his friends, but an overwhelming fear of turning into his father stopped him from getting out of control.

He collected his phone from the chair at the end of the bed and dialled Dobbo's number. He'd known Paul Dobson for three years now, and he was as close to a best mate as he was ever going to get.

It rang a couple of times before a hoarse voice answered. "S'up?"

"Haha! Good night?"

"Fuck you. Why you ringing me at this ungodly hour?"

Billy heard a high-pitched female voice in the background asking where the toilet was. "You dirty dawg! Got your oats then?"

"Fuck off, Bill. What do you want? And where the hell did you get to last night?"

Deliberately ignoring the latter, Billy got straight to the point. "I was going to ask you if you'd give me a lift to the home in a bit, but I can hear that you are otherwise engaged."

"What's wrong with your car?"

"Umm…" Billy scratched his unshaved cheek, lifting the side of his face into a grimace. "It's just not available to use at this precise moment in time is all. Never mind. I'll sort something."

"Yeah, whatever, you lying twat. Fill me in later."

"Laters, buddy." Billy hung up and sat down on the edge of the bed, his elbows on his knees and his hands hanging loosely between his legs. He looked at his phone and speed-dialled the number for Butterfield's, his mother's home.

"Hi, yeah. It's Billy, Jenny Taylor's son." He licked along his bottom lip as Becky, the carer on the other end of the phone, greeted him, asking him if he was well. "Yeah, good thanks. And you?"

The staff members were always very polite, but there was a hint of pity in their voices every time he spoke to them. "Good. Listen, I was hoping to come this afternoon as usual, but I'm having transport trouble. Would you be able to tell Mum that I will get there if I can, and if not, I will try and come along tomorrow?"

Becky assured him she would pass on the message, and after a brief goodbye, Billy hung up. He knew that the message would mean nothing to his mother unless she was having a moment of clarity, but it was that moment of clarity that he held out for every single day. He stuffed his phone in his jeans pocket, collected his jacket and headed out of the front door with no real agenda.

Walking the streets of York, Billy felt like a tourist. He'd lived there for four years but he rarely visited the centre. He strolled down Stonegate, turning his head to take in the delights of the street performers and buskers, and wandered into St. Helen's Square. The sun was beating down, so he slipped out of his jacket, slinging it over his shoulder. He didn't really know where he was going or why he was walking. He'd just needed to get out of the house, away from the constant reminders of the mess he was living in and the torture that came in the form of a grey-eyed brunette who had wrapped her soul around his own and was refusing to let go.

He ducked into the alleyway that led to the Lendal Cellars and lit up a cigarette, leaning back against the wall and taking a moment to just breathe. The sting in his chest as he held onto the smoke gave him the pain he needed to focus on in order to put everything else to the back of his mind for just a moment.

He turned to face the street crossing his ankles he watched the world go by.

A band of lads a similar age to his own had set up outside one of the shops and were tuning guitars and plugging leads into amps. He squinted against the sun and watched with interest and a slice of jealousy as they warmed up, already drawing in a crowd.

There was a time in his life when he had longed to pursue a career in music. At school, there had been a couple of boys in his year group who had been musically inclined, and they'd talked of getting together to follow their dreams. The idea had swum around without materialising, and before they'd made any concrete plans, Billy had skipped town with his family and the dream had fallen apart.

Because he'd been almost eighteen when he moved, he'd never bothered going back to school. His dad had been too busy dealing with his mum to care much about what his son's dreams and ambitions were, so there had been no talk of continuing A-Levels or pursuing a university career. It was assumed he would find work as soon as possible and start getting used to life as a young adult, paying his way and pulling his weight.

A twinge of resentment niggled Billy as he watched the guitarist's fingers dance up and down the fret board while grinning at the lead singer with excitement, a look in his eye that clearly said, *This is us living the dream, mate!* Okay, it was only busking, but they were most definitely on their chosen path.

Billy flicked the butt of his cigarette to the ground, pushing himself off the wall and stepping out of the alleyway into the sun-drenched street. He strolled towards the gathering crowd and listened to *Eboracum Rain* thump out their tunes for a few more minutes, tossing a stray twenty pence piece into the open guitar case that lay begging strangers for change in front of them. He squinted up at the sky and headed up Coney Street towards Lendal Bridge and the Museum Gardens.

Out-for-the-day families sauntered in through the gates, heading for the grassy inclines and the resident ice-cream van. Billy crossed the road and walked through the gates into the city's ten-acre botanical garden.

Young couples lay entwined on the grass, sharing chaste kisses and stroking sun-burned skin, while toddlers and children chased pigeons across the grass, their delighted screams filling the air. Billy tied his jacket around his waist and stuffed his hands in his jeans' pockets, following a throng of teenage girls up one of the twisting paths to the shelter of a large oak tree.

His stomach grumbled and he regretted skipping breakfast, glancing longingly at the ice-cream van as he passed it on his way up the path. An elderly gentleman in front of him stopped in his tracks, causing Billy to nearly bump into him. He smiled fondly as the man turned around to apologise. He reminded him a little of his grandpa, and a stream of sadness and guilt trickled through him as he recalled the last time he had made the effort to contact them. It was a two-way communication failure, but it just needed someone to make the first step to reconciliation. There was no reason why Billy couldn't be that person. He was an adult now, after all. Responsibility lay on his shoulders, too, and with that came the possibility of blame being laid if he did nothing.

He untied his jacket, laying it on the floor, and slid down the trunk of the tree to sit down on it, pulling his knees up and resting his elbows on the top of them. Peering out from under his long fringe, he watched as the lunchtime crowd began to disperse. Businessmen in suits readjusted loosened ties before their dash back to the offices where they would spend the next few hours thanking the Lord for air conditioning.

Towards the bottom of the hill, a large weeping

willow stood, majestic and alone, and Billy's eyes were magnetically drawn towards a pair of shabby Doc Marten boots that peeked out from behind. They were attached to pair of tanned, bare calves that led to a large sheet of paper resting on top of anonymous knees. The owner of the boots was leaning up against the tree otherwise of sight except for a slender hand that gracefully moved across the paper, a pencil held loosely between finger and thumb.

By the way that his heart was racing, he knew instinctively who it was.

He inhaled deeply, placing his hand on the grass to push himself up, grabbing his jacket from the floor and sliding into it more slowly than was necessary. He wasn't even sure what was going to happen next. Cocking his head to the side, he closed one eye and blew a breath up to his fringe.

What if she bolts?

He didn't want to be the cause of another scene, particularly here with people around. She would definitely not want anything to do with him if he was the reason she freaked out again in public. He had no idea what he would say to her if his legs decided to carry him over in that moment. He wasn't even sure his mouth would open or, if it did, that anything would come out. He breathed in through his nose, resisting the urge to light up and walk away, and ducking his head down, he moved cautiously towards the willow tree, looking everywhere but at the girl who didn't even know she was breaking him in two.

As he approached the tree from behind where Eve was sitting, he reached up and scratched the back of his head, stopping in his tracks, dropping his head back and closing his eyes. He chastised himself, telling himself not to be such a pussy and to just walk up to her, to say hi, but his internal pep talk did nothing to spur him on in either direction, and he stood for a minute or two, eyes closed.

What am I even thinking?

Even if he managed to say hello, he was convinced something in her would stop her from responding, just like last time, and it wouldn't ever get past that. He could not control the future, let alone this girl who ran like a damn wild animal anytime he was near her.

He'd dreamed about looking into those eyes again. He'd dreamed of touching the skin on her face, of getting close enough to smell her hair, to brush it from her forehead.

But how could he have ever thought like that? He would be surprised if anyone even got to hold her hand, never mind anything else. Turning on his heel at the last minute, he walked back up towards the gates.

Stupid idiot.

Why he had gotten his hopes up so much that he thought anything would ever come of this was beyond him. She was clearly messed up and would need more than some dead-beat dick head to help fix her.

CHAPTER
six

Waiting - Aquilo

THE LIGHT DRIPPING between the trees was perfect for the feel of the music she was listening to. Eve pulled out her A3 sketchbook from her portfolio and turned to a new sheet of paper. She loved that feel of a blank canvas more than anything and took a deep breath with her eyes closed, a gentle smile playing on her lips. Emptying her bag that morning, she had been devastated to find that the sketchbook she'd been using for the past few weeks was gone. God only knew where it was after the way she had run the night before.

Just in front of where she sat was a teenage girl and her beau. They lay side by side, their hands entwined, staring at the clouds as they imagined them as animals and objects. Every so often, the boy would look over to the girl, and the way his eyes roamed over her face made Eve's heart twinge. She'd never experienced the love, nor the lust of a boy in that way, and she wondered in that moment if she ever would. She selected a drawing pencil from her case and checked that it was sharp enough. The girl's feet were flat on the ground, her knees creating the point of a triangle, and Eve began to sketch the soft curve of her legs onto the paper. After only a few minutes of moving only her eyes and her hand, she became lost in the act of recreating the scene in front of her.

She used her finger to smudge and soften harsh lines, creating light and shadow in all the right places, periodically cocking her head to the side to appraise her efforts. Drawing people was her main interest and indeed her forté. She loved trying to capture a moment: a look in the eye, a facial expression or the way that people interacted... Her drawing style was relaxed and free. She had a real gift. She really saw people and was able to transfer emotion to paper. She often wondered if her obsession grew from never actually getting close enough to experience people for real.

She moved on to looking at the folds in the boy's T-shirt as it pulled across his chest, and using a putty rubber, she moved the marks she had made around the paper to create the illusion of cotton.

As she watched the couple, representing their young love with her pencil, the hairs on the back of her neck stood on end. Someone had walked closer to her—she'd heard the movement in the grass. She swallowed and held her breath, staring straight ahead and not daring to move except to flick her eyes back to her live models and direct her pencil slowly across the paper.

Something was bothering her.

She was desperate to turn around and see who had come so close. It couldn't be someone she knew: they'd have come right around the tree and attempted to sit with her or at least to said hello, wouldn't they? It could just be a nosy passer-by or an art enthusiast who'd spotted what she was doing, hoping for a peek.

As she settled on this probable truth, she relaxed as much as she could back into her task, and after a minute, the sound of the grass rustling behind her picked up again, this time getting further away from her.

She smiled to herself for being right: just an inquisitive stranger, after all.

After spending the majority of her Saturday in Museum Gardens—always the best option for restoring calm to Eve's mind—she was ready for music and a tub of ice cream.

She'd needed some alone time after the incident at the ball the night before but also to minimise any accidental sightings of Billy bloody Taylor, which is why she'd set off early so she wasn't around when he came to collect his car.

She took a round-about route home to avoid bumping into anyone she knew, let alone him, but on arriving back to the house as the sun was beginning to set, she was surprised to see the blue Fiesta still sitting there, awaiting the arrival of its owner.

She shook her head to get rid of the thought that he could even be on his way round right then and quickly unlocked the door, dumping her bags in the hallway and calling out to Rachel to let her know she was home.

"I'm in the bath, bud."

Eve clumped up the stairs and pushed the bathroom door open, leaning on the frame to talk to Rachel who was up to her chin in bubbles, her leg over the side, shaving from knee to ankle.

"That's a lot of effort to go to just for me coming home, sweetness." Eve winked.

Rachel laughed. "Actually, I am going out." She gave

Eve a mysterious look and wiggled her eyebrows. "I have a date."

Eve's eyes widened, and she walked further into the room, sitting herself down on the toilet seat, her ears pricked for more details. "Oh! A date with whom?" She leaned forwards, resting her elbows on her thighs and her chin in her hands as she waited for more information.

"Just a guy from my course." Rachel averted her eyes, a small smirk tugging at the side of her mouth.

"Just a guy, huh? I don't believe that's the truth, missy."

Rachel moved her eyes deliberately slowly towards Eve, pursing her lips to stop the excitement bursting out of them prematurely. "Okay. Okay. No big deal, though. Just Julian."

"No freakin' way!" Eve's hands flew up to her forehead in disbelief. Rachel had been lusting over Julian Walker since Fresher's Week, but as yet had not managed to catch his eye. "How? When? Details!"

Rachel made fists in the water. She scrunched her face up and kicked her feet in the water, causing it to splash over the sides. "He just asked me today. I went to meet Deb for a quick drink after lunch. He was there with some of his mates, and when Deb went to the toilet, he came over and started chatting to me and asked me out. Tonight! He said he'd seen me last night at the ball and was going to come over, but then… Well, then I wasn't there…" Rachel looked down, not wanting to make Eve feel even the slightest bit guilty. Eve smiled tightly and then allowed her enthusiasm to rise back up again.

"Well, what the chuff are you going to wear?"

Rachel grinned. "All sorted. There are three outfits on my bed. Go. Go!"

Eve jumped up, bouncing on her toes and rubbing her hands together before running out of the door. She stopped in the doorway and swung around again, beaming at her friend.

Rachel's room was decorated with purple walls and a grey carpet, and it gave Eve a headache before even stepping inside. She sauntered over to the bed and placed her hands on her hips, rolling onto the sides of her feet and back while eyeing the outfits that Rachel had selected for vetoing. She moved her eyes over the clothes a couple more times and then returned to the bathroom to inform Rachel of the final decision. "I think the coral top but with that beige jacket and leggings. Are you eating out? I'm going to order a Chinese and then eat my body weight in ice cream."

"He's taking me to dinner, so I'll pass thanks."

Eve nodded and grinned at her best friend as she left to get ready for her night in.

An hour later, Eve stood on the doorstep and blew Rachel a kiss as she confidently sashayed out of the gate, onto the street and into the waiting taxi. "Have fun. Be good. Be careful!"

Rachel waved out of the window and Eve smiled fondly. She folded her arms across her chest, hiding her hands under her armpits as she looked up at the darkening sky. The temperature had dropped again, and there were some menacing looking clouds making their way across the city. She stood for a few moments longer, breathing in the smell of the changing air, then ducked back inside the house, closing the front door, forgetting all about the blue Fiesta that remained uncollected.

She loved Rachel, but she loved having time to herself, too. When she wasn't there, Eve could be herself—her true self. The self that loved to dance around the kitchen barefoot, the self that sung at the top of her voice to her favourite songs, the self that came out of that frightened exterior and just enjoyed being...

She took the stairs two at a time, flinging the door to her bedroom open and flopping onto her bed on her stomach to reach across for her iPod before retreating back downstairs. Rummaging in the kitchen drawer, she located the takeaway menu and dialled the number, ordering her dish to be delivered within the hour. She hung up and then padded into the living room, plugging her iPod into the dock that sat on the table.

Her playlists were eclectic to say the least, from Say Lou Lou to REM. She hit shuffle and immediately began to jiggle her legs to the raspy tones of Coco Sumner. She retrieved her portfolio from the hallway and sat down with it on the sofa. Her plan was to add some finishing touches to the sketch she'd started in the park and then see if she could complete a piece for her end of semester assessments.

A low roll of thunder caused her to move to the window and watch the colours of the sky dissipate into new ones, taking photographs on her phone. She was constantly thinking of her next project, and anything that caught her eye would no doubt end up in her ideas book in some form or another. She sat back down, opening her sketchbook, and waited for the knock at the door that would bring her food.

***

SITTING ON HIS own in the pub, nursing a pint he'd managed to pay for with the pittance left in the bottom of his bank account, Billy sat with his head down, the muscles in his jaw flexing as he clenched his teeth to stop him from tipping up the table in frustration. He fingered a beer mat, tearing at the corners and rolling bits of the cardboard into tiny balls, flicking them across the room.

Part of him wished he had just taken control of the situation in Flatlands Park and gone against Rachel's warnings. At least then Eve might have been shocked into talking to him. She might not be so fucking freaked out by him now, and he might not have bottled it every time he thought he had plucked up the courage to go and see her.

He was locked inside his own prison of thought, rolling what ifs around in his head. The hold she seemed to have over him was ridiculous.

He'd woken up thinking about her, and he was pretty sure he would go to bed on the same train again tonight. He kicked the table leg.

Being in possession of her sketchbook was torturous: seeing a piece of her, touching the paper she had held, tracing the lines she had created, following the journey of her pencil and in turn her eyes, seeing what she had seen…

He needed to get rid of it, and with it the thoughts of her. He was through fucking about. She'd either see him or she wouldn't, and he'd just deal with that when he got there. Apart from anything else, he needed his car and keys so he could visit his mother the next day.

He stood, scraping his seat harshly across the stone floor, and downed his pint against his better judgment. Filling his pockets with his *Camel Blues*, keys and wallet, he made the decision to call at home to pick up the cursed leather-bound book.

Nodding over to the barman by way of thanks, he shoved the door open and barged into the outdoors. The evening was creeping in, and with it storm clouds and the beginnings of rain. He tucked his hands deep into his jeans pockets and hunched his shoulders against the weather. It would take him twenty minutes to get there if he walked quickly, five more to get from his house to her.

Checking left and right, he jogged across the road and walked up towards the Minster. Lit up at night, it was majestic, and Billy took a second or two to allow his eyes to roam over its impressive form. He had often dreamed of being able to play his piano in such a grand building with acoustics like the Minster.

He lit up a cigarette, savouring the burn in his lungs that momentarily stopped the pounding in his chest. He was ten minutes away from his door, which meant in fifteen minutes or so, he may or may not get to look at her face.

He had run the different scenarios around in his head: they might not be in; Rachel might be in but Eve might be out; they might be in but they might refuse to answer the door; they might both be in and Eve might refuse to see him…He had thought about rehearsing a speech for each of them but decided that he would only fuck it up and end up sounding like a twat.

Stubbing his cigarette out, he set off at a steady jog to the bottom of the road and past the university buildings. Running through puddles, his jeans became muddy and wet. He flicked his head to remove his hair away from his eyes and the rainwater blurring his vision.

It took him all of a minute to run into his house, ignoring the slurs from his father, to grab the sketchbook and get back out again.

As he turned the corner, the heavens opened, and a torrential downpour hit the city.

"Fuck!" Billy ran and ducked into shop doorway,

shoving the sketchbook up inside his T-shirt and fastening his jacket across his chest in an attempt to keep the pages from water damage.

He was so close now and he took a moment to slow down his movement so he could catch his breath and steady his heartbeat before he arrived. His chest heaved in an attempt to refuel his lungs, and Billy walked purposefully to number seven Elton Terrace—the one with the blue door and the squeaky gate.

Standing in front of the house, a profound and all-consuming need to discover the girl who hid behind the deep sea of emotions that swirled behind the emptiness of her eyes arose inside of him and pushed him forwards.

He couldn't give up this chance at being able to look into them, even if it was just one last time, to at least discover if it was all in his mind or if indeed there was this connection he was feeling so overpoweringly and so deeply. If he didn't take this opportunity, his nerve would go again, and she may be lost to him forever. If he didn't do it now, he never would, and he would spend the rest of his life fucked up about the girl that got away—the girl he never even tried to chase.

Never had a girl affected him in this way.

He paused with his hand on the top of the cold metal of the gate, blowing out his cheeks to eliminate the sick feeling in his stomach. He tilted his head upwards, searching for answers in the stars that were hidden by the storm and ran his hand down his face, resting his finger and thumb either side of the bridge of his nose. He pushed open the gate, cringing at the noise the hinges made.

Each step closer seemed more sluggish and slower than the one before.

He stood facing the door, raised his fist and knocked. It was now or never.

The sound of his blood rushing in his ears was the only thing he could focus on until the rattling of keys jolted him from his paralysis. The sound of one of them sliding into the lock and twisting had him squeezing his fists tight inside his pockets. He clenched his teeth and held his breath as the handle dropped down and the door started to open.

It took a lifetime, but suddenly she was there, as close to him as she was that day in the school corridor.

Fumbling inside her purse, Eve stood on the top step. Her hair hung in front of her shoulders, and her eyes were downcast. Billy sucked in a sharp breath and drank in the sight of her. Her demeanour was relaxed and his cheek pulled the corner of his mouth into a gentle smile. His eyes roamed over her, taking in as much as he could lest she realise he was there and shut him out.

She was dressed in her signature leggings and checked shirt, the outfit he had seen her in dozens of times, but instead of her Docs, her feet were bare, and he noticed a silver ring on one of her toes.

His stomach tightened as he moved his eyes back up to her face and she began to speak.

She spoke into her purse as she continued to rifle through its contents. "Sorry. I'll just be a second. I thought I had a tenner… Oh. Here it is. Sorry." She pulled it out, lifting her eyes until they rested on his face.

She froze, except for a slight widening of her eyes as the realisation that Billy Taylor (and not the deliveryman with her food) was on her doorstep sunk in. Biting down on her bottom lip, Eve straightened up. She dropped her arms by her sides, her heart pounding, and Billy held his breath, locking into her eyes once again.

This time, though, Eve didn't look away—nor did she run—and he hurried his thoughts along as he contemplated the fact that this rendezvous with her could be cut short at any moment.

And then she said his name.

"Billy…" Her eyes shifted to the floor.

His heart thumped hard beneath his ribcage as he fought to release his own words that stuck like thorns.

God, she was beautiful.

His curled fingers made a tunnel at his lips as he cleared his throat. "Eve. Um. Hi."

Glancing back up at him from under her long lashes, she folded her arms across her chest. She wasn't entirely sure of his intentions, but the look in his eyes told her he was not there just to pick up his keys.

Despite feeling a little braver over her own threshold, her body was screaming at her to close the door, so she spoke again before Billy could explain himself, thumbing behind her into the house. "I'll just go get…" She turned away, walking quickly on wobbly legs towards the kitchen, her heart in her mouth and her mind whirling and screaming loudly.

Just get the keys and he'll leave.

She rummaged around in the kitchen, her fingers shaking, with no idea where the damn things were. "Fucks sake, Rachel. Where have you put them?"

"Can I help?"

Eve froze for a second time, spinning around and gripping the kitchen counter behind her. She drew in a breath and glared at Billy, unable to speak.

He stood in the kitchen doorway, his eyes flicking across her face she began to move slowly and further into the house, her face emanating fear and her mouth hanging slightly open.

He didn't follow her. He stood, his hands up in surrender, his brows raised, and nodded to her gently.

She began to shake her head slowly. "I... I can't find them. Please leave."

Billy dropped his head to his chest, shoving his hands in his pockets in an attempt to give her some breathing space. What had he done? Thick-headedness and impatience had overruled his better judgment and now he had more than likely made matters worse.

He waited for her to run.

CHAPTER
seven

Breathe – Rhodes

THE HAMMERING HAD started, and Eve was not able to predict what might happen next. Her escape route was blocked… by Billy Taylor. If her legs started running, she would have to go through him, and she wasn't entirely convinced that he would let her.

He stood in front of her, still and quiet, as she swallowed, getting ready to move. She looked down, remembering she was barefoot and inwardly cursed at herself. Thinking on her feet, she remembered Rachel's shoes that were at the back door.

Billy slowly lifted his cocked head and peered up at her, and her stomach lurched.

That was her cue.

She spun on her heel and took off towards the back door.

"Shit." Billy raked his hands through his hair and followed on her trail. She was fast. He reached the door as she was slamming it shut and locking it behind her. "Eve, I just want my keys," he shouted to her through the wood, hoping she would hear him.

She didn't.

"Fuck! Fuck, fuck, fuck." He swivelled back around and ran for the front door that still stood open, pulling it closed behind him, before jumping down all three steps at once. He put his hand on the wall, vaulting over the top, and ran in the direction of the park. She was bound to be heading in there, right?

Eve's feet, now in a pair of Rachel's Converse, slapped against the pavement as she strode the streets towards Flatlands Park. She cursed the rain as it soaked through her thin clothing and began to numb her hands.

Fucking Billy and his fucking persistence. Why did he not get the hint? Was it not obvious enough last time that she couldn't be near him, and didn't *want* to be near him? Were all men so pig-headed?

It was late again, so the gate, as usual, was locked. She located the gap in the bushes and crawled through, checking momentarily for her sketchbook. She couldn't think where else it might be but didn't hold out much hope that she would find it.

The ground was boggy, and she slipped and slid, the mud splashing up her leggings, and she changed course to locate the path.

Following the one that took her to the far end of the park, Eve slumped down behind a tree and put her head between her knees to regain her breath and to steady her shaking body. The adrenaline that pumped through her when she ran like that was enough to make her forget the feeling of being trapped, the feeling of not being able to control the situation she found herself in. It wasn't often she ran for such a length of time, and just like the night

LLOYD-JONES

before, she was now exhausted.

Her hideouts back home had been closer, and she was able to run faster and harder to get to them sooner because of the shorter distance. She wasn't a runner by any stretch of the imagination, but she'd discovered how fast she was once she started having to get away from a predicament. It took everything out of her, though, which was part of the feel-good factor of it. Her chest burned and she squeezed her eyes together, grimacing at the pain.

Once calm had been restored, she tilted her head back against the tree and looked up at the sky. Some of the clouds had cleared and the stars were more visible again. The persistent drip of the rain cooled her skin, and she closed her eyes to wait it out, hoping to God he wouldn't find her.

***

BILLY HEADED IN the direction of the park and straight to the gap in the hedge that he knew she would have had to use as an entrance. He had no idea how long this was going to take him. For all he knew, she wasn't even there.

Fucking stupid girl.

For the second time in two days, he was sprinting through the rain looking for a stranger. That word seemed alien to him, though: she felt nothing like a stranger to his heart.

This was his final chance to try and explore the possibility of getting to know her. If this didn't work, he had to get over it and move on.

He looked at the ground and saw where someone had recently trudged through the mud and flattened down the wet grass, and his mood lifted a little. The trail reached the edge of the path and then stopped. Billy sighed and stood with his hands on his hips, his chest heaving and rainwater dripping from the ends of his hair onto his face. He ran his hand down to clear some of it away and took off down the path, being careful to keep his footsteps as quiet as he could, ducking his head down against the rain and wind.

The path took a turn to the right down to the far end of the park, and as he walked up it, he finally saw her.

Her back was up against a tree, her legs tucked up with her chin resting on the tops of her knees. He detoured so that he could approach from behind, only this time he did not hesitate. He slid down the other side of it and let his instincts kick in.

"Eve, please don't run. I have your sketchbook."

Eve kicked her head up from her knees, her eyes wide and her stomach lurching. She shifted her position so that her palms were planted flat on the ground either side of her, ready to push herself up and run if she needed to.

"I just want to talk to you, okay? I just want to talk to you without you running away from me. You don't have to say anything back, but please, just listen to me." Billy's mouth was dry, and he had no idea if this was working or not. He pulled his legs closer to his chest, resting his arms on his knees and bowing his head.

She leaned her cheek against the trunk of the tree, tucking her chin into her shoulder and closing her eyes. She could hear him breathing, and the smell of him was almost unbearable: a heady mix of cigarettes, the woody scent of his aftershave and the rain.

Her adrenalin hit had subsided, and she shivered into herself as she waited for his voice again. It was deeper than she remembered and had a gravely tone to it, but she supposed he was an adult now. The feeling of being so close to him was burning into her skin, and she was sure she'd be physically scarred from this moment.

Billy's mouth ran away with him, and his nerves got the better of him. He continued to talk quickly in order to get out what it was he wanted to say before she bolted. He was sure he was still on borrowed time with her and that once the sketchbook was in her possession again, that would be the end of it.

Despite all of this, he was determined to make a go of earning her trust, or whatever it was this fucking crazy, beautiful girl needed.

"So, I am assuming you're still there and that you haven't slipped away like some kind of ninja."

Eve caught herself smiling in spite of herself, and she rolled her eyes at him, secretly. She relaxed a little and moved her hands, crossing her arms in front of her.

"I have your sketchbook here and I wanted to return it. That's why I came tonight. I came to give you this back and to get my car keys. I really kinda need my car back. I don't have your number so I couldn't call in advance to warn you, so that's why I just turned up. That's why I was on your doorstep. My plan was to return your book dry and intact, but seeing as you had other ideas, I am going to have to return it wet and soggy. I'm sorry. I'm sorry for just turning up, I'm sorry for scaring you and I'm sorry about the rain."

Eve heard him fumbling about and turned her head a little when she saw his arm twist back around the trunk, her sketchbook in his hand. She reached around and took hold of the book, hesitating before pulling it towards her and out of Billy's grasp.

It was heavy with rainwater, and Eve sighed. Some of

her most recent and best sketches were inside of those pages, and her heart sank as she contemplated the amount of work she was going to have to put in to recreate the ideas for her coursework.

Billy's heart was thumping in his chest as he passed over the piece of her that he had treasured since the previous day—the little piece of her soul that he had clung to… And now it was gone.

His only excuse to find her and see her again had been handed back, and all hope seemed to be ripped away with it.

She turned her head sideways again, whispering almost inaudibly. "Thank you."

Billy, with his head between his knees once again, smiled to himself.

This was a start. It might also be the end, but at least she wasn't running. He sucked in another breath and pushed the boat out further. "You're incredibly talented."

Eve swallowed and closed her eyes, sucking in a breath and holding it for as long as she could until the feeling of betrayal subsided. She hadn't even considered the fact that he might have looked inside. She was about to let loose and ask him how he dared to pry inside a book that didn't belong to him, but then sense kicked in. If he hadn't opened it, he wouldn't have known what it was, and she wouldn't have it back in her hands now. She leaned her head backwards, another smile tugging at her mouth at the ridiculousness of the situation: the two of them sitting back to back against a tree in the rain, in the middle of a park, in the dark, soaked to the skin because she was too scared to look into his eyes in case he came too close. What a fuck up.

Billy continued talking to her, and she listened. "Your sketches are pretty fucking awesome. It's like you see what people are feeling and then you draw it. How the hell do you draw a feeling?" He looked up at the stars that had come into view, the rain beginning to ease off at last. His question was rhetorical, so Eve didn't answer.

Pulling his cigarettes from his top pocket, he struck a match and lit one up, sucking hard on that first pull and squinting as he waited to blow it all away. "Sorry. Do you smoke? Would you like one?"

Eve had no idea how to respond to such compliments from this boy, this man, and had slipped into a bit of a daydream as she listened to his voice and his movements behind her. She was jolted from them and sat up straight, the need to answer him now like a shard of glass in her throat. "Umm, no. Thank you."

She shuffled and allowed her legs to straighten out across the wet grass, placing her sketchbook on her lap. She pulled her shirt closer and wrapped her arms around her body, waiting. For what, she had no idea, but what she did know was that she was calm, and her blue light had stopped spinning.

Billy fingered a handful of leaves that sat damp and muddy next to his legs. He wracked his brains for the next thing to say as Eve was clearly not going to lead the conversation. How he was going to get through to this wounded soul, he had no idea, but he was damn well going to try given that she had allowed him the chance to start at all.

He already missed her eyes after holding her gaze again tonight. When she had first opened the door, she'd been relaxed and so bloody beautiful. That split second when she lifted her face to him, when she thought he was someone else, he saw her. He felt like he saw the Eve he was sure was locked away behind the fear. And then the penny had dropped, and she'd shut down. She'd physically shut down.

What was wrong with him that meant she disappeared from view whenever he was around? Why did he have this effect on her?

"So…" He blew out a lungful of smoke and wiped his top lip with the back of his hand. "You were clearly expecting someone else when you opened the door to me, right?"

Eve cleared her throat. This was beginning to turn into a conversation, something she was not used to having with a stranger. She wasn't comfortable answering questions at the best of times, and he was pushing her boundaries in quick succession tonight. She didn't like it one bit, but here she was, sitting within arm's reach of him, forming answers in her head. She licked her lips, biting the inside of her cheek before responding. "I thought you were the delivery man. I ordered Chinese food." She looked into her lap, that blue light switching itself to 'standby' in the background in preparation for any emergencies.

Billy laughed to himself and took another drag on his cigarette, blowing the smoke into the air. "Well, technically, I was the delivery man. I just didn't bring food." He held his breath and waited for her response.

Eve laughed unexpectedly and the sound filled Billy's heart with something he could not describe. He'd made her laugh. A grin spread across his face. It was the sweetest sound he had ever heard. His stomach lurched with excitement and desire. Bravery started to grow inside of him, and the hope that he'd felt float away earlier whispered to him gently.

Do not give up on her.

"Oh, fuckity fuck!" Eve sat bolt upright and got to her feet.

Billy sensed her movements and did the same, jumping to his feet and ducking around the tree without thinking. "Shit, you okay?" He stopped short once he realised what he had done, brushing the mud from his backside, and looked at the stunned and silenced Eve who was mirroring his movements, both sets of eyes wide and flickering.

They froze.

Backing off slightly, Billy held his hands out in front of him. "I'm sorry. Sorry. Don't run. Please. Please don't run." He took the final drag on his cigarette, holding the butt between finger and thumb, and flicked it away, his left hand still out, pleading with her to stay put. "I thought something had happened to you." He cleared his throat and lifted his eyebrows. "When you shouted out, just then. A bat. Or something. Y'know, like…" He twirled his finger near his head and Eve dropped her guard out of confusion and frowned at him, no idea what he was talking about. "Y'know, caught in your hair or something perhaps?" He squinted up at her from under his fringe and grimaced another apology. "I'm sorry if I scared you again."

Eve hid an amused smirk that took her by surprise. She looked down at Rachel's mud-covered Chucks and scratched the side of her face, her mouth twisted to one side. "Um. The Chinese?" Her sarcastic rise in intonation caused Billy to tuck his tongue into the well of his cheek and nod slowly, a smile playing at the corner of his mouth.

"I—I just remembered I wasn't there for the delivery, so…" She flicked her eyes back to his face and stared up at him, biting her top lip to stop herself from laughing.

Billy couldn't take his eyes off her. She was something else, and the mischievous look on her face tugged at a primal need inside him. His eyes roamed across her features, resting on her full mouth, her lip that she was biting on, and he subconsciously licked across his own before pulling himself together.

Eve's heart was fluttering in her chest. This was a new feeling. She was just as scared as usual, but she didn't want to run. Not right then, anyway. She definitely wanted to stay right where she was.

"Well, I think you might have missed out there." Billy stood tall and pushed his hands into his pockets, taking a deep breath. He couldn't allow this to end now. He was sure that this girl was something special, and the needs inside of him had multiplied over the last half hour. The connection was not just in his imagination as he sometimes made himself believe in order to get her out of his head. It was fucking real, and he was damned if he was going to let this opportunity fly away. He needed to proceed with caution, and he knew it could be a long, tiring and painful road, but he was already packing his rucksack and tying up his laces ready for the trip.

There was no doubt in his mind.

He wanted her, all of her, and completely. "So, what happens now?" He hunched his shoulders up and kicked the dirt under his feet.

Eve's eyes widened again.

She did not have a plan for the next move. She never did. She would always run with patent disregard for the consequences. She'd gotten herself into a quandary that she had no idea how to get out of. As much as she felt calm in the strangest of ways, she wasn't sure that she would be able to manage the half hour walk back home alongside Billy Taylor, let alone whatever else he was hoping for.

"I can't…" She breathed in, lifting her eyes to the starless sky and wishing upon an invisible one. "I don't know how to do… this." She wagged her finger between them and winced slightly at the awkwardness that seemed to fall over her like a dark shroud.

This…

What was he even asking? Did he want to befriend her? Spend time with her? Did she dare assume he wanted more? There was chemistry, she knew that—she'd always known that—but how the hell would she be able to find the right way to explain to this guy who had her all fucked up that she was the biggest freak he'd ever meet and that getting close in any way would be a huge problem?

She was too crazy to be wanted—too crazy to be needed or loved.

Billy squinted at the ground and fought to find the right words.

Don't fuck this up, dickhead. Don't you dare fuck this up.

He blew out a breath and leaned his shoulder against the tree, crossing his ankles, one over the other. Eve stood, her arms limp by her sides, the pulse in her neck twitching as she observed him from the corner of her eyes.

"I'll help." He looked up at her and her stomach clenched tight.

What was he doing to her? What was that look he was giving her?

"Where I can, I mean." Billy pushed himself off the

tree and took a step towards her, ducking his head a little to look into her eyes, his hands firmly in his pockets. "You just gotta guide me, okay?" He searched her face for an answer, his bright blue eyes reflecting the moonlight, intense and honest.

Eve shuddered involuntarily, not from the cold, but from the feeling that was pulsing around her body. He was so, so close to her. She could feel his body heat, and that smell…

"I'm not here to make life hard. I don't want to make you hurt or to frighten you. If you want me to leave, I can, but I did notice that you're not wearing a coat, so you really should get dry soon or you're going to be ill. So, let me walk you home. That can be step one. No more, no less… no expectations. Deal?" He raised his eyebrows to accentuate his question and pleaded with every fibre of his being for her to agree.

Eve's light started whirring, and the ringing in her ears pierced the quiet of the park. She wiped her palms down the front of her leggings while her eyes refused to stay on his face and darted around. She breathed in deeply, blowing the air from her cheeks.

Don't do this now. Don't do this while he is watching again. Don't let him see what a freak you are.

The noise became unbearable and she pressed her hands to her ears in an attempt to block it out, crouching down, her head dropping between her knees.

Billy bent down with her and took in a shaky breath.

What the fuck was he trying to get into here? Every nerve ending should have been screaming for him to leave her to it, but instead, the wave of sadness that washed over him like a tsunami knocked him for six and welded him to the spot, an overbearing need to protect her galloping across his chest. She seemed so vulnerable and so fragile. The need to wrap himself around her to shelter her from whatever evil lurked beneath her surface was almost tangible. He wanted to hold her hand while she tipped out her bucket of broken pieces and then sit cross-legged next to her and help her to put them back together.

Whatever had this amazing girl locked away was something he wanted to confront head on with her.

He wasn't going anywhere.

CHAPTER
eight

Carried – Kt Tunstall

THE PAIR SAT in silence for a few seconds as Eve battled with herself and fought to stay put. She was mentally and physically exhausted, and having Flight in the driving seat, it was almost impossible to push back against it. She refused to let him see her freak out again. This rocking like a baby thing she had going on was bad enough, and she was determined for the fight in her to make an appearance and take charge tonight.

She was at a crossroads: she could either run again and be haunted by 'what ifs' for the rest of her life, or she could scoop up the feelings he was instilling in her and whisk them into something positive. She had no idea what would come of it all, but for crying out loud, she was nineteen and she needed to start living.

She was going to let Billy walk her home.

She counted backwards from thirty to steady her breathing. She could do this. She'd done it before. She had flicked the switch the other way and pedalled backwards. Her mind flashed back to the fields at home, her safest safe place, and she inhaled through her nose, holding the air in her lungs in a bid to feel alive. She locked her fingers behind her head, her elbows swinging around to the front of her head and blew it all away.

Billy watched protectively as her body relaxed a little and she dropped her arms so that her elbows rested on her knees, her forearms extended and palms open. Her head remained low and he eyed her dainty hands, a silver band on the index finger of her left, and an assortment of others on her right hand. Her wrists were wrapped with leather cuffs and bangles and, a tiny tattoo peeked out from between them, the outline of an elephant with musical notes drifting out of its trunk. Billy almost reached his hand out, aching with a need to trace it with his finger. Thinking better of it, he sucked the desire and need back in through his gritted teeth.

Gentle patters of raindrops fell onto the underside of Eve's arms as she exposed them. The calming feeling of the water soothed the burning of her skin, and the ringing in her ears began to subside. With it, the hammering in her chest quieted and she breathed in and out deeply. She lifted her head to find Billy watching her in his crouched position. She met his hooded eyes with her own and gave him a tight-lipped smile. He reciprocated and raised his brows slightly, his face asking the poignant question. She nodded, and Billy nodded in response.

Eve felt real peace for the first time in such a long time. The way he was responding to her and her actions was sensitive and intelligent. She'd been running from him for so long—running from her memories of him, her dreams of him and his look. She'd been running from his eyes that bore a hole right into the depths of her—his eyes that her hand and pencils had recreated over and over in a bid to empty her soul of the intense blue—and here he was showing more understanding than her own mother ever had. He could have left her here. Hell, he could have not bothered following her at all, but he'd persisted, and he'd found her, and he was here.

He saw her. She knew that now. She knew that this was the connection.

Eve dropped her eyes again, and Billy stayed put, giving her the space she needed, waiting patiently for her to let him know she was done. She let her arms fall between her legs and pulled at the grass. She needed to trust him, first of all to get her home, and she needed to start that process now. So, in a move that surprised both of them, she reached out her arm and screwed one eye shut, looking up at him with the other, her head cocked onto one side. "Pull me up then."

Billy gave her a crooked smile that made her stomach lunge in a brand-new way and pushed himself to his feet. Her outstretched hand gave him a newfound confidence in the situation, and the wings of hope that had begun to flutter towards him rested on his shoulders, giving him a gentle shove. She was offering an olive branch. This was her way of saying 'hello' and he was going to literally grab it with both hands. He bent forwards slowly and looked into her eyes.

Holding out his arm, he smiled gently as she gently rocked forwards, curling her fingers around his hand, her eyes never leaving his. Her tiny frame pulled itself up, using his strength as leverage, and within a couple of seconds the two of them were standing face to face. Eve awkwardly planted her hands on the small of her back and looked down at the floor, unsure how the next bit would work.

Billy realised quickly that he would need to take control of the situation and leaned his head to one side, ducking slightly to look into her face again. He reached out and moved her hair, tucking it behind her ears, causing Eve to close her eyes and inhale. She lifted her face, fluttering her eyelids open as Billy spoke to her again.

"You okay?"

She smiled tightly and nodded. "I just need…" She sighed and shook her head gently. "I don't really know what I need. To get home, I suppose."

He held out his hand again. "Come on then. Let's get you back."

She looked down at his outstretched hand and back up at his face. It was a kind face, his bright eyes the focal point until he smiled.

Without another word, she slipped her hand in his, biting down on her bottom lip nervously, flicking her eyes back up to him, waiting for him to make the first move towards the bushes where they would both have to crawl out of the park again.

Billy breathed in deeply in a bid to distill the ache that rushed through his body when her skin connected with his.

He knew he would never let her run from him again.

**

BILLY AND EVE picked their way across the wet grass to the path that led towards their exit. The only sounds were their breathing and the patter of rain in the trees. He pulled a packet of mints from his pocket, popping one into his mouth before offering one to her. She shook her head, smiling in thanks, and continued to walk peacefully next to him.

"Are you warm enough? Do you want my jacket? I'm not sure it will do much good. It's pretty damp."

Eve eyed him curiously and shook her head with a smile. "Thanks, though."

She let her head fall backwards, allowing the rainwater to cool her face. Billy looked over at her and blew the air from his cheeks. What was she doing to him? He stared at her, his eyes following the curve of her neck and the line of her jaw. He was becoming hungry, greedy for her. He needed to get to know her, to learn everything there was to know about her. He wanted that above all else, but in that moment, the animal in him was awake, and his basic needs were fighting to the front. Her hair tumbled down her back, glistening with rain, and it took all of his inner strength to not pull her to him.

He shook his head to clear his thoughts and dropped her hand in a bid to disconnect his dick and engage his head again. He missed the feel of her, though, and regretted it immediately. It might have been his only chance to touch her, and he swore through his teeth.

"Fuck." His curse was barely audible, but Eve heard him and tilted her head forwards, giving him a wicked glance from the corner of her eye.

"Fuck what?"

"Fuck, nothing." He smiled at her inquisitiveness, grateful that she was feeling comfortable enough to talk to him and pushed his hands into his pockets.

She jutted her chin out and squinted up at him from his side. "Why don't I believe you?"

Billy laughed, shaking his head. If he was even the slightest bit lucky, this beauty was going to get him into all kinds of trouble, and he was chomping at the bit to get started. He turned to look at her and decided to just let it all out. "Fuck, you're incredible," he said, matter-of-factly. He held her eyes with his, pleading with her to not look away, and reached out with his hand, stroking down her nose with his thumb. "You're incredible."

Eve dropped her head so her hair covered her face as her heart thudded away behind her ribcage. She was not accustomed to receiving such comments and had no idea how to react. Billy stopped in his tracks and reached out to hold Eve's elbow so that she would stop beside him. She threw her head up, unsure what was going on, and looked at him, searching his face for answers to the questions her body was posing. Her skin felt too tight for her and she wanted to climb out of it.

Billy gently placed his hand on Eve's cheek, allowing the not-so-smart part of his brain to take over. She prepared herself for flinching away and fucking things up once again, but to her surprise, she stayed put. The feel of his warmth against her skin seemed to appease the interrogation of her own mind and body. All the answers to all the questions were in his eyes, in his smile and the feel of his hands.

She waited for what was going to come out of his mouth, rooted to the spot, her mind a blur of new feelings. Her skin tingled and a tightening in her stomach matched the tightening in her chest.

He moved in closer and lifted her chin slightly with his finger, brushing her hair from her forehead. Devoured by his look, as he took in every inch of her face, she felt like she was being consumed by him. She was completely exposed and vulnerable, yet she had never felt more protected in all her life. If anyone else had come even half as close to her as he now was, she would have gone. She'd have turned and run away.

Billy struggled to let the words escape that he was holding in his throat. He was fucking petrified that once they were out and they couldn't be taken back, that this, whatever this was, would end right fucking here, in this spot, and he couldn't bear it. He couldn't stand the thought of never looking into those grey pools of hurt and anguish ever again, knowing he could maybe have helped save her before she drifted away.

Eve swallowed.

He was delving into her soul and ripping open boxes of memories and secrets that she hadn't even remembered were there. She had no idea what was in them and she needed him to close them quickly.

"Say something." She rested her hand on top of his and licked her lips, holding onto her bottom one with her teeth as she waited for him. She saw his eyes change, becoming dark, and her breathing changed with them.

He moved his head towards her, pleading with her for permission to come closer still, holding her eyes with his. She had nowhere to go and he needed to say even just a tiny bit of what he was feeling.

"Eve…" He closed his eyes and exhaled, his minty breath warming her face. "Eve, I barely know you, but this is the craziest I have ever felt around anyone. I can't make you any promises and can't predict the future, but right here with you is the most alive I have ever felt." He pursed his lips, freaking out inside for how stupid he must sound to her. Only hours ago she was legging it away from him, desperate to put as much space between them as she physically could, but now she was here, so close to him that he could feel her pulse against his skin.

Eve slowly prized her fingers underneath Billy's and eased his hand from her face. He opened his eyes, searching for her reaction to his words and found nothing. She was saying nothing and was backing away from him, her hands placed across her forehead and her mouth in a thin line. Billy linked his fingers behind his head, staring up at the darkness.

Fucking dickhead. You absolute dickhead.

What on earth had possessed him to be so forthright, he would never know. He began to walk backwards, giving Eve the space she clearly needed as anger and frustration bubbled up inside of him. He blew out the air from his cheeks and squatted to the floor, digging into his pockets for his cigarettes and matches. He shielded the flame from the light wind and took that first drag.

"You know what?" He spoke through the exhale of smoke and squinted up at her, then back down at the floor. "I don't know what to do for the best. I don't fucking know what to do, Eve. It's like a game of fucking tug of war, and quite frankly, I don't know if I can keep running to catch hold of the end of the rope." He sucked greedily on the cigarette and threw it into the wet grass, pushing himself back to his feet.

Eve stood stock still, taking in the scene before her. He seemed angry. His eyes were different than before. What the hell did he want from her? Confusion buzzed around her head, and she walked a few paces away to get some distance from him and the sudden change in his mood. He'd said he would walk her home: nothing more, nothing less and no expectations. So why this?

She leaned her body up against a nearby tree and

pushed her hands back through her hair, lifting her foot behind her to rest it flat on the trunk. The sky had cleared again, and she focused her eyes on the clusters of stars that were now twinkling in full view. She felt him come closer and deliberately avoided looking over to where he stood, head down and hands in his back pockets.

"Look, I'm sorry, okay? I didn't mean to… I just—I just feel so frustrated." He glanced up through his squinted eyes at her and waited for her to acknowledge him.

"What do you want from me, Billy?" Eve had dropped her head back down to look at him now, and she folded her arms across her chest. He flicked his head up, eyebrows raised. Pulling his hands out of his pockets, he shrugged.

"How the hell am I supposed to answer that? I've told you how I feel when I am even remotely near to you, but every time I do get close, you shut down or you run, so regardless of what it is I want from you, it's highly unlikely I'm going to get it really, don't you think? What do you want from me?"

Eve gave a sarcastic smile and shook her head. "We've barely ever spoken to each other and we are already fighting. Doesn't really bode well for anything more, does it? What happened to no expectations? What happened to helping me to do whatever it is we are doing? What happened to just walking me home, Billy?"

He shoved his head to the side and breathed impatiently. Impatient was his middle name right now and he knew it. He had promised to help her take it slow yet here he was pushing her boundaries and making things worse.

But she drove him fucking insane.

He wanted to scoop her up and take her home with

him, but any progress seemed nigh on impossible. How was he supposed to break down these walls that she built taller each time? Why wouldn't she just release it all, whatever it was that was balled up inside of her? He wished she would open her eyes and see him—see that he needed her with such intensity that it was making him dizzy, stupid. He'd been so sure she was with him a moment ago—the connection that had been so evident, so electric…

Surely, she couldn't have missed that.

He turned his head back to face her, dropping his arms by his sides and clenching his back teeth. "You feel it, though, right?"

Eve's heart pattered and her mouth went dry.

Well of course she fucking felt it. Why did he think she was still standing there? She pushed herself away from the tree and walked towards him slowly, her pulse rate quickening with every step she took. She wasn't entirely sure what she was doing or what was going to happen when she got close to him, but she held his eyes with her own and continued forwards regardless.

Billy stayed where he was and watched as Eve's slender legs moved towards him. Her hair was still damp, and it hung limply over her shoulders. As she got closer, a gust of wind grabbed a hold of her shirt and blew it open. She was wearing a vest underneath, and the skin on her collarbone became exposed for a split second. Billy sucked in a lustful breath, willing himself not to move.

She stopped about a foot away, wrapping her shirt around herself and taking a deep breath. Her face tilted to his, she looked into his eyes and lifted her hand to Billy's fringe, moving the long strands gently off his forehead.

He flinched and every muscle in his body tightened

with the burning of desperate need. Balled inside his pockets, his fists clenched tightly so as to stop himself again from reaching out and touching her. She needed to take control of this moment. He could see it in her eyes, and he needed to stop being so fucking pigheaded and let her.

What the fuck had he been thinking just now, going off on a rant like he did?

The light from the moon allowed him an illuminated view of her eyes that now seemed more alive than they had done previously. The shutters were up, and the grey swirled with something he couldn't define.

She poked the tip of her tongue out, resting it between her lips, and breathed in through her nose as if preparing herself for a jump.

Ready to let go, she dropped her hand down and flicked her eyes back and forth between each one of his as she exhaled. Her voice, when it finally seeped out, was barely a whisper. "I feel it."

The breath that he'd been holding was released into the air, and a relieved smile played at the corner of Billy's mouth. He lowered his head and moved his hands to rest on her upper arms. Raising his eyebrows, he silently asked permission to come a little closer, and she nodded, biting down on her bottom lip.

Billy closed his eyes and rested his forehead on hers, smoothing his thumbs across the apples of her cheeks. God, she felt so good under his touch, and it took everything he could muster not to claim her lips right there.

Eve stood, looking up at this strange man who had collected every one of her emotions, filled a basket with them and invited her on this roller coaster of a picnic. She knew now that she was going to have to unwrap some of them and lay them out for analysis, but she needed to make it clear to Billy that it was going to be at her convenience. He couldn't push her on this. It was new for her, being close to someone physically, but being close emotionally was going to be a whole other ball game. If this was going to turn into something, then he needed to know it would be slow and probably painful. He needed to assure her that he could handle her pace and understand that if she freaked out, pushing her would push her away. There was nothing she could do about that.

"I can't…" Eve dropped her eyes to the floor and huffed out a breath. "I can't promise anything, Billy. This…" She gesticulated around both their heads. "This needs to be so slow. I've never done this before. Ever. Okay?"

He continued to stroke her cheek, inhaling her and just thanking his lucky fucking stars for this one moment in time. "I know. And I'm sorry. I just want to know you, Eve. I just want to learn you by heart."

CHAPTER
nine

Under Streetlights – Brooke Annibale

STANDING IN FRONT of Billy, with his hand on her face and his body so close, Eve was transported to a parallel universe—a universe where she didn't run from her demons because there, she had none. There was something about this man that made her forget about the craziness in her head.

Those first encounters had scared her shitless, but she hadn't allowed herself to actually be near him then, to feel him. It was as if him being close just soaked up all her fear and restlessness, leaving her calm and at ease with herself and her own failings. It wasn't that she was not scared—she was petrified of the possibilities this opened up—but it wasn't the type of fear that she needed to run from. This was a fear of the new reactions her body was having to this stranger who had seemingly taken hold of her and was, so far, refusing to let go.

She'd never experienced that feeling of breathlessness when getting close to a guy she liked; she'd never enjoyed the sensation of having her body turn to mush at the mere mention of his name, so all of this was brand new. She'd never before even considered the fact that she might, in fact, find Billy Taylor attractive as it was something else about him that had her hooked. But looking into his face now, her body was telling her loud and clear that she found him incredibly attractive indeed.

Eve felt naked under the intense look in his eyes as they searched her face. Not entirely sure how to react, nor how soon to, she needed some time to get used to the idea of having him around if that was how this was going to play out. Getting home was now a priority so she could find some headspace to deal with the evening's events on her own.

She closed her eyes and stepped out of his touch, glancing up at him. "We should probably get home."

Billy ran his hand down his face and blew air from his cheeks. "Yep. You're probably right."

Embarrassed and feeling awkward for ruining what seemed like another perfect moment, she inwardly chastised herself. However, she had no real control over her reactions to emotional situations, and there was no telling what might happen if she allowed the obvious chemistry to explode a little further right now. There was a distinct possibility of making real headway here. Determined to at least try not to fuck it up, she glanced up at him. "I just need to take baby steps, y'know?"

Billy nodded in understanding, his skin aching to touch her again, and the pair sauntered towards the bushes.

As Eve prepared to drop to her hands and knees, she stalled and looked up at Billy with wide eyes. "My sketchbook... I left it."

He frowned comically, a small twitch in the corner of

his mouth as he slipped his hand inside his jacket and pulled out the leather-bound art book. "You mean this sketchbook?"

Eve pursed her lips, squinting with mock annoyance. "Hmm. Thank you."

"Well you didn't think I was going to make a third trip to the park in the dark and rain this week, did you?"

Eve laughed sheepishly. "Sorry. Though, I don't think you'll find that anyone forced you."

He smirked at her feisty side. It was almost as if he was unwrapping a gift at Christmas. Each corner of the paper that was torn off revealed a little more of the delights inside. She was a box of excitement that he couldn't wait to discover.

"Touché! I'll keep it inside my jacket. Try and keep the majority of the rain off it at least."

They climbed out of the other side, brushing down their legs to rid themselves of the leaves and soil. Eve huffed out a breath and prepared herself for the forty-minute walk with Billy beside her.

She guessed that small talk would be the order of the day and decided to break the ice, a first for her. "So, you live in York. Are you studying?" She gave him a quick glance from the corner of her eye before wrapping her arms around her body, concentrating on putting one foot in front of the other without tripping or running, unsure whether or not the flight instinct would kick in at any minute.

He stuck his hands into his back pockets and looked up to the sky before answering. "No."

Eve frowned.

Registering her confusion, he elaborated. "Sorry. I

121

mean, yes. I live in York, of course." He smiled at her. "But I'm not studying. I just live here. With my dad." The latter slipped out without much actual thought at all, and he winced at the hesitation in his voice before he released the words, hoping that Eve wouldn't pick up on it and start asking questions.

"How long have you lived here?"

The pair crossed the road, and Billy placed his hand in the small of Eve's back protectively as they weaved between a couple of oncoming cars. She inhaled through her nose as a shiver of something shot up her spine when his hand pressed against her. She'd only been physically touched by her mother and Rachel, for as long as she could remember. This was different. This was electric.

He cleared his throat. "Umm, since I was seventeen."

"So…" She scratched the side of her cheek to give herself thinking time. "You came here after you left Bishop High?"

"Yeah. Packed up and moved here to be near my mum's parents. She's not well. My mum that is."

Eve's expression softened and she looked at him properly. "I'm sorry. I—I hope things are looking up for her."

Billy's smile had her stomach lurching again, and she tugged at her bottom lip with her teeth.

Get a bloody grip.

"Thanks." He didn't feel like it was the right time to launch into a spiel about the complications of his life. Eve clearly had her own ton of shit to deal with, and he wasn't about to burden her with his own. "So, how about you? You're studying art, right?"

Eve nodded.

"And how's that working out for you?" He knew fine well how it was working out for her because he had been in possession of her artwork for almost twenty-four hours. He'd poured over every page so that each drawing was etched in his memory. Flashes of images passed in front of his eyes—images he had conjured up of Eve's hands moving across the paper, creating the lines and curves, of her eyes moving to follow the strokes of the pencil and charcoal...

"Yeah. Good, thanks."

"Good. That's really good. You'll do really well. You're unbelievably talented."

Eve smiled up at him again, a full beaming smile this time, and his body twitched with desire. He clenched his teeth and pulled his cigarettes out and lighting one, he blew the smoke upwards and scratched the back of his head.

What he wouldn't do to this girl wouldn't even fill the back of a postage stamp. He let his eyes slide down the side of her face to her neck and her exposed collarbone. Her skin glistened with a light smattering of rain and he could only think about how fucking good it would feel to taste it.

Taking another long drag to clear his thoughts, he blew them away to the side, mentally adjusting himself. He wanted to make her his own. He needed to be really careful, though. She was on a tightrope right now, and one stupid look, a sudden move towards her or a thoughtless, throwaway comment could have her toppling to the ground.

Eve's heart was hammering. She read the look on Billy's face perfectly and knew that what she was feeling probably matched it. She was not ready for this in the slightest, though, and she needed to get home fast.

***

DEALING WITH HIS family situation had hardened Billy's heart and he'd lost all optimism for the future. He'd settled for a life of looking after others and had shoved his own ambition, his own happiness and his own desires to the back seat of his life. Being so close to her that night was something he had not even dared to dream about since their first encounter at school.

After he moved away, he'd had to try to forget about her and the way she had made him feel that day in the corridor when he was seventeen. The memory of her, though, had often floated around his subconscious, and last night in the union bar, when his eyes found hers again, the lid on his box of hopes had flipped open and he'd been able to look inside it for the first time in a really long time. Tonight had been another roller coaster, and during the dips and loops, he'd honestly thought they might fall out of the carriage, but Eve had been so strong in the park. She had pushed through, and now he was walking her home. He almost dared to believe that she might trust him one day.

They neared number seven, Elton Terrace, and Billy's stomach rolled with loss and emptiness as he thought about the fact he'd be saying goodbye to her when he'd only just said hello.

He slowed a little and turned to face her.

They'd walked two miles together, but that moment was the most important part of their journey. It was possibly the most important moment of his life so far. He could say the wrong thing now and fuck it all up, throw it all away.

He ran his hand through his hair and rested it on the back of his neck, squinting across at Eve as he perched on a garden wall. "So, I guess this is where I leave you to go and get dried off." He gave her a tight smile.

"I guess you're right."

"You'll… be ok though, yeah?" He unbuttoned his jacket and handed her sketchbook over, his face a little more serious.

Eve avoided his eyes and toed the pavement. "I'll be fine. Thanks for walking back with me."

"Of course."

Rolling onto the sides of her feet, she lifted her face and studied him, losing herself there for a few seconds, and then shifted her gaze to the side as it became overwhelmingly uncomfortable. She pulled her book tight against her chest and wrapped her arms around it. Giving him a shy smile, she swivelled around on her toes and walked towards the house. "Night, Billy."

He couldn't look away, following her with his eyes as she opened the gate and walked up the path to her front door.

"Eve, wait!" He pushed himself off the wall and walked towards her. She stopped with her hand on the door handle. He was fidgety, and she quietly enjoyed the thought of him being as nervous about this as she was.

"Can I…" He sighed and rubbed his hand across his chin. "Can I have your number, maybe?"

Smiling into her chest and then back up at him, she pointed to the front door. "It's number seven."

And with that, she was gone.

Billy spun around with his eyes closed.

This girl was going to be the death of him.

He walked back up the road, lifting his arms slowly into the air and placing his hands on top of his head, leaning his head back and closing his eyes. He sat back on the wall and lit another cigarette, savouring each pull before he blew it out.

Well, at least that was progress.

***

LEANING BACK WITH the length of her body pressed against the door, Eve huffed out and closed her eyes. Her whole being was tingling and her skin was on fire. She slid down to the floor and let her legs flop out straight in front of her as they turned to jelly, refusing to hold her weight any longer. Her mind was a whirr of white noise and questions, and she struggled to focus on her fingers that were tangled up on her lap in front of her. Whatever it was that had just happened between her and Billy had taken its time to register and her body was almost going into shock. She'd spent nearly two hours in the company of a stranger and had come out unscathed.

Tipping her head back against the door, her eyes to the ceiling, she scrubbed her hands slowly down her face.

Exhausted from the emotional tsunami and the second two mile run in as many days, Eve wanted nothing more than to slip underneath her duvet and sleep until noon the next day. Maybe then she would find the head space to take stock of what had happened over the last forty-eight hours.

She pushed herself up and walked gingerly to the kitchen, opening the fridge. She found a clean knife in the drawer and sliced herself a chunk of cheese, plucking an apple from the fruit bowl on her way past.

Taking a bite out of each, she plonked herself down on her mattress and leaned forwards to remove Rachel's chucks from her feet. Her fingers fumbled at the knots in

126

the laces, and after the third useless attempt, she gave up, swinging her legs onto the bed and lying her head on the pillow, mentally apologising to her mother for getting mud on the bedclothes.

***

EVE'S EYES FLICKERED open, the onset of a headache already evident as she groaned and pulled the duvet over her head. Astutely aware of another's body heat emanating from behind her as the previous night came flooding back, she froze. She didn't dare look. Listening to the soft breathing of whoever it was that lay comatose at her side, a wave of nausea crept over her. She'd been tired, but surely not so tired that she was delirious?

Crap.

She tried not to move, but the more she tried, the more restless she became, the need to stretch her legs irrepressible. Slowly, she began to uncurl herself, when, without warning, a voice rang out and almost stopped Eve's heart from beating.

"What the fuck happened to you last night?"

Rachel was still laid on her side, her eyes closed. She fumbled on the floor for her phone and pulled it under the covers. Opening one eye, she checked the display and then dumped it back on the floor with a huff.

Eve lay back and stared at the ceiling with a sigh, the hint of a smile creeping across her face until she felt Rachel's arm smacking her across the chest.

"Oi! That hurt." She twisted her body around to face Rachel's back and poked her in the ribs. "Why are you in my bed?"

Rachel didn't move. "I asked you a question first. What the hell happened to you last night?"

127

Eve frowned and flopped her hand over the covers. "What makes you think anything happened?"

Rachel flipped over to face Eve and gave her a stern look. "Because, smart arse, there was a note on the doormat saying that the Chinese delivery guy couldn't deliver because there was no-one in, you're still in last night's clothes and you're wearing my Chucks—which, incidentally, are covered in mud, which in turn suggests that you went for a little jog around the park." She eyeballed Eve with her eyebrows raised, making her squirm and scrunch her face up. "Spill. Now."

Eve sighed, took hold of Rachel's little finger with her own and regaled her with the events of the night before. She was careful to leave out the parts where her heart and body had come alive through his touch or the look in his eyes. She wasn't ready to share him that way just yet. These feelings were so new to her, and she wasn't sure if she was interpreting everything correctly. If Rachel got even a hint from her that there was more to this than she realised, that would be it. She would try to force things that Eve was not ready for out of friendship, trying to do the best for her. "When he came to the door, I thought he was my Chinese takeaway."

"Think you need to get to the opticians, my love."

Eve rolled her eyes and flicked the end of Rachel's nose.

"Well, I'm glad that you're not frightened of him anymore. At least we can go out now without you being worried about bumping into him."

Eve blinked her eyes across to Rachel. "Mmm."

"How did you end up with my Converse on then?"

Eve lifted her leg out of the covers and held it in the

air, wiggling her ankle around. "I could get used to them actually. They're quite comfortable." Rachel gave her a warning look and Eve laughed. "I had to go out of the back door and your shoes were the closest thing. I'm sorry. I'll clean them."

"Damn right you will." Rachel sat up and threw the duvet back. "So, did you give Billy his car keys then after he walked you home?" She scraped her hair back off her face and tied it up with a bobble that sat around her wrist.

Eve stared at Rachel, her eyes growing wider and wider.

Rachel glanced at her. "I'm going to take that as a big fat no. Did he not ask for them?" She swivelled her legs over the side of the bed and planted both of her feet on the carpet, turning her head back to Eve who sat with her face in her hands.

She was in no way, shape or form ready to come face to face with Billy again just yet. She needed some time to wallow in her own thoughts, to get lost in her drawings and get used to the idea of him being somewhere nearby without freaking out. If he was to come knocking on the door again today, she wasn't quite sure what would happen. She couldn't run. Jesus, if she ran again, she would look like a fool; she would look like the crazy, incapable girl that she was trying so hard not to be. She pulled her face from her hands and looked over at Rachel, who was now frowning at Eve's reaction.

"What's up?" She turned her body and held Eve's eyes with her own to keep her friend from drifting or shutting down. There was something she was not telling her, and it was Rachel's job as Eve's best friend to keep chipping away until she opened up.

***

ON RETURNING HOME, Billy managed to avoid his father's attention. Neville was sitting comatose, snoring like a brown bear in the chair, the TV remote in his hand and an empty glass nestled in his crotch, his large weathered fingers loosely wrapped around it. The television flashed with bright colours as the late-night casino show enticed gullible and mindless victims with its large-breasted hostess, her shiny hair and blowjob lips.

Billy walked over to the screen and switched it off at the plug, wincing as his father stirred at the shift in the room's volume. Pulling at the threadbare blanket that lay habitually on the back of the sofa, he folded it double and lay it gently on his father's sleeping form before carefully sliding the glass out of his hand.

Moving towards the kitchen, he dropped the glass into the washing up bowl and opened the fridge. There was nothing more than a half-eaten packet of ham and a pint of milk on offer, and he rued the moment he had chosen to skip lunch, and dinner come to think of it, and he would blame Eve when he saw her next. A contented smile found his lips as he thought of her, and he replayed the evening's events as he buttered himself a slice of bread, shoveling it hungrily into his mouth. He remembered the softness of the inside of her forearms, the jewellery and the tattoo that he was so desperate to touch. The feeling that zipped through him when her hands had been on his skin sent his hormones into overload, and he allowed his mind to empty and fill up again with thoughts of her.

Washing his 'meal' down with a swig of milk from the bottle, he wiped the back of his hand across his mouth and closed the fridge, his eyes connecting with the picture of his mother that was stuck with a magnet in the centre of it. He reached his hand up and stroked the worn photograph with the back of his finger, pursing his lips and bowing his head as he mentally planned his visit the next day. That was until the realisation that his car keys were still sitting in Eve's house jolted his head back up.

He closed his eyes and laughed to himself. "For fuck's sake.

CHAPTER
ten

Always In My Head - Coldplay

SITTING AT OPPOSITE ends of the sofa, nursing warm mugs with their legs curled underneath them, Eve and Rachel discussed the big date with Julian. Rachel had been glued to her phone all morning, checking and rechecking her messages for anything from the now elusive boy.

"So, what did he say when you left him in the taxi?" Eve sipped noisily on her hot tea and blinked over the rim of her mug at Rachel who was staring wistfully into her own. The date had seemed to go well in her opinion.

They'd laughed and chatted easily with one another over a perfectly lovely dinner and then spent the remainder of the evening sitting pretty damn close on a slouchy, leather couch in one of the bars. Rachel sighed and took a gulp of her coffee. "He said…" She sighed again. "'Don't call us; we'll call you.'" Her eyes rolled and then, catching sight of Eve's face, incredulous and gob smacked, she sprayed coffee across the back of the seat with laughter.

"Are you taking the *piss*?" Eve's eyes followed the spray of hot liquid and then moved slowly back to Rachel's face, her mouth hanging open.

Rachel struggled to compose herself, and Eve snorted, joining in with the laughter.

"Oh, mate. I think you maybe need to nip this in the bud before it gets any worse. Don't call us; we'll fucking call you? What a dick!"

Rachel stretched her legs out in front of her and curled her socked toes into fists. "He's bloody gorgeous, though. Can I not just try and keep hold of him for a shag at least?" They both laughed again, and Eve got up for a refill and to fetch a cloth.

"What happens if you break the rules and call him first?" she shouted from the kitchen while she flicked the switch down on the kettle and pottered around, cleaning surfaces and putting cutlery to bed.

"I don't know, but we will soon find out. If he hasn't got in touch by lunchtime, I'm dialing."

"Make sure I'm there with you when you do."

As she picked the boiled kettle from its resting place, a knock at the door disturbed her flow. Turning absentmindedly towards the sound, Eve moved the kettle away from her mug, pouring scalding water onto the counter.

"Fuck!" She thrust her body backwards and out of the way as it trickled towards the edge of the counter and onto the floor. "Rach, can you get the door? I've spilled hot water everywhere." She heard a sigh and the scuffle of Rachel prising herself from her corner of the sofa. She shook her head, smiling fondly, as she pulled reams of kitchen paper from the roll and bent down to mop up the spillage.

Rachel's voice from the hallway alerted her to the fact

that she was inviting the visitor inside, so she assumed it would be Deb coming to get the low down on Julian. She swirled the paper across the kitchen tiles for the final time and pushed her hair off her forehead with the back of her hand.

"Hi, Deb. Cuppa?"

Rachel cleared her throat, not so subtly, flicking her eyes to the visitor as they both stood in the kitchen behind her. "Umm, Eve? Billy is here for his car keys."

Eve froze for the second time that morning, her eyes trained carefully on the floor tiles, her skin prickling. Very slowly, she looked down at herself, wearing last night's clothes, and registered that her arse was in the air. Her arse… was in the air.

Fuckity. Fuck.

She slowly bent her knees, lowering herself so that she was sitting in a crouched position, her legs trembling and making the job stupidly difficult, before leaning forwards to collect the paper towels from the floor to distract herself from the ringing that had begun in her ears.

This was not happening. Surely this was not happening.

Billy Taylor was in her house, and she had greeted him with her arse. She needed to break the silence before she was taken over by her instincts.

Do. Not. Freak. Out.

She kept her focus on the floor and the wet paper towels that were now dripping in her hands. She could not see Billy right now. Not like this. "Umm. They're in the top drawer. Just there." She pointed to the kitchen drawer, tapping her index finger in the air for emphasis without turning her head in their direction.

There was no noise coming from behind her, so she took it that the information hadn't been received loud and fucking clear by Rachel or Billy. She repeated it, more firmly this time. "The keys"—she pointed again in the direction of the drawer—"should be just here, in this drawer. Just here. Where you put them, right?" She spat the words out firmly. "Rae, please get them for… for Billy. I'm—I'm just a little busy here with this spillage." Her mouth was dry, and she swallowed down in an attempt to stop the feeling of choking. It was the best she could do, short of diving up to get a glass from the cupboard and cool her mouth with water. She still didn't dare turn around for fear of giving everything away with her eyes and the reaction she knew she would have if she looked at him.

Rachel walked towards the kitchen drawer, spinning round and walking backwards, eyeing Billy with raised brows "Ohhh… kay!" She mouthed silently at him, and he shrugged. She really wasn't sure what was going on with Eve but was damned sure she was going to get it out of her later on. She pulled the drawer open and rifled around under takeaway menus, pegs and biros, but there were no keys. "Nope. They're not here, bud."

Eve dipped her head, leaning her arm on her thigh, and sighed through her nose. She squeezed her eyes tight and pinched the bridge of her nose before standing up and turning towards the counter where Rachel stood with her arms crossed. Every fibre of her body twisted in an antagonistic fight against her heart's urge to turn and face him. She silently ordered Rachel to move away from the drawer with a flick of her wide eyes, and her teeth clenched into a fake smile. She yanked all the menus out of her way and spun her fingers around in the chaos that was lying at

135

the bottom. Rachel was right. The keys were not there, which, if she's had her wits about her, she would have remembered from the previous evening.

She closed the drawer and put her hands on the top of the counter, hunching her shoulders over and bowing her head to think. "Rae, please could you have a look in your room?" She spoke quietly, knowing that she was in for an interrogation later when they were alone again. Rachel nodded once, firmly, her mouth turned down, and walked out of the kitchen.

Eve took this opportunity to brace herself in preparation for finally facing Billy. She couldn't leave it any longer because she was beginning to look like an absolute weirdo, but with Rachel out of the room, she could now look at him without giving anything away to her. She lifted her hands from the kitchen top and dropped her arms to her sides, sliding slowly round in her socks to face him. As her eyes found his, her throat released a gentle gasp. He was dressed in a crisp white T-shirt and a pair of grey joggers, his hair was wet from what she presumed was a recent shower, and his bright eyes were alive.

"Hi."

Eve pressed her lips together and inhaled deeply before opening them again to reply. "Hi."

Billy ran his hand through his hair and rested it on the back of his neck in that way he did, looking at her from under his shaggy fringe. "You okay?"

She smiled and nodded, folding her arms across her chest and tucking her hands under her armpits. This was okay. This wasn't scary—just unexpected. Her heart was still hammering in her chest, but it was from the sight of him, nothing more. "I'm…" She gestured with her head in the direction of the stairs. "I'm sure she will be back with them in a minute."

"That's okay. I can wait." Billy scratched the side of his cheek before sticking his hands into his jogger pockets, and Eve snapped to attention, forgetting her manners.

"Sorry. Um… would you like a drink? Kettle has just boiled." She looked over to the counter and then the still damp floor. "Even if half of the contents are all over the floor."

Billy laughed and her stomach lurched at the sound. What the hell was she doing?

He stood, not moving for fear of scaring Eve. She was different this morning. She'd been almost relaxed with him by the end of the walk the night before, but this morning she was guarded, and he wondered if he should just leave once he had his keys so as not to push his luck.

Eve shifted her weight onto her other foot and waited expectantly for him to speak. There was a part of her that wanted him gone, out of her house and away from her so she could sort through all of these confusing emotions that she was harbouring, but there was so much of her that was singing a cathedral song because he was here, in her kitchen.

"Well, I'm actually heading out once I get my car." He thumbed back towards the door. "So I should really—" He stopped, looking deeply into her eyes. Could he bear to tear himself away from them again after such a brief encounter? "Tea. Milk, no sugar. Thanks." He coughed, curling his fingers to his mouth, his eyes shifting to the side to hide his embarrassment. His street cred would be in tatters.

The pulse in her neck definitely started twitching faster, she could feel it, and someone grabbed an invisible string that was seemingly attached to the corner of her mouth and yanked it so that she was grinning on one side of her face, dimples in place and a sparkle in her eye. It was to herself of course, behind her hair. She wasn't going to let on to Billy or anyone else for that matter that him being there was exactly what she wanted. And she was going to have to start embracing and dealing with that fact herself.

She re-filled the kettle from the sink and moved around the kitchen, grabbing a mug and teabags, the milk from the fridge, and Billy could not take his eyes off her. He couldn't look away from her petite form, moving and stretching and twisting.

She's making tea, for fuck's sake. Get a fucking grip.

More and more, this girl was taunting his sexual desires. He needed time with her on his own. He needed to earn her trust completely so that he could be one step closer to the day when she would let him hold her.

Rachel appeared in the doorway, dangling a bunch of keys from her hand with a smile on her face, yanking his attention away, and he walked over to her to retrieve them.

"Cool. That's great. Thank you," he smiled. Now that she was back downstairs, the magic in the air seemed to swish back into the top hat, and his need for tea was dwindling.

"Umm, Eve, I actually think I'm just going to get off. I need to go see my mum. But thank you for the keys, and—" He stopped short with no idea what he was going to say next until it came out of his mouth. "Maybe I could come round later on. We could go for a walk or something?"

Eve leaned back against the sideboard, her hands behind her gripping the edge. Was this a date he was offering? She couldn't think fast enough of a reason to say no, and she heard herself agreeing. Within 30 seconds, Billy was no longer in her kitchen, but Rachel was standing in front of her, arms folded and a frown on her face.

"Speak."

Her interrogation lasted a good half an hour and comprised of question after question regarding Eve's behaviour around Billy. "So, what you're actually telling me is that you like this guy, and he likes you, but you are too scared to do anything about it?"

Eve sat on the armchair, her knees pulled up to her chest and her chin resting on the top. She looked up at Rachel and nodded, her lips pursed and brows raised. "Pretty much."

"Well I'll be goddamned. Eve Swallow has a crush."

She rolled her eyes. "He's not a crush. I've explained this. It's different."

"Ohhh it's different. Okay, I see. So. How, may I ask, do you know it's different when you haven't ever had a crush before? Huh? Explain that one."

"It just is. It's more than a crush. It is in fact ridiculous the way I react when he gets close to me. Like, I don't know. I can't really explain."

"Sounds like a crush to me. And anyway, I don't understand how this has transformed when not twenty-four hours ago you were doing a Usain Bolt and sprinting through the park to get away from him. How the hell are you now crushing on him?"

"Rachel. It's not a crush. It's more. It's…" Eve sighed. She had no idea how to put it into words seeing as she couldn't even explain it to herself. She thought back to the moment in the park where she knew she wasn't going to run away from Billy again—the moment where she reached out her hand so that he could help her up. What was this power he had over her? Or was she completely insane? "It's a connection." She flicked her eyes up to monitor the look on her friend's face.

Rachel wasn't a born romantic. She scoffed at the idea of love at first sight or soul mates, and Eve couldn't imagine she was about to take her seriously.

"A connection? You mean you want to be connected to his dick?" She laughed and Eve threw a cushion at her, causing her to duck and laugh harder.

"I'm not discussing it with you at all if you are just going to mock me. I can't explain it. I just know there is something deeper than me just finding him attractive, that's all. Can you just be satisfied with that until I figure it out myself?"

"Okay, okay. Fine. But if there are any developments, physical or otherwise, you have to fill me in."

"Rach, you are not allowed to force this, right? I know you think you know what's good for me, but I need you to let me do this by myself. It's really important." Eve dropped her legs to the floor and leaned forward, clasping her hands on her lap, checking that Rachel was looking at her as she spoke. She was so lucky to have her in her life. She was in a much better place all round because of Rachel's love and friendship, but there were times when she might describe the help as meddling a bit, and she knew that Rachel would want to take this on as a little project.

Her friend sighed, tucking her hair behind her ears. She could see the pleading in Eve's eyes and knew better than to push further. She plonked her arse on the arm of the chair and picked up Eve's hand, linking their little fingers together. "You know I wouldn't interfere with something like this. I'm your best mate. I do know what you're like. I promise I will leave this to you."

Eve smiled gratefully, squeezing their joined fingers and whispering a thank you, not missing the tiny pang of guilt that shot through her for doubting Rachel's ability to be sensitive and discerning where she was concerned.

Rachel nodded.

"Have you heard from Julian?" Eve changed the subject quickly to direct attention away from her own predicament and so Rachel would become distracted and refrain from asking any more questions. Rachel frowned and pulled her phone from her back pocket, checking the screen.

"Nope."

"Maybe he just doesn't want to seem too keen or something?" Eve certainly didn't have a PhD in the mind games of men, but she figured that maybe they didn't want to be caught being too forward if they liked a girl. However, when she thought of Billy, he didn't seem bothered about letting it be known that he was keen. In the park the previous night, he had professed to feeling alive when she was near—that he hadn't ever felt it with anyone else. If that wasn't keen then she didn't know what was. It was in fact her who was playing it cool as backwards as it seemed when she thought about it properly. If you like someone, why pretend you don't?

To guard your heart, of course.

To stop people getting in and to keep the gates locked.

"Hmm… maybe. I'm going to give him another hour and then that's it."

Eve smiled and let go of Rachel's finger, pushing herself up from the chair. "I'm sure he will be pleased to hear from you. He was the one to ask you out, remember?

Must like you. I'm going to get a shower and then make some lunch. Want anything?"

Rachel shook her head and spun herself round, falling backwards into the chair that Eve had just vacated, leaving her legs hanging over the arm. She rested her head on the cushion and made grabby hands towards the remote control that lay inches from her grasp on the coffee table. Eve rolled her eyes, picked it up and threw it at her before making a sandwich and running up the stairs.

Sitting cross-legged on her bed with her sketchbook, her plate of food to one side and her art box to the other, Eve began drawing the faint lines of a featureless face. She spent a lot of time life drawing, taking a snapshot in time and eternalising it in charcoal or inks, but today, she felt compelled to draw from memory. Sometimes, she didn't know where her pencil would take her. Her hand would glide across the paper on an unknown journey, and the end product would sometimes surprise her. It was as if the pencil had a mind of its own and needed her skill and talents to help tell its stories.

Today was no exception.

She periodically reached blindly towards her plate and took a bite out of her cheese sandwich, never once taking her eyes from her work.

Working without music was one of the things that Eve couldn't do. It didn't matter where she was, music was always playing either from the iPod dock or directly through her headphones. She had opted for headphones today so she could focus and drown out any external noises, or indeed any internal ramblings. Listening to music was another coping mechanism, and after the events of the past few days, she felt the need to lock herself away for a few hours, releasing what she wasn't yet able to describe or explain away with words. Often, songs would tell Eve's stories for her, so there she sat in a world of mutual and cyclical story telling between her, the pencil and her current favourite playlist.

She drained her glass of juice and continued to follow the instructions the pencil was whispering to her, shading cheekbones and eye sockets, making wispy strokes for eyebrows and hair that fell into the so far non-existent eyes. Losing herself in the music and the path of the pencil, Eve felt like she was regaining a bit of balance in her mind. She wasn't sure she would ever understand how just one look could send her careering down a path of such uncertainty, but it was one that she was learning slowly to enjoy travelling. It was like a magical mystery tour. She was blindfolded and had her hands held out, one to feel her way, the other held tightly by a stranger who was urging her to let go and fall towards him.

She hardly knew him, yet she was already deciding that she didn't want him going anywhere anytime soon. What possessed her to agree to seeing him later that day was becoming more and more clear the more she thought about him and the way he made her feel.

As she continued to lose herself in her artwork, her eyes widened as the features she was drawing became more and more recognisable. She dropped the pencil as if it were poker hot and leaned away from the paper, placing her hands on the bed behind her, knocking her plate to the floor. Her head darted to the side and down to the crumb covered carpet. "Shit."

Cautiously moving her eyes back to the paper that had now slid forwards off her drawing board, she squinted at the story her pencil had spilled across it. The eyes were unmistakable, and her heart began to thump a little harder in her chest as she struggled to look anywhere else. She hadn't realised her memory of his face was so clear; it was almost perfect, the only thing missing being the bright blue colour. Eve lifted her knees quickly to remove the board, swinging her legs to the floor and moving to her desk that sat in the corner of the room under the window.

She grabbed the sketchbook Billy had returned to her the night before and, stepping over the mess she had made on the floor, opened her wardrobe door. In the bottom sat a cardboard box filled to the brim with similar books. She knelt in front of it, pulling them out one by one. Lowering her bottom to the soles of her feet, Eve flicked through each and every one, stopping on the pages that caught her attention because of the bright blue eyes that sang to her from various corners and spaces. Every book was the same: pages and pages of pencil and charcoal drawings, interspersed with representation after representation of the same blue eyes, both large and small.

She pushed herself slowly to her feet, mesmerised by the most recent ones on the last used page of the now damaged sketchbook—the ones she had drawn and painted only hours before getting ready for the summer ball. Her own eyes not leaving the page, she walked back around the other side of her bed, slumping down on the edge and absently pulling the paper she had just been working on towards her. Side by side there was no denying it. She flitted her vision back and forth, taking in the shape, the curl of the dark lashes and the way they were looking into her very soul.

CHAPTER
eleven

Every Little Thing She Does Is Magic — The Police

AS SHE SAT on the edge of her bed, sketchbook on her knees, she was almost unsurprised when she saw her bedroom door push slowly open, a large male hand curling around the wood. She smelled him before she saw him, and her eyes closed involuntarily, her lungs opening wide to accept the inhale of breath from her nose. Her lids lifted gently and fluttered to allow her vision to settle and adapt so that she could take in all that was in front of her. She was positive he could hear the hammering of her heart against her ribs. Her hands gripped the edge of her sketchbook more tightly and she sat, waiting, as he appeared from behind the door in excruciatingly slow motion.

First, one of his denim clad legs appeared, long and quite obviously muscular, and no sooner had she swallowed that part of him whole than his arm and shoulder appeared, wrapped tightly in a pale blue T-shirt that pulled against the taught muscles in his upper arm. Eve found herself blowing air slowly from her cheeks, her mouth forming a circle as she got used to the butterflies that were waltzing around in her stomach.

Just as she was settling into the feeling, the dark strands of his hair showed themselves. They were flopped forwards as his head ducked a little lower than his usual six-foot frame, hiding a sheepish and almost shy replica of the eyes that lay in the pages of her art books. His eyebrows were raised slightly as if asking permission to come further into the room, a gentle smile dancing on his lips.

"Hey, you." Billy's smile rose a little higher as his eyes rested on Eve's, the now familiar need beginning to build and race through his body. He pulled his brow a little further up for a second to reiterate his question, hoping to God she would let him in.

When he'd arrived at the door minutes earlier, nervous as hell, he hadn't held out much hope, fully expecting for their 'date' (or whatever it was she wanted to call it) to be put off or cancelled. Being in her room now meant she perhaps wouldn't be able to turn him away as easily, so he allowed himself to be optimistic about his visit.

Eve continued to clutch the sketchbook and nodded in answer, causing Billy's whole frame to walk inside the now tiny room. The walls seemed to have moved closer together and the carpeted floor had surely halved in size. The antagonistic prickling of her skin and the thumping of her heart were feelings that Eve was beginning to associate with Billy being close by, but as he stood there looking at her, she felt like the only thing in the room, and all of the anxieties from earlier on dripped away with each blink of her eyes. There was a calmness that continued to wash over her that was reminiscent of how she felt when she was drawing.

He stood near the open door and pushed his hand into his pocket, his left one thumbing behind him as he glanced over his shoulder. "Rachel said I should come up. I—I hope that's okay?"

She nodded again and Billy's eyes moved around the room, taking in the details before dropping back down to Eve who sat motionless on the edge of her bed.

He pointed and nodded to the book on her lap. "What are you working on?"

Her eyes followed his to the page and panic rose in her throat until she remembered that he had already seen this sketchbook and had therefore probably already seen the pages and pages of blue eyes.

She huffed out a breath through her nose and cleared her throat as she slowly closed the cover over. "Nothing much. Just a bit of sketching for my course." She moved to stand up from the bed to put the book on her desk, and as she did, the large sheet of paper that she had filled with his face floated in slow motion, like a feather, to the floor.

Her reactions were not as fast as Billy's and he got there first, bending forwards to collect it from the carpet. Pulling it towards him, he was about to hand it over when his eyes fell to the pencil marks.

He gasped.

He couldn't take in what he was seeing fast enough.

His eyes moved from the drawing up to Eve's face and back again, until she dragged her hands over her hair, allowing her head to fall back into them, and turned away from him. She stood still for a minute and then spun round again to face him, her eyes scrunched closed.

"It's really fucking good, Eve. I mean… Wow. It's like looking in a mirror."

147

Eleanor **LLOYD-JONES**

She snapped her eyes open and fixed them on his face for a minute while he drank in the image once more before swiping it from his grasp and flinging it onto the bed. "It's nothing is what it is. Just experimenting." She gave him a tight smile, sliding her hands into the back pockets of her jeans as she tried to take control of the impossible situation. "So, where do you want to go?"

Billy nodded. He could see she was embarrassed. He was doing so well so far at not fucking this up, so he let it go and didn't mention it again, even though inside he was dancing at the idea of her thinking about him when he wasn't there.

He stood still and allowed himself to take in the curve of her neck and the line of her jaw. He moved his eyes to the way her long dark lashes framed those grey eyes and the dimples that tucked themselves in when she smiled. He watched with a halted breath as she trapped her lip between her teeth while she waited for him to respond.

He cleared his throat and scratched his cheek, twisting his mouth to the side. "I was thinking we could have a wander into town, perhaps? Maybe grab a takeaway coffee and sit in the park. How does that sound?"

It was an almost perfect suggestion, and she relaxed now that she knew she wouldn't have to dodge crowds of people or sit in a stuffy cafe. She cocked her head to the side and nodded in approval, smiling this time with more genuine warmth. "Tea."

Billy laughed. "Okay, tea it is."

"I'll just grab..." She moved towards the door, stopping in front of him. "Um. Can I just...?" She pointed to the hook on the back of the door.

"Oh, shit, sorry! Yeah, sorry." He sidestepped and

148

placed his hand on the back of his neck, narrowing his eyes as he fought to cope with being so close to her that he could smell her hair. Eve took hold of the door and yanked a hoodie from the hook on the back. She slid her arms in and shoved it over her head, collecting her phone from the bed as she slipped her feet into her boots and swung her bag over her shoulder.

"Ready?"

"Ready." She smiled again and led the way downstairs. Billy followed and forced himself not to watch her arse as she trundled down the steps. This was starting to become unbearable. He could only dream of the day that she would let him touch her properly and, even then, he wasn't so sure it would ever happen. He sighed to himself with frustration and swore he would die trying.

"Rae, we are going out." Eve popped her head around the living room door to find Rachel pretty much where she had left her earlier: slumped in the armchair, wallowing in self-pity and eyes glued to the television. "Dude?"

Rachel looked up and gave a half-hearted wave. "Have fun, you crazy kids."

Eve rolled her eyes and stood back up, nearly bumping into Billy as she turned around and he caught hold of her arms to stop her from toppling over.

"Jesus! Stop creeping up on me." She pulled herself away and then looked to the floor, embarrassed at her outburst. "Sorry. I didn't mean to shout."

Billy smiled a lopsided grin and reached out to tuck Eve's hair behind her ear. "Come on, funny girl. Let's go."

***

WALKING INTO TOWN next to Billy felt more and more natural the further they went, and the conversation rolled between them with ease this time. Eve discovered that Billy was also an only child, and that he worked in the independent record store on the edge of town. She had sometimes wandered in there when it was quiet and wondered why she had never bumped into him—not that it would have been a particularly pleasant meeting if her reaction to seeing him the other night was anything to go by. She also discovered that he seemed as passionate about music as she was and that his favourite band of all time was The Police.

"Did you know that Sting trained to be a teacher originally?"

Billy looked at Eve and nodded. "I did."

"My second cousin went to the school where he did his teaching practice, in Northumberland. Apparently, he was told that he would be better off spending time with his guitar than trying to educate children." Eve's mouth was running away with her, and Billy smiled, a warmth spreading through him the more she relaxed in his company.

"Did you also know that his daughter, Coco Sumner, has an album and that it is one of my favourite albums at the moment?"

"I did not know that." He smiled down at her. "I will have to check that one out."

"You should. It's great. You'll love her." She grinned up at him, and Billy's stomach twisted. Eve looked away, catching the glaze of his eye, and blushed at the pavement.

The pair walked into an independent coffee shop and Billy ordered a latté for himself and a tea for Eve. He reached into his back pocket and pulled out the ten-pound note that he had managed to scrounge from Dobbo just a couple of hours earlier. He'd made him beg like a dog and promise that he would go out for drinks with him after payday the following week as interest. He'd then cuffed him around the back of the head and told him to 'go get 'er'.

As they entered the Museum Gardens, the clouds that had threatened to settle in for the whole day began to disperse, leaving patches of blue sky and the promise of a warm afternoon. The pair of them took up residence underneath the weeping willow where Billy had seen Eve the day before.

"This is my favourite spot in the park," she mused, pulling her hair in front of her shoulders as she leaned back against the tree. Billy sat down next to her and stretched his long legs out parallel to hers. "It's a good spot."

He contemplated telling her that he'd seen her here but thought better of it. If she thought he was stalking her in any way, he was positive that she would end whatever this was before it had even really started.

Eve cradled the warm drink between her hands and turned to look at Billy, the profile of his face capturing her attention. He had a strong, straight nose, not too long, not too short, and his square jawline jutted out slightly below the tip of it. His philtral dimple was deeply carved and paved the way to full lips and a beautifully defined cupid's bow.

Billy could feel her eyes moving down his face and sat still, intrigued by her attention. She put her tea down on the grass and formed a square shape with her fingers. Closing one eye, she made clicking sound, imitating the shutter noise of a camera, causing Billy to turn his head slowly, a smile forming on his lips.

"Committing my face to memory, Miss Swallow?"

Eve blushed. Again. "I'm an artist. I commit everything I see to memory." She smiled from behind her hair, took another sip of her tea and reached inside her bag.

Billy watched as she pulled out a small book and a pencil case. His body was rigged with satisfaction and happiness at being with her. It was calm, it was natural and it was positive. He was having a hard time holding in his need to touch her, as was becoming standard practice, but his need for her to stay right where she was sitting was the need that seemed to reign supreme, so he held in his desires in exchange for ensuring she felt safe.

Eve opened up the A5 sketchbook that she carried everywhere and found a blank page.

"Are you going to draw me again?" Billy looked over her shoulder at the page, hoping for a peek at some more of her sketches.

"If that's okay? You have a really strong profile, and drawing people and faces is my main interest."

"Of course it's okay. How do you want me?" Billy's lip curled slightly, not unnoticed by Eve, and she almost spat her tea out at the innuendo, her cheeks flushing for the umpteenth time in a couple of hours.

"Just look over there at the river. And keep still."

"Okay. Am I allowed to talk to you?"

Eve sharpened her pencil onto the grass and swivelled herself around so she was sitting facing Billy. She crossed her legs and rested her pad on her knee. Leaning forwards slightly, she pulled a couple of strands of hair from Billy's forehead so they curled around to the side. The cool of her fingers on his skin caused him to inhale deeply, and he closed his eyes as he blew out through his mouth.

"Yes, you can talk to me, but you have to keep still

and have to let me concentrate, okay?" She gave him a smile from the side of her mouth, the dimple in her cheek winking mischievously at him. He held her gaze for a moment, allowing his eyes to flick from hers to her mouth, and then he nodded in agreement.

"Okay. Let's do this." He rolled his shoulders back and cracked his neck to the side as if warming up for a fight, and Eve laughed, causing goose bumps to rise on his arms. Once he had settled himself, Eve moved her pencil across the paper, capturing the sculpted lines of Billy's face.

"How come you were at the ball the other night?" Eve had been meaning to ask him last night, but the opportunity hadn't arisen. Now she knew she'd been in the same city as him for nine months, she couldn't help but scoff at the timing.

Why had he waited until now to make himself known to her. Why had he not tried again back then?

It was what she called bad fucking timing.

However, sitting there with him, she was beginning to think that, despite her horrendous reaction to seeing him, it was going to have a positive outcome. She felt safe in his presence and that was a good thing. There were very few people who made her feel relaxed, and adding him to the list was definitely something she could deal with.

"My pal, Dobbo, is mates with a couple of the final year students there and they got him a pair of tickets. Not really my scene normally."

"Normally?" Eve flicked her eyes up to his nose and back to the paper as she shaded the shadow that fell across it.

Billy ran his finger and thumb around the sides of his mouth. "Well. It wasn't something I was particularly looking forward to. Until…"

Eve looked back up, her eyes resting on his eyelashes that dusted his cheek as they blinked.

"Until I saw you."

Eve felt her heart stop, she was sure of it, and she held her breath as Billy turned towards her. Without any warning, her hand shot up and grabbed his chin, forcing his face back to the position he was in. "Keep still." She blew out through pursed lips and allowed herself to smile a little at his disobedience.

Billy looked straight ahead and unfolded his fingers that were entwined in his lap. He began to tap a beat out on the sides of his legs with his hands, and Eve glanced over.

"What you playing?"

"The drums."

Eve snorted. "Clearly. Which song?"

"A song by The Police."

She smudged her finger along the brow, filling faint lines back in once she was happy with the shade and sighing with a smile on her face. "Which song?"

Billy didn't miss a beat. He kept stock-still and answered her quickly. "Every Little Thing She Does is Magic."

Eve's eyes moved back to his face, concentration etched across it, and followed Billy's hairline to his ear, her pencil mimicking what she saw.

"Eeeh oh oh, eeeh oh oh, eeeh oh oh." Billy's voice was low and husky, and a smile spread across his face as he turned his head towards her again. He managed to catch Eve's eyes that were crinkled with laughter before she frowned at him and squinted her eyes.

She wiped her hand down her jeans to remove the smudges of charcoal. He was so brazen. She was sure he knew exactly what he was doing, and she was equally sure that he knew he was having this effect on her. Her heart was refusing to beat in a steady rhythm, and she was positive it would burst out of her chest at any moment.

"Keep bloody still." She dipped her head back down to the page and smoothed out the texture of the lips she had just shaded. She moved slowly with the pad of her finger across the bottom one, and Billy watched out of the corner of his eye. Her learned perceptiveness scanned the whole drawing and her tongue poked out of her mouth to wet her own red lips, sucking her bottom one inwards before dragging her teeth along it as it slid back out.

Billy had to look away, turning his eyes to the sky in an attempt to clear his mind of debauchery.

She was going to be his undoing.

"Close your eyes." Eve held the finished drawing to her chest and sat up straight, looking Billy in the eye. He reached out to try to take the sketchbook from her, but she wouldn't let him near.

"Close your eyes!"

Billy huffed out with mock annoyance. "You're so bossy. Just let me see it."

"You will see it."

He surrendered and let his lids fall over his eyes, his arms folded across his chest.

Eve pulled the book away from her chest and picked up her pencil and began to write…

Billy, thank you for a lovely day and for your

understanding...

She scrawled her signature at the bottom of the picture, looped around the final 'e' of her name to create a daisy and then tore the page from the book, placing it on Billy's lap.

"Open." She sat back against the tree, stretching her legs back out and clunking the toes of her boots together while she waited for Billy to look.

He opened his eyes and looked down at the paper, picking it up and taking in the incredible talent that jumped from the page. He read the message, allowing his finger to trace her name as he had done the night he'd found her sketchbook.

Turning his body to face Eve, he moved his hand forwards to take hers from her lap, running his thumb over her knuckles and waiting for a reaction.

Eve looked down at their joined hands and then back up at his face. She was unsure how to react to the closeness they shared and bit down on the tip of her tongue. Her body was reacting just fine, but her mind needed to catch up. She had no idea what his next move was going to be, but there was a whole bunch of nerve endings that hoped he would move even closer as her heart pounded faster.

Billy placed one hand on the ground near her leg and leaned forward. She closed her eyes and squeezed her hand into a fist so tight that her nails almost broke the skin of her palm.

Taking advantage of the fact her eyes were closed, his gaze lingered on her face: the fine wisps of blonde hair that grew from her hairline, the apple of her cheek, the milky skin that was tinted with pink from the fresh air and he guessed shyness, the curl of her long lashes, the smattering of freckles across her nose and the gentle bow of her full lips.

He moved closer still and pressed his own lips to the top of her head, whispering into her hair. "I love it. Thank you. And, you're welcome."

There was no way he was going to fuck this up by rushing into things that she might not want or be ready for. He would wait. He would follow her lead and go at her pace in the hope that one day, he would be able to tear down her guard and wipe away the sadness and hurt that were so obvious to him when he looked into her eyes.

Eve released the breath that she had been holding and allowed her eyes to flutter open. Billy's face was so close to hers.

He reached up to brush the hair from her forehead and squeezed the hand that he was still holding onto. "More tea?"

She nodded and smiled sheepishly as Billy stood up, pulling her to her feet. Eve bent down, picked up her bag and sketchpad and handed Billy his drawing. He folded it carefully with his free hand, using his lips to assist, and slid it into his back pocket.

There was no way he was letting go of her hand today unless it was absolutely necessary.

CHAPTER
twelve

A Real Thunderbolt – Paul Cook And The Chronicles

ALMOST EVERY DAY over the next month or so, Billy arrived on Eve's doorstep. Some days, she had to send him away until she got back from her art classes; other days, Billy had to call twice or three times to catch Eve in. On the days when he had been working, he picked up a tea and a coffee on his way home and the pair sat on Eve's doorstep together. Whenever possible, though, they walked into the city centre and whiled away the hours in Museum Gardens, even if it was in the evening.

Sometimes Eve would sketch; sometimes they would sit in silence while the pair of them read a book or listened to music together, sharing headphones. But each time, Eve grew more and more sure of Billy and how safe she felt when he was close.

It was a Saturday afternoon at the beginning of August, and they lay on the grass under the tree, side by side. Billy rolled over, propping himself up with his arm, and plucked a long stem of grass, grasping it between his teeth. Eve's face had fallen to the side and her eyes were closed. The sun was high, and the warmth of its rays beat down on Billy's back as he allowed himself the rare pleasure of just looking at her without her squirming. He'd had to be so patient with her. These months had felt like years, but sometimes the days would pass without him even realising because he was so wrapped up in her company.

Her hair fanned out around her and caught the light of the sun that created golden streaks near her face. He let his eyes roam from her hairline to her closed eyelids, and he longed for the day when he would be allowed to trail kisses across them to wake her up. Her skin was perfect, milky soft, and he flinched as his hand found a life of its own, reaching out to stroke it. He stopped himself before the backs of his fingers connected with the apple of her cheek.

Fuck, she was edible.

Eve sensed that Billy had come closer and didn't dare open her eyes. They had spent so much time together recently, and she was growing fonder of him every day. The connection between them was so strong and she felt it every time he was near. Her favourite time of day was when she heard him knocking on the door, and she couldn't quite fathom how she had come so far in just a couple of months. She knew that their closeness had jumped way over the boundaries of just friendship—the heat and chemistry between them were undeniable.

They were attracted to one another, there was no doubt about that, but the imminent physical element of their relationship so far was smothered by the electric storm that their minds and souls created together. They fit somehow. Billy was her missing piece, and she wasn't sure how she'd managed without him being there before now.

She often thought back to her days at school and wondered how different things might have been had she allowed him in back then. With Billy by her side, she felt she was able to take on the world. A busy shopping mall? She was there.

Acceptance.

He accepted her exactly how she was and expected nothing from her. She was the one leading this merry dance, and he was more than happy to take it as slow as she needed. He wasn't going anywhere; she knew that. He wasn't going to leave her to pick up any pieces, and he wasn't going to tell her she wasn't good enough.

The warmth of the sun on her cheek was soothing, yet her heart was about to burst through her ribcage. Billy had touched her before: he'd moved her hair from her face, stroked her cheek and held her hand. He'd even kissed her hair, her forehead… but there was something intense about that moment right then. He was watching her. She could feel it, and it was all she could focus on.

She swallowed slowly, hoping he wouldn't notice—that he would think she was asleep. She knew it was going to happen someday soon, but she still wasn't sure if she was ready today, even though every nerve ending in her body was screaming otherwise.

Billy curled his fingers into a fist to try to ignore the aching in his groin as his eyes rested on her mouth. Her lips parted ever so slightly, and he bit down on his own. Pulling the grass from his mouth, he slowly moved his hand to her arm that lay by her side, her palm to the sun exposing the tiny elephant underneath the bangles and cuffs.

He started at her wrist and dragged the grass along her arm with a feather-light touch, up to the crook of her elbow and back down again. Eve's fingers gently curled and released, and Billy noticed the slight shift in her breathing, causing his own breath to hitch in his throat.

Her body was on fire.

She'd never felt this intense longing before and struggled to compose herself. She wasn't even sure if it was normal to feel this good. He was only stroking her arm, for fuck's sake. Had she not already been alerted to the fact that Billy had moved closer to her, she may have freaked out and sat up to ask him what the hell he was doing, but she'd been prepared. Moving now would urge Billy to stop and she wasn't sure she wanted him to. However, she wasn't sure she wanted him to continue, either, because if his heart was beating as fast as hers was, she knew he would want more than this.

She might freak out. She didn't want to fuck this up, but her body and her mind were at loggerheads.

Billy watched Eve's face carefully for signs of movement. Her chest rose and fell with every breath she pulled in as he continued to caress her skin. Her eyes stayed closed, but he knew she wasn't asleep. The corner of his mouth curled up and he blinked heavily, knowing that she was enjoying this as much as he was. He would have been happy to stay in the same position all day, part of him hoping she would stay just as she was, too.

The animal in him wanted her to invite him closer so he could taste her lips for the first time, and he needed to remove those thoughts quickly before he did something stupid. He moved the grass higher up this time, along her shoulder and across the skin on her chest and collarbone. Eve sucked in a deep breath, in response to fresh skin being brushed, and held onto it as Billy moved up her neck and along her jawbone. No sooner had he reached the skin on her soft cheeks, he swiftly shifted the grass to her ear and tickled the inside, breaking the spell and ending the agonising lustfulness that he could not have controlled much longer.

Eve squealed and sat bolt upright, batting his hand away and rubbing the inside of her ear. He fell backwards onto his elbows, filled with deep laughter, and she turned to him with squinted eyes and pursed lips. "You are evil, Billy Taylor. Plain evil." She playfully punched his arm and he grasped hold of it as he rolled onto his side, moaning in mock agony.

Eve pulled her hair around her shoulders and leaned back against the tree. "Tell me about your mum."

Billy flopped flat on his back, folding his hands across his forehead. He hadn't volunteered the information as yet, but he knew she would ask at some point and was already prepared to satisfy her curiosity—he just hadn't practiced what he was going to say. Sighing, he pulled his lips in, biting down on them from the inside.

"You don't have to if it's too hard for you to talk about." Eve looked into her lap and twisted the silver ring that lived on her left thumb.

"No, no. It's okay. I don't mind talking about it. I just need to find the right words to start really." He pushed himself up onto his elbows and looked down the length of his body to where she sat, bathed in sunlight.

She sensed him looking and turned her face towards him, giving him a smile that spurred him on.

"When I was quite young, things started to get a bit weird with her. She started to forget stupid things like buying toilet roll, switching lights out. It might seem trivial, but Mum never forgot anything really. She was pretty organised and always on the go, so she had lists and calendars, and to me she seemed like a bit of a superwoman. One time, a while later, I woke up to no clean uniform for school, and I ended up having a rant at her. She'd just forgotten to do any washing. Dad and I didn't notice 'cause it was something that we both usually left to her—took for granted. Anyway, to cut a long story short, things got worse. We'd be having a conversation and she'd just forget what words to use. Another time, I walked into the living room and she was standing by the window with a fork in her hand, just turning it over and over with a look of utter confusion. I asked her what she was doing, and she looked at me, face as straight as anything, and asked me what it was." He sat up and pulled his legs towards him, the soles of his feet facing each other, and leaned forward to pick at the grass in front of him, bouncing his knees.

"That's so sad." Eve's eyes were filled with care and an empathy that tugged at his insides.

"Yeah. I mean, it's a disaster, an absolute tragedy really, but you gotta move on, I guess. I try hard every day to thank whoever it is up there that she is still alive and that I still get to see her, even if she doesn't know who I am most of the time."

Eve tried to read the expression on Billy's face, but there was nothing. "What about your dad? How does he cope with it?"

Billy's whole body tensed at the sound of the word 'dad'. He didn't want Eve to have to walk through that door of his life, so he lied. "He does well, considering. We get by." He smiled, tight-lipped, and avoided looking at her.

***

SAYING GOODBYE TO her on the doorstep this time was absolute torture for Billy. The feelings that had gushed through him in the park were not yet dormant, and his raw needs were getting hungrier and hungrier the more time he spent with her. Opening up to her about his mum, it was as if he was holding a magnet out and watching as she moved nearer and nearer to him. He felt so close to her after today, and now more than ever, he was determined to claim her as his own.

As he dawdled along the road back to his house, he toyed with the idea of just going for it next time. They could pussy foot around for months the way they were going, and he just wasn't sure he could last that long. He needed to taste her, to feel her. He needed her to be closer still.

Pulling a cigarette from his pack, he lit it and took a drag, dialling Dobbo's number as he blew the smoke back out of his lungs.

"Yeah?" A clattering of cutlery and crockery winged its way down the phone and Billy laughed as Dobbo swore.

"Mate, what the hell are you doing?"

"Washing up."

Billy laughed again at Calamity Jane and took another drag on his cig. "I'm going home for a shower and then I'll come round yours, yeah? I'll be about forty-five minutes."

"Forty-five minutes? You puff. It takes me ten minutes to get ready."

"That's 'cause you don't take time to wash your dick properly. See you in a bit." Billy hung up with a shake of his head and a grin on his face. He was looking forward to getting together with the guys, despite the pang in his chest that had been there since he walked away from Eve's house.

As he approached his own house, he saw that his

dad's van was parked on the street. He sighed and mentally prepared himself before pushing the front door open. Walking down the hallway, he heard Nev's voice talking to someone. He continued to the door of the living room and pushed it open to reveal his father pacing the carpet, his head bent and his hand on the back of his neck. Billy frowned and moved into the room, resting on the arm of the sofa as he tried to make out the conversation.

"Chris, please. Listen… No…" Nev sighed and dragged his hand across his head, and Billy looked on, brow furrowed. "You can't just… Chris, please." Neville straightened up and pulled the phone down the side of his face to look with despair at the now blank screen. He closed his eyes and inhaled deeply through his nose. Without another breath, he spun around and launched the phone across the room in the direction of Billy, letting out an almighty roar of anger. Billy's face dropped as he ducked his head and shielded his face with his arm. His reflexes were definitely improving as the years went by.

"Jesus Christ, Dad! What the hell was that?" Billy stood up and retrieved the miraculously intact phone from the floor. Neville slumped into the chair, falling forwards with his head in his hands.

"Dad, what was he saying? What's going on?" He moved to the chair and crouched down next to his father, resting his hand on his forearm. "Dad?"

"It doesn't matter, Bill. Just leave me. It doesn't matter. I'll sort it. Just go. Leave me alone."

Billy knew better than to push his father when he didn't want to be pushed, so instead he pushed himself to his feet, bending down to kiss his dad's head and leaving the room. He took the stairs two at a time, ducking into his bedroom to grab his towel before heading to the bathroom.

Standing in the shower, Billy wracked his brains for an answer to his dad's rage. He didn't know who Chris was, but whoever he was, he had pissed off the wrong guy. Neville in a rage was not something he would wish on anyone. As a kid, Billy had had a great relationship with him, but there had always been a tainted feeling of mistrust hanging around. He'd never been able to put his finger on it, but he'd always been wary of him. There had always been a sadness in his mother's eyes that she tried so hard to hide from him. As he grew older, it had become clear that the sadness was for his father. His mother was sad for him because he was hurting. She didn't know why he was hurting, but the aggression that was released from his core wasn't because he was a monster.

Now of course, the hurt had been joined by heartbreak since the deterioration of the love of his life. Nev had loved Jenny from the moment he'd laid eyes on her at the school dance, and within four weeks of dating had dropped to his knees and asked her to be his wife. Losing her to the devil's foot soldiers was worse in his eyes than losing her to the grim reaper.

Billy turned his face up to the shower spray and closed his eyes. Tonight was about forgetting his worries and spending time with his friends and he pushed worries about his dad to the back of his mind.

It was only on rare occasions that Billy would make an effort to wear a shirt and a pair of shoes that were not Chucks. Bent at the knee to see himself in the bathroom mirror, he rubbed his waxed hands through his hair, tousling it into a style of sorts, and then brushed his teeth, turning to lean back against the sink as he did.

"Bill!"

He closed his eyes and replied through a mouthful of toothpaste. "Yeah?"

"I'm going out. Don't wait up."

"Okay. I'm off out, too. See you tomorrow."

There was a pause before Billy heard the front door open.

Neville stood on the doorstep, his hand on the doorknob, his head dipped. "See you tomorrow, son."

Billy's eyelids opened slowly, and his heart pulled at the smallest hint of tenderness in his father's voice. The door slammed and it was gone.

After spitting in the sink, he looked in the mirror, searching them for a bit more fight, a bit more backbone, a bit more determination to stand up to him... It wasn't there. He placed his hands either side of the sink, head down, and emptied his lungs. Pushing back to stand straight and adjusting his collar, he walked out of the bathroom and down the stairs before grabbing his coat from the hook in the hall. He checked his pockets for the essentials and stepped into the warm evening air.

Dobbo lived only a couple of streets away, and he and the other lads were meeting there before they headed into town. Billy stuffed his hands into his jeans pockets and strode along to the end of the street, jogging across the road.

Apprehension ran down his spine as he contemplated his current mood. A night out with the lads was always something that he enjoyed for the first couple of hours, but as soon as he'd sunk two or three pints, it became a tennis match of playful abuse between him and his friends as they tried to cajole him into staying for just one more—cajole him into letting go and relaxing.

It that he wasn't relaxed: it was about him staying in control. He never lost control. He needed that. He needed to be sober as he walked back through his own front door. He needed to ensure that he had his wits about him just in case, but more than that, he didn't trust himself. He was his father's son, and there was no telling what a skinful of alcohol would do to him.

Knocking on Dobbo's door, he lit a cigarette and leaned against the frame. It opened, and he, Jamie and Charlie piled out, cans in their hands. They each slapped Billy on the back as they walked past him.

"Good to see ya, Willi-a-a-a-m!" Charlie drew out the vowel in Billy's Sunday name as he grabbed his hand and shook it warmly. He was the clown of the group and by far the best looking. Whenever they went out, Charlie was the one who left early with a smoking hot chick under his arm and a wink to the lads.

The four of them walked into the city centre and arrived as a throng of laughter and camaraderie at The Old White Swan.

"I'll get this round." Charlie moved to the front of the bunch and leaned on the bar, winking at the pretty girl behind it.

"Absolute charmer, that one." Dobbo laughed and turned to Billy, resting back on the bar with his elbows. "So, go on then. Who is she?"

"Who is who?" Billy avoided looking at him and pretended to dig around in his pockets for his wallet.

"The chick that's got you all fucked up." Dobbo swiped across his nose with his thumb and raised his eyebrows in question, waiting for Billy to respond.

"I dunno what you're talking about."

Jamie watched on, amused, and folded his arms across his chest, a grin on his face and his eyes darting between the best friends.

"Bullshit, Bill. I've not seen or heard from you for over a fortnight, your face looks like a slapped arse, and I know when you're lying. That tenner I lent you back in July must have done the trick, eh?"

At the last remark, Billy looked up under his fringe and rolled his eyes. Dobbo was a great mate but was definitely one of the lads when it came to ribbing and taking the piss. He was also a nosy fucking twat.

"*She* is nobody that you need to concern yourself with at the moment, thank you, Mr. Dobson. If and when she becomes significant enough, I will be sure you're the first to know." Billy cuffed him playfully across the jaw.

"I knew it! Is she worth a squirt?"

Jamie cracked up, bending over as he laughed at Dobbo who shrugged his shoulders, holding his palms up.

"What? It's a reasonable question. If she's not significant enough to you yet, Bill, she's fair game, right? So, I'm just asking if she's worth a squirt?"

"Shut the fuck up, Dobbo," Billy snapped, much to the continued amusement of Jamie.

"My, my! Someone needs to get laid. Maybe you should make her significant, tonight."

Charlie turned around from the bar, handing pints to each of them, and noticed the change in mood. "Jesus. Who fucking died while I was gone?" He lifted his glass up to say cheers and took a swig. Billy held his glass to his lips and knocked it back, downing half of it in one. He lifted his arm and swiped it across his top lip to remove the froth, not taking his eyes from his best friend. He'd needed him to be his rock tonight, but that clearly wasn't going to happen.

CHAPTER
thirteen

Unsteady – X Ambassadors

STUMBLING OUT OF the taxi, Billy leaned forward with his hands on the wall outside his house. Charlie and Dobbo slammed the doors and walked over to make sure he was still standing up as the cab rolled off down the street.

"Geezer, you gonna be okay?"

The concern in his voice was evident to Charlie and he glanced over, furrowing his brow as if to ask for more information. Dobbo subtly shook his head, warning Charlie to keep his mouth shut for the time being but with the hint of a promise to fill him in later on.

"Just go home. I'm fucking fine." Billy's words slurred out of the side of his mouth as he fought to lift his head up.

"Are you sure you want to sleep here tonight?"

"Just fuck off. I said, I'm fine."

Dobbo sighed and placed his hand on Billy's shoulder. His teasing earlier seemed to have tripped Billy over the line he would usually refuse to cross, and he was feeling guilty. It had all been fun at first. The lads had cheered him on every time he bought another pint, but it had become clear very quickly that it wasn't the cheering and back slapping that was pushing Billy back to the bar each time. Something else had a hold of his collar and was dragging him there.

He knew Billy's history. He knew his dad was a bastard. He knew Billy's loyalties were skewed, but he knew he had to back him up wherever he could. He'd often opened his doors to him when the door at home had been too daunting for Billy to walk through, but it seemed that tonight, he'd been digging his heels in.

"Just be careful, okay?" He dropped his head low and gave Billy's shoulder a squeeze before standing up and tipping his head to the side to instruct Charlie to follow him and leave Billy to his own devices.

Billy wasn't aware of any passage of time as he stood swaying, bent over the wall. Coherent thought had left him, and all that remained was the buzzing in his ears from the music he'd been subjected to all night and flashes of what had gone down in the club. He had no idea how many drinks he had consumed, nor what they were, and his chest heaved up and down as anger at himself began to rise like a demon from the pit of his stomach. He was in no fit state to do anything about his current situation, but he knew he'd been stupid—a self-fulfilling prophecy, perhaps. Clenching his jaw, he struggled to keep his eyes open, continuing to sway from side to side. He felt his fingers curl into a fist and tried hard to jolly his thoughts along to catch up with his movements. He managed to stand himself up for long enough to open the gate and slowly walked towards the front door. However, his body didn't cooperate, and he fell into the hedge along the side of the path.

Closing his eyes, Billy drifted off to sleep in a twisted

heap on the path, but only moments later was woken abruptly by the sounds of something he at first couldn't identify.

"What the fuck are you doing, Bill?" Nev stood, swaying his six-foot-three frame above his crumpled son, his words slurring from the side of his mouth. Billy lifted his head and scrunched his face up, opening one eye to see what the hell it was that had woken him. Struggling to focus on anything, he stared up at his dad's face for a much longer time than was necessary in Neville's opinion, and that flicked his switch. He leaned down and grabbed hold of Billy's arm, dragging him to his feet.

"Jesus, Dad. Get the fuck off me!" Billy stumbled and fell into Nev, who used his other hand to grab Billy's hair and pull his head backwards so that he had no choice but to look at him.

"Don't fucking swear in my house, Bill. Where the fuck have you been?"

Billy brought his shoulders up with the pain of having his hair pulled, his hand instinctively lifting to protect his scalp.

Dutch courage took a hold of him and shook some bravado into him. "We're outside, you dumb fuck. I'll swear as much as I like. Fuck, Dad. Get the fuck off me!"

"Don't you fucking swear! Where have you been? Look at you. You're a fucking mess."

Billy winced as his father pulled harder on his hair. He gritted his teeth and put his hand on top of his dad's in an attempt to release the pressure, a mistake he quickly learned from as Nev pulled harder, yanking his head further back and pushing his face into Billy's. The alcohol on his breath was fresh tonight, a top-up from the night before, and the bloodshot eyes that stared into his own held no love, no compassion.

This wasn't his dad. This was someone else.

"I've told you before, you don't fucking come and go, treating this place like a fucking hotel. D'ya hear me? You pull your fucking weight."

Something inside Billy snapped, and curling his lip, he looked up and spat in his father's face causing Nev released his grip quickly to wipe it away.

"You little fucker." He reached out to grab him again, but Billy's adrenaline-filled body was able to duck underneath his arm. As Neville lunged forward, Billy's rage bubbled to the surface.

Hatred for himself, for being so weak

Hatred for his dad, for being so weak.

Hatred for God—or whoever the fuck it was who was up there sitting on his fucking throne playing puppet shows with the people in his life.

And yet more anger for himself: for stooping to his father's level, for giving in to the temptation of alcohol—that empty promise of forgetfulness and peace.

Whoever said that alcohol was an escape had some shitty sense of humour. Fucked up was what it made you. It offered nothing but the doom and gloom of being trapped in your own head with a warped view of everything going on around you. Sure, some people were lucky enough to get a buzz out of it to a certain extent. Not here. Not in this house. Liquor was the devil here.

He bit down with his back teeth and stood tall as his father's body loomed towards him. As he jutted his chin, the demons he had been dodging for most of his life poured into every muscle, every fibre, and flooded his blood stream. He saw nothing but the red mist of fury in front of him. His head was burning, and an invisible force was pushing him forwards. His shoulder pulled backwards, his fingers curling into a tightened ball, and before Neville could grab for him, his fist swung around and smashed into his father's jaw.

As his strength followed through on the punch, he watched his dad's face flop to the side, his neck twisting and his mouth dropping open from the force. Splatters of blood flicked through the air, and the grunt of pain that was released from somewhere deep down bounced back and forth. It all played out in slow motion to the faint sound of the Nutcracker Suite in the back of Billy's head—a beautiful moment, like a scene in a fucking blockbuster movie where the hero gets his own back and life becomes sweeter.

All these thoughts running through his head as it dawned on him what he had done, took him off the ball. It was the game changer. His attention had slipped for a second too long, and the next thing he knew was darkness—darkness and pain.; a whole world of fucking pain; repeated pain…over and over, on his face and in his ribs.

He moved his limp limbs in an attempt to shield himself from the blows that kept coming.

But the damage was done.

And then it stopped.

All that was left was the heavy breathing of a monster, an ogre, a man Billy didn't recognise, and the whimpering cries of a small child—a small child who was hurting, in pain and broken.

It took a moment for him to realise those sounds were

coming from his own mouth, and he breathed out heavily, concentrating on the sting of unshed tears behind his eyes as he lay there.

"Try again when you're sober, Bill." Nev turned and spat at Billy's face, leaving blood and saliva sliding down into his son's ear. "Little cunt."

He pulled his keys from his pocket and disappeared into the house.

There was no point trying to get up to start with. There was no desire to. Staying still meant that the pain was just about bearable. He lay with his arms tucked around his body and his eyes shut tight. His tongue ventured out of his mouth to lick the cut on his lip, and it was then that he realised it wasn't just a cut. His lip was at least twice its normal size.

The pounding in his head, from the noise of his own mind—the chattering that was criticising him, telling him he was a fucking idiot, telling him to get up and fight back—and from the onset of what he assumed was going to be a horrific hangover, was almost comforting. It meant he was still alive and hadn't slipped under the blanket of death, even though death was what he felt like.

A buzzing in his back pocket took his thoughts elsewhere, but he didn't have the energy to reach for it.

After a while, however long a while was, he attempted to open his eyes. It worked. For one of them. The other remained shut. Billy pushed himself up with one arm, the other cradling his ribs, and stood to his feet. Straightening up was not going to happen, so he began a slow, delicate limp towards the gate.

It wasn't a conscious decision not to go into the house, but it wasn't subconscious, either. His body just moved the way it did. Survival, perhaps? He pushed on the metal and turned right out of the gate.

It took him a good five minutes of painful walking to realise where he was going. He wasn't entirely sure it was the best decision of his life, but it was the only place he wanted to be. The shock of the beating had gone some way to sobering him up and as he approached number seven Elton Terrace, his heart picked up its pace and spurred him on up the path.

He had no idea of the time, and he had no idea if she would answer the door, but hers was the only face he wanted to look at. There was some voice behind his self-assured subconscious that was telling him what a stupid idea this was, though: this was bound to frighten her; this was bound to fuck everything up after all the progress they had made... But he dismissed them all because he knew they were wrong; he knew that this was where he needed to be. He needed to quit hiding, quit making excuses for other people's choices and he needed to start living life on his terms. There was only one person that could change the path of his future, and that was him. Eve was going to be part of that future, even if she didn't know it yet, although he had a feeling she did. He needed her like he needed water, like he needed air, and he needed her to need him, too.

Billy reached up to knock on the door, but the pain that shot through his side as he did so nearly floored him. He climbed onto the first step and tried again. It was a feeble knock, and he wasn't sure that she would hear it at all. He stood patiently, listening out for any movement, and when there was nothing, he tried again.

After three attempts, he gave up and retreated back down the steps to the path in front of the house. He lifted his head and breathed in deeply. As he moved his eyes back down, they rested on the pale blue curtains that he recognised from Eve's room that first afternoon. He bent at the knee and stretched his arm out to scoop up a handful of stones from the ground. He wasn't sure this plan would work. His upper body had no strength left, and if his ribs were broken as he suspected, he would not have enough leverage. Grasping hold of the stones, he gently straightened up, but the sound of the front door opening stopped him.

"Billy? What the…? Oh, fuck." Eve jumped down the steps and rushed to where he stood, his face frozen with surprise from seeing her at the door. "What the fuck happened?" Her face crumpled as she took in the scene before her. Billy's left eye was completely closed, the flesh around it bulbous and red, his beautiful long lashes matted and stuck together with blood and goo. There was dried blood streaked down his face, and his bottom lip was huge, a cut running down the side of it. She brought her hand to her mouth to stop herself from gasping.

Billy attempted to smile at her, but it hurt too much, and he winced, the back of his hand reaching up and pressing on his lip.

She snapped to it. She was going to have to help him, which would mean wrapping her arm around his body, but she knew what she had to do. Eve swallowed. "Here, let me help you. Come on, inside." She cautiously slipped her arm around Billy's broad shoulders and cupped his forearm with her hand.

"You smell incredible." Billy turned his head, his good eye sparkling mischievously, and Eve blushed and shook her head.

"And you smell of beer. You're pissed, Billy. And talking rubbish. Come on. We need to get you cleaned up."

Moments later and sitting on a stool in the kitchen, Billy leaned forward, resting his arms onto the counter, watching as Eve searched drawers for first aid items.

"I'm sure there's something in here." She opened the cupboard under the sink and found antiseptic wipes and a box of plasters. She reached further in and pulled out a new, unused dishcloth and deftly ripped it in half. She ran it under the hot tap for a couple of minutes and then moved over to where Billy sat, still watching.

"This is gonna hurt. I just need you to sit still, okay?"

Billy nodded sleepily. The exertion was catching up with him, on top of the belly full of beer, and he fought to keep his eye open.

"Can you sit up?" Eve stood in front of him and he turned to face her, swivelling his body around and straightening his back. He winced again, his face scrunching up with pain, and he rolled his shoulder to try to ease some of the tension there.

Eve reached her hand out to move Billy's hair from his forehead, but his knees were in the way. She went to move around to the side, but before she made it, Billy moved his legs apart to create a gap. She looked at it and back up at his face, chewing the inside of her mouth, an uncertain feeling rushing up her spine. She reached deep down into her core and pulled out as much courage as she could find, took a deep breath and stepped forwards between Billy's thighs, resuming her role as nurse as quickly as possible so that there was no confusion as to why she had moved so close.

She could hear his breathing, laboured and tired, and

she flicked her eyes to his. "I'm going to wipe the blood from your face, okay?"

Talking was too much effort and he didn't want to spoil the moment. His stomach rolled with nerves in response to the tiny space they shared. She really did smell incredible, and he couldn't take his eyes from her face. She worked slowly and softly, wiping the warm cloth on the skin of his cheek. She smoothed it across his forehead to remove what he assumed to be more blood, and then down and round by his mouth.

He sucked in a breath. This was too much.

Her eyes flitted across his face as she examined every inch of skin for cuts and dried blood. She was so close, almost touching him, and his skin was on fire.

"You okay?" Eve stopped moving and steadied her breathing. She looked down at the cloth, which was no longer white, and back up at Billy's broken face. "What the hell happened, Billy?" She frowned softly, her face exuding genuine concern. "Who the hell did this to you?"

Billy dipped his head and brought his hands up from his side, clasping them in front of him. If he told her, this could change everything. It could open the door to his own life. It could pave the way to a whole new future. But if she knew, if she knew what a monster his father was, she would insist they informed the police. She would make him do the right thing, and he wasn't sure—despite the deep-rooted hatred he had for the man that had beaten him tonight—that he was ready to let go of the dad that he knew was inside of him somewhere. If Eve knew, he would probably lose him, too.

He bottled it for the time being, pointing to his lip and shaking his head.

"Too sore to talk?"

Billy nodded again.

"Okay. Okay, I'm going to rinse the cloth and get you a drink."

Billy prepared his body for the cold he would feel when she moved away from him. He watched again as she moved across the kitchen to the sink. Her body was hugged tight in jersey pyjamas and his eyes roamed over every last curve of her. This was not the time for wicked thoughts, but everything about this girl flicked every single switch for him.

Eve walked back over, handing him a cold glass of water that he sipped tentatively before resuming her place between Billy's legs. She liked it there. Her heart was hammering, but the closeness of him was nothing like the closeness she feared from others. His body heat was a comfort. She'd never seen him in a shirt before, and the open neck acted as a window to what might be beneath it.

Shaking her head, she laughed to herself as she cleared the ridiculous thoughts. He needed a nurse, not a horny virgin.

As Eve started the ritual again, Billy's body took over impulsively. His arm lifted slowly from his lap and reached towards Eve's face. She moved her eyes away, concentrating on dabbing the blood from the side of his face so she could pretend she hadn't noticed, holding her breath in anticipation of what he might do next.

He fingered a strand of her hair absentmindedly, his eyes searching her face for something. He was so close. The smell of him made inhaling deeply as a coping strategy pretty futile—the woody mix of cigarettes and aftershave made even more intoxicating tonight with the hint of alcohol—and the effect was antagonistic. Every hair on her body was standing on end with something she couldn't define. She was petrified, but it was different. Rooted to the spot, her breath was heavy and her knees were weak. She placed the cloth on the counter and dropped her hands to the side.

"You're so fucking beautiful, Eve." Billy's gaze felt like fire on her skin, and the breath from his whisper sent rockets coursing the length of her spine. She swallowed, rolling her fingers into fists and pressing her nails into the flesh on her palms. She attempted to move her thoughts away from the old feelings that she associated with being close to anyone. She was not about to let this slip away. She was determined to win this. The flight inside of her was beginning to weaken and the fight was stepping in. She was fighting for herself, for her future and by the looks of the broken and bruised man who had her transfixed, she was now fighting for Billy, too.

CHAPTER
fourteen

This Time — Rae Morris

EVE'S EYES CLOSED, and he knew she was fighting the urge to stop this before it had even started. His own eyes moved from her lips to her hairline, across her cheeks and back down to her pretty mouth.

She was perfect in every way.

His fingers continued to wind around the golden-brown strands of hair that framed her heart-shaped face, and he softly brushed them to the side so he could look at all of her. He could barely contain himself as he contemplated being able to taste her skin, to take her mouth with his. The ache inside of him was becoming too much, and if he didn't act on it soon, he might explode.

He moved to the side of her face, brushing down and around to her chin, taking hold of it gently, and stroking across it.

Eve's heart raced and the deep-down feelings of what she was now certain were lust and desire were pulsating and urging her to open herself up freely to this moment. Her fists clenched tighter as the soft feeling of Billy's fingers smoothed over her skin.

She took hold of her bottom lip with her teeth and let out an unexpected sigh. Was this really meant to feel so good when all he was doing was holding her face? She couldn't bear to open her eyes in case he moved away, although she was sure that if he was feeling what she was, he wouldn't be going anywhere.

Billy gently pulled her lip from between her teeth, running his thumb over it. Tentatively, he moved his other hand down to Eve's waist and around to the small of her back, gently pulling her closer to him.

She didn't resist, although her insides were screaming to get out and run away.

The thin material of her pyjamas leaked the heat of her body onto his hand, increasing his need to touch her. He was sure this was going to go so wrong, so quickly, but for now, he was thanking his lucky fucking stars for her willingness. Moving his hand to push his fingers through her hair off her face, he cupped the back of her head, and Eve leaned into his touch, breathing in deeply.

"Open your eyes." Billy's whispered breath was close to her mouth.

"I can't," Eve whispered back, her body beginning to tremble slightly. Her mouth was dry and every attempt to swallow made it worse.

"You can, beautiful girl. You can." He stroked the back of his hand down her cheek. "I need to see you."

Billy's whisper was like an electric shock running the length of her body. She took another deep breath and allowed her eyelids to flutter open, gasping gently as she became privy to how close their faces were.

He gave her a lopsided smile. "There you are."

Eve dipped her head shyly, a coy smile playing on her lips, and shook her hair in front of her face. Billy was beginning to learn her little quirks, and he laughed softly at her attempt to become invisible.

The two of them had spent so many hours together recently, and his feelings for her had multiplied each time. He couldn't define it just yet, but the connection was so real, so intense, that there was no doubt in his mind where it was headed. He could only hope that she was feeling the same. Billy took hold of her hand and pulled it to him. He turned it over, exposing the tiny elephant that he'd been desperate to touch in the park, tracing it with his index finger and making Eve shiver. He brought his lips to meet the sensitive skin and tipped her face back gently so that her eyes met his again.

Uncurling her fingers, and with a nervous energy coursing through her veins, she rested them on Billy's thighs to steady herself.

"Hi." She smiled straight at him this time, her eyes darting from his good one to his battered one, and his stomach lurched. The dimples in her cheeks winked at him, and he softened as he took her in.

"Hey, you." Stroking the apple of her cheek, he followed the invisible trail his thumb had left with his eyes. "You okay?"

Eve nodded. "I think so."

"Good." He smiled again, twisting his side to ease the ache in his ribs. "Because I'm going to kiss you in a minute, and I need you to be okay with it. Okay?" He raised his eyebrows and tilted his chin down to reiterate his question.

There was a new look in his eyes this time, and Eve blew all the air from her cheeks and nodded. He was so in control of this, and she was like putty in his hands.

"Okay."

"Okay." Billy smiled again and pulled her closer still, allowing his eyes to drink in every inch of her face another time. Her bare feet moved easily towards him, and her body flickered with a deep need as it connected with his.

That deep grey had had him hooked from day one, and he was no closer to freeing himself now. Moving his left hand, he cupped it under her ear and round the back of her head, continuing to smooth his thumb across her cheek.

His gaze was intense now, homed in on her eyes, flicking back and forth from one to the other, and her whole body lit up like a beacon. Eve's breathing became shallower, and she counted backwards from thirty to try to control it.

She could not lose it now. Not now.

Billy was lost in a trance as the feeling of need and lust engulfed him. He almost had to fight to move forwards because there was a voice in his head screaming at him, warning him that if he did this, if he gave in to his animal desires, that it would be the end. It would scare her off. It would ruin everything they had.

Could he not just be satisfied with having her as a friend? Why risk pushing her away just for a kiss? But it wasn't just for a kiss. He knew that once he had claimed her mouth, he wouldn't ever be able to let her go. It wasn't just for a kiss: it was for every other kiss he would ever give. It was for skin on skin, for nights of closeness, for, dare he say it, a chance at love…

It was for all of her… body, mind and soul.

As much as she was petrified of the feelings she was experiencing—petrified of them intensifying and petrified of losing herself to them and him—the powerful pull that this man had was rooting her to the spot. She locked her eyes with his. She needed to do this. She needed to leap, put her trust in him and give herself a chance to move forward.

She needed to fall.

Eve stepped closer, and with that—that sweet invitation—Billy needed no more persuasion. He moved his face close and claimed her mouth with his own, pressing his lips to hers gently, and with so much tenderness. He winced silently with the pain in his own lip but swallowed it quickly.

Eve let out a breath against his mouth, her lips parting slightly and her eyes closing involuntarily. Her body weakened underneath her, and she felt herself fall into Billy.

Pulling her body closer, he moved one of his hands to steady her, their hearts beating against each other's chests. He ran his thumb across her cheek and inhaled deeply, desperate not to break the connection he had finally made.

"Fuck." Billy spoke quietly against her lips, barely able to contain the rush though his body at the taste of her. Her hands instinctively squeezed tightly on Billy's thighs, another breath inhaled, and he smiled cheekily against her mouth.

Eve's body seemed to take control, way ahead of her thoughts and insecurities, and the need to be closer still was overwhelming. Her breath came more forcefully, and her hands gained a life of their own. She moved them slowly up the front of Billy's torso and over his shoulders, holding her breath as she felt Billy groan against her mouth while their lips continued to move together. She fingered the soft black hair at the nape of his neck and let out a sigh as Billy's hands moved into her own hair.

He had kissed so many girls over the years, but this was something else entirely. Moving his mouth from hers, leaving her breathless with what he hoped was lust and need and not because she was scared, he flicked his brow up, his head tilted downwards, catching the look in her eyes. They weren't the pain-filled pools of grey that he was used to looking into. Instead, they were filled with a life and a fire he had never seen before.

"Okay?"

She nodded, sucking on her bottom lip where he had just been, causing Billy to move back to where he now knew he belonged. He opened his mouth against hers, parting her lips slightly, and dipped the tip of his tongue just inside, catching the end of hers.

Eve gasped, a feeling of utter desire sweeping through her body. She had no idea how this worked, and panic rose in her throat as she contemplated getting it wrong. Quickly though, as if the two had been partners for life, her own tongue learned the dance, and she got lost in the delicate figure-eighting.

Billy pushed closer, greedy for more, and slid his hands from her waist, smoothing them over her jersey clad buttocks.

Moving her hands back down the front of his chest, she felt the taught muscles beneath the cotton that covered it. Her head was spinning with nothing but him. She couldn't think. She could hardly breathe. She was where she now knew she had always longed to be but had never known how to get there. This guy had spun like a whirlwind into her life, made her run harder and faster than she'd ever felt the need to before, captured her soul and made her never want to be apart from him… and now this. Now, he had set her whole body on fire and it was the most amazing feeling she had ever known. His lips had stolen her away to somewhere she never wanted to return from. His touch was gentle, and she melted in his hands.

Billy moved back up to Eve's waist, his breaths coming short and fast. He wanted all of her. He needed to explore every inch of her and learn her curves by heart, and before he had time to think about what he was doing, he had slid his hand underneath her pyjama top and onto the naked skin of her lower back. It was like velvet, and he wanted more. He pulled her closer still, moving his other hand to join it before journeying to the side of her body, his hands beginning to tremble with nerves.

He'd done this so many times, but it meant so much more this time.

Billy's thumbs caressed the soft skin of her stomach back and forth as he held onto her waist and kissed her slowly, drinking in the taste of her, and slowly, his hands started their excursion north.

Eve froze, her lips still pressed against Billy's. She sucked in a breath and opened her eyes.

His hands were warm and soft, and she really didn't want him to move them at all, but something broke. Some spell was shattered the moment they moved up her stomach and she stepped backwards out of his reach.

What if they weren't right?

What if once he'd touched them, he decided that she wasn't the girl he wanted anymore?

What if once he'd touched them, he wanted more and she couldn't do it properly?

Her mother's voice rang through her head over and

over as she lowered her head and stepped away from Billy, leaving his hands to flop down by his sides, both their chests heaving.

What if she just wasn't good enough?

Billy ran his hand through his hair, his eyes dancing across her face, concern and a touch of frustration sketched across his own as he tried to slow his breathing back down.

"I'm sorry. Sorry. I… Are you okay?" He frowned.

Eve breathed through her nose, counting backwards. She swallowed down and lifted her face to meet his. "No, I'm sorry." Her whisper was full of sadness and it tugged at Billy's heart.

"Hey. Hey, no, no, no. Don't be sorry. There's nothing to be sorry for. Come here." Billy held his hand out to her, coaxing her closer.

She looked down at it and shook her head.

"Eve, what is it? Did I hurt you?"

Looking back up at him, confused at his question, she frowned. "No. Of course you didn't hurt me. I—I'm…" She sighed and fiddled with her fingers as she fought to find the words. "I just…" Huffing out a breath, she became frustrated at her inability to tell him how she was feeling.

Billy slid from the stool to his feet, padding slowly towards her, ignoring the searing pain in his ribs. She looked up at him as he gently took her face in his hands and smiled.

"We don't have to do anything you're not ready for. That includes this. Kissing, touching, anything… You just say and we will slow it down, okay?"

"I liked kissing you." Eve blinked slowly and bit her lip as she remembered his mouth on hers just moments ago. Her eyes turned upwards at him like that were sexy as hell, and it took every inch of self-control that he had inside of him to resist picking her up and carrying her to her bedroom.

He breathed out of his nose, stroking her cheeks with his thumbs. "I liked kissing you, too."

Eve moved her hands to cover Billy's, and she held her breath as he bent down to cover her mouth with his again. This time, it was with a softness that wrenched at her heart. He lifted his head back up, kissing the tip of her nose, and pulled her gently to him, nestling her head against his chest, stroking his fingers through her hair.

This simple act caused a waterfall of backed-up emotion to fall from Eve in the shape of tears that ran silently down her face. She'd never been held like this before, not for as long as she could remember, and the fact she was standing there with Billy's arms wrapped around her—feeling safe with no urge to run—washed over her like a warm blanket.

As her shoulders began to shake, Billy held her tighter, kissing the top of her head. This girl needed protection from her past, he was sure of it, and he was damned if he was going to let anyone else have the job. He swore he would do everything in his power to keep Eve from hurting—from anything that made her run.

They stood in each other's arms for a few minutes until Eve's tears gave up. She moved away from him, wiping at her face with the sleeve of her pyjama top, and smoothed her hair away from her face, laughing gently with embarrassment.

"Wow. Sorry. Bet you weren't expecting that tonight, huh?"

Billy reached out and tucked her hair behind her ears.

"I wasn't expecting a lot of things tonight, but I don't want you apologising for anything. I want... I *need* you to be yourself and do whatever it is you need to do when you're with me, okay?" He raised his eyebrows at her.

She wiped a last stray tear from her cheek with the back of her hand, nodding at him. Blowing out the air from her cheeks, she tucked her hands under her armpits and rolled onto the sides of her feet.

"Do you want a drink?"

"I should go home—leave you to get some sleep."

Eve looked to the floor, wriggling her toes, and then looked back up at him. "I'd really like it if you would stay for a drink? If you don't mind, that is."

Billy smiled. "If that's what you want, then of course. I'd like nothing more." He bent down and brushed her lips with his. He couldn't get enough and was exploiting the fact that she was so close. To his surprise, Eve responded more passionately than he expected, taking hold of his face and opening her mouth to receive his tongue. He wrapped his arms around her waist and pulled her closer. The softness of her mouth on his was too much and he pulled back, breathing heavily and searching her eyes for an answer to the question that was on his lips but that he didn't dare to ask. He didn't want to push her on this. She'd been scared before. She was emotional, and it would be unfair of him to take advantage of her fragile state right now.

The two of them maintained eye contact for what felt like forever, their chests rising and falling steadily. He needed to back down here before she started something she might regret, or something she didn't feel like she could stop.

He needed to go home.

"I'm going to go, beautiful girl. I don't think it's a good idea if I stay."

Eve swallowed and blinked at him, her brow furrowing. "Did I do something wrong?"

Her worst nightmare.

Her mum's prophecy.

Was it true?

Was she right?

Her heart beat a little faster in her chest as she searched Billy's face.

"Wrong?" Billy laughed. "Funny girl, I don't think you could do anything wrong even if you tried. You have done nothing wrong. It's me who has done the wrong thing. I have outstayed my welcome, and I think if I stay any longer, I might not be able to leave you alone, and I don't want to put you in a difficult position. So no. You haven't done anything wrong. You have in fact done everything right, okay?" He ran his knuckles down the side of her cheek and Eve leaned into his touch.

"I'd still prefer it if you stayed." She wasn't sure where the bravado was coming from, but she knew that the minute he walked out of the door, she would miss him terribly, and right now, she needed to feel safe. Billy was the one person who could help her with that. He sighed and rubbed the back of his neck, sucking in a sharp breath as the pain in his side reminded him of his earlier encounter with his father.

If he did go home, there was a chance he would run into him again. He would obviously have to face him in the morning at the very least, but he wasn't sure that he was up to it yet. He loved him—of course he did—but there were days where he despised him. He'd never wished him dead, but tonight, when he'd been filled with the devil's liquid, he came pretty close. The thought of going back to that house where the beast lay sleeping filled him with anger, and he didn't want to be that person.

Looking back down at Eve's face, her eyes seemed to plead with him, and it was then that it became clear he needed to stay just as much as she needed him to.

He took hold of her hand and kissed the back of it, smiling mischievously from under his lashes. "Milk and two sugars, please."

Eve grinned and spun on her toes, trotting across the kitchen tiles to the kettle, and Billy groaned to himself as he watched the glory of her arse walk away from him. What the fuck he was doing he had no idea. How the hell was he supposed to keep his hands off her now that he'd held her, now that he knew how her skin felt, how soft her lips were and how she tasted of strawberries and vanilla?

He slumped onto the stool, resuming his position against the counter, and pulled out his phone from his back pocket. On clicking the screen, he saw a message from Dobbo.

Hope you're OK, buddy. Make sure you sleep it off and I'll ring tomorrow.

Billy sighed, tucking his phone back where it belonged, and continued to watch as the girl he was falling for pottered around the kitchen.

"Let's go in the living room. It's warmer." She handed him a mug of steaming tea, wrapping her hands around her own cup, and led the way through the kitchen and into the living area where she tucked her legs under her and sat curled into the corner of the sofa. Billy plonked himself down next to her, but not too close, and the two sat in silence for a few minutes, sipping on their tea.

Billy trained his eyes forwards as he felt her gaze burn into the side of his face. It was the longest she had ever looked at him, aside from the times she had sketched him, and it became clear that there was something she wanted to say but was building up the courage to do so. After waiting for as long as she could, Eve broached the question again that Billy had avoided earlier. She now knew that his mouth didn't hurt so much that he couldn't talk, and she brushed her bottom lip with her thumb, her mind drifting back to the kiss she'd shared with him not ten minutes before.

"Who bust you up, Billy?"

His head dipped and he inhaled deeply, caressing the mug that he held in both hands on his lap.

"I get if you don't want to talk about it, but it's a pretty nasty beating you have taken there and, I dunno, I guess I want know what idiot thought it was a good idea. Tell me to keep my nose out, though, if you want." Her eyes didn't leave his face, taking advantage of the fact he wasn't drilling into her own soul with his.

Billy's long lashes rested on his cheek and curled upwards as he dropped his lids closed, composing himself for a response. He lifted his head and let it loll backwards so he was staring at the ceiling, and dropping his mouth wide open then closing it, he clenched his back teeth before lowering his head again and turning to face Eve.

His eyes found hers and with them, he found his courage.

"My dad."

CHAPTER
fifteen

Unguarded – Rae Morris

SLIDING THE KEY into the lock without making a noise, Billy closed his eyes and rested his forehead on the cool wood as he took the final drag of his fifth cigarette that morning. He glanced at the grubby white van that was still parked on the other side of the street and prayed to every fucking god he could think of that this would play out calmly, without any shouting, without any flying fists or inanimate objects. He wasn't holding his breath, though.

As he pushed the front door open, he heard the whistling of the kettle and bit down on the insides of his cheeks. He slid his shoes off and hung his coat up in the hallway, pulling his belongings from the pockets. He considered slinking off upstairs to avoid bumping into his father but decided that he needed to get it over and done with.

Releasing the breath he'd been holding, Billy took the bull by the horns and walked through the door to the living room, placing his phone and keys on the coffee table.

"Morning, Dad." His voice came out as a confident

boom, and he stood in the doorway, watching his father move around the kitchen, fixing a sandwich.

Neville placed his lunch into a carrier bag and didn't look up. "There's fifty quid under the bread bin and a shopping list. Make yourself useful if you're not working and see if you can pick up some extra shifts at the shop. I've lost my job, and I don't know how long it will take me to get another. I've got two months left before we are screwed."

Billy didn't move. He continued to watch his father's lack of remorse as he busied himself like nothing had happened the night before. Incredulous, he folded his hands in front of his chest and waited—waited for his father to turn around, waited for him to notice him, waited for an apology… He had a feeling he might be waiting all his fucking life, but as sure as hell was on fire, he was not going to roll over this time.

Neville walked to the fridge and pulled out a carton of juice, shoving it in his bag. He turned to walk out of the kitchen and came face to face with Billy's rigid frame in the doorway. He stopped in his tracks and lifted his head slowly. Billy's heart was in his mouth, and every muscle in his body was tensed and ready for a fight, regardless of the aches and pains from the night before. He watched carefully as his father's eyes moved up to his face, taking in the damage done by his own fists: the bust lip, the black eye. He watched his mouth, his chest, waiting, hoping and praying for a hint of something.

Neville walked forwards, planting his big hand on Billy's chest and pushing him out of the way before grabbing his coat from the back of the sofa and marching towards the hallway.

"Fucking hell, Dad. Are you shitting me? Seriously?" Billy was pumped. There was more than anger rolling around his veins now, and his stomach lurched with a ladder of emotions. Hate had reached the top first. He began to walk towards his father, but Neville stopped and looked back over his shoulder, his head low, his gaze to the floor.

"Don't push me, Billy." He strode out of the front door and slammed it behind him. Billy flinched with the sound, bowing his head and closing his eyes against the anger that was threatening to take control of him. He clenched his fists, lolled his head backwards and roared to whoever was listening

"Fucking knob head!" He strode quickly out of the living room and up to his room, the door slamming against the wall as he threw it open. He walked straight to the other side of the room and threw his fist into the wall.

"Fucking wanker!"

The pain that ran along his forearm felt good, so he did it again. And again.

Panting with a mixture of exertion and emotion, Billy flopped onto his bed and hung his head, his forearms resting on his legs, and steadied his breathing.

***

AS HER EYES fluttered open, the sunlight making them squint, Eve took a moment to work out where she was. It wasn't until she heard Rachel's voice that she was certain she was at home but still unsure why she wasn't in her room and why she had clearly slept for a longer time that normal given that Rachel was already up. Pushing herself up onto her elbows, she turned a confused face towards where her friend stood, a mug of tea in her hand.

"Morning." Rachel raised her eyebrows at Eve, who reached out for the mug and took it from her, manoeuvring herself to a sitting position.

She cleared her throat before answering. "Um, morning."

"Didn't fancy your bed last night then?"

Eve looked along the length of her body, at her duvet that was across her legs, and smiled at the thought of Billy covering her up before he left. She bit down on her bottom lip as the memory of kissing him came back to her in glorious technicolour.

"Erm, nope. I fancied sleeping down here. Clearly." She smiled sweetly up at Rachel, who stood with her hands on her hips. There was no way she was getting away with not spilling the beans.

"And the rest, Juliet."

Eve threw her head back and groaned. She was going to have to tell her, but as soon as it was out, she wouldn't hear the end of it. There would be constant nagging and constant pushing for information.

"Okay. Billy was here."

"I knew it."

"Whoa! Hang on. Before you jump to conclusions, we just kissed. JUST kissed."

"*Just kissed* for Eve Swallow is a big deal! So why the duvet?"

Eve looked back at it. "I dunno. I didn't get it. I must have fallen asleep and he must have got it."

"A gentleman, hey?"

Eve smiled and threw the quilt over her face, kicking her feet and grinning to herself before flinging it back and standing up.

Rachel grabbed hold of her little finger and squeezed it gently, her eyes softening as she stepped closer to Eve. "So, he managed to knock a couple of walls down then?" She flicked her eyes from one to the other of Eve's and smiled tightly.

Eve nodded and swung their arms together. "He seems to have knocked down a whole load of walls. Not quite sure how or why, but something happens to me when he's around." She stepped even closer to Rachel and squeezed her finger tighter before letting it go. She placed her mug down on the coffee table and blew the air from her cheeks. Lifting her arms, she looped them around Rachel's neck and pulled her close. Her heart beat fast, but as soon as Rachel's hands wrapped around her back and pulled her closer still, she relaxed and laughed.

"Oh my God! Look at us, Swallow. Look at us!" Both girls laughed again, and tears sprang up in Rachel's eyes. She buried her face in Eve's shoulder, rubbing her hands up and down her friend's back. "I love you mate. I love you."

Eve squeezed her eyes tight and sniffed. "I love you, too, Rae. Now let me go before I freak out."

Both girls laughed again and dropped their arms by their sides. Rachel let out a little squeal and wiped her cheeks. "Okay. I'm going to Deb's to study. I'll catch you later, yeah?"

Eve nodded and smiled at her best friend. "Any news from Julian?"

"Nah. Next!" She winked and turned on her heel. "Love ya."

Eve watched as Rachel disappeared out of the living room, backpack slung over her shoulder. She hadn't spent

200

much time with her over the last couple of weeks and made a silent promise to rectify that very soon.

Taking the stairs two at a time, Eve reached her bedroom and grabbed her towel from the back of the door. Under the shower, she closed her eyes and let the spray of hot water soothe every part of her. She contemplated the information Billy had given her the night before about his dad, and her heart tugged. He'd been reluctant to go into any detail but had said enough for her to understand that he was in a pretty messed-up situation.

As she pottered around her room in her towel, her eyes fell on her bedside table and to a scrap of paper that lay on the top of it. She picked it up, her eyes scanning the unfamiliar handwriting.

Eve,
Thanks for last night. Didn't want to wake you.
P.S. You really do smell incredible. ;)
Billy x
07895146764

Eve grinned and lifted her arm to her nose, breathing in the skin where she had just rubbed coconut body cream. Rolling her eyes at herself, she re-read the note before sitting on her bed to dry her hair. She reached over and picked up her phone, keying in Billy's number and hitting save.

Curling her feet under her, she sat in the rocking chair that had once belonged to her grandmother. She'd had it stripped, varnished and recovered as a 'starting university' present, and Eve would spend many an hour curled up in it reading or sketching. She pulled a pad onto her lap and began to draw.

Billy's dad was obviously harbouring a whole load of guilt and grief that he didn't know how to deal with, and maybe lashing out at Billy gave him a release of some kind. She was no psychologist, but she was intuitive, and her interest in human beings meant she spent a lot of time studying them, their mannerisms and characteristics. Most of what she learned from them was then captured on paper.

She rarely got close enough to anyone for it to be of any use to them. However, she was feeling closer to Billy than she ever had done with anyone else and couldn't just get away with drawing what she saw.

She was involved now.

***

AS HE TURNED the car engine off, Billy leaned his head forwards, resting it and his hands on the steering wheel before closing his eyes. He needed to prepare himself for walking through the double doors of Butterfields with a smile on his face when all he actually wanted to do was burst through them, run to his mother and have her hold him and tell him everything would be fine. Facing up to the fact that he would never have that again was a very real pain in his chest today, and he wasn't sure he would even make it up the front steps.

The past few weeks had flown by in a blur of lust for Eve and avoidance tactics where his father was concerned. After the night in her kitchen, Eve had relaxed more and more, and the two of them had spent a lot of time in each other's pockets. Being off for the summer, she had loads of free time, which she filled up with sketching and lazy hours with him. He couldn't get enough of her. She was proving to be a welcome solace, her house a special place that he could visit and forget. But forgetting meant forgetting about his mum, too. He had neglected coming to see her more than he cared to admit since meeting Eve and promised that he would rectify this. Of course, he laid all blame for that with his father. Just thinking about him caused the blood inside of him to boil. There had been very little verbal exchange between them since the night he left Billy bleeding on the pathway outside the house—only the odd meeting of his fist.

Inhaling deeply, the rumble that had been pushing him in the wrong direction all morning made it to the top again. He pulled his hand away and slammed the heel of it back down on the dashboard with angry force.

"Fucking bastard!" He threw his head back against the headrest, his back teeth clenching, and ran his hand across his mouth before opening the car door. Slamming it hard behind him and locking it, he stuffed the keys in his jeans pocket and sauntered around to the front of the building.

On approaching the main reception desk, his eyes wandered behind the counter to the carer who often looked after his mum.

"Hey, Becky." Billy waited until she turned around and lifted his hand in a small wave. She returned his greeting with a warm smile, shuffled some papers and walked over to where he stood.

"Hi, Billy. How are you?"

"I'm good. Thanks."

Becky smiled again, this time more warmly as her eyes discretely took in the remains of a bruise on Billy's cheek. She'd seen him like this before, but it wasn't her business.

"How is she today?"

The receptionist slid the visitors' book towards Billy, who lowered his head to sign his name, checking the clock on the wall for the time.

"She's good, Billy. Really good." It was a bog-standard response that she always gave because what else could she say?

'She still doesn't know who she is or who anyone else is, and she hit three members of staff last night'

It just wasn't worth it.

Billy nodded and smiled again.

"I'll walk up with you." She lifted the hatch and the two of them strolled the long corridor towards the stairs. Billy glanced sideways at Becky as they made small talk. She was a pretty thing. Her shoulder length blonde hair swung as she walked, and her kind brown eyes smiled when she did. He'd always been really glad of her fake optimism, the way she would always leave out the details that caused awkward silences and apologies.

He looked her up and down discretely as she spoke about what the residents had had for their dinner, dismissing the thoughts of pushing her into a store cupboard for ten minutes that popped into his mind. He rolled his eyes at himself and trained them forwards: the curse of a pent-up, horny twenty-something.

The pair approached the door to Jenny's room, and Becky smiled up at Billy, placing a light hand on his arm. "I'll leave you to it. See you later, Billy."

Sitting in the armchair that was set near the window, Jenny Taylor's head was resting to the side, her eyes focused on the view outside, a book open on her lap. As the door was pushed open, she gently turned to see who was coming through the opening.

As Billy walked inside her compact living space, Jenny smiled up at him and held out her hand. She'd know those bright blue eyes anywhere, even though his hair was darker and longer. They had been what she'd noticed the first time she laid eyes on him all those years ago. That was until the first time he had smiled at her—that had been the day she'd lost her heart to him forever.

Billy walked over to her, taking her hand and kissing the top of her head.

"Hi, Mum." He let his lips linger in her hair for just a moment, breathing in the comforting smell of her shampoo.

"Neville, darling, I'm not your mother. God knows I'm not that old yet!" She patted Billy's hand and moved the book from her lap. He sighed into his mother's hair, closing his eyes and swallowing down a lump of emotion.

"It's Billy. I'm Billy, Mum."

"Who?" Jenny snatched her hand away sharply and looked up at the man who stood in front of her, her brow furrowed.

Billy moved further back and pulled the spare chair up so he could sit in front of her and make eye contact. He leaned forwards onto his knees and waited for her to look at him.

"It's me, Mum. It's Billy. I'm your son. Remember? We went for a walk in the gardens last time?" He waited patiently for her to process what he had just said and smiled kindly as the recognition behind her eyes began to surface.

"Oh, Billy! My big boy. You're getting tall. How old are you now? Eighteen? You must be at least eighteen, I'd say." She leaned closer and took one of his hands in her own. She allowed her eyes to roam across his bruised face, a shadow of sadness drifting across them as she frowned at the rainbow of colours under his eye.

"Twenty-two, Mum. Twenty-three after Christmas."

"Well, I will have to be sure to get you something nice for your birthday then, won't I?" She smiled tightly at him. Her memories of him as a young child were often quite prominent in her mind, so wrapping it around the fact that this tall, muscular young man was her little boy was so difficult.

Billy read the familiar expression on his mother's face and pulled the pack of photographs from inside his jacket as he did every time he visited. It was a chronological pile of dog-eared prints, spanning from when he had been just eight years old, to just a few weeks ago—a new one every six months. Jenny pulled one to her of Billy dressed in shorts and a T-shirt. A dark and curly-haired boy grinned up at them both, ice-cream around his mouth and a football at his feet.

Jenny ran her finger over the fading photograph and smiled wistfully. "I remember that summer. We'd just taken you to see Monsters Inc. at the cinema with Grandma and you managed to persuade us to go to McDonalds on the way home."

Billy grinned up at his mum. Her old sparkle danced across her face, and for a fleeting moment, he felt warm and loved.

They flicked through the other photographs together, each one depicting Billy a little older, each picture less familiar to her.

Jenny took some time to look deep into Billy's eyes in

a bid to see the child she remembered. His face had lost its puppy fat and was all straight, chiselled lines. The smattering of facial hair on his unshaven face made him look rugged and handsome. He had been a beautiful boy. She lifted her hand up and cupped his cheek, a pained expression on her face.

"Look, Mum. This is Eve." He turned the final photograph round.

"She is very beautiful."

Billy smiled. "She is. She's amazing, Mum. Maybe I will bring her to meet you next time."

Jenny smiled. "I'd like that very much." She handed the picture back to him and her eyes scanned the bruises and swelling again. "What happened to your face, Billy?"

He clasped his hands in front of him. She'd asked the same question the day before and he'd avoided answering, but she was waiting expectantly this time. He closed his eyes and huffed out through his nose, trying quickly to formulate an acceptable response. It wouldn't matter what he told her. She would have forgotten again by the time he came back, but he couldn't bear to give her the truth. It was only on very rare occasions that Billy and Jenny discussed Neville. The passage of time confused her, but she had some sort of awareness that she'd not seen her husband in quite a while. The conversation regarding him was always very vague and devoid of much detail, and Billy was always very careful to control his facial expressions and tone of voice so that nothing could be misconstrued.

"Just a bar brawl, Mum. Nothing to worry about." He smiled up at her briefly. He'd never been able to get away with lying when he was younger. His poker face had been underdeveloped back then and Jenny had rumbled him on more than one occasion, but these days, he was able to deceive anyone. Living a lie made that easy.

Jenny's eyes glazed over as she lost herself in some distant memory of her husband after a night in the pub. He had often come home with cuts and bruises across his knuckles, a black eye here and there. He'd been such a gentle lover to her, but there was a darker side to him that he had never flipped over for Jenny's benefit. There was something in the bottom of a glass that sneaked into his soul and twisted his resolve, ensuring he would come home troubled and distant.

"Shall we go for a drink in the day room?"

Jenny moved her head slowly towards Billy's voice, a small frown knitting at her brow as she struggled to hold onto the current situation, squeezing the black hole shut so that she didn't lose sight of who it was that was sitting in front of her.

Billy was patient and allowed her this moment, but it was short lived.

He'd lost her again.

CHAPTER
sixteen

Pieces - Red

KICKING OFF HIS boots, Billy crouched down and dug around in the pile of music that he had dumped on his bedroom floor all those weeks ago. He was searching for a particular piece: one that his mother had often played for him as a very young child—a piece that he had learned to play as a young musician.

When Jenny's eyes had glazed over for the third time that morning, Billy had called it a day. He'd kept up his promise to himself and had visited her every day for the past two weeks now.

He'd cautiously said goodbye, leaving a promise with her that he would be back the next day. Whether she would remember that or not was not something he wouldn't waste any time thinking about. She was so hit and miss.

Hit and miss. Hit and miss. That was his life.

Hit and miss.

Hit and duck.

Hit.

Hit.

Duck.
You missed…
Hit…
Hit…

The music wasn't there, and the pile was now spread across the floor in an untidy jumble of paper. Billy let himself fall backwards to sit on the floor and flung his arms up in annoyance. He shot his right one out, fist clenched, and hit the side of his bed. Running both hands across the top of his head, he let out another roar of anger.

He wasn't coping very well. He knew that. Things were starting to fall apart around him, and he was struggling to find the mechanisms to deal with family life.

Picking himself and the papers from the floor, he made his way down to the dining room. He'd made a promise to himself that he was going to start playing again, but that had not happened so far. Billy grabbed a dining-room chair and placed it down in front of the piano. He randomly pulled out a score and stood it up, his heart beating a little faster as he contemplated lifting the lid again. Huffing, he wiped his hands down the front of his joggers and raised his head to see the music.

He began to play.

It was a classical piece by a little-known Yorkshire composer—one he had always loved losing himself in. His fingers moved gently, muscle memory taking over instinctively as he followed the notation on the faded score. Recollections of learning the difficult chords came flooding back as he moved effortlessly along the keys as if he had never been away. Flashbacks of simpler times invaded his senses and urged him to play on.

As minutes turned into hours, he found himself

wading through his entire catalogue, picking out his favourite pieces to play.

The room grew slowly darker as dusk set in, and Billy stilled.

He felt lighter.

A tingling remained inside of him as he lowered the lid of the instrument and collected his music back up, stacking it neatly before slipping it inside a cardboard folder. With his eyelids closed, he bowed his head in an attempt to contain his calmer feelings a while longer.

Keys in the front door jolted him from his reverie, the tension in his shoulders returning immediately, and he sighed.

He wasn't sure what mood would greet him as his father stepped over the threshold, but something inside him made him hang around to find out. He needed to resolve things somehow. His dad was hurting too, he knew that, but he was supposed to be the protector, the adult, the one to keep him safe and he felt that Neville needed a reminder of that.

Huffing out through his nose, he stood up, placing the chair back where it belonged underneath the dining room table, and turned towards the hallway. Nervous, he stood and waited for his dad to walk in. As the sound of Nev's boots hit the tiles, Billy braced himself and stepped out into the passageway, stopping him in his tracks.

Billy clutched at the folder under his arm, lifting his eyes to meet his father's. "Dad."

"Not now, Bill. I'm beat."

"I think we need to talk."

Nev blew air from his cheeks and dropped his head down to his chest. "I'm not sure there's much to talk about, son. It is what it is. Let me past."

If he'd known what was good for him, Billy would have left well alone, but something was pushing him and urging him to continue. He swallowed down and locked his stance, bracing himself. "I think there's loads to talk about if I'm honest, Dad."

Nev's head whipped up and his brow furrowed. He wasn't used to Billy being defiant, and it came as a shock to him today. He was feisty to say the least, but normally compliant and just let him get on with things. This was a Billy he wasn't used to dealing with.

"Let me past. I'm not in the mood."

Billy stuffed his hands into his pockets and stared with conviction at his father. "Why won't you let me in? Why are you pushing me away? Literally."

The blackness of fury filled Neville from the ground up. There was no room for this in his life. He was on a downward spiral that he felt powerless to stop. Things had gone too far, and he had no idea how to start fixing them now. He'd lost his wife for fuck's sake. How do you come back from that?

"Move."

Billy held his father's gaze with his own for a few seconds longer to try to read him, to try to understand what was behind his eyes. Seeing nothing but ice and anger, he backed down, pursing his lips and shaking his head as he stepped to the side to let him pass. The next words on his lips were released before he had time to think about them.

"We're done, Dad." He sighed. "We're done."

Neville stopped in his tracks, his hand on the living room door handle, his head bowed. Billy squeezed his eyes shut waiting for his father's response, but there was nothing.

Nothing.

Neville pushed the door open, walked into the living room and closed it behind him.

***

THE VIBRATION OF the phone in his pocket cut through tears that sat like a film across his eyes as Billy walked down the street to the local Spar. He blinked furiously to try to release them, swiping the back of his hand across his face with anger and frustration. There were no words, no thoughts, just emptiness…

There are ten stages of grief, so they say. This felt like grief. He'd just thrown away the chance to patch things up with his dad and had effectively lost him in the process. Those words had tumbled out without a second thought, and he doubted very much if there was going to be any coming back from that.

He stood outside the shop, breathing deeply to compose himself before shoving himself through the door. He strode to the counter and waited impatiently in line. His gaze shifted around the shop in the hope that no one he knew would be lurking behind shelving. He was in no mood for conversation, and in less of a mood for being questioned.

It was finally his turn, and he waited as the lassie behind the counter finished tucking the receipt from the previous customer into the till. Billy clenched his teeth in the hope that she wasn't one for small talk and avoided eye contact at all costs. He asked for his cigarettes and paid for them quickly, instructing that she keep the small change for the charity box before pushing his way out of the door, head down and hands stuffed deep into his pockets.

The rain had started again, the weather a constant

reflection of his mood these days, and he turned his collar up, lifting his shoulders in an attempt to stay dry.

Trotting across the road, he headed back towards his house. Part way there, however, he instinctively changed direction. His chest heaved inside his clothes and the tears that had threatened to fall just a few minutes earlier finally tipped themselves down his cheeks. He stopped dead and threw his head back, letting out yet another roar of agony and desolation. The nothingness and the pain collided in his heart and his limbs took over the fight, sending Billy jogging towards Elton Terrace.

When his mind caught up with what was happening and where he was going, it all made sense. It was the only place he wanted to be, the only place he could be. A place where he knew he wouldn't be judged or criticized for the way he was dealing with things—somewhere he could let it all out.

He stood at the gate and looked up to Eve's bedroom window, the rain from his hair falling into his eyes and mixing with his tears as he allowed them to fall freely. His face scrunched up as he walked towards the front door, and Billy wiped at his nose with his sleeve before reaching up and knocking. Dropped to his sides, his arms hung limply as he turned his head in an attempt to contain his emotion - at least for the time being.

"Jesus, Billy. What the hell are you doing? Get in here. You're soaked." Eve moved forwards and grabbed his arm, pulling on it to urge him into the house. His reluctance was obvious, and even Billy wasn't sure what was stopping him from moving, despite the fact that his legs had carried him there. The tears that had subsided for the time being welled again, stinging his eyes as he fought desperately against them.

"Billy?" Eve stepped out into the rain and reached up to cup his cheek, gently moving his head so that he was facing her. He blinked, forcing the tears to fall, and she frowned with concern, wiping a stray one with the pad of her thumb.

Desperate to pocket the grief and battle against his trembling lip, Billy turned his face skyward as he blew out of his cheeks, struggling to keep it together.

"Hey." Eve pulled herself onto her tiptoes and kissed his cheek. "Hey. Look at me." She slid her hand into his and squeezed his fingers. Her tenderness weaved its way into Billy's demeanour and he lowered his head. A kind smile sat on her lips, her eyes wide and full of questions that she was sensitively refraining from asking.

"Let's get you inside. You need to dry off."

Billy gave a small nod and let himself be led into the house as Eve walked backwards up the steps and into the hallway, still holding onto his hand. His heart was thumping in his chest from the torrent of emotion that was charging around his body, and he swallowed to steady himself. He kicked off his shoes at the door and awaited his next instruction.

Eve moved behind him, stretching onto her tiptoes and tugging at his jacket, pulling it off his broad shoulders and sliding it down his arms. She moved to the kitchen area and hung it on the back of one of the chairs.

"Come on. You can use the bathroom to get sorted."

Billy still hadn't said a word, and Eve didn't want to push him. Things were complicated in his life, and she of all people knew that sometimes, it was easier just to say nothing. He would pour it out if and when he was good and ready.

Turning her head as she walked up the stairs to make sure he was following her, she smiled gently. "You go into the bathroom and I'll get you a clean towel."

The pair reached the landing and Eve pointed to the bathroom. She retrieved a large towel from her bedroom drawers, handing it to Billy who stood deflated in the doorway. He still hadn't murmured a word.

"I'll look for something you can change into. You get dried, okay?"

He nodded and she turned around towards Rachel's bedroom.

Billy walked into the bathroom and closed the door. Standing with his hands on the sink, he leaned in towards the mirror, watching his own face for a little while, moving his eyes to take in the blotchy redness that now covered it. He bowed his head and then pushed himself off, lifting his T-shirt over his head and dropping it to the floor. Sitting on the toilet seat, he rubbed his hair with the towel, scrubbing at his face to clear the emotion.

Eve slumped down on Rachel's bed.

"What's up, chuck?" Rachel looked at her over the top of her glasses and closed her laptop.

"Umm… I don't suppose you have any man-sized T-shirts or anything lying around here, do you?"

Rachel maintained eye contact, studying the look on Eve's face. "And pray, what might one need a man-sized T-shirt for?"

"For Billy."

"Ah." She got up and walked towards her wardrobe. "I have Dillon's old rugby shirt. I wear it for bed sometimes."

"Thank the Lord for older brothers." She smiled and

took the shirt from her friend who eyed her suspiciously.

"He's wet."

Rachel's brows lifted.

"From the rain, dick head."

"Ah." Rachel shoved her glasses on top of her head. "You guys have fun then." She winked and slumped back onto her bed.

Eve rolled her eyes and left the room, a small smile sweeping her face. She wandered across the landing and stood outside the bathroom door, her head low and her knuckles poised and ready to knock.

Without warning, the door opened and Billy stepped out, almost walking into her, his naked chest now in place of the chunk of wood.

Eve stared, clutching the rugby shirt tightly, her stomach lurching.

"Um…" She swallowed and blinked, not daring to meet Billy's eyes as they burned into her skin. Raising her hand slowly to indicate the shirt, she opened her mouth to speak. "I've brought you this." She watched the rise and fall of his broad chest, his breathing heavy. He looked different.

Bigger.

Stronger.

Primal.

Her pulse raced this time because of his masculinity, his body, not because of the way he made her feel in her heart.

He moved to take hold of the shirt that she still clutched tightly, but instead, he closed his hand over the top of Eve's tightly curled one. A clenching in her abdomen caused her bite down on her lip, and reaching out, Billy pulled at it to release it from its hold, the pad of his thumb lingering on its softness for just a moment. He pressed her knuckles to his lips, causing her to look up at him, those pools of grey that swirled with something more this time.

Taking a step closer, he snaked his arm around her waist, gently guiding her to him. He was on fire with need, and as he registered her pressed up against him, he released a lust-filled moan from the back of his throat.

She let go of the rugby shirt and rested her fingers on the door frame to retain her balance, the muscles in her legs becoming weaker. Billy's eyes were hooded and dark, and the rush of desire that swam across her lower stomach increased.

Unable to delay tasting her any longer, Billy leaned forward and took her mouth with his as she placed her hands on his naked chest, releasing a breathy sigh at the feel of his skin under her palms.

Eve let go: her whole body crumpled into him and she responded with her tongue, swirling and dancing it with his.

He growled into her mouth, his greedy hands moving impulsively up to her face, smoothing into her hair and pulling gently at the long brown strands that fell from the nape of her neck.

There was both urgency and a passion that had sat dormant until now, and Eve was embracing it with her every fibre.

They pulled away from each other, panting, eyes to mouth and back again. Pain seared across Billy's chest as the enormity of the situation he was in came crashing down on him yet again. Something in him had changed today, though. He'd become a man. He'd stood up to his father, not with fists, but with his words and with his head, and he felt alive in that moment, despite the tears and the heartache, despite the hurt that was bound to continue to follow.

He couldn't bear for the closeness to be broken, and he drew Eve to him again, this time with his hands up her back. He had lived every waking moment for this day to come. There had been a time when he'd thought that it never would, but here he was with the most beautiful fucking girl in the world, and her eyes seemed to be telling him to take her to bed.

He'd had "come-to-bed" flashed at him hundreds of times: girls panting and prancing in front of him to get his attention. He'd taken some of them home and fucked them because of the feeling they'd given him in his dick, because of a pretty smile or a short skirt that left nothing to the imagination. He was twenty-two, a red-blooded male, and he wasn't ashamed of that, but this was something else entirely. His need to consume Eve was overpowering. He didn't just want her body—and God did he want her body—but he wanted her soul, too. This was all the right kinds of right. She was his everything. With her, he could bury his existence and forget that he was alone.

Wasting no more time, he walked forwards swiftly, guiding her backwards towards her bedroom door. Once inside and kicking it closed with his foot, he felt a fierceness raging up inside of him, and Eve, although petrified of how quickly this was escalating, followed his lead, allowing herself be manhandled until she felt the backs of her legs hit the edge of the bed.

Billy's hand cupped her head as he lowered her onto the mattress. He lifted his knee and crawled up to straddle her, never once breaking contact with her mouth. Her bubblegum tongue swirled and flicked, teasing him and making him ache for more closeness. He couldn't get enough of her smell and the way she tasted—the way she felt in his hands.

Eve closed her eyes and let out a sigh of pleasure as Billy's mouth and tongue travelled gently and slowly along the length of her neck. The scent of him had her careening into a coma of desire and want. Each time his lips found a new bit of skin, her back arched and another groan escape.

Her responses spurred Billy on, his greed and need heightening each time she tilted her head back. He pushed her vest upwards, pulling his mouth away only to silently search her face for permission, and watched as she licked her lip and nodded.

Billy's touch was gossamer as he dragged the flimsy material up her torso and to her breasts. She lifted her arms in the air and blinked nervously at him as he drank in the scene laid out before him, flinging the vest to the side.

She looked so good lying beneath him it almost hurt.

Unsure now what to do with her arms, she began to fold them in front of her, to hide herself away, but there was something about the way Billy was looking at her that empowered her and made her feel beautiful. Instead, she let them fall to the mattress beside her. He ran a feather-light trail up her stomach with his fingertips, and she almost cried out as ripples of pleasure tiptoed through her. Sliding his hand underneath her back, he deftly undid the clasp of her bra, slipping the straps gently down her arms and tossing it to the floor.

Goosebumps prickled Eve's skin as he smoothed his hands across her chest, dragging the backs of them down the mounds of her breasts, the tightening in her stomach becoming more and more intense.

Never once breaking eye contact, he dipped his head and circled her taut nipple with the tip of his tongue, watching her react to his touch.

After a slow and delectable assault on her breasts, he took a journey south and Eve's breathing altered. This was where she might lose it completely. This was the bit she hadn't allowed herself to think about so far, and she fought hard against her mind that was screaming for her to grab his wrists and tell him to stop. She stared up at the ceiling, her fists clutching tightly to the sheets, and tried hard to focus on the deliciousness of Billy's touch.

Running his hand across the flat of her stomach, the milkiness of her skin tempting him, he kissed below her belly button. Just a centimetre or two further and he would be at the waistband of her leggings. He'd reached a point of no return. If he could not have all of her tonight, if she closed down, he wasn't sure he would be able to handle it. She was exquisite, untouched by anyone else, and here she was allowing him to discover her, to be the first to make her feel good.

As he leaned his head forwards to lick and kiss the very lowest part of her stomach, he raised his eyes to her face. She was nervous, and it was his job to make sure she was comfortable.

"Hey, you." Billy smiled from the side of his mouth and Eve bit her lip. It drove him wild, and he clenched his teeth in an attempt to have some release. "You okay?"

Eve nodded gently and moved her hand slowly to the top of his head where she ran her fingers through the soft, dark curls of his hair. She was determined to stay in the moment, and looking into the bright blue of his irises, she knew that she was in the safest, most gentle hands. Billy would protect her. He would make sure she wasn't hurting.

She trusted him completely.

She swallowed down nervously and blew out a breath from her lips as she plucked up the courage to release the words that she felt Billy needed to hear.

"I want this."

With a low groan of pleasure at her invitation, he slipped his fingers under the waistband and pulled them down, kissing each millimetre of skin as it became exposed. Eve's breathing quickened as she lost herself in the heavenly feel of his mouth on parts of her that no-one else had ever seen.

As he trailed butterfly-soft touches along her inner thighs, Eve inhaled sharply. He crawled back up to the top of the bed, watching her face intently as he finally slid his hand into the cotton material that covered Eve's last bit of modesty.

Eve's body lit up like the fourth of July at his touch, unable to get enough of the aching that pulsed through her, and the fire in Billy's eyes raged as he continued to watch her respond to him—the way her body arched each time his fingers moved.

As her body trembled in climax, her forehead damp, her chest rising and falling with each moan that escaped her lips, he pulled away and pressed his lips forcefully to hers, inhaling deeply through his nose at her reciprocation.

He dipped his head to her ear and whispered, "Damn, baby."

Kneeling above her, he shed his remaining clothes, kicking them to the floor, and Eve dragged her gaze down the muscles of his stomach, anticipation thumping through her. He walked to the end of the bed and leaned forwards, stripping Eve of her final piece of clothing before stalking to meet her body with his once more.

He gazed lovingly at her, frowning slightly at the furrowed brow that she wore for a split second. He ran his fingers down the crease and to the tip of her nose, smoothing the backs of his fingers across her cheeks.

"You sure?"

Eve gave him a shy smile and nodded. She reached up and pulled him closer. "I've never been more sure about anything in my life."

Billy fell into her kiss as he tore open a little silver packet, slipping his hand underneath her back and pulling her naked body flush to his. He gently parted her legs with his knees, and her whole body trembled as he moved nearer still, slowly entering her.

Both of them closed their eyes, inhaling sharply at the connection.

Feeding off the feel of her, he held still, her body touching every inch of his.

The eye contact they shared confirmed everything he had ever been too scared to hope for as he moved deliciously inside of her.

This was where he belonged.

CHAPTER
Seventeen

Your Body Is A Wonderland – John Mayer

BASKING IN THE afterglow of her first sexual experience, Eve battled to find the right words to say. She was pretty sure that her physical reactions had said a thousand of them much more eloquently than she could muster, and she didn't want to spoil the hazy atmosphere that hung around them both in the dim light of her bedroom.

Billy's hand dusted over her arm as she lay tucked into him, her head resting on his chest and her own fingers smoothing lightly over his skin. It was the strangest transformation. Her body seemed to know exactly what to do now, even though it was such an alien experience for her.

His other arm was slung back behind his head, his eyes turned to the ceiling and a cigarette hanging from his mouth; Eve could not drink him in fast enough.

She wanted to climb inside his head and work out what had carried him away from her for the last few minutes. He had been in a state when he arrived only a couple of hours earlier, but now he seemed calm and serene.

She secretly hoped she'd had something to do with that. However, there were questions dotted on her tongue, and even though she didn't feel like now was the time to pry, she was desperate to discover what was causing him such anguish.

Billy took a final drag on his cigarette and moved his arm lazily to take it out of his mouth. He blew the last of the smoke towards the window and sat up to stub out the butt. Eve reached over to her bedside table and passed him a candle. He pushed the butt into the top of it and leaned over her to replace it on the table. As he moved back, he hovered above her, his eyes bright and hungry as they roamed over her still-naked breasts. His head bowed slowly towards her and he took her mouth with his, his tongue swirling softly on the tip of hers.

That now familiar feeling of need twinged between Eve's legs again, and her squirming body gave Billy the cue he was hoping for.

He kissed her neck and breasts, biting at her nipples softly, groaning deeply as Eve ran her hands up his back. He could stay here forever, devouring this beautiful woman, claiming her as his own and doing everything in his power to make her feel as good as she was making him feel.

As he moved inside her for the second time that evening, their bodies tangled up in one another, Eve cried. Silent tears of an undefined emotion trickled from her eyes, down the sides of her face, soaking into her pillow.

Billy frowned, kissing the tracks they made, slowing his pace as he searched her eyes for an answer to the unknown questions.

She smiled up at him sheepishly, whispering through her red lips that were exquisitely sore from kissing him all evening. "I'm okay."

He nudged her nose with his own. "Are you sure? I'm not hurting you, am I?"

"No. I'm fine. Honestly." Eve wrapped her hands behind Billy's neck and pulled him to her, forcing him to kiss her. She squeezed her eyes tight to dispel the uneasiness and to lose herself in this man who had her all tied up in knots.

Tiptoeing back from the toilet, hours later, Billy sat on the edge of the bed and watched as Eve slept, her hair loose around her face, her tiny body curled into itself on its side. Her breathing was soft, and his skin ached to touch hers again. They had barely spoken tonight, words not seeming necessary as their bodies connected with one another. She was almost too good to be true, and thinking back to only a couple of months earlier, he could hardly believe his luck. This girl was his now. All those years he had wondered and almost grieved over the lost chance to get to know her were insignificant. He was here with her, she was here with him, and it was better than he could ever have imagined.

Pulling on his boxers, he lay back down beside her, staring up at the ceiling for the umpteenth time that night. The words he had spoken to his father as he'd left the house were rattling around in his quiet conscience. Could he go back? Would his dad let him back?

He sat up quickly and searched for his phone in the pocket of his jacket. Sitting on the edge of the bed, he switched the screen on.

Nothing.

Ragging his hands through his hair he sighed. What a fucking mess.

The moonlight dripped into the room through the

thin curtains that hung in front of the window, a barrier between the two of them and the world outside that seemed to be hell bent on twisting the knife at every turn in the road that they called life. Eve would be going back to university in a couple of weeks, and Billy was determined to spend as many of his hours with her as he could. She was the only person that he wanted to be around, and if she would have him, he would arrive at her front door on the morning of every day that he was not working, and he would stay there until he was sure his father would be too drunk to be woken. He didn't want to take liberties and expect to be able to sleep at her house every night, but right here, right now, this was the one place he felt at peace.

He lay back down on the bed, rolled onto his side and gently pulled Eve's naked body into him, wrapping his arms around her and nestling his nose into her hair. She didn't stir, and Billy smiled, closing his eyes and hoping to God he could switch off his thoughts long enough to fall asleep.

***

"SWEET FUCKING MOTHER of Mary, Eve!" Rachel did an about turn in less than a millisecond, her hands clapped over her eyes as she realised what she had walked in on.

"Fuck!" Billy jumped up, dragging the duvet with him in an attempt to cover himself as Eve squealed, reaching out to snatch it back, her eyes ablaze with embarrassment and annoyance.

"Fuck's sake, Rae. Ever hear of fucking knocking? Jeeeeeesus!"

"I'm sorry! I'm sorry! I didn't know he was still here." Rachel stood with her back to the bed, her hands still across her face.

"Just go." Eve flung her arm out, pointing at the door. "Go. Now!"

"I need you to help me with something, though."

"Rachel… GO!"

Rachel scooted out of the door, slamming it shut behind her and shouting a further apology through the wood.

Eve sat naked and cross-legged on the bed, her head in her hands and Billy remained standing, his eyes wide, looking from the door to Eve and back again.

"She… What the…? Why…? Why would she…?"

Eve slowly raised her head to see Billy bumbling around, the duvet slipping from around his waist. She pressed her lips together and looked up at him, amusement crinkling the corners of her now dancing eyes.

"What the hell is so funny?" Incredulousness slapped Billy across his face as he watched Eve's crumple into laughter.

"You." She pushed herself to her knees and crawled over to the edge of the bed, taking hold of the duvet and yanking it from him. "Come on. Let's get dressed and go get some breakfast from somewhere that sells stuff that's really bad for you."

"I was enjoying having *you* for breakfast until she walked in." Billy was deadly serious.

Eve snorted. "You've had me every day for the past three weeks, and for lunch and tea, but right now, my belly needs food, and that—regardless of your obvious talents— is not something you can supply. Get dressed and take me for breakfast."

Billy shook his head and smirked at Eve, leaning forwards to kiss her on the mouth. She had this uncanny ability to dissolve his temper with a tiny flash of those grey eyes.

Just as he reached her, she smirked and pulled away and he watched, a broken man, as she sashayed into the bathroom.

"You're killing me, Eve," Billy shouted after her, clutching his heart and shaking his head. He pulled on his boxers and jeans and shook the duvet out so that it lay smooth on top of the bed.

As he was sitting on the edge of it pulling his socks on, Eve walked back in, her hair scraped into a messy pile on top of her head while she applied her face cream. He was used to seeing her with her hair falling into her face— a shield, a safety blanket, a curtain—but with her hair off her face, her beautiful heart-shaped face was open with all her guards down, and it took his breath away.

He stood slowly and walked to her, inhaling every inch of her. She was so at ease and so relaxed now, even though she was completely naked, and he was mesmerised.

Billy reached his hand up and ran his thumb down the soft skin of her cheek, under her chin and let his fingers trail across her collarbone.

Eve held her breath, never once breaking eye contact with Billy. She felt alive, she felt beautiful and she felt safe.

However, after nearly three weeks of being holed up alone with Billy where they had devoured each other, not really coming up for much air, the act of getting dressed and actually going outside proved more daunting for Eve than she expected.

Stepping into the street, she pulled her hoodie closer to her as the early September air whipped around her face before linking her arm around Billy's.

"Can we eat in the park?" She looked up at him, catching an adoring look in his eye as he moved his arm around her shoulder.

"Anything you want, beautiful girl. Anything you want."

After a visit to McDonalds, the two sat on a bench with doughnuts and milkshakes and watched the world go by. Eve wiped sugar from the corner of her mouth, licking her fingers clean, and turned to look at Billy. The questions that had been ready to burst out of her mouth when he had turned up on her doorstep three weeks earlier were still there. She'd given him all the space he had silently asked for, but now it was time to talk.

She sucked the last of the sugar from her thumb before squinting up at Billy cautiously. "Why were you upset when you came to my door?"

Billy lowered his head and screwed up the paper bag that had held his food. He narrowed his eyes and looked out across the gardens, searching for the words. "My life is just a bit of a mess at the moment, baby."

Eve's head dipped to match Billy's. She reached over and took his hand in hers, squeezing it gently.

Billy sighed and squeezed back. "My mum doesn't know who I am most days, and that never gets any easier to come to terms with. And my dad… Well. I don't really know where to start." He inhaled deeply and glanced across at Eve. "I pretty much told him that I was washing my hands of him the day I came to your house."

Eve nodded silently as Billy fought to keep himself composed.

He looked down at the ground, removing his hand from hers, clenching his back teeth causing the muscle in his jaw to flex. Leaning back into the bench and propping himself up with his elbows on the top of the backrest, he stared out to the middle distance, a glazed and shut-away look in his eyes.

"He didn't fight for me, Eve."

A frown crumpled Eve's face as her heart broke a little at the sound of Billy's cracked voice.

"He didn't fight for me."

She blew all the air from her cheeks as she tried to stay strong for him. Leaning her head on his shoulder, she closed her eyes. She had nothing of any worth to say to that. How on earth was she supposed to respond? There really wasn't anything appropriate *to* say. This amazing man who had so much love inside of him was being left to the wolves because the people who were meant to protect him were unable to or were choosing not to.

Billy sniffed up and squared his shoulders. He was not about to cry again over his dad. Not anymore. He needed to man-up and move forward with his life, even if Neville didn't want to help him with that. He wrapped his arm around Eve's shoulders and pulled her to him, squeezing her tight and turning his head to press a kiss into her hair.

"Thank you."

She gazed up at him, her brow still furrowed. "For what?"

"For being you."

Eve pulled at the lapel on Billy's jacket and leaned up to kiss his cheek. "So, what are you going to do now?"

Billy shrugged. "I dunno. I have spent my whole life trying to please him, doing anything and everything to make sure that he was okay, regardless of what I wanted. I have visited my mum almost every day since I was seventeen. I have a dead-end job that although I do kind of enjoy, is definitely not my chosen career."

"What is your chosen career? What would you choose to do if you could?"

A wistful look drifted across Billy's face. "Music."

"You'd do music?"

"Yep. I would 'do' music." He laughed at her expression. "In any way, shape or form. I would take any job that allowed me to write and play music."

Eve sat up and twisted her body on the bench so that she was facing him, excitement dancing in her eyes. "So do it."

Billy laughed. "Yep. It's that simple. I will just get up off this bench and go and *do* music."

"Why be so negative about it? You have to start somewhere. So, get off your sexy backside and do something about it."

He gave her a sideways glance, weighing up the seriousness of her demands. "How?"

She shrugged. "I don't know. You play the piano, right? Not that I'd know 'cause I have never heard you play. What else do you play?"

Billy shifted his position so he was mirroring Eve's, facing her. His pulse began to quicken in response to being able to talk about his passions freely and without guilt. "Guitar. I play the guitar, too."

"Okay. So, are you any good? I mean, you must be, I s'pose."

Billy chuckled and cuffed Eve's cheek playfully. "Yes, actually. I am pretty good."

Eve gazed adoringly into his eyes, her own shining with pride and a smirk forming on her lips.

"What are you grinning about, beautiful girl?"

"My boyfriend is a pretty good musician." She giggled and scrunched her nose up.

"Your boyfriend, huh?" He squinted at her, a lopsided grin on his face. "So, I'm your boyfriend now, am I?"

Eve blushed, her eyes dropping to her hands that were now fumbling a little in her lap. "Umm…" She cringed up at him from behind her hair and shrugged. "Well, I kinda assumed you already were."

Billy continued looking at her with the same expression on his face, causing Eve to squirm under her skin. She was so beautiful and so perfect. He lifted his hand to her face and smoothed the back of his fingers down the side of her cheek.

"Of course I am."

She looked up at him, sliding her hand over to take hold of his and bit down on her bottom lip.

Billy reached out and released it from its snare, moving his head forwards and instead trapping it gently with his own teeth. "Only I'm allowed to bite that lip. I'm your boyfriend, so there's no need for you to be worried or unsure anymore, okay?"

Eve closed her eyes, savouring the feel of his mouth on hers, and nodded in compliance.

Walking hand in hand through the winding paths of Museum Gardens, Eve and Billy continued to chat about the music that he was so keen to make. She looked up at him as he spoke to her about his passion and told her how he had written lots on the piano, but that since moving to York, all of that had taken a back seat. It was so refreshing to see him fired up and animated about something, and the warmth that spread through her because of his happiness felt right.

"I'd love to hear you play."

Billy laughed. "Unless you have a piano somewhere, I am not sure that's going to happen."

"I could come to your house." Eve regretted the words even before they tumbled out of her mouth.

Billy froze. He pinched the bridge of his nose with his finger and thumb and closed his eyes.

Bowing her head, she played nervously with the ties on her hoodie. "Sorry."

"No, it's okay. I—" Billy sighed, stopping her in her tracks and turning her by her shoulders so that she was facing him. He kissed the top of her head and pulled her close, her forehead resting on his chest. "I can't let you in on that part of my life, Eve. I can't have him knowing about you."

She looked up into his eyes and nodded, pushing her lips together and turning away without saying anything.

Billy sighed. "Eve, it's not you, okay? I just can't let him spoil what we've got. And he will, Eve. He will spoil it somehow. I need to keep you and him separate so that when I come to you I can forget. You're the best thing in my life right now, and I don't want to tarnish that." He leaned his forehead against hers and tucked a stray strand of her hair behind her ear. "Does that make any sense?"

Eve looked up at him again, this time with more understanding in her eyes, and nodded for a second time. "Yeah. I get it. I do. It's just so sad, that's all.

"I need to keep you safe."

"I know. I do. But how will I ever hear you play?"

"We'll sort something. I'll bring my guitar around next time I go home, yeah?"

Eve nodded. "I'd like that very much."

"Maybe I'll even write you a song." Billy gave her a lopsided grin and kissed her nose.

"Seriously?"

"Sure. Why not? You're my girl. That's what musicians do for their girls, isn't it?"

Eve threw her head back and laughed. She stood on her tiptoes to kiss Billy's mouth. "I love you, Billy Taylor."

He halted. "What!"

"Hmm?"

"What did you just say?"

"I didn't say anything, dufus. I kissed you."

"You kissed me, but just before you kissed me, you said something. What did you say?"

Eve frowned and cocked her head to the side. "I think you are hearing things, Mr. Taylor."

Billy pulled her to him roughly, crushing her lips with his own, losing himself in the taste of her and the feel of her body under his hands. She melted against the firmness of him and the feel of his mouth on hers as he moved down her neck and back up to just below her ear.

Billy spoke with barely a whisper. "I love you, too, Eve Swallow. I love you hard."

CHAPTER
eighteen

Monsters — Angus Powell

THE SOUND OF people talking when you are underwater is the strangest of sounds. The echo of children's laughter and the movement of water around kicking limbs from underneath had always calmed Eve in the same way as sitting in the middle of a field with her sketchbook.

She sat on the bottom of the university swimming pool now, her loose hair attempting to float back up without her. She had already counted to ninety and was hoping to get to one hundred and twenty before she had to give up and return to the land of other people.

A small child—who could easily have been a mermaid in another life, or indeed Eve when she was little—came swimming past, her leg brushing against Eve's arm and knocking her off kilter.

Her eyes snapped and she watched the tiny body fly through the water until she remembered she was holding her breath. Blowing the air out of her mouth quickly, released bubbles that she then followed to the surface, and bobbing like a cork, Eve shook her hair out and ran her hands down her face to clear the water from her skin.

"Not even two minutes that time." Rachel sat on the edge of the pool, her perfectly manicured toes splashing the water.

Eve pushed herself up and out to sit beside her, deliberately running her cold wet arm down Rachel's side, who in turn screwed her nose up and flicked water at Eve.

"Cow."

"Moo." Eve laughed.

"You okay?" Rachel nudged at Eve.

"Yeah, I'm good. I'm really good." Eve turned her head to face her best friend and gave her a genuinely warm and contented smile. Rachel held her pinky out and Eve grabbed it with her own. They squeezed gently and Rachel laid her head on Eve's shoulder.

"You seem really happy. He's good for you."

"I think you're right. I think he is perfect for me." Eve grinned shyly. She wasn't naïve: she understood about love and relationships, even though this was her first one. She knew that lust could sometimes be mistaken for other emotions, and that just because she was feeling this now didn't mean that she would always feel this way. From what she could remember, her mother and father had always appeared to be so in love, but look at them now. She didn't even know where her father was, nor did she know if anyone did. However, the feelings that ran through her whenever she thought about Billy could surely not be diluted? Surely this was the real deal, the last-forever stuff, the 'nothing can tear us apart' kind of love? She shook her head to herself as she concentrated on Rachel and what she was saying.

"I'm really pleased for you, babe. Really pleased. Not

so pleased that he's had you to himself for ages but pleased for you nonetheless."

Eve grinned. "Sorry. We have been... getting to know one another a bit better."

"Really? I would never have guessed." Rachel's face was completely straight, her voice monotone. Eve looked down, embarrassed. They sat in companionable silence for a few minutes, kicking their feet in the water until goosebumps rose on their arms.

Rachel lifted her head and looked out of the window, blowing air noisily from her lips. "So-o-o... has he got a big dick?"

Eve's eyes and mouth widened as a grin spread across Rachel's face, and without warning, Eve shoved her in the back, pushing her into the water. She slid in after her and held her head under the water, Rachel's arms and legs thrashing about as Eve counted loudly.

"Five... six... seven... shall we go to one-twenty?" Laughing loudly, she let go and allowed Rachel to surface, spluttering and cursing, splashing as much water in Eve's face as she could.

"You BITCH!"

Eve laughed again and ducked under the water, swimming a length and slicing through the surface at the other end like a fish. She waved sarcastically as Rachel flipped her the bird and climbed out of the pool.

Walking back to the house, Rachel searched Eve's face from the corner of her eye. She was serious about being pleased for her. Eve had changed over the last few months: she was happier, more content. There seemed to have been less anxiety, and Eve just seemed more at peace. However, as her best friend, it was Rachel's job to lurk in the corners and over her shoulder, just to ensure that there was someone there to pick up the pieces with her if something went wrong—not that she had any reason to doubt that Billy's intentions were anything but honourable, but he was a bloke after all.

Rachel's opinion of blokes wasn't entirely positive, so she decided to keep her guard up, for Eve's sake. She also missed her. She missed hanging out with her and wanted to steal a bit of her best friend back.

"Fancy a girly night tonight?"

"Hmm?"

"Hello? Earth to Swallow? Jesus."

"Sorry. I was just thinking."

"Do. You. Fancy. A. Girly. Night. To-o-o-o-night?"

Eve snorted. "Okay, okay. I'm not deaf. Yeah, let's have a girly night. We haven't done that in ages. I'll tell Billy I am unavailable for snogs and shags tonight."

Now it was Rachel's turn to snort.

Once inside the house, Eve ran upstairs to get changed and to wring out her swim stuff. She pulled her phone from the bottom of her bag and checked the screen.

Hey, beautiful girl. Missed you today. I finish work at 6. Wanna do something fun? x

A wave of triple-edged disappointment washed over Eve in a heartbeat. She had spent nearly every waking minute with Billy for what seemed like forever. She couldn't remember a time without him. He had taken some owed annual leave from work, and today had been his first day back. She should really have spent the day sketching and putting finishing touches to her coursework ready for returning to university the following week, but an hour in the pool had been just what she'd needed after being locked in her room for so long.

She'd missed him, though.

The thought of seeing him in just two hours overtook the need to spend time with Rachel, but if Billy was to come over, she would no doubt lose the next day, too, and then have less time to do work. She sighed and threw her phone to the bed while she made a decision.

Picking up her sketchbook she flipped to a clean page. The image of the little girl swimming past her earlier sparked an idea, and she began to draw soft lines and curves, the movement of the child's legs through the water. She fell into her work and lost track of time, her hand taking her pencil for a walk across the paper until it was filled with a swish of water and limbs.

Eve cocked her head at the abstract creation and held it up to the light. It was unlike anything she had attempted before. She felt it needed a little colour and jumped off her bed to get her art box. Her phone beeped with a message.

Just leaving work now. Shall I pick up some chips? X

"Ah, shit." It was too late now to cancel on Rachel. She was going to have to tell Billy that he couldn't come round, and her heart sank. She hit 'reply' and typed out her message.

Really sorry—my pencil distracted me! Promised Rae that we'd have a girlie night. Do you mind? x

She picked up a blue pastel and smoothed it across the paper, creating a sheen of colour waiting for Billy to reply. Her phone chimed and she looked at it with one eye shut.

You break my heart, baby! OK. You girls have fun. Will text later x

***

BILLY SHOVED HIS phone in his back pocket and sighed. He'd known the day would come where he'd have to spend the night at home. He'd been back and forth to the house during the days to change clothes and sort the mail out, confident that his father would be at work, but he hadn't slept in his own bed now for so long. He wasn't entirely sure that his dad would have noticed he wasn't there, nor was he sure that he would care either way. Fumbling in his jeans for some loose change, he opted for a bus ride back instead of the twenty-five-minute walk. He planned on grabbing food and then hiding in his room until morning.

Neville's notice was nearly up at work, and Billy was prepared for bad moods and more drinking when his father had nothing to keep him out of trouble. Whether or not he had sorted himself out with another position, Billy had no idea, and the thought of having to try to pick up more shifts at the shop didn't fill him with joy. It meant more money, of course, even if most of it would be taken from him, but it meant less time with Eve. He wasn't sure it was the best trade off.

Reaching the front door fifteen minutes later, Billy pushed it open after the realisation that his father was at home and not at the pub hit him square across the chest.

He pursed his lips in preparation for the shit storm that he was now expecting and braced himself before walking with purpose into the living room.

Neville sat in the armchair watching the television, a mug in his hand and the newspaper in his lap.

"Dad." Billy nodded in his direction and walked through to the kitchen, dumping the bag of chips he had picked up on the way home onto the counter.

"Where have you been, Bill?"

Billy gripped the kitchen work surface and leaned forward. "Work."

"You been living in the shop, have you?"

Billy smirked to himself at his ability to predict, almost to the last word, what would come out of his dad's mouth. He closed his eyes and gritted his back teeth before replying, desperate to keep his cool. Had Neville forgotten the last conversation they had? Conversation wasn't even an accurate description of the exchange in the hallway that day, but surely he had heard him when he'd told him he was through.

"No, Dad. I had some holiday owed, so I took it." Billy waited patiently for his father's comeback.

"Took it where? 'Cause you sure as hell haven't been at home of an evening. So, where have you been, Bill?"

Billy was losing his cool. He was a grown man now—old enough and responsible enough to make his own life choices—yet here was his deadbeat, dickhead of a father trying to dictate to him his comings and goings. Who the fucking hell did he think he was? He pushed himself from the counter and walked to the doorway, standing stock-still and staring at him.

"Why the hell do you care, Dad?"

Neville's head snapped up, his brow furrowed and his eyes dark. He let them wander over Billy's face for a minute before spitting out his words. "Because I'm your fucking father, that's why, and I want to know where you have been."

Billy regretted the snort of laugher that escaped before it even registered with Neville, but incredulousness took over and he stood there shaking his head with disbelief.

"My father? My *fucking* father? Are you shitting me? You haven't been my father since we moved here, *Dad*." He spat the last word out venomously as he started to stalk towards the chair. Neville's eyes grew wide as he watched his son's solid form come towards him, buffed with anger.

Billy slapped his hands down on each arm of the chair, leaning into Neville's face. "Fathers look after their children. Fathers show love towards their children. Fathers don't use their fucking children as punch bags. So, fuck you and your supposed concern about where I have been sleeping. Fuck you, Dad. I told you. We are done." And with that, Billy stormed from the living room, taking the stairs two at a time up to his room. He threw some clothes in a bag, packed up his guitar and music and marched out of the house, his mouth dry and his heart pounding in his chest.

Neville remained in the armchair, stunned into silence at Billy's outburst, but just before the door closed, he pushed to his feet and shouted after him.

"If you walk out of that door, lad, you don't get to come back."

It slammed shut, and Neville bowed his head, his huge frame sagging and the sting of tears pricking the backs of his eyes.

***

"MATE, LONG TIME no see." Dobbo's cheerful voice on the end of the phone wasn't really what Billy was in the mood for, but as he rounded the corner at the end of his street, there was a quiet understanding that being with him was going to be the closest thing to normality he'd had in a while, and that, at least, was something to be thankful for.

"Hey, dude. Yeah, sorry. Been a bit tied up. Listen, are you in? I'm in a bit of a fucking mess, bro, and I need a bed for a couple of nights."

You know who your real friends are in times of crisis, and Dobbo was one of the good guys. Despite Billy going AWOL since meeting Eve, he was still his friend, and as far as Dobson was concerned, mates were mates and you helped them out when they needed it. He was well aware of Billy's situation at home, and although he would never presume to interfere, he had an open-door policy ready and waiting for when Billy needed to escape.

"Sure thing, buddy. Come on round. We'll chat then."

"Thanks, man. See you in a bit." Billy hung up, shrugged his bag higher onto his shoulder and walked the ten-minute journey.

Just before he knocked on the door, he thought of Eve. He was going to have to lay low for a few days. He was quietly glad that she was occupied for tonight. Mindless guy time with Dobbo was needed along with some serious alone time to sort his head out. He had no idea what his next move was going to be. He had no idea if he had any courage in his convictions.

His heart was still thumping in his chest after his outburst: he'd never lost his temper like that with his dad, always compliant and dutiful for the sake of his mum, and a twinge of regret began to surface as he pulled his phone out of his pocket. It was all for her. Everything he ever did was for her, and the lump that formed in his throat nearly floored him as he absentmindedly typed out a text message to Eve.

> *Staying at Dobbo's for a few nights. Will explain tomorrow. Hope you're having fun. I love you. X*

Pocketing his phone for the second time, Billy walked up the path to Dobbo's house and knocked on the door. As it swung open, a strange feeling of relief washed over him, and he allowed himself to believe in himself for just a few seconds. How long it would last, he had no idea, but he would clutch hold of it for the time being until he had sorted through the sack of other emotions he had packed along with his toothbrush.

"Hey, bud. Come in." Dobbo took hold of Billy's guitar and led him into the belly of the house that Billy would call home for, he hoped, the next few days at least.

Maureen Dobson stood at the sink washing dishes. She never asked questions. She always welcomed him in with open arms, treating him as she would her own, but Billy was certain she knew more than she let on. Whether that was because Dobbo had told her or due to her mother's intuition—that powerful sixth sense that all mothers seemed to have—he wasn't sure. Once a mother, always a mother… he'd read that somewhere, and his gran had always joked about sleeping with one eye open, even when Neville was old enough to have kids of his own. Mothers seemed to have a special ability to know when things were unhinged… He missed that.

"Hi, Billy, love. I've just put the kettle on. Do me a

favour and get some mugs out, will you? Make yourself useful."

Billy smiled at her very unsubtle attempts at making things seem normal and for giving him something to do straight away. He moved around the kitchen like he'd lived there for years, filling mugs with milk and sugar and emptying a packet of biscuits onto a plate.

"Have you eaten, love? I've some liver and onions left. Will that do you?"

"Perfect, Mo. Thank you. I'll get some in a bit." He moved to her and gave her a kiss on the cheek and she reciprocated with a gentle squeeze of his hand, communicating to him, in her own way, that he was very welcome to stay as long as he needed, that she would listen if he wanted, but that she would mind her own business if he didn't feel like talking.

He gave her a tight smile as a thank you and carried the tray into the living room.

The three of them sat in comfortable silence, the television humming quietly in the background. Maureen dozed in the chair while Dobbo read the sports pages of the Daily Mail. Billy allowed his head to fall back against the cushion, losing himself inside his own head. He closed his eyes and exhaled with a sense of accomplishment.

There were no elephants here today, just mutual respect and understanding.

Polishing off a plate of the finest Yorkshire grub a couple of days later, Billy wiped his mouth with a napkin and patted his belly. "Marvellous, Mo. Bloody marvellous." He stood up to wash his plate.

"Pleasure, darlin'. I'll go make you up a bed on the floor in Paul's room." She scooted upstairs, leaving the boys to themselves in the kitchen.

"So, I don't want to pry, mate, but are you gonna tell me what's happened?"

Billy stopped, his hands limp in the dishwater, his back to his friend and his head low.

He was sick of doing all the fighting, sick of keeping everything together for the sake of others and he realised he had no energy left.

He gave up.

Squeezing his eyes tight he attempted to stop the sudden threat of tears, but they were past the point of no return before he had even registered their presence. He blew out, his shoulders beginning to shake, and he crumpled.

"Shit, man." Dobbo jumped to his feet and pulled him into a bear hug. "Shit."

Billy buried his face into his mate's shoulders and let go.

He gave him a friendly thump, grabbing the back of his neck and squeezing supportively. He'd known Billy for nearly four years, and in that time, they had become really close. Billy was always the sensible one, the one who never lost his cool, the one who took everything in his stride... However, this was the second time recently that he'd seen him out of control, and he was pretty sure that it wasn't going to be the last.

Dobbo never asked. He had always wanted to reach out, but Billy wouldn't ever admit to needing any support other than a bit of space now and again.

This was different.

He could feel it in the heaving of Billy's chest and the fierceness with which he clung to him. He moved backwards, slowly releasing himself from Billy's desperation, and held him at arm's length. "Okay?"

Billy nodded, wiping his forearm across his eyes. "God. Sorry, mate. Don't know what came over me."

"Bill, you don't have to pretend. I know this is bad. Talk to me, buddy."

Billy sniffed up, swiping his thumb under his nose and nodding at the floor. "Okay." He pulled a chair out at the kitchen table and sat down, resting his elbows on the wooden surface and rubbing his hands back and forth across the top of his head.

Dobbo joined him and sat forwards, clasping his hands in front of him, waiting patiently for Billy to find his voice.

He finally lifted his head and looked at the clock on the wall. "I've had it with him. I've moved out." He flicked his eyes sideways to look at his friend. "I told him weeks ago that we were done. He smashed me up after that night out and never once showed any remorse. I walked into the house last night after staying with Eve for a few weeks, and he spoke to me as if nothing had happened—he spoke to me like I had some kind of duty to answer to him. Like fuck I have. So, I fucking told him. I tried to keep calm. I tried to appease him, but he kept asking and probing, and I lost it. I told him straight that he was a sorry excuse for a father. And here I am. And I don't have a fucking clue what to do. I can't go back."

Dobbo leaned forward and gripped the back of Billy's neck affectionately again. "You've done the right thing, bro. I know it's shit and it's hard, and you now have a ton of bollocks to work through, but you needed to get out. He's no good for you, man."

A lone tear—one that seemed to have held itself back, knowing and understanding the pain that would sear through him at that moment from the crack in his heart—rolled over the rim of Billy's eye as he blinked. "Yeah, but he's my dad."

CHAPTER
nineteen

Something In The Way She Moves – James Taylor

SITTING CROSS-LEGGED ON the blow-up bed in Dobbo's room, Billy strummed at his guitar, his fingers finding a life of their own as they remembered the frets and strings. He played a few riffs and bars of familiar songs that he had committed to memory and then thumbed through his pile of music.

He'd rung in sick at work, not really in the right frame of mind to stand smiling and being polite all day and had the house to himself with Dobbo at the contruction yard where he worked and Maureen off cleaning.

He pulled out his 'Brit Pop Hits of the Nineties' book from the front of his guitar case and spent a carefree hour reacquainting himself with old favourites before his phone chirped with a text from Eve.

Missing you. Hope you are okay. I love you xx

The warmth that covered him whenever he thought of her enveloped him as he typed out his reply. He had given her a brief rundown of the events from the evening before when he rang her that morning but had managed to persuade her to leave him to his own devices for a couple of days, as much as it pained them both.

It gave Eve an opportunity to get some artwork completed and spend time with Rachel, and it meant that Billy didn't have to talk.

He put his phone down and picked at his strings again, experimenting with chord sequences, humming along to them until a melody began to form in his head.

Rolling forwards onto his knees, he grabbed a pencil from the shelf and scribbled words down on the back of a classical score. It had been a while since he had done any song writing, and he realised how much of his creativity had been stifled and curbed due to everyday life and the fuck ups it threw him. More often than not, the songs spoke to him, not the other way around, so he wasn't sure what would come of it, but for the next two hours, he sat there, pencil in his mouth, periodically changing words, adding verses and tweaking the melody.

When Dobbo and his mum returned home from work, Billy set his guitar down, smiling at his day's productivity, and jogged down the stairs to greet them. He helped Maureen with some shopping bags and to put the food away.

"I'm just off for a quick shower and then I'll help with tea, Mum."

"Okay, love." She flicked the kettle on and then indicated that Billy should sit down at the table. He swallowed, unsure how this conversation was going to go. They had never spoken before about life and its tribulations.

Maureen sat in the chair beside him and reached out,

covering Billy's hand with her own. Her voice was calm but firm. "You have a home here for as long as you want it, love. I will clear the spare room and you can stay."

Billy blinked heavily, unsure of what to say. He opened his mouth to start, but Maureen cut him off.

"I'll have no protestations. If you've nowhere to go, you will stay here. However, if you are staying, you are part of this household and you will pull your weight. I will expect money for food, but nothing else, and I will expect help with cooking and cleaning and the like. You hear me?"

Billy nodded, feeling like a child and liking it very much. He went to open his mouth again, but Maureen pulled him to her in a firm and loving hug, squeezing the bones of him and kissing the top of his head.

Getting to her feet quickly, she walked away from him to the fridge. "Now, get some mugs. We need tea." She pulled the hem of her cardigan to her face, and Billy caught her wiping her eyes. His own throat constricted, and he stood, moving to the cupboard, pulling three mugs out slowly, his head low and his heart beating slowly and calmly.

"Thank you."

Maureen turned to him, a closed-lipped smile on her face. She nodded and took the mugs from him, and nothing more was said.

The rest of the evening was spent cooking and sorting out the spare room together. The three of them moved boxes and fitness equipment into the shed at the bottom of the garden. Billy couldn't remember the last time he had done mundane things with his family. For the first time in a while, he allowed himself to hope for a light at the end of a very dark tunnel. If he could set himself up here, he would have some much needed distance from the ache in his father's heart, and in turn he might be able to start collecting the wood and girders that could one day be styled into bridges that would lead him home again.

He carried the last box down the stairs as Dobson was coming back up. "This is the last one, I think."

"Cool. I'll go find some bedding." Dobbo squeezed past him on the stairs and slapped him on the back. "Good to have you here, mate."

***

STANDING IN FRONT of the mirror, Eve huffed out, annoyed at her lack of creativity when it came to hairstyles. Ever since she could remember, she'd worn her hair long and loose, mostly to hide herself away from the rest of the world, but she had clocked the look on Billy's face when she walked in from the bathroom with it piled on top of her head. She hadn't seen him now for nearly a week, but tonight he was taking her on a date. It was probably the first official date they had been on, other than the umpteen coffees and walks in the park. Tonight, he'd promised, it would be a proper date.

"Rachel!" She balled her fists at her sides, scowling at herself in the mirror as she shouted for assistance.

Rachel burst into her room and looked at the bird's nest that was now Eve's hair. "Jesus Christ. What on earth are you doing?"

Eve held her arms out and shrugged. "What does it look like? I am trying an up-do."

"A what now?"

"An up-do. A freakin' up-do."

"Again, a what?"

Eve swivelled around, planting her hands on her hips. "I am trying to put my hair up."

"Oh." Rachel bit her lips together to stop herself from laughing and walked forwards, taking chunks of back combed hair in her fingers and letting them fall again. She scrunched her nose up sympathetically and whispered near Eve's ear. "I think we need to start again, chicken."

Eve buried her face in her hands and let out a wail. "Help me!"

Rachel turned her around to the mirror by the shoulders, grabbed her chair from her desk and plonked it behind Eve. "Sit."

After about twenty minutes using a comb, hair spray, straighteners and goodness knows what else, she had created a beautifully messy bun with braids and tendrils.

"Oh my God, Rae. That's amazing." Eve moved her hand up to touch the top of it gently. "Where on earth did you learn to do stuff like this?"

"Oh, I get around. Now get dressed. He will be here in fifteen minutes."

Eve grinned at herself in the mirror. She looked so different. Her mind cast back to the summer ball, and she remembered that the first time Billy had laid eyes on her again since school: her hair had been tied up. Perhaps that's why he loved it so much.

She fumbled around in her wardrobe for something that wasn't leggings and a shirt or paint covered denims, eventually settling on a black knee-length broderie anglaise skirt. She slipped into it and pulled on a white vest. Digging around in her jewellery box, she found a pair of her grandmother's droplet earrings and neared the mirror again to put them in, standing back to look at herself.

She was weirdly nervous about seeing him, which she knew was ridiculous. Slicking on a layer of mascara, she grabbed her leather jacket and walked into Rachel's room for appraisal.

Rae looked up from her book and nodded, a smile on her face. "Perfect. Chucks? Or Docs?"

"I don't own Chucks. It will obviously be Docs."

"You can borrow my Chucks."

Eve laughed. "Thanks, but I'll stick with my old faithfuls. So, I look okay?"

"Honey, you look stunning. Now go have fun."

Eve spun around and ran down the stairs. She checked the clock on the kitchen wall. Twenty-thirteen. He would be there any minute.

She opened the back door to let some air in and stood for a moment, her eyes to the stars. The nights had become darker over the last couple of weeks, and the skies were an inky blue. She wrapped her arms around her body, a breeze cooling her skin.

Things were good. Life was good and she was feeling good.

The sound of the doorknocker jolted her from her thoughts, and she turned and pattered down the hall to where she knew Billy would be standing waiting.

Smoothing her hand down her skirt, she closed her fingers around the handle, pulling gently. She could not conceal her excitement when her eyes found his, her face beaming. He was so beautiful, dressed in a blue shirt that matched his eyes, and jeans. His sleeves were rolled part way up his forearm, and he looked happy and relaxed.

"Hey, beautiful girl."

She stepped forwards and took his face in her hands, kissing his lips softly. She whispered against them as she closed her eyes, losing herself in his smell. "I missed you."

Billy found the back of her head with his hand and crushed her body against his, his lips parting to allow her tongue to dance with his. "God, I missed you, too." He pulled away gently before he decided to call the whole thing off and just take her to bed, holding her at arm's length. "You look amazing. Look at your face!"

"You like the hair?"

"I love the hair." He stroked his thumb down her cheek and across her lips. "I can see you."

Eve dropped her eyes shyly. "Let's go." She looped her arm into his and the pair set off down the street. It was then that her heart picked up pace again and she realised that it wasn't so much seeing Billy again that had been worrying her, but more where he was taking her.

"Am I allowed to know where we're going?"

"Nope."

"Nope?"

After a few yards, Billy stopped in front of his car that was parked on Eve's street. She looked at him, surprised. "We're driving?"

"We are." Billy smiled down at her and lifted her chin so he could taste her lips again. "Is that okay?"

Eve nodded before her thought processes had time to kick in. He opened the passenger door and closed it behind her once she had forced herself inside, her heart thudding. Running around the back of the car, he dived into the driver's side and started the engine.

"You ready?"

Eve fiddled with her fingers nervously and nodded. Billy's had been the last car she was in, and she remembered only too well how that had worked out for her. She wasn't at all sure how this was going to go. Back then, though, she had been more skittish, more afraid of herself and everything around her. She hoped that having Billy by her side would mean she was less likely to have an adverse reaction.

"Hey." Billy pulled her face around and searched her eyes. "Trust me. Okay?"

She smiled and nodded. Of course she trusted him. She would go as far as saying that she trusted him with her life. She'd had such a good run of it recently: no outbursts, no anxiety attacks and no running. That was the biggest deal. He completed her, made her whole and grounded her. She couldn't imagine a scenario where she would ever run from Billy again, and unless he felt the need to run from her, she couldn't imagine a scenario where they wouldn't be together.

"Right. Before we set off, I need to blindfold you."

Eve's head turned slowly towards him so that she was facing him, her eyes full of disbelief. "You... are *shitting* me?"

"Umm, nope!"

"Billy, do you not know me at all?"

"Eve, trust me, okay?" He had wracked his brain for solutions to the problem of Eve not liking cars, and then it became apparent that his idea to blindfold her may well just be dual-purpose. With her eyes covered, she would hopefully forget she was in a car and be calm and collected. He had laughed to himself, shaking his head and crossing his fingers that his theory would work.

"Nuh-uh." She shook her head and folded her arms.

"Baby, please." He moved towards her gently, a cream, silk scarf in his hands that he softly draped across her eyes, tying it at the back being careful not to trap her hair in the knot.

Eve swallowed down hard and bit her lip.

"Oi." He pulled it free and leaned over to take it between his teeth. "No lip-biting. You're my girl. Trust me. Please."

She felt blindly for his face and cupped her hand around his cheek. before blowing the air from her cheeks and forcing a smile. "I trust you."

As the engine shut off ten minutes later, Eve's breathing began to quicken. She fumbled and reached out for Billy's hand and he took it, squeezing gently.

"We here?"

"Yep. I'm going to get out of the car in a sec and open the door for you, okay? Stay there and don't peep."

Eve rolled her eyes inside the scarf. It was a risky little game he was playing here. She heard him getting out of the car and waited for the slam of the door, holding her breath. Praying to God, and every other spirit, that she didn't vomit all over her shoes, she recalled again the ridiculous scene after climbing out of the very same car a few months earlier. Although the fear had been incredibly real that night, she was tempted to chalk it up to being in a heightened state of emotion. Cars were still most definitely not her favourite places to be, but she was feeling okay, considering. As these thoughts were rattling around in her head, she listened to the sounds that Billy was making. He was in the boot of the car, also rattling around.

"What are you doing back there?"

He spoke to her through the hatch back. "Two minutes, baby. Stay there."

"Where are we, Billy? Can I take this thing off yet?"

"Nope. Patience."

She sighed and slumped back into her seat. This was

not her idea of fun at all and hoped for Billy's sake that the rest of the evening was going to be a little more exciting.

Billy swore, catching his hand on the side of the boot. It wasn't as perfect as he had hoped. He'd wanted everything ready for her for when she got out, but at this rate, she was going to be ready to go home before he had finished. He moved bags and other items out and walked away from the car.

Eve sensed the quiet and panicked. "Billy?" Her hands flew up to the scarf on her eyes.

"I'm here, you daft bugger. Stay there, and do not peek."

She let her hands flop back down and squeezed them into fists for something to focus on.

Finally, after a few more minutes of setting up, he was done. He slammed the boot shut and walked around to Eve's side of the car, opening it and picking up her fist.

"Ready?"

She smiled, her annoyance dissipating immediately with the touch of his hand. "Ready."

Billy helped her out of the car and turned her around to face the way they were going. The ground felt soft under her feet, and the cool air kissed her face. The smell of woodland and wet soil invaded her nose, along with the wafting of lit matches on the wind. She relaxed, and as Billy wrapped his arms around her shoulders and moved her forwards a few feet, a spark of excitement ignited in the pit of her stomach.

"Okay, I am going to help you to sit down. Lift your foot up. Up more. Okay, now step forwards and do the same with your other foot. Yep. That's it."

Eve was shaking. She was at his mercy right now and

had to give all of herself to him to ensure she was safe. This was a different kind of trust. She had no idea where she was, no idea what she would be faced with once she opened her eyes and had to believe that he had her best interests at heart.

"Right, I want you to sit. I'll hold your arm while you lower yourself down. That's it. Right. Wait one second, and then I will take your blindfold off, okay?"

Eve nodded. She spread her palms out on the surface she was now sitting on, the soft feel of wool, and resisted the temptation to explore further. After more shuffling, Billy moved forwards and carefully lifted the scarf from her face.

"Okay. You can look now."

She sat for a few seconds, her eyes screwed tight and her lips pursed. Billy watched her, a nervous smile on his face.

"Open your eyes, beautiful girl."

Eve inhaled. "I daren't." A dull light appeared to flicker in front of her eyelids, and the sound of an owl hooting caught her attention.

"Open your eyes."

Eve bit her lip and linked her fingers before allowing her lashes to flutter and her eyes to open. They widened as they took in the scene in front of her. They were in the middle of the park where they first properly met just a few months earlier. Tea lights housed in little paper lanterns lined the perimeter of the blanket she was sitting on, giving the dark night a flickering ambiance. In the middle were blocks of wood on which stood a bottle of wine, two plastic glasses and a selection of picnic foods. But what really took Eve's breath away was Billy. He sat opposite her, his face bathed in candlelight, his guitar on his knee, wearing the cutest lopsided grin.

He blinked slowly and licked his lips. "Happy Date Night, beautiful girl."

Before she had chance to respond, he began to gently pick at the strings on the guitar, rendering her speechless. The haunting sound of the chords in the open skies immediately permeated her skin, and she couldn't take her eyes off his hands. That was until he started to sing. Gravelly tones were released effortlessly from deep within him, and when it became clear that Billy was singing to her, for her and only her, a lump formed in her throat.

He was spellbinding.

The final strum of the strings was her undoing, and tears that had so far waited on the edge spilled over and down her cheeks as she blinked. She wiped them away, half laughing at how deliriously happy she was and how ridiculous it was that she was crying. Billy put his guitar down on the ground and opened his arms to her. She crawled across the blanket and into his lap, curling herself up into her safest place on earth.

He wrapped himself around her and kissed her wet cheeks.

Eve looked up at his face, beaming at him. "Did… Did you write that for me?"

Billy nodded and rubbed his nose with hers before winking. "You're welcome."

She leaned her head further back and reached for his mouth with hers, hungry for him all of a sudden, her breath shaky and impatient. She whispered against his lips. "It's beautiful. I love it."

Billy pushed his fingers into her hair and leaned down

261

to give her what she wanted. The taste of her after so many days gave way to overwhelming lust, and he was unsure they would even get to eat dinner.

"Are you hungry?" he whispered against her mouth.

"Only for you."

Billy groaned and closed his eyes, running his hand up the smooth skin on her leg, an open highway to his favourite place to be. He shifted his weight, lowering Eve to the blanket and pinning her hands above her head. Her chest rose and fell with anticipation as she watched the hunger in his eyes devour every inch of her face. The fact that they were outside, in a public place, crossed her mind for the briefest of moments, but the thought dissipated as she homed in on the feeling of being aroused purely by the look in his eyes.

He watched her as she reacted, her lips parting and her pupils dilating. He was greedy for her tonight, desperate to take her and remind her how much he needed her, how much he loved her—every inch of her. The tightly coiled spring inside of him that was ready to release after the tension of the last few days was revealing itself as intense sexual desire. The roller coaster of emotions he had ridden had churned him up, and he found himself feeling freed, wild.

Even if it was fleeting, even if it was just for tonight, he needed to forget. He needed to lose himself in this incredible woman who had stolen his heart. He lifted his eyes momentarily to the stars, thanking his lucky ones for bringing her to him, for allowing him this chance to know her, to be hers.

His hand travelled back down to her bare legs, smoothing over them before running up the inside and underneath her skirt. He let out another moan in appreciation for the ease of access. Pushing it up and around her waist, still holding Eve by her wrists, he clenched his teeth in order to control his animal instincts that bared themselves.

By way of invitation, Eve gently bucked her hips to meet Billy's hand, and he crushed his lips to hers, teasing them open so that he could dance his tongue with hers.

If anyone had told her that she would be engaging in such heated sexual activity before she was twenty, she would have laughed them away. It was something she had almost resigned herself to believe was never going to be possible. There had been no dreams of meeting the right guy because close physical contact had never been an option. It was almost surreal, and for a moment, she found herself looking down on her own body, watching herself be smothered, licked and worshipped by this six-foot man.

She moved her face to the side, moaning breathily in his ear and it was too much for him. He yanked at the button on his jeans, wrapping his arms underneath her in an attempt to bring her closer to him.

He was never letting her go.

CHAPTER
twenty

Can't Go Back Now – The Weepies
I Don't Want To Be – Gavin Degraw

LYING WITH HER back tucked into his front, Eve licked her fingers clean of strawberry juice and pushed herself up on her elbow. She reached for her glass, taking a sip of the now warm liquid and laughed as some of it dribbled out of the glass and down her chin.

Billy took a hold of it, turning her face to his. He leaned his head forwards and licked and kissed the sticky liquid from her skin, then kissed her hard on her mouth. "So, you enjoyed date night?"

Eve's eyes crinkled as she smiled up at him. "It was perfect. Everything was perfect. And I forgive you for blindfolding me and forcing me into a car."

Billy laughed and traced his finger down her arm. "What is the deal with that anyway, you and cars?"

Eve shrugged. "Just part of the ridiculousness that is me, I guess. I used to ride in cars all the time when I was really little, I'm sure. My dad always had a car, I think. I don't know. I just seemed to develop a fear of them. I'll go in my mum's. I don't like it, but I'll do it. I just feel... restricted."

"You weren't sick this time, at least."

"No, I am not usually sick. I think last time was a special case. I was forced to go to the Summer ball, which I really didn't want to do; I was wearing a dress, which I really didn't want to do... and then I got chased by this really, really hot guy and I think it all got a bit too much."

Billy grinned. "A really, really hot guy? Is that so?"

"Yeah, he was pretty hot." She wriggled herself around so that she was facing him. "He had chocolate brown hair." Running her hand through his dark curls, she continued. "The most amazing blue eyes." Eve brushed her thumb delicately across the top of his eyelid, and then leaned forward and pressed her lips to his, "And these lips. Man, his lips were just..."

Billy shushed her by pressing harder and tangling his tongue with hers. She exhaled against him and her body weakened in his arms.

"You need to leave me alone, Miss Swallow, or I am going to end up being a very bad boy, right here on this blanket. Again. And we need to get going." He kissed the end of her nose and rose to his knees, pulling her up. The two of them began clearing away the picnic and Billy picked up his guitar, zipping it away in his case.

"Thank you for my song." Eve smiled up at him as she closed the lid on a Tupperware box.

"You're welcome."

"You really are very good. You definitely should *do* music."

Billy laughed. "That was the plan back in the day."

"I'm serious. You really should. People would

265

definitely pay to hear you play and sing."

"I'm not sure it's as easy as that, baby."

"But you need to start somewhere." She stood and shook the blanket. "There must be a way to get started."

Billy shook his head and smiled. "You really want this for me, hey?"

"Of course I do, but that's not what matters. *You* want this for you and that is what should be driving you forwards. Music is in your soul, and if you don't use it, you're never going to be truly content. This could be a fresh start now. You have a place to call home, and you don't have to answer to him anymore, so the world is your oyster. Go and do what makes you happy."

"You make me happy."

Eve grinned and lifted the picnic bag into the boot of the car. "You make me happy, too. But drawing and painting also make me happy, and I couldn't be happy with you if I wasn't able to do that every day. You are only half of yourself if you are not doing what you love."

Billy searched Eve's eyes. She continued to amaze him, and he felt himself falling more and more in love with her every day. "How did you get so smart, hey?"

Eve shrugged, packing more items into the car as she spoke. "Because I've spent the majority of my life running away from other people, holed up on my own with too much time to think and philosophise, I suppose. I read a lot. I observe a lot."

Billy watched her lips as they spoke, his eyes running over her body as she moved. She was so unassuming, so unaware of how incredible she was. He moved towards her and tucked a strand of hair behind her ear. "So how do you propose I 'do music' then?"

266

She stopped and looked at him, perching on the edge of the boot of the car. "York is like the busking capital of the world. Take your guitar and your flat cap down Stonegate and release yourself on the people of the world."

"Release myself…" He chuckled.

Eve rolled her eyes and laughed. "Show them who you are. If they see even half of what I see, they will fall in love with you instantly."

***

THE MORNING WAS unseasonably warm, and waking up in the box room at Dobbo's, a day off work ahead of him, he reached across to the bedside table for his phone. It was Eve's last day of freedom before returning to university, and she had convinced him to try his hand at busking, promising to go with him.

Eve: Are you up?

He hit reply and waited impatiently for her next message.

Eve: I'm awake… but my bed is too comfy.

And my bed is too cold without you.

Eve: Come get in mine then. It's toasty…

He rolled his eyes and bit down on the inside of his cheeks at her mischievousness.

Don't tempt me…

Eve: Mmmm… soooooo warm…

Billy laughed and flopped back down on the pillow as his phone beeped again. He opened up the message to find a photo of Eve, sleepy-eyed, with bed hair, looking sexy as fuck and the duvet only just covering her breasts. He groaned loudly at the thought of being under there with her naked body.

You're fucking killing me, Swallow. Behave!

Billy closed his eyes and scrubbed his five o'clock shadow with his hand as he dropped his phone to the floor—a raging hard-on threatening to change the morning's plans—and forced himself to get up and shower.

He'd made a point of practicing a repertoire of popular songs the night before and had created a list ready to take with him. Packing up his guitar and his music, he shrugged on his coat and headed out to meet the sexy minx that his girl was turning into.

Sundays in York could often be heaving with people—shoppers and tourists alike. Today was no exception. Weaving in and out of the throngs, Billy held Eve's hands tightly, her body stiff and nervous. She wondered if she would ever get to the point where she was completely comfortable around lots of people. Had she been on her own, she would have panicked by now, and it was only because of Billy that she was able to bear it. He dominated the situation, keeping her close and directing her confidently through the gaps between shopping bags and pushchairs. It was snail's pace for everyone else. People would stop dead in the middle of the street to point and stare in awe at some building or other, or to gaze open-mouthed at a street performer.

Before long, they arrived in St Helen's Square, the same spot that Billy had stood all those months before watching 'Eboracum Rain', the band who seemed to have it all together. He smiled to himself, allowing his dream to take over for just a moment, thinking about how one day it could be him drawing in the crowds.

Setting his guitar down, he unzipped the case.

They had sat a couple of days before, poring over the twelve-page document entitled "A Guide to Busking in York" that outlined the dos and don'ts for buskers and businesses alike. It was suggested that performers introduce themselves to the nearby shop owners to inform them of their intentions. Billy had positioned himself outside Betty's Tea Rooms, and once he had set out his 'stall', he pushed politely to the front of the ridiculously long queue of people who waited in line to buy over-priced scones and miniature sandwiches, and bobbed inside to speak to the proprietor.

There had been a whole section in the document that suggested ways of resolving conflict, and Billy was hopeful that whoever was in charge today was able to engage in 'constructive dialogue'. As luck would have it, they were more than happy for him to perform outside their shop. The area was already a favoured spot by the regular buskers, and Billy was secretly smug that he had managed to bag it before anyone else.

The guidance document had also suggested that a repetitive set list would be sure to encourage complaints. He had a list of twenty songs, but he knew that if he got to the end of it, his back catalogue of pieces could be pulled from the corners of his memory and dusted off. If it came to it, he was more than confident enough to take requests and play less familiar songs by ear. He was aware that other buskers may come along and wait for a chance to have his spot, and it advised to spend no more than two hours in the same place.

A trickle of nerves made their way down the small of his back. He wasn't worried about playing, he knew he was good at what he did, but would people like him? Music was so subjective and reliant on personal taste.

Wiping the back of his hand across his forehead, he pulled his old Levis up at the thigh so he could crouch down and sort out his music. Eve stood awkwardly at the side of him, unsure of what to do to help. She was so excited for him, but being in the middle of town on a busy Sunday went against every red flag she'd ever flown. She was unsure where to put herself. If she sat near him while he played, she would essentially be the centre of attention, and that was not something that filled her with joy.

She had packed her bag with an empty sketchbook and her box of pencils and charcoals and fully intended to take advantage of the time. She planned to capture the essence of the spectators as they listened, hoping to portray wonder and enjoyment in her drawings. After some deliberation, she decided that if she was going to have to endure the public anyway, being as close to Billy as was possible was indeed the best option.

"Can I sit here?" She pointed to a spot just a few feet behind where he was organising himself, a spot where she would be able to lean back against the walls of the shop.

Billy sat cross-legged on his coat, writing on the back

of a piece of cardboard box with a marker pen. He glanced over. "Sure. Sit wherever you like."

"I just figured I'd catch up on some sketching while you play."

He smiled and held up his makeshift sign.

Hi - pleased to meet you!
Shout up if you have any requests
Thank you in advance for your kindness
Billy :)

"Perfect!"

He leaned it up against his rucksack and placed his guitar case in front of it. Bending at the waist, he plugged the guitar lead into his amp and then stood up, blowing the air from his cheeks.

Eve stretched onto her tiptoes and placed a lingering kiss on his lips, her eyes closing and her hand curling round the back of his neck. "You're amazing. Go get 'em."

He snaked his arm around her waist, pulling her close to him so that their bodies were touching at every nerve ending. He gazed into her eyes, smoothing her hair back from her face. "How did I get so lucky, hey? I love you, beautiful girl. Thank you."

Eve snuggled under his chin and squeezed him. "Ready?"

He nodded. "Ready."

For the first couple of songs, Eve sat and watched with a newfound emotion. She was almost bursting with pride, watching her man—the man who wanted her above

271

Eleanor LLOYD-JONES

anyone else, the man who stood there, so damn talented—
and she could barely breathe.

At first, shoppers merely slowed down, their heads
turning to watch as they sauntered past. Billy stood, his foot
against the building, his hair tousled, his sleeves rolled up
and his eyes closed. He had no mic, but he didn't need one:
his strong, gravelly voice projected across the square, and
after the fourth song, people began to stop.

There were benches along the pavement, and some
people sat down, taking a load off their weary shopper's
feet and watched, listening. Eve's eyes flicked over their
faces, their eyes glued to his mouth or his hands. She caught
the end of a whisper from a couple who sat jigging a
toddler on their knees to the beat. "He's really good, isn't
he?"

She beamed wider.

Before long, he had drawn quite a crowd. Eve sat back
and let him enjoy his moment, pulling out her sketchbook
and starting to move her pencil across the paper. The
fluidity of the lines of heads and shoulders scooted from
one end to the other, and she captured the movement of a
little girl who came to the front and began dancing to Billy's
sound.

Two hours was all he planned to stay, but two turned
into three. The crowd kept evolving into new ones. People
clapped, put money in his case and went off to finish their
shopping or to drop into a cafe for lunch. They were
quickly replaced by other fascinated people who loitered
around the edges and bounced on their tiptoes to catch a
glimpse of the artist who'd managed to lure people to him.

Eve stood, grabbed her bag and whispered into his ear.
"You're like the Pied fucking Piper! I'm going to grab us

272

some lunch."

Billy smiled and nodded through the lyrics to 'One More Song' by Tyler Hilton, and Eve sucked in a huge breath and fought her way through the audience and out the other side. She clutched tightly at the strap on her bag and disappeared up Stonegate, on her own…

Billy's heart had slowed to a relaxed pace as he fell into a state of utter happiness and enjoyment, bouncing off the crowd's reactions to his songs. He couldn't believe he hadn't done this before now, and he vowed to never leave music behind again. He would not put aside his own happiness for the sake of others. Eve had been right. How could he be the whole of Billy Taylor if half of him was missing? He'd spent so long believing that he had to make sure everyone else was okay that he'd forgot to check if he was okay himself. How could he have possibly sorted everyone else out to the best of his ability if he was only working at half capacity?

As his musings dwindled, he saw Eve returning through the middle of the crowd, a carrier bag held close to her chest as she nervously squeezed past people with quiet 'excuse mes', apologising for knocking into people. He loved her with everything he had, and a wicked idea came to him.

He stopped playing and pulled a plectrum from his back pocket, clearing his throat and addressing the crowd. "This one's for my girl. She rocks my world."

Looking down at the strings, he strummed the first chord of 'Every Little Thing She Does is Magic' by The Police at which point, Eve's head raised in slow motion, her eyes narrowed with an 'I'll get you for this' look across her face.

As she emerged from the crowd of people, Billy pointed to her and everyone clapped and cheered.

She was going to kill him.

Four hours of playing and eighty pounds later, Eve and Billy were packing up ready to go home. A couple of stragglers came over to thank him, pushing some more change into his hand, and a little boy walked over shyly and dropped a hand full of silver into his case.

"I told you they'd love you."

"I know, but I didn't expect that. Eighty quid?"

Eve beamed. "What you gonna spend it on?"

"I'm going to take you out for a posh meal."

Eve frowned. "The fuck you are! That's your money. I don't want you spending it on me."

He gave Eve a kiss just below her ear, slinging his guitar onto his back "We'll see." He went quiet and then moved his eyes back to her face. "I should probably give some of it to my dad for bills and stuff." They set off walking.

Eve shook her head. "No, Billy."

He frowned at her. "Why not?"

"No. He is not your responsibility. He is a grown man who needs to sort himself out. You have done everything for him. Leave him."

Billy bowed his head and squeezed Eve's hand a little tighter. "I know you're right. I just… I dunno. He's my dad."

"He is your dad, and I completely understand why you feel you have a duty of care, but he beat you, Billy! He beat you black and blue. And then he beat you again!" She became animated, her voice hitching up a notch. "And he still hasn't shown any remorse. You owe him nothing. You've got to change your outlook on this." She stopped walking and tugged on his arm to stop him, too. She spun him to face her. "I love you, Billy, and I won't stand by and let him hurt you anymore. You have to keep fighting. For you." Her chin trembled slightly as she spoke, and a little v formed between Billy's eyebrows.

He ran the pad of his thumb gently across the pink flesh of her bottom lip, searching her eyes that were shining with unshed tears.

"I can't see you messed up again like that night, Billy. I just can't. It was hard enough then, but that was before I realized I'd fallen in love with you." She rested her hand on Billy's that was still near her face and spoke more softly. "Don't put yourself at risk anymore. I couldn't bear it if something happened to you."

Billy bowed his head and kissed her forehead. "I won't. I promise. I'm done with him now, but I do feel like I need to help him. I'll get the money to him without having to see him. I just…" He couldn't find the right words to describe the need in him to still protect, even when he was the one that needed protecting. He guessed that, deep down, he knew his dad had just chosen the wrong path when he reached that crossroads, and that he probably just needed a little assistance in getting back on the right road.

He had always made sure that his mum's illness was at the forefront of his thinking when trying to deal with Neville's moods. Nev was the way he was because he was dealing with constant grief. He had lost his wife in the worst possible way. The worst of it was that there was still the shell of the woman he fell in love with. She was still able to look at him with the same eyes that shone when he'd kissed her for the first time, still able to touch him with the same silky skin that had caressed every part of his body as they had made love under the stars as teenagers. Her voice was the same voice that she used when she'd said 'I do' all those years ago, making him the luckiest man on the planet, but Jenny, the beautiful soul he had lived for, was gone.

"He's just a man who has lost his wife. I need to support him if I can."

Eve's eyes darted back and forth between Billy's, reading the hardship behind them, the sadness and desperation of a young man who should not be carrying all of this shit around with him. "Billy, you lost her, too! You lost your mum and look at how well you cope."

He pulled her into him, her head resting on his chest. "I don't feel like I cope very well at all. I fall apart almost every time I walk through the doors of that home. I pray to every deity there is that the next visit will be the one where she looks up at me with love in her eyes and says, "Hi, Billy!" but it never happens. I'm much more like my dad than I care to admit to you or myself. This is why I don't drink. This is why I try to keep the peace, because if I lose it, I don't know if I will ever get it back. And I think that's what has happened with Dad. He has gone so far under that he has forgotten the way out. That's if there even is a way out. How do you come back from that?"

Eve had no words to offer him. She hadn't had to deal with anything like this before. Yes, she had lost a father somewhere along the line, but her memories of him were not as real as Billy's were of his mum. There was a gaping hole in her life, but it was one that she was able to paper over without too much distress as long as she buried it at the bottom of one of the memory boxes in her mind. She hadn't allowed herself to dwell on that part of her life for a good few years. Asking her mother to fill in the gaps was a fruitless exercise: it only caused arguments, and their relationship was strained enough as it was.

Billy kissed the top of her head and breathed in the scent of her. He looked out into the emptiness of the streets and pursed his lips. She was right in what she was saying, but if he cut the ties completely now, there would be nothing for him to hope for. "I just feel like I have to keep him in my sights, you know? Keep a hold of the end of the rope so that when the time comes, I can use it to help build the bridges."

Eve squeezed him a little tighter.

"I know, but sometimes holding on can be more painful and damaging than letting go."

CHAPTER
twenty one

The Christmas Song – Denis Solee

CHRISTMAS WAS THE worst time of the year for Billy and for Eve. It was approaching fast and they had not yet discussed their plans for December twenty-fifth.

For Eve, the months that had passed were a blur of assignments and cold afternoons on the streets of York listening to Billy light up as he bloomed into this confident and charismatic performer. They'd been filled with nights of heated desire, where they would swim in a sea of tangled blankets, where the lightbulbs were the stars, inhaling each other like their lives depended on it, and it was a night like this where Eve brought up the subject of Christmas.

She lay on top of Billy, every bit of her touching every bit of him. His hands smoothed over the skin of her naked buttocks, the tingles of climax still pulsating between her legs. She was instantly aroused again, just from being this close to him. The prospect of spending two weeks apart was not something she was willing to wrap her head around just yet.

"You are too sexy, Mr. Taylor." She bit gently at his

nipple, inhaling and tasting the mixture of salt and that unique flavour of 'Billy'.

He smiled down, sweeping her hair away from her face. "You're insatiable, Miss Swallow."

"I am. I can't get enough of you. You have woken me up inside." She kissed his chin and gazed into his eyes for a minute. "So… what are your plans for Christmas Day?"

Billy groaned and lifted his eyes to the ceiling. "I hate Christmas."

"Not my favourite time of the year either."

"Obviously I am staying at Dobbo's now, so I think Mo will expect me to be there—not that I don't want to be. It will be lovely, I'm sure, but it will be endured half-heartedly, I think. Part of me will be wondering what Dad is doing, wondering what Mum is doing, and then, obviously, I'd like to spend some of it with you."

Eve smiled into his chest. "I'd love to spend it with you, too, but I will have to go home to my mum's."

"For the whole holiday?"

"It will be expected that I stay for a week of it, probably. Especially as I stayed here all summer."

Billy sighed. "What will I do without you?"

Eve ran her hand down his side and back up, staring at the Laura Ashley curtains her mother had picked out for her. She lifted herself up onto her elbows and looked at him. "Come back with me."

"To your mum's?"

"Why not?"

"Well, from what you have told me about her, I'm not convinced she would approve, that's all."

"I'll talk to her. I'm sure she will be fine."

And she was. Eve rang her that very night and

managed to arrange for Billy to come down for two nights. So, when the festive period began, plans were made. Billy would spend Christmas Day with the Dobsons and then drive to Leeds on Boxing Day to spend two nights at the Swallow residence.

The two had agreed to exchange gifts the night before Eve was due to leave for home.

Billy called in a favour from an old friend and managed to book a recording studio for the price of a crate of Carling and a promise to visit again soon.

He nipped out of work at lunchtime the day before and ducked, cloak and dagger, into the store where he had ordered another gift he'd saved his busking money to buy and he'd had the call to say it was ready to collect.

He stood at the counter waiting to be served, his hands shoved into his back pockets turning to see the shop door opening and Eve walking in.

They both stared at each other, unsure what to do or say.

"What…?"

"I…"

"How come you are in here?" Billy continued to flick his eyes to the back of the shop, hoping that the assistant would take a few more minutes.

"Um…" Eve stumbled over her words. "Looking for… a present for… Mummy Dear… Yep. That's it." She blushed and Billy gave her a knowing smile, playing along to help her out.

"Fancy grabbing a drink?"

"Sure."

"Ok. I'll just pay for this and meet you outside when I'm done?" He was damned if he was going have the surprise ruined.

"Okay, I'll see you outside Starbucks in ten." She stepped out of the shop, shaking her head. She would have to go back after Billy had left.

She had been dreading shopping, and she'd hoped having Rachel with her would help her to cope, but her friend was leaving early to spend Christmas in Japan with her family and was stuck at uni finishing off a last-minute assignment. So, seeing Billy in the shop was nice, and after spending half an hour on a bench sipping hot tea with him, she felt ready to take on the mission of having to start a conversation with the retailer.

Stepping up into the shop, she dropped her gaze towards the floor. She was the only customer—centre stage and completely vulnerable to the invasive questions and the pandering of the assistant.

Eve had seen the gift she had in mind a few times before and knew exactly where to find it, but instead she procrastinated. Skirting around the edges of the store, she fingered items that would normally hold her interest, but that served only as distraction—procrastination to avoid her conversation with the stranger behind the counter. A bead encrusted headdress, an array of silk scarves, a row of tiny porcelain swans… She gently nudged the end one flush against the shelf, perfectly parallel to its brothers, rolling her eyes at how much of her mother had rubbed off on her without her realising it. Only then did she look closer at the details: the gloss finish, the exquisitely painted feathers… Slipping her hand into the oversized pocket of her velveteen coat, she curled her fingers around the wad of notes that lay like a scroll of secrets at the bottom.

The bell above the shop door tinkled and she whipped

her head around. When it became apparent that the culprit was a stranger, it gave her the push she needed to walk to the glass cabinet that stood tall in the middle of the shop floor. Her fingers automatically lifted to the glass and rested there delicately. Eve's fist tightened around the money as she inhaled deeply and strode with an unfamiliar confidence towards the counter. She'd never spent this much in one go, but for Billy, it was worth it. She would deal with the wrath of her mother when the time came.

***

THE FOLLOWING EVENING, they sat cross-legged opposite each other in the corners of the sofa at Eve's house, grinning like school kids.

Billy picked up the two neatly wrapped packages that he had placed on the cushion in front of him. He slid the small, box-shaped one towards Eve, who looked at it with nervous excitement, her bottom lip trapped between her teeth.

"Merry Christmas, beautiful girl."

"Eeek! What is it?" She squealed before picking it up gently.

"Well open it and you will see, won't you?"

She flashed her eyes at him and carefully slipped her finger underneath the flap of paper, lifting the tape up. She did the same at the other end and unfolded the top. A blue box with silver flowers embossed on the lid now sat in her hand. It was about the size of a matchbox, and she didn't dare look.

Billy clasped his hands together tightly, his face twitching into a smile in anticipation of Eve's reaction when she saw it. She slowly moved her hand to lift the lid and stared into the box for a few seconds before unfolding the silver tissue paper. Lying inside on a bed of cotton wool was a hand stamped copper keyring, a heart shaped hole in the corner with the words 'Take care of my heart. I left it with you."

Eve's eyes lifted to Billy's and dangling from his fingers on a delicate chain was a beautiful silver heart pendant that fit the hole perfectly. Eve inhaled, a sheen of tears spoiling her view of it. She swiped at them and reached out to take it from him.

She turned it over in her hands and found an inscription on that, too. 'All yours'.

She looked up at him again, this time letting the tears roll freely.

"It's beautiful." Her voice was gossamer, and Billy reached out to wipe the tears from her cheeks. She passed it back to him and moved forwards onto her knees, sweeping her hair around her shoulder so that he could fasten it for her. As she moved back to her sitting position, Billy handed her the second present to unwrap.

Paper off, she looked at the CD cover, her eyes pouring over the words on the front and the copy of her own sketches from that first day busking.

"It's your song." Billy pointed to the song title by way of explanation. "I've got a mate who owns a studio, and I called in a favour." He smiled up at Eve, who was still speechless. "I figured that I needed to find a way of letting you hear me play the piano. So, there you go. Your song, with me on the piano."

Eve jumped up from the sofa and ran to the CD player in the corner of the room. She slid the disc onto the tray and pressed play. Standing there in front of the speakers, she was unsure what to do. She wanted to be as close to the sound as she could possibly get, but she also wanted to wrap herself around Billy and never let go. Instead, she was rooted to the spot, staring at the CD player as the notes from the piano filled the room and washed over her.

Billy moved to her and enveloped her within his arms from behind, swaying her gently to the music, whispering the words along with himself into her ear. He couldn't imagine there being a time where they wouldn't feel this close to one another, and for the thousandth time since he first laid eyes on her again, he thanked his lucky fucking stars.

Once the song ended, Eve spun around in his arms and hugged him tightly. "You are amazing." She released her hold on him regretfully and ran to get the gift bag that she had stuffed behind her on the sofa. She bounced on her toes and held it out for him to open.

Billy moved back to the sofa and sat on the edge, pulling open the ties on the bag. It felt heavy in his hands, and he narrowed his eyes, smiling at Eve who knelt at his feet, her face grinning like a Cheshire cat. She clapped her hands together as he began to unwrap the tissue paper from around a small cardboard box.

He read across it and his jaw opened, his eyes flicking back to Eve.

He lifted the flap open and pulled out a sterling silver Zippo lighter.

"Jesus, baby. These things cost a fortune."

In a dancing swirl from the bottom left corner to the top right, just below the lid, was an engraved stave of musical notes, an intricately fashioned treble clef at the start of it. He turned it over in his hands and held his breath as he read the inscription.

'Follow your heart… I'll be right behind you following it, too'.

***

BILLY UNLOCKED THE door and walked into the hallway at the Dobson residence. The usual delicious smell of something horribly bad for him wafted through from the kitchen, and he shouted to let Maureen know he was home.

Dropping Eve at the train station just an hour earlier had been difficult. It was the twenty-first of December, and he wouldn't see her now until the twenty-sixth. He hung his coat on the banister and sauntered in to where Mo was laying the table.

"She get off okay, love?"

"Yeah. All good thanks, Mo."

"You'll miss her these next few days, won't you?"

Billy took the place mats from her and began to lay them out. "I sure will, Mo. Sure will."

Eve was such a massive part of his life now that time without her just wasn't ever quite right. She was his rock. That alone was amazing when he remembered how he had found her, wide-eyed and trembling like a frightened animal, bolting as far away from him as she could get. That night under the tree, he had almost given up—the chance to get to know her almost slipping through his fingers—but now she belonged to him, and she was strong enough inside for both of them.

He smiled and continued to help Maureen get organised for dinner.

As he and his new family sat around the table, filling their bellies with the meal that Maureen had lovingly cooked, the conversation turned to busking and whether it was going well or not. Billy told them of his success, that he seemed to be gathering crowds almost every time he was out there. The money he was earning was sometimes an extra hundred to hundred and fifty pounds a week if he busked over a weekend. He had started putting some of it away for a rainy day and had managed to save nearly a grand now. However, he decided to leave out the part where he planned to give at least some of the money to his father.

The preparations for the big day in the Dobson household were well underway, and Maureen had roped the lads into helping to dress the tree, hang decorations from every corner of every room, and fetch the monstrosity that was the turkey from the butchers. There would be turkey broth, turkey curry and turkey salad for weeks after the event.

Billy busied himself with writing music and pulling in extra shifts at the shop in the days that Eve was gone. He threw himself into busking, taking advantage of Christmas shoppers and the festive cheer that people seemed to carry around with them in every gift-filled carrier bag that hung from their hands.

The weather had turned bitter, and although there was no snow, there was definitely a Christmassy feel in the air.

Visiting his mother had become more difficult over the past week. He wanted her home. He wanted to pull a cracker with her around the table and clink his glass with hers. He wanted to kiss her cheek in the morning, hand her a present before dancing her across the living room to Chris Rea. This year was worse because it was going to be a real Christmas, the first one for a long time.

He should be sharing it with her.

He made plans to go to the home on Christmas Eve

and leave her gift with the receptionist. He couldn't bring himself to go and say hello. If she didn't remember him this time, he was sure his heart would snap in two.

He'd found a little shop that sold handmade music boxes. The guy made them to order with the music of one's choice. Billy had chosen a wooden, hand-carved one and paid extra money for an inscription on the bottom.

I love you always, Mum.
Billy x

He was sure that it would mean nothing to her on most occasions, but on the days where the light ran through her and she woke from her nightmare, it would be there, reminding her who he was and that she would always be in his heart.

He wrapped it carefully in gold paper, tying a bow around it, and popped it in a gift bag with her name on it.

On the morning of the twenty-fourth, he got up early and drove to Butterfields. As he approached the ward desk to sign in, Becky rounded the corner, tinsel in her hair and festive snowman earrings hanging from her earlobes.

"Hi, Billy. Merry Christmas."

"Hi. Merry Christmas, Becky." He gave her a sad smile and lifted the gift bag by way of explanation.

"I'll walk you down. She will be pleased to see you."

Billy shifted his weight to his other foot awkwardly. "I—I was just going to leave it here. I hoped someone would give it to her for me. I've got to—" He dropped his eyes to the floor and sighed.

"I understand. Here. I'll take it."

Billy looked at her from under his fringe. "Thanks."

She took it and squeezed his hand as she walked past. "Have a lovely day tomorrow, Billy."

He turned back to look at her, smiling in thanks, and walked towards the main reception desk.

A quiet knock on the door of her room caused Jenny Taylor's eyes to move slowly from the window to the source of the sound. It was cold today, and the blanket across her knee was a comfort. Her fingers were in knots on her lap and her pale face was sallow. Dark circles under her eyes indicated a sleepless night, and the clump of knots at the back of her hair were a sure sign that she had been tossing and turning.

"Come in." Her voice was soft and tired.

"Good morning, Jenny. It's Becky. How are you this morning?" Becky walked carefully towards her, pulling at her bedcovers to straighten them up as she walked past.

"It's cold today." Jenny smoothed her hand over the blanket as she spoke, looking back at the window.

"It is. Christmas is definitely around the corner." Becky pulled the chair from the other side of the room to where Jenny was sitting and held the gift bag out to her. Jenny turned and lifted her eyes in question, searching the young girl's face for an explanation.

"It's a gift. For you. A Christmas present."

Jenny looked back down at the bag and reached for it tentatively. She pulled gently at the green ribbon that held the bag closed. The tag that swung from it caught her eye, and she read the word that was scribbled on it.

Mum

Her eyes lifted again quickly to meet Becky's, her mouth opening slightly to say words that she was not sure had yet formulated properly in her mind. She pulled out the present and ripped the paper off carefully.

The wooden box sat cool in the palms of her hands, and she moved one of them from underneath, tracing the ravines and crevices of wood that swirled intricately across the lid with her finger. She pulled the box to her and smelled the wood, inhaling deeply and allowing it to fill her senses.

Becky swallowed down, watching this broken woman interact with the beautiful gift. She wanted to speak but didn't dare in case the spell that seemed to have been cast happened to break.

Jenny carefully lifted the lid. A mother and a small child held each other tightly and spun slowly around the inside as the tune of 'Here Comes the Sun' by The Beatles flowed through the air and wrapped itself around her like a blanket of love. A river of tears lined up behind her eyes, creating a sheen that threatened to spill over at any second. She couldn't take her eyes from the figurines in the middle.

And then she spoke.

The words that were hidden away in the depths of her mind came rushing to the front and tumbled off her tongue into the room.

"My son. Billy."

Becky's eyes widened and a smile spread across her face. "Yes, Jenny. It's from Billy."

She got to her feet carefully, excusing herself and moving slowly out of the room and once outside, she ran. She ran hard and fast down the corridor, almost tumbling down the stairs, shouting Billy's name at the top of her voice.

"Billy? She's here! Billy?" She pulled up at the reception desk and stopped. "Sandra… Billy Taylor. Did he leave yet? I spoke to him up at the ward desk and I hoped he might still be here."

Sandra looked up from her computer, glasses perched on the end of her nose. "I guess you might catch him in the car park. He was chatting to me for a bit but left about two minutes ago."

"Thanks." She ran through the revolving doors and down the steps, scanning the car park quickly with her eyes. There were only three cars, and she wasn't sure if any of them were his until an engine started. A beat up, blue Fiesta began to drive towards the exit and Becky screamed, waving her arms to try and catch the driver's attention in the rearview mirror.

"Billy! Billy, come back. Your mum is here. Billy!"

The car moved out of the gates, indicated left and drove off. Becky dropped to her haunches and covered her face with her hands, a lump in her throat and a pain in her heart.

CHAPTER
twenty two

Silver Bells – Sam Levine

"HAVE A GOOD few days, bud. Drive carefully. Say hi to Eve from me." Dobbo slapped Billy on the back as he slammed the boot shut. Maureen moved forward with a tin foil covered plate. "You may as well take this leftover turkey, love. We have plenty here, and Eve's mum might be glad of it."

Billy laughed and took it from her, leaning in to kiss her on the cheek. "Thanks, Mo. And thanks for yesterday. It was really great."

Maureen had ensured that Christmas Day was fun with no time to dwell on sadness, and Billy had enjoyed every minute. He had sneaked off after dinner to call Eve, but that was short lived as her mother had summoned her after just a short time. His heart was ready to burst at the thought of seeing her today, and he just wanted to get going.

He shook Dobs' hand again and climbed into the driver's seat. "See you in a few days. Cheers!"

Dobbo and Mo waved at him from the doorstep, and a smile spread across his face as he contemplated how lucky he was to have landed on his feet with this family. They had been nothing but accommodating, and it was as if he had lived there all his life now. He'd tried to offer more money to Maureen but she'd refused to take it, saying that it was enough for her that he was getting back on his feet and that he was safe.

As he drove down Lowther Street, he took a left and travelled towards the house he had shared with his father for four years. He turned the engine off a couple of houses away and sat with his hands on his thighs, staring at the glove compartment. After an internal pep talk, he leaned forwards and pulled out a thick envelope. He opened it for the hundredth time and reread the message he had scrawled inside the Christmas card.

> Merry Christmas, Dad.
> Hope this helps towards some bills 'til you get back on your feet with work.
> Billy.

He had written half a dozen different variations on scraps of paper, changing his mind each time. He'd tried long-winded explanations as to why he left, he'd written even less than what was in the card now, but in the end, he'd settled for something to the point, but with a touch of sentiment.

He fingered the notes that lay in the crease of the card: two hundred pounds. He would send more again soon, but for now, this would do. This would hopefully show his dad that he still thought of him, that he still loved him and that he hadn't completely let go.

Tucking the card and money back into the envelope, he licked the seal, smoothing his hand over it so that it stuck.

Getting out of the car and walking up the path was the next hurdle to cross. It was Boxing Day, so he could have assumed that Neville was at the pub, but due to the loss of his job and money being tight without Billy's wage, he instead assumed that he would be home. He wanted to deliver the envelope unnoticed so that he could make a quick exit, deciding not to post it to ensure its safe arrival due to the amount of money inside. He opened the car door and clicked it closed gently.

Arriving at the front door, Billy sucked in a nervous breath and pushed his fingers through the letterbox. If he dropped it from this height, it would clatter on the floor, so he pushed his whole hand in as far as it would go, hoping the shorter fall would be less conspicuous. As soon as he let go, he turned and left, jogging to the car and turning the engine quickly. He was on the road that took him to his girl and would push thoughts of his father to the back of his mind until another day.

Creeping down the tree-lined road that led to the Swallow household an hour and a half later, Billy's stomach tightened with nerves. As he checked the address one more time and pulled up at 45 Beechwood Crescent, he allowed himself a couple of minutes to compose himself.

Meeting a girlfriend's mother was daunting enough as it was, but he likened the idea of meeting Eve's mum to entering the lion's den. He was sure that Gillian wasn't going to make him feel as welcome as he would like. The animosity between the two women was clear from the way Eve talked about her.

Billy got out of the car and walked around to the boot.

He slung his rucksack over his shoulder, picked up the turkey and the bunch of flowers that he had bought for Mrs. Swallow, and took a deep breath.

"Here goes," he muttered to himself under his breath as he approached the front door.

Before he had chance to ring the bell, the door flew open and Eve nearly knocked him backwards from the doorstep as she flung herself around him. Her face was in the crook of his neck, her arms wrapped tightly around it, and she inhaled him deeply, whispering into his skin.

"God, I missed you."

Billy held his arms out to the side so as not to crush the flowers or drop the plate as his heart thumped and the smell and closeness of her threatened to change the shape of the bulge in his pants. He could not walk into her house and greet her mother with a hard on, so he gently pulled away from her—committing the lustful look in her eyes to memory for another time—and kissed her.

She grinned up at him and took his elbow, leading him into the house. "Mum?" she shouted through the hallway and turned back to look at Billy again, unable to take her eyes from him for long. "Mum, he's here."

A tapping of heels across tiles came from further down the hallway, and within a few seconds, an almost perfect replica of Eve walked through the door at the end, wiping her hands on a tea towel, a smile taking over her face.

"Billy, hi there. So nice to finally meet you. Come in, come in!" She waved her hand to hurry them along and put the dishcloth, folded perfectly, back over the handle of the oven door.

Billy couldn't move at first. It was like looking at a set of twins. The only differences were the length and style of

Gillian Swallow's hair, and that her eyes were blue, not grey. Eve shoved him in the back and jolted him. He walked forwards, shaking his head and holding out the flowers for Mrs. Swallow.

"Hi, Mrs. Swallow. It's nice to meet you, too. These are for you."

Gillian touched his arm and leaned in to peck his cheek. "It's Gillian, please. It makes me sound so old when you call me Mrs. These are beautiful, Billy, thank you. Eve, pop them in some water?" She smiled at Eve who rolled her eyes and took them from her, walking into the large kitchen area.

"Let me take your things, and then we can make a drink and sit down to get to know each other a little bit, seeing as Eve has told me nothing. Did you have a lovely day yesterday?"

Billy let his rucksack fall from his shoulder, catching the strap with his hand, and passed it to Gillian. He shrugged one arm out of his coat and dropped his eyes to the turkey. "Lovely day, thank you. Umm, this is for you. Leftover turkey. Maur... Umm... We thought you might be able to make use of it."

Gillian laughed. "I have turkey coming out of my ears, Billy, but thank you very much. I'll pop it in the fridge."

Once the kettle had boiled and mugs were filled, the three of them sat around the kitchen table while Gillian chatted to Billy, asking him questions that he had already mentally prepared for.

"So, what do your parents do, Billy?"

He cleared his throat and swiped his thumb under his nose, readying himself for releasing the rehearsed answer. He leaned his elbow on the table, his other hand in the crease of his thigh joint. "My mum was diagnosed with early onset dementia when I was just thirteen. She has been in a home since I was seventeen. Dad has recently lost his job due to cutbacks so is just working on finding another one at the moment, but he works in construction." He looked down and took a sip of coffee to indicate that he was done and that there wasn't much more to say.

"That must be really hard for you both, Billy." Gillian's eyes held genuine concern as she spoke. "Good that you have each other to lean on."

Eve pursed her lips, waiting for Billy's response.

"Actually, I moved out from my father's house a couple of months ago. We were getting under each other's feet a bit, so I figured I'd give him some space. But yes, it is hard. I just have to try to stay positive."

Eve gave him a supportive smile from across the table, and Gillian turned to her, smiling for Billy, too. She reached over and straightened the collar on Eve's shirt and tucked a stray strand of hair behind her ear.

"I used to insist that she dressed like a girl, but it seems she has her own ideas these days."

"Mum." Eve's eyes were wide.

Gillian ignored her plea, glancing to where Eve had placed the flowers in a vase on the table and dragging them to her. She stood up and tore off a piece of kitchen roll, pulling the flowers out and laying them down on top of it. One by one, she placed them back in the vase, rearranging them. "Like this, Eve. Look. I've shown you before. It's not difficult."

She'd turned back to Billy now, and was moving the topic of conversation along, recognising that this was difficult for him to discuss.

Eve scraped her chair back and closed her eyes, her fists balling at her sides. "Billy, I'll show you where you'll be sleeping."

He awkwardly excused himself and followed her through the lounge area and up the stairs with his things. She walked without speaking, but once inside her bedroom, she threw herself face down on the bed. "Ugh." She let her arms flop either side of her, and then rolled onto her back and wriggled and kicked and made fists like a tantruming child.

"Jesus, Eve! Chill out. She only…"

She interrupted him immediately, sitting up, her legs sticking out over the end of her bed and held her finger up to stop him from talking. "No. No, no, no, no." She glared at him through narrowed eyes, and he stood there, hands on his hips, flabbergasted at this feisty little thing looking at him like he was the enemy.

"Do not stick up for that woman, Billy. She is relentless. Nothing that I do is good enough for her. I am not dressed right, I cannot flower arrange, my hair isn't neat enough, the milk is in the wrong place in the fridge, I didn't arrange the washing in the right order on the line, I don't say my words properly… I have had it all my life, and I just thought for once, while you were here, she might let up, but no. No. She is already starting. Do not tell me she is just anything. She is suffocating."

"Wow."

"Wow, what?" She let her hand drop to her side, looking up at him, steely determination and anger shining back at Billy.

"Wow, you."

"Wow, what me?" She was starting to get irritated.

"Wow, you're incredibly hot when you're cross." Billy stalked towards her and pushed her down against the bed, moving between her legs and pinning her hands above her head.

"What I wouldn't do to you right now, Miss Swallow. God, what I wouldn't do…" His eyes roamed all over her body, and he leaned in and kissed her deeply, a primal groan releasing from his throat as Eve's breathlessness caught his ears.

"I want you right here, right now, and the fact that I know I can't makes me want you even more." His eyes were on fire, hooded and dark, and Eve almost whimpered with need.

She swallowed down hard, moistening her lips before trying to speak. "I… I think we should, probably go downstairs before we do something really, really silly."

Billy pressed his forehead to hers and growled again in defeat. He pulled her to her feet and crushed her against his body. "I want this…" He smoothed his thumb across her mouth. "I want this…" His hand travelled down her neck and across her chest. "And I want this…"

Holding her breath, Eve closed her eyes as his hand skimmed down her stomach and between her legs, the thin material of her leggings acting as a useless barrier to his touch. If she thought they would get away with it, she would not hesitate for one second in letting Billy take her right there. He trailed his fingers to her waistband, tiptoeing them inside and sliding them into the cotton of her pants.

Eve tried hopelessly to resist, weakly pushing his arm, before throwing her head back and moaning in a whisper. "Billy, no. We can't. Not here. Please…"

"Please?" Billy grinned, his eyes not leaving her face

as he watched her expression change from horror to utter pleasure. It took less than two minutes, and Eve fell against his chest, giggling with embarrassment and mischief, not quite believing she had allowed Billy to bring her to orgasm with her mother sitting downstairs.

He kissed her slowly and gently, his hand wrapped softly around her throat, and he whispered against her lips. "I missed you, too."

Hours later, Billy glanced down to where Eve was curled, fast asleep in the crook of his arm after the three of them had eaten Chinese takeaway and the women had polished off a couple of bottles of wine.

Leaning on the doorframe, her arms folded, Gillian watched Billy as he tried to wake her. "I think she's out like a light there."

Eve stirred gently at the sound of her voice, huffing out of her nose, her eyelids fluttering but not opening, and Billy stood, letting her tiny body rest against the cushions. "I'll just nip to the loo and then I'll carry her up."

Gillian nodded.

On arriving back downstairs, Billy sat on the edge of the sofa, smoothing Eve's hair from her face and stroking the backs of his fingers down her cheek.

"She looks like an angel when she sleeps, doesn't she?"

Billy smiled and nodded. He couldn't work Gillian out. Her tongue could be so sharp, yet there was love shining from her face. He slid his hand under Eve's legs and wrapped his other arm around her shoulders, her head lolling gently into the crook of his neck. Filled with his own love for her, he leaned and placed a kiss on her cheek.

Gillian held the door open for him as he climbed slowly up the stairs to Eve's bedroom, a lump in her throat.

Once her body hit the soft mattress, Billy gently removed Eve's leggings and socks, pulling the duvet over her shoulders.

"I love you, baby."

He kissed her cheek and returned downstairs. Gillian was at the kitchen counter, the kettle boiling away beside her. Opening a cupboard, she pulled out two large mugs and popped a teabag into both.

He watched her move around the kitchen. Her body language was guarded, but her face told a thousand stories. She had been crying.

"Hey, I can do this, Gillian. Sit down and I'll bring it to you. How do you take yours?"

She stopped, her hand resting on the fridge door, a slight tremble in her fingers. Her eyes glassed over with another serving of tears as she looked up at Billy, and her hand dropped as she cleared her throat, wiping at her face. "I'm sorry, Billy. Milk, no sugar. Thank you."

"You don't need to be sorry. Sit down and I'll make it for you." There was something so typically British about believing that a good old cup of tea would solve all the world's problems.

They sat opposite each other at the kitchen table, their hands curled around the warm mugs of steaming tea. Gillian's head was bowed, and Billy watched her, waiting patiently for her next move. There was a feeling in his gut that this was about Eve.

After a few minutes, Gillian began to talk. "I was just watching you with her then, Billy. You love her very much."

Embarrassed, he bowed his head and smiled into his tea. He lifted his eyes and smiled. "I do. Very much. She's amazing."

Gillian's voice was quiet at first, just above a whisper, as she chatted gently to Billy about Eve as a young child. He knew Eve well now, and the mischievousness that Gillian talked about resounded loudly as he thought of his girl when she was relaxed and happy. It didn't ring true when he remembered the frightened girl that ran and ran to get as far away from him as she possibly could, however. He listened attentively, laughing along with the funny stories she regaled him with about the things that she used to get up to, but he knew that it was all just a prelude to something more ominous.

After a little while, Gillian's eyes clouded over, and her lip quivered. She looked up at Billy for the first time since she'd started talking.

"I've failed her, Billy."

CHAPTER
twenty three

Boat Song - The Miserable Rich
Gillian

IT WAS UNLIKE Eve to shy away from people. She was such a sociable little girl, always happy to make new friends and share her thoughts and experiences with anyone who would listen. But lately, she had become clingy. It was the day before her fifth birthday when I decided it was something not to ignore. Our relatives had been invited to a tea party at our house, and on the day of the event, they arrived with gifts and kisses for my little girl.

She had two cousins on my side of the family (my brother's kids), and Dave's older sister had three children. Shauna and family lived at the bottom end of the country, so I forgave Eve for being a little wary when they first charged into the house. However, unlike other times when they had met and she had dragged them all up to play with her toys, she hid behind my leg for the majority of the party.

As I was tucking her into bed that night, I stroked her cheek and searched her deep grey eyes for her troubles.

"What's the matter, poppet? You seemed sad today. Did you not have a lovely time at your birthday party?"

She wrapped her little hand around my neck and nodded.

"I liked my party, Mummy."

"Oh, I'm so glad you did," I whispered excitedly, smoothing her hair from her forehead. "What was your very favourite part?"

She looked up at the ceiling, thinking. "I liked the jelly and ice cream. And did you see the new dolly that Auntie Shauna gave me? She has blue eyes like you, Mummy."

"I did! I saw it. It's a very beautiful dolly. What are you going to call her?"

"I named her Polly."

"Well that's a perfect name."

"Can I sleep with Polly, Mummy?"

"Yes, of course. Where did we put her?" I got to my feet and dug around in the carrier bags full of presents that we'd packed up and brought to Eve's room, ready to find homes for them tomorrow.

"Here she is." I kneeled down again by the bed and tucked the doll under the covers next to her.

"It's time to go to sleep now, little chicken. I'm going to give you a big kiss, and then I need to go help Daddy clear away all the party things, okay?"

"Okay, Mummy. I need to tell Polly some secrets before I go to sleep. I will just whisper them."

I smiled at her innocence and nodded, though a chink of my heart came loose at the prospect of her opening up to her toys instead of me.

"Okay. Sleep tight, my darling girl. See you in the morning." I kissed each cheek, her forehead and her nose, and then gave her the biggest kiss on her tiny puckered mouth, just as I did every night.

"Love you, Mummy."

As Dave and I pottered around, dumping crumb-filled paper plates and plastic forks into the bin liners that stood homeless on the kitchen floor, I mentioned my concerns to him.

"Do you think something is wrong with Eve?"

Dave tipped a cold mug of tea into the sink and pulled the door to the dishwasher down. Shrugging, he turned the tap on and rinsed his fingers. "I don't know, love. What do you mean by 'something wrong'?"

I frowned and lifted one side of my face as I tried to put my finger on what my gut was shouting at me. I flicked the kettle on and wiped the table down. "She just doesn't seem herself lately. Today, she definitely wasn't herself."

"She seemed a little subdued, but maybe she's just coming down with something."

"Hmm. Maybe." There was no conviction in my response. I wasn't convinced that it was because she wasn't feeling well. It had been gradual, but today was definitely a turning point. I knew my daughter, and something was troubling her.

The next morning was Sunday, and Eve's birthday. Dave and I were more excited than her, I think, and we woke early to surprise her with a family breakfast in bed. She climbed bleary-eyed under our covers between us, and Dave placed a tray of ridiculously bad-for-you food on our knees. It took a moment for her to notice, but when she did, I threw my head back with laughter at her reaction, her childish mimicking of adult phrases.

"Ice cream for breakfast, Daddy? What on earth are you playing at?"

I grabbed her, pulled her backwards into a snuggle and kissed her cheek.

"Funny girl! It's your birthday, darling. We can have whatever we want."

She squealed with delight and grabbed a spoon. "This is the best birthday ever!"

After more ice cream, a slice of leftover birthday cake and a chocolate milkshake, we took Eve downstairs to open her presents. The look on her face when she opened the living room door and saw *the pile of gifts on the sofa was worth all the stresses and strains of organising the surprises. By this point in the day, my worries about her behaviour had dissipated a little, and I threw myself into giving her a perfect day.*

It wasn't until bedtime again when she became a little distressed and teary.

"I think someone is tired." Dave picked her up and sat her on his knee. "It's been a busy weekend for this little princess, hey? Let's get you in the bath and then we can snuggle up and read stories."

Eve nodded, sticking her thumb in her mouth, and I gave Dave a look that said 'see what I mean?'

He nodded to me and carried Eve upstairs.

The giggles and splashes that came from the bathroom indicated that Dave had managed to turn Eve's concentration away from whatever was playing on her mind. I smiled at the scene I pictured… The rubber ducks would be out, the watering can would be in use, and there would no doubt be some kind of water fight emerging. That didn't fool my mother's intuition, though. She was usually so vocal when things were bothering her, but this time she seemed to be hiding something away.

As I stood folding little T-shirts and pairing little socks, the doorbell went.

"Hey, Pete. Come in. He's just upstairs bathing Eve."

Dave's brother walked into the house and kissed my cheek. "Hi, sis. Just wondered if he fancied nipping out for a beer."

It was endearing that he called me sis, even though it was only by law, and I wondered as I often did, where it had all gone wrong between him and Dave. It didn't keep Pete away, though. He called in at least once a week, sometimes more. He was either oblivious to the antagonistic relationship he shared with his brother or was trying his best to fix it.

"We've had quite a weekend with Eve's birthday. I'm not

entirely sure he will be up for it, but you can ask. Go up. Eve will be pleased to see you."

Eve and her Uncle Pete had always had a fun relationship. He'd doted on her when she was first born, and now, their happy-go-lucky personalities seemed to bounce off each other anytime they were together. He nodded and moved past me to go upstairs. I turned back to folding washing and tried to focus on making a mental list of mundane jobs I needed to get done the following day.

After a few minutes, Dave came back downstairs. His T-shirt was soaked, and I laughed. "Had fun?"

"Yeah, she's a little tinker." He ragged his hand through his hair, and his cheek pulled to the side in a defeated smile. "He wants me to go for a beer."

I looked up at him, shrugging and folding yet another item of clothing. "Maybe you should go. It might do you both good to spend some guy time together out of the house. He's your brother, love. That has to count for something."

Dave's brow rose in agreement as he nodded. "Yeah, I guess so." He leaned against the kitchen counter as he waited for a cold mug of coffee to heat up in the microwave. "Okay, I'll get her to bed and then we'll nip to The Acorn for a couple." The microwave pinged. He pushed himself from the cupboard and walked over to where I was standing. "Is there a clean towel down here? There aren't any in the airing cupboard."

I dug around in the basket at my feet and pulled one out. "I'll put her to bed if you want. You go get sorted and take Pete out. I'll just finish off here, and then I'll get her out of the bath."

Dave nodded and sipped on the now hot drink. "Okay, love." He walked past me and kissed my cheek, his hand skimming my bottom. "Perhaps we can have some girl and guy time when I get back." He winked, and my stomach lurched as it always did, even after all that time together. I shook out the pillowcase in my hand and smiled. Dave walked into the dining room to collect a clean shirt that was hanging on the curtain rail with all the other items I had ironed the night before and hadn't had time to put away.

I heard the sound of the door clicking closed behind him.

I heard coat hangers clanging.

I heard my husband swear under his breath as he knocked a couple of items to the floor.

I heard next door's cat crying on the wall outside and made a mental note to speak to them about it shitting on our grass all the time.

I heard the ticking of the living room clock as I picked up a bundle of clothes and carried them to the utility room ready to be ironed the next day.

I heard Dave exit the dining room and slump down in front of the TV.

Pete had been with Eve for a good fifteen minutes before I managed to tear myself away from the washing pile, and it wasn't until I got to the top of the stairs that I realised I had heard only silence from the bathroom in all that time. The sounds that a little girl playing in the tub should make, the sounds that should have been made by a loving niece and her favourite uncle, the sounds that I had most definitely heard when Dave was up there with her, had all been non-existent in those minutes, and to me, that was very strange.

That intuition that wouldn't let me drop the niggling feelings I was having was sitting on my shoulder, whispering things I didn't want to hear.

I moved like a zombie down the landing towards the bathroom.

Stopping halfway, I focused all of my energy on that eerie sound of nothingness, that stillness that did not make sense when I thought of my bubbly little girl. I bowed my head, the soft, blue towel that I planned to wrap my Eve in hanging from my limp arm, and I listened. I listened so very hard for that sound of innocence amongst the silence.

But it wasn't just silence. I was wrong…

I could now hear the quiet, constant swish of water, and when I squeezed my eyes shut to block out all other stimuli that were burning every one of my nerve endings, it was there… and my heart stopped.

I could hear breathing.

I could hear grunting.

It was deep, it was laboured, and it was coming from Pete.

I shook my head to clear it, batting at the whisperings from my shoulder, frowning at what I hoped were tricks being played on me by my mind, and I tried again, my ears begging and pleading, so very desperately, to pick out the sound of laughter and fun.

But all that was there was a menacing calm, and the grunting, and the methodical swishing of water.

lifeless | ˈlʌɪfləs |

adjective

1 dead or apparently dead: his lifeless body was taken from the river.

• lacking vigour, vitality, or excitement: dull and lifeless hair.

2 devoid of living things. the lifeless landscapes of the moon.

No life. It had been sucked out of me so that I was unable to react, rooted to the spot. The panic rose higher in my throat, and I fought frantically to swallow it down. I needed to go to her, but I couldn't move my limbs. My breaths came in short, shallow bursts. I tried not to focus on them and instead on what I should do to get to my baby.

Why wasn't I moving? Why wasn't I running in there and saving her?

There were a thousand words on my tongue and the same

amount stuck in my throat, but none of them would release themselves.

It was the sound of Dave running up the stairs that broke me. My knees gave way and I collapsed to the floor, my mouth opening wide and releasing a soundless scream.

I pulled at my hair and bit at the skin on my arm.

"Jesus, Gill. What the hell are you doing?" He bent down and pulled my arms away from my body. And then it happened...

I heard the sweet sound of Eve's laughter drift through the door, but it was too late.

I heard the sound of water splashing, just how it was meant to be when I walked up the stairs. But it was too late.

Pete wasn't grunting anymore. He was laughing, too, and asking Eve if she'd had a lovely birthday.

Dave picked up the towel that I had dropped and walked to the bathroom, throwing it through the doorway as he peered around it to speak to his brother.

"Get Eve out of the bath for me. I just need to deal with something. Be there in a minute."

My mouth opened to scream again. I just needed to say no, that one word, just one little word, but someone had tied my throat up with string.

Dave scooped me from the floor into his arms and carried me to the bedroom. He scanned my face for signs of something, anything. There was nothing.

Tears wouldn't fall.

Noise wouldn't come forth.

I sat motionless.

Silent.

Lifeless.

CHAPTER
twenty four

Silhouettes — Adam French

THE ONLY SOUND in Billy's head was his blood pumping, thudding. He'd barely touched the drink that now sat lukewarm in front of him, and he hadn't said a word in fifteen minutes.

Gillian Swallow still sat opposite him, a shell of the woman who had greeted him at the door just hours before. Her floodgates had opened, and words and memories that had been locked away in complete secret for thirteen years came tumbling out like a swarm of locusts.

"Wh… Why?" It was all Billy could manage.

Gillian didn't meet his eyes with hers.

"Why are you telling me this? Why is this coming out here, now, to me?" Billy pushed his chair away from the table and stood up, walking with his hands on his head towards the kitchen window. He stared out at the garden, the stars, and tried to rid his mind of the images it was now conjuring up.

"I was watching you with her. I was watching how much you love her. That's all I have ever wanted for her: to find a man who will take care of her body like it should be taken care of." She stared into her mug.

Billy spun around. "Where is he?"

Gillian's head kicked up. "Who?"

"Pete."

"Oh, Billy. No good will come of that. He has learned his lesson now. He doesn't come around here anymore. Not since…" She trailed off and blinked to alert another army of tears to their duty.

Billy sat back down on his chair. "Since what?"

"Nothing. It's all history that you don't need to be burdened with."

Any good behaviour he had planned on during his stay had gone out of the window. Eve was the only thing that mattered now, and he forgot his manners.

Billy hissed through his teeth, leaning forwards with fire in his eyes. "You're fucking kidding me, right?" He pointed to the ceiling. "That girl has my heart, and I am not fucking leaving with half a story. Since what? Tell me."

Gillian got to her feet and walked to the fridge. She pulled out a half-full bottle of Pinot Grigio and a large wine glass, pouring it and lifting the glass to her mouth, her hands shaking, her body defeated. She tipped her head to take the cold liquid but crumpled before it touched her lips. With a grimace, she hurled the drink at the wall, the glass smashing into a thousand pieces that resembled those of her broken heart. She moved to sit on the floor, her legs no longer willing to bear the weight she had been carrying alone for so long. Pulling them to her, she rocked back and forth like a baby, an all too familiar noiseless scream hurtling from the back of her throat.

Billy moved slowly to her and sat on the floor next to

her, smoothing his hand over her shoulder.

He was numb. There were no thoughts. There was no feeling.

They sat side-by-side, their backs against the cupboard doors for what felt like an eternity until Billy found his voice again. He let his hand drop, resting both arms on his knees, his head bowed between them. "Since what, Gillian?"

Her chin sat on top of her knees, her eyes glazed and empty. "I've never told anyone. Just Dave, Eve's father. I lived with it killing me from the inside for three months before I spoke to him. He didn't believe me."

"But you stopped it, right? You stopped Pete from hurting her anymore?"

Gillian didn't reply, and Billy's eyes grew wide. His head whipped to the side and he grabbed Gillian's chin, forcing her to look at him.

"Tell me you stopped it, Gillian."

She looked deep into his eyes, her brow crumpling, her mouth turning down as she prepared to cry again. "I don't know."

"What? What the hell do you mean, you don't know?" Billy's face was creased with anger and confusion. How could she not know? How could she not have done everything and anything in her power to ensure, without a shadow of a fucking doubt, that that monster never ever touched her daughter again?

"I let Dave go to the pub with him that night, told him I had a pain in my head that floored me. And after their bonding session, they seemed to get on a bit better. I couldn't take that away from Dave, so I kept it to myself. I let Pete back in the house but made sure he was never alone with her." Her tears began to roll again as she recalled the living nightmare that had eaten away at her, hour after hour for so long.

"But…"

"I know, Billy. I know. He could have got to her somehow."

"Jesus, Gillian." Billy ragged his hands through his hair and squeezed his eyes shut. She continued to speak, her voice hoarse and laced with hurt.

"I brought it up one night after I couldn't hold it in anymore. He got angry and told me not to be ridiculous, that Pete wasn't like that—that Pete loved Eve. But then, not long after, I'd been out with friends and I came home to Dave sitting at the table, just there where you were sitting…" She pointed at the kitchen chair. "And Pete was knocked out cold on the floor, blood everywhere, a broken nose, broken ribs… He was barely breathing. Dave had left Pete with Eve while he went to answer the phone and walked back in on him…using her tiny body…"

Billy's head was turned to the side, his eyes trained on Gillian's face. Bile rose up in his throat, and he dived up to the sink to be sick. He ran the tap and took in as much cold water as he could swallow before wiping his mouth with the back of his sleeve.

"We had to get him to the hospital. We made up some story about finding him like that."

Billy spun round with a venomous fury. "Why the hell didn't you tell the truth?"

Gillian bit back, "Because I'd have lost Dave! He would have been sent down. Pete isn't the kind of person to forgive and forget. They made a deal. He wouldn't come to the house anymore, he wouldn't get to see Eve anymore and the secrets would stay with us—all of us. We buried them." She smiled sarcastically. "Not so easy to bury the memories, though."

Billy turned from the sink and slid to the floor. "And where is Dave now?"

Gillian pinched the bridge of her nose, squeezing the fingers on her other hand into the flesh of her palm. "Gone."

"Gone where?"

"Gone. Left. Packed up and walked out."

"When? Why?"

Gillian let out a trembling sigh. "He was the love of my life. We were so happy. And Pete ruined everything. Dave spent longer and longer in the office and less time with us over a period of a few months, until one night, he came home and just broke down. He couldn't cope. He couldn't bear walking into his house and seeing his beautiful little girl, knowing what had happened to her, knowing it was his brother who was the cause of it, knowing he had been unable to stop it from happening. He was riddled with guilt. So, he left. He left us and left me to pick up the pieces."

"But what about Eve? Why did he leave Eve?" Billy couldn't wrap his mind around this hurricane of information that was spinning around his head.

This was her father.

How could he leave her?

It wasn't until he asked himself that question that his mind wandered to his own father and how really, if you looked at it with your head cocked, he had left him, too.

"And you had to pick yourself up too, huh?"

"I had to make a life for my daughter so that she forgot. I didn't want her to have memories of this horrific

314

time. I wanted everything to be perfect for her. Too perfect. I scrubbed and cleaned this house to get rid of Pete and what he did. I washed and scrubbed our clothes, and I bleached our life. No one would know. No one would think we were anything less than perfect. People would comment on 'oh, what a beautiful, happy, normal little girl you have' before I was done. And I smothered her. I know I did. But I didn't know what else to do!" Her voice became higher and higher, until it cracked. "She grew further from my reach, started running away, was scared to go out in public, scared to get in cars, though I suspect that has more to do with Pete than my overbearing parenting."

Billy looked up at the clock that ticked on the wall. It was two am.

"Have you heard from him?"

"Who? Dave? No… Not since he left. I don't talk about him with Eve. I refuse to. He left us here, and as far as I am concerned, she doesn't need to know anything else. If she starts to remember her father then she might start to remember Pete and what he did to her, and I can't have my baby hurting like that."

A rumble of anger started at the pit of his stomach as he watched Gillian's features sag with a weariness he had never seen on anyone before. "I disagree. I think she deserves to know everything. How the fucking hell do you sleep at night?"

Gillian laughed almost manically. "Medication is a magical thing… Listen, I know you have her best interests at heart, Billy, but this is my daughter we are talking about. I know what she needs better than some boy she barely knows. No offence."

He sat still and stared at his fingers. Starting an

argument right now wouldn't do anyone any good, so he bit his tongue. Hard. "So, she is the way she is because of Pete, because of you, because of her father."

Gillian nodded and pushed to her feet. "I had to do what I thought was right at the time, Billy. So please don't judge." She moved slowly towards the kitchen door. "I'm thrilled she has you. You can show her how it is supposed to be. I trust you to do that. But I also need to trust you to keep this to yourself. She doesn't need to know. I'm sorry it has come out like this tonight, but you need to bury it now. Just like I had to."

Billy got up and moved to the table, sitting on the edge of the chair. He went to speak, but she cut him off before the words left his lips.

"I have spent thirteen years trying to erase all the bad. Please don't start penciling it back in now." She walked around to his side of the table and placed a light hand on his shoulder. "Goodnight, Billy."

And just like that, she walked out and closed the door, shutting Billy inside the kitchen, alone with her ghosts.

He sat at the table for another hour.

He watched the second hand move around the clock and counted the ticks. They were comfortingly regular every time, even though he tried to catch them out, hoping that one of them would slip or that it would miss a beat. He struck his finger on the table on the offbeat, trying to fit two, then three taps in before the next tick, never quite managing it.

It was the creak of the kitchen door that eventually made his head move, turning slowly and lazily to the side to watch Eve pad into the room, rubbing her eyes sleepily, her vest crumpled and twisted around her body, her hair tousled. She yawned and walked towards him, sliding onto his knee and curling up against his chest.

Lifting her arms, she linked them round his neck. "Take me to bed, handsome."

Billy's arms lay limply around Eve's waist, his eyes back to the clock. Half asleep, she was not really aware that he had barely moved and had not even acknowledged her arrival.

She breathed in deeply and closed her eyes against his smell and listened to his heartbeat.

Ten minutes more passed, and Eve became uncomfortable and chilly. She shifted her position and looked up at Billy's face. A frown twitched between her eyes and she ran her finger across his brow and down his cheek, cupping it gently with her hand. "Hey, Billy? What's the matter, baby?" She sat up to get a better look at him. There was a blankness to his usually bright eyes, and Eve's pulse quickened when he didn't look at her. "Billy?" Her voice was sharper this time, more urgent, and it snapped him out of his trance.

He dropped sad eyes to her face, both of them scanning the beauty of her. "Hey, you."

And then he couldn't breathe.

The conversation he'd had with Eve's mother came charging back at him, a raging bull with horns that stabbed him in his heart. He pulled Eve tightly to him, pressing his lips to her head and almost allowing himself to cry into her hair.

"Shit, baby. What is it? What's happened?" She panicked, pulling away from him, feeling claustrophobic all of a sudden and climbing from his knee.

His arms dropped to his sides and he stared at her, his

eyes glistening.

"What the hell, Billy? You're scaring me. Talk to me."

Something inside yanked at him, pulling at his collar, forcing him to get a grip and take a hold of the situation, and he stood to his feet.

Gillian had been clear in her instructions: she did not want Eve to know anything, so he had to respect that, for now at least, as much as it was ripping him apart from the inside. He walked to the sink and splashed his face with cold water.

Eve watched him, trying to figure out what was wrong.

Billy stood with his hands on the sink, leaning forwards with his eyes closed. He took a deep breath and pushed himself back, grabbing a tea towel from the oven and drying his face. Walking towards Eve—avoiding looking at her bottom half, legs naked and in only a tiny pair of briefs—he pulled her to him, his skin burning as he touched her. Every hair stood on end as he thrashed around in his memory for the feelings he'd had when he touched her that very same morning, before he knew.

"Hey, beautiful girl. I'm okay. I'm sorry." He kissed her forehead and ran his hand up and down her back. "I'm tired, and I think things just got on top of me. I'll be fine. Let's get you up to bed."

He followed her up the stairs, grimacing as his face contorted and screwed itself up in preparation for crying. He held it together and sat on the edge of the bed while Eve climbed in and curled up facing him. She reached out and fingered the curls that fell onto his forehead, smiling gently at him as she committed his face to memory for the hundredth time, just in case she forgot it while she slept.

"Everything will work out someday, Billy. It will. I'm

sure of it. He's not a bad man. He's just lost his way, like you said. But you gotta keep safe until he finds his way back, okay?" Her fingertips traced down the side of his face, causing Billy's eyes to close against the feel of them, his heart and his head pulling against each other antagonistically. He opened them and caught hold of Eve's hand, pulling those fingertips to his lips as he kissed each one in turn.

"You talk so much sense, Eve. You are so strong and so beautiful. Look at you."

Eve blinked, not able to tear her gaze away from him. "Sleep with me tonight."

Billy sucked in a breath. "I can't. Your mum…"

"She won't know. We can get up before her in the morning. Sleep with me."

Billy's eyes poured all over her. God, he loved her with every cell in his body, every hair on his skin, every nerve ending that ignited with a passion so raw, so intense… He loved her too much.

"You're thinking too much, mister. Just get in."

Billy gave her a half-hearted smirk and sighed out loud. The old him—the one before he knew—would have been under the duvet like a shot. She would start to ask more questions if he didn't act like the old him, and he wasn't so sure he would be able to hold his tongue if she started.

He stood and turned his back to her to unbuckle his jeans and let them fall to the floor, stepping out of them carefully and folding them over the arm of the chair. He reached down for the hem of his T-shirt to pull it over his head but stopped halfway, letting it drop back into place. Scraping his fingers through his hair, he turned around and looked at her tiny body curled up, her beautiful face lit up with naughtiness and anticipation.

Sitting on the floor next to the bed, he took her hand in his. He turned her palm over and leaned in to kiss the elephant that sat, as always, trumpeting his sounds on her wrist.

"I never did ask you what this meant." He rubbed his finger over the spot of delicate skin that he had just kissed and waited for her to answer him.

"Elephants never forget." She smiled up at him, watching the expressions on his face flit from one to another.

"What does this elephant never forget?" He was careful not to look into her eyes as he asked her, for fear of betraying Gillian's trust. He continued to run his finger up and down the soft skin of her wrist, up to the crook of her elbow and back down to the tooting elephant.

"Well, that's the thing. I'm not so sure. There is so much about my early childhood that I don't know because I've forgotten. And Mum refuses to discuss my dad, so I guess—and it might seem silly to some—that one day, this little elephant will remind me of some of it."

Billy nodded, kissing the palm of her hand.

There were two kinds of elephant: those that never forget, and those that sit there while people sidestep them awkwardly as they go about their daily lives.

"My life seems to be filled with them."

Eve frowned.

"Elephants."

"What do you mean?"

"You know, massive, real-life issues that are patently there, in the way of everything, big enough for us all to trip over, fall out over, fight over. Big enough to hurt each other for. Yet not one of us chooses to acknowledge them. Did you know that I haven't spoken to my grandparents in over eight months?"

Eve shook her head, her eyes wide, taking him in.

"Hmm. They are my mother's parents, but they never call. They never come and see me, and I don't go to see them, either. And the elephant in the room there is…?"

Eve took in a shaky breath. "Your dad."

"Yep. My dad. Certainly fucking big enough and ugly enough for us to know he's there, but no one comes forward to help resolve the issue. They won't come around because they're scared of him—not scared enough to try to protect me, obviously. I won't go to them because I don't want to sit there, quite deliberately avoiding any conversations that might lead to talking about him and in turn making the goddamned elephant even bigger. And then there's my mum, who is also a big fuck off elephant in everyone's room. Dad and I don't discuss her, because it's too hard, even though we both know we are hurting so, so fucking badly because of her. You'd think that two grown men would be able to organise themselves so that they didn't have to skirt around this great grey beast that is quite frankly in the way of every fucking thing…" He shook his head and laughed. "Quite funny when you look at it like that." He looked again at the tattoo on Eve's arm. "That's a really tiny elephant…" He wanted to tell her that she needed a bigger elephant to symbolise her Uncle Pete—tell her that she had been living for thirteen years without realising this great African beauty was standing tall and trumpeting so loudly that when they got up the next morning, neither Billy nor Gillian would be able to bear being in the same room together now that she had spilled her heart out.

"Every time I handed my pay packet over to my dad and he scoffed at the pittance I was earning, another elephant would walk into our living room, squat and shit all over my life. I gave up everything I loved for that man to help him get by, to give us both a bit of hope. And he knows it. He knows that I stopped doing all the things that made me happy because I loved him and Mum, and he has thrown it all back in my face. But it never gets talked about. So, there it sits on the carpet of every room we go into, obvious and in the fucking way. So, look at the pair of us… elephants coming out of our fucking ears."

Eve had never seen him this negative about life, and she needed to be close to him, to make him forget about things that were out of his control for now. She put her hand over his and pulled him to her. "Hey. Get into bed with me. You're too far away down there."

Billy complied begrudgingly. He hopped over her and slunk under the duvet. Eve rolled over and tangled her legs with his, tucking into his torso. The feel of her on his skin, the warmth of her seeping into his bones, drove his body fucking wild, but his head was screaming at his dick to back down.

Not tonight old boy. This is too raw. You can't touch her like that tonight.

Until he was able to function without unsavoury and quite frankly disturbing images flashing across his vision, until he was able to bury this—just like Gillian said—he was going to have to come up with a bucket load of excuses…

CHAPTER
twenty five

Shut Us Down – Freddie Dickson

IT WAS THE shaft of sunlight that edged its way into the room that woke Billy from the horrors that had plagued his slumber. The sanctuary that he'd hoped for once sleep arrived didn't come. There were monsters, incubi and elephants lurking in every corner, ready to start a new nightmare before that last one ended.

Sleep had evaded Billy for another hour after he climbed in next to Eve. He'd laid on his back with his arm slung across his eyes as he fought to ignore the feel of her body. Persuading her that sleep was a good idea, he'd stayed still and silent as she dropped off almost immediately.

How the hell was this going to work now? How was he supposed to go back to how things were, worshiping this girl's body like a temple, exploring, discovering and rediscovering every inch of her skin until he knew it by heart?

As his eyes adjusted to the change in light, and the mugginess in his head cleared enough for him to focus on his surroundings, he became aware of the sound of Gillian pottering around upstairs. The bedroom door was thrown open, which meant she had been into the room and seen him in bed with her daughter.

He looked down to see the duvet had slipped off the bed, that Eve was wrapped around him, her barely covered breasts pressed into him, that his T-shirt had ridden up. He was also sporting the most resplendent display of morning glory he had ever seen.

Oh, holy fuck.

Carefully, he prized himself away from Eve, desperate not to wake her, and slid out of the bed. He quietly slipped into his jeans and tiptoed out of the bedroom, almost knocking Mrs. Swallow off her feet as he did.

"Shit!" He grimaced as he grabbed the tops of her arms to steady her. "You okay?"

Gillian pulled away from him, embarrassed, and straightened herself up. "Yes. Sorry. Good morning. I trust you slept okay?"

Billy bowed his head. "Look, I'm sorry. She got up in the middle of the night and begged me to slee—"

"It's fine, Billy. It's fine. She's nearly twenty. I trust you. I just… Well. Never mind. But it's okay. Just, you know, be careful. Sensible." Gillian ducked her head and walked past Billy towards the bathroom. "I'm going to jump in the shower. Ten minutes or so and you can use it."

He nodded and walked down the landing, sitting on the top stair and rubbing across the top of his head with his hands.

The door to Eve's bedroom opened and out she walked, a vision of sexuality in her tiny briefs and vest top, her head turning to look at him. His eyes roamed from her feet, up her long, slender legs—resting for so much longer than they should have done on the curve of her perfect arse—and eventually up to her face. She had piled her hair on top of her head, loose tendrils escaping around the nape of her neck and around her face, and that hard on that had started to subside sprung back to life immediately.

She padded over to where he was sitting, and before he had a chance to shake himself out of it and stand up, she had swung her leg around him and sat on his lap, straddling him on the stairs, a ridiculously dirty look in her eye.

Billy swallowed hard and clenched his back teeth together, his hands twitching at his sides, desperate to reach up and touch her.

"Good morning, gorgeous. You look so handsome in the mornings." Eve smiled sexily and leaned forward, combing her fingers back through the front of his hair and planting a trail of kisses along his stubbled jawline.

He inhaled, his eyes closing involuntarily.

Shit…

Eve continued to seduce him with her mouth, moving to the underside of his ear and down his throat.

"Eve."

"Shhh" She hushed him against his skin, causing a ripple of nerve endings to ignite.

"Eve, your mum—" He squeezed his eyes tight and inhaled again, the smell of her intoxicating and turning him on more.

"Shhh."

Snaking her arms around his neck, she moved her lips to his, teasing his mouth open and beginning the dance of tongues that he loved so much. A primal groan released itself from the back of his throat, and Eve took the invitation with pleasure, slowly beginning to rock her hips back and forth in his lap.

"Eve." His voice was barely a whisper as his hands moved from the floor, smoothing up her legs to cup her buttocks as she moved in a gentle rhythm, driving him crazy. Their kisses became more urgent as Billy's animal desires promised to take the rap for any repercussions, while his head fought against images that threatened to fill it.

The noise of the shower being turned off snapped Billy to attention and he stopped still, pushing Eve by the shoulders and leaving her wide-eyed and breathless.

"Eve. Stop. Your mum is about to open that door. Just cool it, okay?" His irritated tone confused her, and she frowned, climbing off his knee and walking without a word back to the bedroom.

Billy sighed heavily, adjusting himself in his jeans as Gillian exited the steam-filled bathroom and went into her room. He got to his feet, and just as he reached the bathroom door, Eve came back out. Her vest was off, and her eyes were wild.

She was annoyed.

She pushed at him so hard he almost fell backwards, stumbling into the bathroom. Closing the door behind them, she slid the bolt across slowly. She reached over the bath and turned the shower on, the noise of the water hitting the enamel loud and distracting. Walking over to him, she began to lift his T-shirt.

Billy was speechless. She was so fucking sexy right now, and there was nothing his head could say that could change the way his body was reacting to her uncharacteristic dominance. He lifted his arms and stood with hooded eyes, watching her face as her newfound confidence took control.

Throwing his T-shirt to the floor, she trailed her fingers from his chest to the narrow path of hair that led to the waistband of his jeans. One by one, she popped the buttons open, hooking her fingertips over the top of the denim, pulling them and his boxers down his legs.

He stepped out of them, watching her face, his chest heaving as she took in the sight of his arousal.

As she stood back up, her eyes full of something he could not define, he could hold off no longer. Grabbing her face and pulling it to him, he crushed his lips to hers, devouring the taste of her. His hands could not cover her quick enough as they ran down her back and up her sides to her breasts.

Eve was on fire. Every inch of her burned with desire and burned even more at the feel of Billy's hands as they explored her skin like it was brand new to him. His fingers pushed into her underwear, discovering her wetness, and she tipped her head back, exposing her neck to Billy, who nipped and licked at it as he moved his mouth down to her hardening nipples.

The steam filling the bathroom and the noise of the shower spray took Eve out of herself, and she felt herself transform.

It was the most uninhibited she had ever been.

The look in Billy's eyes said he wanted every inch of her; it said she was beautiful; it said she was good enough in every way, shape and form.

She was good enough. And she was not ashamed.

Without warning, Billy grabbed underneath her thighs and lifted her up, her legs wrapping themselves instinctively around his body and her arms draping around his neck. She whispered her desires into his ear, her ragged breaths sending shivers down his spine.

"Jesus, Eve." Her carnal demands tipped him over the edge, and he locked his head and all its thoughts far away in the depths of his consciousness. He spun around and slammed Eve's back against the tiles, one hand under her buttocks, the other pushing his thumb into the material of her briefs, ripping angrily at the seam. The need to feel where deep down he knew he belonged was taking precedence over anything his head was trying to say. He needed to do this now or he might never get to have her again. If he allowed his head to lead, he could lose her by pushing her away.

He needed to get it over with.

Flinging the scrap of material to the floor, he adjusted his hold on her, roaming her body to search for the woman he loved. With an urgent and desperate kiss, he slammed into her, both of them inhaling with the force as the wave of initial pleasure hit their bodies. As he pushed harder and deeper in response to her moans, he lost himself. He fought with his mind, focusing hard on the rhythm, not allowing himself to look in her eyes. He squeezed his own shut and closed himself off.

It was raw, it was dirty and it was wanton.

This was grown up sex with a consenting adult, and he was damned if he was going to let his stupid conscience ruin the best thing that had ever happened to him.

Lowering her gently to the floor, her body limp and weak from exertion and climax, a contented smile on her face, Billy stood, one palm pressed against the bathroom wall, his head low and his breathing hard and heavy.

His eyes locked onto her naked body.

The primal need in him had subsided, and all that was left was the shell of him and his heart—his heart that beat furiously for this beautiful woman who he had just used for his own satisfaction, to try to clear his own guilt and frustrations. The longer he looked, the more furiously the anger bubbled inside of him. He shook his head to clear it, but it kept coming.

Eve lifted her arms to wrap them around his body, but he stepped backwards out of her reach. He continued to stand there, his chest heaving, his back teeth clenched and his fists now balled at his sides.

Eve's fingers reached for him again.

His eyes quivered and shifted to the floor. He couldn't look at her. Utter disgust was thrown at him from within. The flash of words and images that didn't belong there zoomed past the periphery of his vision, like the blur of trees and houses from a train window.

"Billy?" A frown pushed itself onto Eve's face and she whispered so softly, his heart nearly broke.

His nostrils flared and the hatred he had for himself in that moment surfaced.

She came towards him yet again, and he held his hands up to stop her, grabbing her wrists and pushing her back. Snatching up his clothes, he shoved his legs into his jeans and tugged at the door handle, forgetting the bolt was on.

It was the icing on the cake.

Exasperation took over, and in his heightened state of emotion, he let loose and smashed his fist into the wood, a roar of pure anger raging from the depths of him.

"Billy!" Eve flung herself forwards to grab at him, her hands shaking, her eyes wide. "Billy, stop!" A river of tears fell freely from her eyes, her mind a whirr of confusion.

What have I done wrong?

Billy shoved the bolt across, opened the door and left.

Eve's knees gave way and she sunk to the floor, lip trembling and her naked body feeling more exposed than ever.

Storming along the landing, Billy thrust his arms and head into his T-shirt as he ran down the stairs, bursting into the living room.

Gillian sat in the armchair, a cushion on her knee and a tear-stained face staring blankly at the wall. "I'm sorry, Billy."

He ignored her, walking to the other side of the room to retrieve his coat from the back of the sofa. He dug his hands into the pockets, pulling out his Camel Blues and the beautiful Zippo lighter that he was now the owner of and turning towards the kitchen and the back door, he gritted his teeth. "Tell her. Or I will. I'll give you a week." He slammed the door behind him.

Making his way down the path to the bottom of the garden, Billy lit up and sucked in the first drag of smoke and held it. He held it until it burned, until he was forced to choke it out, and he fell to his haunches, roaring to the sky. "Fuck you, mother fucker!"

Gillian continued to stare at the wall, silent tears following each other down the same tracks on her cheeks. Living the nightmare alone for thirteen years seemed like a walk in the park compared to this. Sharing is caring, right? Not this. It was like an old wound had been ripped open and everyone was standing over her, staring at it, taking their turn to lift the saltshaker.

What had she done?

Her whole life since the incident had revolved around

making Eve's existence perfect, whitewashed, clean. What was her purpose now? What was she supposed to do with herself now?

A week, he said. She had a week to tell her or he was going to do it himself. She had no idea what to do with this demand. Her eyes fell to her fingers that lay twisted in her lap. There was not much chance of her being able to brush this under the carpet now. Eve was up there, probably crying. Billy was in the garden, screaming with anger.

"Oh, it's nothing, dear."

She found herself starting to laugh maniacally, her body shaking and rocking back and forth until the mania switched to heartbreak and she sobbed. She sobbed like she had never sobbed before, and this time, for the first time, the screams were not silent. That little word that had been lodged in the back of her throat since Eve was five came hurtling out, echoing around the room and bounced around the walls. "No!"

And so they sat—each of them alone, each of them wrapped up in grief, terror, guilt, confusion, sadness…

Eve was the first to move. She picked herself up from the floor of the bathroom, her body shivering, and walked to her room. The tears had stopped now and all that was left was emptiness. She wasn't sure what she was meant to do next.

All of a sudden, she wasn't sure who she was.

Billy completed her, and he had just pushed her away.

She pulled on a pair of old joggers that she found in her closet and slipped into a clean vest. Unsure what she would be faced with when she got to the bottom, she took each step slowly and carefully, listening to the cries of her mother that didn't seem to subside. She reached the last step and pushed the door to the living area open.

The sight of her mother rocking back and forth, her face contorted, was horrific. She had never heard her mother cry. Gillian had always been a 'together' kind of person.

Eve moved closer and knelt before her on the floor, taking her hands in her own. The closeness she was sure they had shared when she was little—that she'd tried so hard to recall—had never come and sitting here, showing compassion towards this woman who had pushed and shoved at her to be more, to be better, was an alien thing.

"Mum?"

Gillian's eyes opened and her shuddering body stopped rocking. She lifted her hand and smoothed it down her daughter's cheek. The tenderness in her touch caused Eve's breathing to falter, and she closed her eyes to avoid crying in front of her.

"What's happened, Mum? Where is Billy? I don't know what's going on and I'm scared." She covered her mother's hand with her own and waited for her to speak, listening to the sound of her own heart. She wasn't sure she wanted to hear what she had to say. There was a sinister feel about the whole situation, and she half wanted to get up and run—run to the fields, to her safe place.

But her safest place was here. He was here with her, even if he felt a million miles away from her right now. She couldn't give up on this until she knew what was going on, and if she ran now, she might never come back, or worse, he might never come for her.

She pulled both their hands from her face and knelt

up, taking her mother by the shoulders and shaking her. "Mum." Her voice came out more forcefully than she expected, shocking her and Gillian. "Tell me what the hell is going on."

Her mum sighed and wiped at her face, sitting up straight and pushing her hair back. She blew all the air from her cheeks and pushed herself to her feet. She wasn't ready for this yet. How the hell was she supposed to start this conversation? She had no idea where to begin. This was going to break her little girl's heart. This was going to sever any remaining ties they had, because once she found out what had been hidden from her for so long, she was going to be filled with hate and anger, and she would lose her for good.

She got up slowly and walked towards the kitchen, words refusing to come, and Eve watched her incredulously, eyes wide and mouth open.

"Mother!" Eve jumped to her feet and followed her quickly, catching hold of her arm and spinning her around. "Tell me. What the fucking hell is going on?"

At that moment, the back door opened and Billy stepped into the kitchen. He stopped with his hand on the door handle and looked between the two women. Eve's face was riddled with anger, an emotion he had never seen her display before now, and Gillian was about to break.

He needed to leave. He needed to go back to York and let the pair of them sort this out, and then, when Eve had been stripped of everything she thought she knew and needed him more than she ever had before, he would be there to hold her in his arms until she was at peace again.

He cleared his throat, and the two women turned to him, Eve's eyes alight with a fire that caused his heart to break a little more. In a short time, that fire would die out and there would be nothing there. It would be his job to ignite it again, somehow.

"Baby, can I just talk to you for a minute?"

"Damn right you can. At least *someone*"—she turned and spat the words at her mother—"is willing to tell me what the hell is going on." Spinning on her heel, she stormed into the living area and up the stairs, Billy following her, deep breaths attempting to calm his nerves.

Eve sat crossed-legged on the bed, a storm raging across her face, and Billy stood in the doorway, not daring to go near her in case he crumbled.

"I'm going back to York."

Her head flung to the side to look at him. "When?"

"Now."

"What do you mean, now?"

"I'm going to go home now and leave you here with your mum for a few days."

"Why? Why are you leaving me here and not taking me home with you?"

"I…"

"What have I done? What the hell have I done wrong between last night and this morning that means you don't want to be near me anymore?" The anger in her was leading this, but her voice cracked and gave her away. The slight wobble in her bottom lip was Billy's undoing, and he stalked over to her, sitting on the bed and pulling her to him, squeezing her body against his and kissing the top of her head.

Eve's arms were tucked into her chest between them, and she clutched at the material of his T-shirt.

Billy's heart thundered and Eve's resolve disappeared,

the tears falling freely.

"Why aren't I good enough?"

"Oh, beautiful girl, my beautiful Eve. You did nothing wrong. You did nothing wrong at all. God, I love you so much. You are so much more than good enough."

"So why are you leaving me? Why won't you take me home with you?"

Billy sucked in a breath and fumbled around in his brain for the right words to say. He was not doing this for Gillian unless she flatly refused. He would give her the week, and then he would come back and get Eve and ensure that she found out somehow, but not here. Not now.

"Because…" He stopped and bit down on the insides of his lips to stop the words tumbling out. "Because you and your mum have some bridges to build. She needs you here. She needs to talk to you."

Eve pushed gently at him so she could look at his face. "About what? Do you know what it's about? Is this why you're so angry?"

Billy avoided her eyes and looked out of the window. "This is not for me to get involved with just yet, baby. You need to stay here, okay?"

Eve shook her head. "No. I don't want to." She pushed at him harder so that he released her. "I don't want to stay here in this house with her."

"Eve, you've got to tr—"

"Trust you, right? You always say this. I have to trust you. Well how about I trust myself for once? I don't want to stay here."

Billy ragged his hand across his head and huffed out through his nose. "Eve. Listen. I am going home, and I am not taking you with me." He got up and stuffed his belongings back into his rucksack. Eve climbed off the bed and grabbed at the T-shirt he held in his hand, refusing to let him pack it. Billy pulled it back, but she was relentless.

"Fine!" He held his hands up. "I won't take that one. Keep it." He tried so hard to keep his cool, but her fierce stubbornness was itching at his skin. He slung his bag over his shoulder and turned to look at her. Her body was so small next to his, and he reached out to touch her. She flinched away, walking to the door and standing in front of it. "Take me home with you."

"Eve, you are acting like a child." He shook his head as the words fell at his feet, but when she shook her own head and folded her arms across her chest, resting the flat of her foot on the door, he lost all patience.

"You know why you can't remember anything, Eve? Because your mother has hidden it all from you for thirteen years. Your elephant can't remember fuck all, Eve, but your mother remembers every little bit."

Eve's arms dropped slowly to her sides, her face twisting in confusion. "What?"

"I'm sorry." He scrunched his eyes closed, pursing his lips. "I'm sorry. I shouldn't have said that." He stuffed his hands into his pockets and sighed, opening his eyes to look at her. "Talk to her, Eve. I've got to go." He stepped forwards and Eve backed down, moving from in front of the door and watching him leave.

CHAPTER
twenty six

Bones — Josh Record
Sundown — Charlie Simpson

THE DECEMBER SUN was low, and Billy squinted his eyes against it as he tuned up his guitar. It had been five days since he'd left Eve at her mother's, and New Year's Eve had come and gone with little significance. He had made a point of not contacting her at all, and in turn had heard nothing from her. It was ripping him apart inside. He had no idea if she knew yet or not.

He had spent the last three days in this spot, playing till his fingers hurt so he didn't have time to sit and think—to sit and remember. Music was the only thing he could focus on without lapsing into thoughts of her. He'd returned to the Dobson's only to sleep and eat and had holed himself up in his room in the evenings, refusing to talk to anyone.

Maureen was respectful and didn't pry and Dobbo knew better than to ask questions of him, so they passed like ships in the night with very few words, most of which were related to food.

A couple of local buskers had begun to recognise Billy now and would wave good morning or pitch up near to him. One young girl had spent an hour or so performing a duet with him the day before, but one band in particular had taken an interest in his sound.

Eboracum Rain had come to watch him play on a number of occasions. They'd chatted to him and said how much they liked his music. As he plugged his amp in that morning, the lead singer walked over and patted him on the back. "Morning, Bill. You doing okay?"

"Hey man. Yeah. I'm good, thanks. You?"

"Yeah good, ta. Listen. Me and the guys were chatting last night, and we wondered if you'd like to tour with us."

Billy's jaw dropped. "Wh...? Wow. Seriously?"

"Yeah, man. We love your sound, and well we need a support act and are invested in finding new talent. We like to support the underdog, and you've caught our eye."

"Wow." Billy rubbed his hand across the top of his head, grinning from the side of his face. "Fuck, I'm flattered."

"So that's a yes?"

Billy shifted his eyes to the side and huffed out. "I mean, fuck."

Eve's words echoed in the back of his mind and the inscription on the back of his lighter flashed before him.

'Follow your heart… I'll be right behind you following it too'.

She would come with him.

"Yeah, sure. I'd fucking love to tour with you." He held out his hand and shook Matt's.

"Awesome. It's small gigs around London over the

338

period of about two months. We will be bunking on floors and in the van most of the time, but it will be a good laugh. Gimme your number and I'll be in touch. We'll need to hit the road around the nineteenth of Jan. Is that cool?"

"Yeah, yeah, cool."

Billy swapped numbers with him and waved him off as he walked away.

Shit.

He grinned at his shoes and scratched the back of his neck.

This was unreal.

But mixed with the elation he felt was a nagging feeling that he was jumping the gun and should be concentrating on priorities closer to home.

He plugged the lead into his guitar and strummed the opening chords of a song he had written in the weeks running up to Christmas. He sang for the gathering crowds, and it wasn't until lunchtime, when he had chance to check his phone, that the excitement he had allowed himself to feel all morning came plummeting to the floor.

She was the one person he'd wanted to contact after Matt walked away, but as the text messaged flashed on the screen, he realised she was the last person he wanted to hear from. Her getting in touch meant that either her life was now in tatters, her soul sucked out of her and with no idea how to start living again, or it meant that he was going to have to be the one to shatter her heart by telling her the truth. He wasn't even sure there was a lesser of the two evils, and he didn't even know what he wanted the text message to say.

I'm coming home.

She was coming home to him, and that was the best news to hear, but the message was tainted with an incredible sadness that he had no idea how to respond to.

He read the message over and over. This was the longest they had gone without exchanging words, and he was struggling. She'd given no indication as to whether she wanted to be alone when she got here, whether she wanted him there, whether she needed picking up from the station.

He hit reply and typed, letting his instincts kick in.

What time do you get in? I'll come and pick you up. X

Her reply came back immediately.

Eve: I'll get myself home.

OK. If you're sure. Do you want me to come round when you get back?

This was the most mundane and normal conversation, but one that was skirting around the most horrific elephant of them all that hung in the air like a bad smell. Billy was clueless as to how to handle this, how to approach it, and he needed her to give a little so that he knew what to do for the best.

Eve: No.

An arrow shot through Billy's heart, almost flooring

him. He dropped to his haunches and hung his head between his knees. This was going wrong before it even started, and he was beginning to wish he had stayed there with her, ready to wrap her up and help her begin to heal her from the moment the words touched her ears. That was if she even knew. His own desperation rose above his ability to be sensitive, and he hit reply again.

Baby, you're hurting. I need to see you.

Eve: I need to be alone. I'm sorry.

He conceded defeat and stood up, picking up his guitar and slinging the strap over his head as he typed out his final reply.

I'm sorry, too. I love you x

He shoved his shoulders back and forced a smile at the old couple who were sitting on the bench in front of where he was set up, their eyes and faces expectant. He fished his plectrum from his back pocket and picked at the strings, the opening to 'Something in the Way She Moves' by James Taylor drifting through the air and causing a lump to rise in his throat.

***

GLAD OF THE empty house with Rachel still away, Eve closed the door, turning her key in it, dumped her things in the hallway and climbed the stairs.

That box of memories that she'd known had been buried deep but that she'd had no idea where to start looking for had been flipped open by the words that had tumbled from her mother's heart. Stumbling and falling with each new one, Eve had kicked the box over, and it was now spilling its contents all over the floor of her life. She now had to wade through them to get to the other side. There was no way around them, and she was not strong enough to stride or jump. So here she was tripping over them, bumping into them, bruising her broken soul with each collision.

She entered her bedroom, closing the door behind her and drawing the curtains across the bright light of the winter sky that stung her eyes, painfully reminding her that she was still alive. Pulling back the duvet, she climbed underneath, curling into a ball and closing herself off to the rest of the world.

***

TWO DAYS PASSED without a word from Eve, and Billy began to worry. He paced the floor of the box room that had become his whole world over the last week and chewed the inside of his cheek. He could risk pushing her away if he turned up unannounced, but there was no telling what would happen if he stayed away. The initial plan for the day had been to visit his mother and then attempt to get into his father's house without him realizing in order to collect more clothes and a few other items that he wanted to have with him if he ended up going on tour with Matt and the band.

He decided to skip going to see his mum. The thought of looking into her eyes and her not recognising him was even more painful this time. Becky had rung him after his visit the week before, and even though he hadn't witnessed it, he had scratched that incident into his memory bank and didn't want to risk replacing it with blank expressions. He'd wrapped the conversation in a scrap of cloth and tucked it into the pocket near his heart, a moment he could look back on. He wanted to keep that sacred, and ruining it with a visit that gave him only a reminder of the fact that she was locked away from him would spoil the images he had created in his head of the look on her face when she'd realised who the gift was from.

He decided instead to go Eve.

It was a split-second decision, and if he'd allowed himself to think about it for any longer, he was sure he would have talked himself out of it. He could have messaged ahead, but he was scared of what her response might be, so he grabbed his keys and jacket, ran down the stairs and headed out of the door.

As he approached her house, a sliver of worry ran down his spine. It seemed eerily still and quiet. He lifted his eyes to the window of Eve's room where the curtains were drawn across. He knew Rachel was still away but thought Eve might have contacted her.

Peering through the letterbox, he took note of the letters and junk mail on the mat before knocking lightly on the door and standing back to wait. He peered up again at the curtains that he was sure were hiding his girl.

After a couple of minutes, he knocked again but with no response. Moving along the wall of the house, he stood on his toes to look into the living room. It was deserted, and it seemed obvious to him that no one had been in there recently.

Sighing heavily, he considered walking through the alley to check the back door, but he knew it was always kept locked from the inside. Pulling out his phone, he dialled her number, and the familiar sound of her ringtone sang back at him from behind the door. His heart leapt and he peered again through the letterbox, the phone still pressed to his ear. It was then that he noticed Eve's bag dumped on the floor, her phone obviously inside it.

"Eve! Eve, baby, are you in there?"

Nothing.

Determined to get into the house, he rattled the door handle, but as suspected, it was locked. Thinking on his feet, he pulled his wallet out of his jeans and located his AA card. He had no idea if this was going to work, but he'd watched Charlie do it enough times when he had locked himself out of his mum's house after a night on the lash.

He wedged the card between the door and the frame, ensuring it was flush. Pressing it against the smallest part of the lock, he pushed and bent the card away from the door handle, waiting with his breath held. The latch slid back, and he lifted his head and closed his eyes in thanks. "Yes!"

Pushing the door open, he stood a moment in an attempt to steady his heartbeat. He needed to not scare her, but the need to make sure she was okay took control and he ran up the stairs and straight to her room his eyes remaining closed and breathing irregular as he gently pushed the door to her room open.

As he dared to lift his lids, the relief that washed over him at seeing her tiny body curled inside a cocoon of blankets was palpable. He stood for a moment, just watching the duvet rise and fall with her breathing and smiled.

She was here.

He moved forwards and sat on the floor near the head of the bed. Her face was covered with her hair, so he gently fingered the strands away so he could see her properly. She didn't stir to start with, her deep slumber sheltering her from stimuli, and he smoothed the back of his hand down her cheek, pulling in a shaky breath.

He savoured the moment, knowing that the second she opened her eyes, his world was going to come crashing down around his ears. A part of him considered leaving before it happened, but he had to face it sometime and now was as good a time as any.

Looking around the room, he concluded that she had been here since she'd arrived home two days before. He closed his eyes and shook his head, standing to his feet, leaving the room quietly to fill a glass of water.

Eve's eyelids attempted to flutter open, but the brass band playing in her head forced them to stay shut. She poked her tongue out and grimaced at the dry skin on her lips. Stretching her arms above her head, she rolled onto her back and pulled her body into a straight line, releasing all the tension that plagued her muscles. Lying there, eyes still closed, she focused her ears on the sound of running water. It didn't seem strange to her until it stopped and the sound of footsteps replaced it.

She sat bolt upright and gripped hold of the duvet with her fists, her eyes trained on the door to her bedroom.

What the fuck?

The sound of shoes on the stairs came next, and Eve froze, paralysed with fear. When the door moved, her mouth opened voluntarily, and she screamed.

"Jesus fucking Christ, Eve!" Billy jumped as he pushed the door open, spilling half of the water up his arm. He found his nerves again and walked towards the bed, Eve staring at him with wide eyes and a frown.

"How did…?" Her voice was croaky, and she cleared it. "How did you get in?"

Billy sat on the bed and handed her the glass that she almost snatched from his hand, gulping it down like it was amber nectar.

"Umm…"

She frowned over the glass at him as the cold liquid revived her.

"I kinda broke in."

Eve spat the water out, spraying it over Billy's face. "*What?*"

"I broke in. I was worried about you."

Sleeping for so long had temporarily buried the pain and she had woken up feeling like it was an old dream. But it was with Billy's words that reality and the events of the last week came rolling back into Eve's memory, a tsunami of hurt and betrayal swishing around her world, causing her to drop the glass and crumble, her face contorting with pain as. The tears still wouldn't come, but her body had lost all the fight in it and refused to support her.

"Oh my god, baby. Here, come here." He wrapped himself around her as he had done just a week ago on her bed at her mother's house, but this time with a strange weight lifted from his shoulders. The elephant was gone and he could mend her now.

"Billy… I…"

He squeezed his eyes shut, pressing his lips to the top of her head. "I know, beautiful girl." His whisper was barely there. "I know."

Eve allowed herself to be held tight and they sat in silence, wrapped around each other, Billy running his fingers gently over her skin and in her hair.

"We will get through this, baby. We will fix you. I promise."

***

THE NEXT COUPLE of days passed by in much the same way, except Billy barely left her side. He rang work and got some more time off, despite his boss' annoyance. He also rang Dobbo, who brought his guitar and some clothes round, and he set up home in Eve's bedroom.

As ever, Dobson was the perfect mate. He didn't pry: he just gave Billy understanding looks and a supportive slap on the back before leaving with a promise to pop round in a couple of days. Maureen called twice and dropped off some homemade dishes that could be heated in the microwave, and Billy would be eternally thankful to her for her kindness.

Eve didn't want to talk, and he was almost glad of it. They both knew the harrowing details, and there was not much more to say, although Billy knew that one day, she would need to open up—probably to a professional—in order to ensure that the wounds closed properly, even if they scarred. Instead, he left her to sleep.

There was so much literature surrounding the topic of sleep and its healing powers, and he would give his right arm if it were true. There were subtitles to articles such as *'Sleep Brightens Your Mood', 'Sleep Revs You Up', 'Sleep Heals You From the Inside Out'* and *'Sleep Makes Tough Decisions Easy'*. But his favourite of all, and the one that he hoped to God was the one bit they had got right, was *'Sleep Guards Your Heart'*.

There were times when Eve would sleep calmly, her head on his lap while he read or watched the TV with the sound turned low. There were others where she would stare

347

blankly at the walls while he tinkered away at the strings of his instrument. The worst times, though, were when she would wake up from a fitful sleep, screaming and lashing out, panicking if he was not right there. He tried his best to get her to eat, but nothing much would go or stay down, so he settled on keeping her fluids up.

On the third day, Billy made the decision to try and get Eve up and about, starting with a bath. He left her sleeping peacefully whilst he ran it. He sat on the edge of the tub as the water filled it and allowed his mind to drift home.

He hadn't spoken to his dad now for weeks, he'd heard nothing from him regarding the Christmas card and the money he sent him, and he was starting to feel the need to talk to him. Was there too much water under the broken bridges or was this something they could salvage? He'd seen a glimmer of the father he remembered from childhood on the odd occasion, but those moments were always tainted and ruined by the monster he had become.

He made a decision to go to see him after Eve's bath and try to speak to him. He couldn't remember the last time they had had an actual conversation that meant something and that didn't involve fists or venomous words.

Standing, he turned the taps off, settling his mind back to the matter in hand: how he was going to coax Eve out of bed and into the water.

As he entered the bedroom, she was sitting up. She was a mess.

"Hey, baby."

She turned her head slowly and looked up at him, blinking her big eyes at the man who was holding her in the palm of his hands.

"Hey."

"Feeling okay?"

She nodded noncommittally, and then changed her mind, shaking her head to the side, her face finally crumpling and allowing her to let go.

The tears came silently, but at least they came. He sat down next to her and took her hand, letting her empty herself of the emotion that had shut her off. The numbness was wearing off, and that was good. He allowed himself to smile a little to himself at this milestone. It meant she was feeling again, and he needed her to feel so that she could start living past this nightmare.

Helping her to her feet, he pulled her to him and enveloped her with all the love he could emanate from his bones. She lifted her arms, weak from lack of sustenance, hanging them limply around his waist as she sobbed into his chest.

After a few minutes, he leaned down and scooped her legs up and carried her to the bathroom. She stood quietly while he undressed her, watching him move around like he did this every day. He reached past her to the window ledge and grabbed her hairbrush. He gently ran it through her now greasy hair, and then held her hand so she could step into the bath.

After he had sponged her skin, he encouraged her to lean back to wet her hair so that he could wash it. Eve followed all his instructions silently, her heart slowing to a steady rhythm.

When she looked at him, the world seemed okay. She could do this with Billy at her side—she was sure of it. He loved her. She knew that. He wouldn't hurt her, and he would be patient. He was displaying proof of that right now, and she was in awe of him.

"Thank you."

"What, baby?" Billy tipped another jug of warm water on her hair as she leaned backwards.

"Thank you."

"Hey, you don't need to thank me. Anyhow, you were starting to stink." He winked at her and she allowed herself a little smile.

"I don't know why I shut you out. I can't do this without you." She sat up and folded her arms on the side of the bath, leaning her chin on top of them and looking up at him.

"Well you don't have to because I'm not going anywhere."

"Promise?"

Billy looked at her and stroked her cheek. "I do need to go and see my dad today."

Eve's eyes flitted back and forth across his face.

"But then I will be back. That I will promise, okay?"

She nodded, her eyes welling with tears. She swiped at them angrily.

"Hey." Billy frowned and kissed her forehead softly. "Don't cry. I'll be back. I promise. Let's get you out of this water before you shrivel up." He stood and held out a towel, wrapping it around her and handing her a smaller one for her hair. The pair walked back into the bedroom while Eve got ready. She wrapped the small towel, turban style, on her head and rummaged around in her drawers for something to wear.

Once she was dressed, Billy made her a drink and some toast.

"What's your favourite film?"

"What?"

"Your favourite film. What is it?"

Eve shrugged. "I've got loads of favourite films."

"So name one."

"True Romance."

"Great choice." Billy opened Eve's laptop and typed in the web browser. Within a few minutes, he had rented True Romance and had it loaded up ready to play. "By the time this has finished and you have eaten this toast, I will be nearly back, okay? So, settle under those covers and show me that beautiful smile."

Eve rolled her eyes at him and took a bite from the toast. It was like a brick in her mouth after refusing food for so long.

Billy kissed the top of her head, grabbed his coat and walked to the door. "See you later, beautiful girl." He winked, and then he left.

CHAPTER
twenty seven

Song For Zula - Phosphorescent

THE VAN WAS parked outside the house, and Billy approached slowly, his hands curled tight in his pockets. He wasn't even sure if he was doing the right thing, and his own words reverberated in the back of his head.

"We are done…"

But of course, those words were empty. As he had said on so many occasions, this was still his dad, and he needed to hold on to something. Without him, he was just Billy. Yes, he had his grandparents, but when would those bridges be rebuilt? Yes, he had Dobbo and Maureen whom he loved dearly, but they weren't his family.

He was missing a sense of belonging. He didn't belong with his mother. She didn't have a clue what was going on with his life, and even when he told her and she listened and nodded and was pleased for him, it only had to be repeated the next time he saw her. What was the point?

He didn't belong with his father, either, but he was so fucking desperate to be loved unconditionally by someone that he could not give up. Yes, Eve loved him—he didn't doubt that for a second—but that was a different kind of love. That was an all-consuming, can't-live-without-you kind of love that could break or fall apart at any moment. The love of a mother or father was everlasting, right? So there had to be something deep down inside of his father that he could retrieve. If he dug deep enough, maybe he could pull out that slow burning love of a father for his son.

As he neared the house, the front door flew open, stopping Billy in his tracks.

Neville was drunk.

He fell into the wall and his foot slipped, causing him to tumble down the front step.

"Fucking bastard." He was muttering under his breath and steadied himself, digging around in his pocket and pulling out the van keys.

Billy frowned, and without another thought, edged towards him. "Dad?"

Neville's head swung lazily towards Billy's voice and he sneered. "What the fuck do you want?"

"Where are you going?"

"Leave me alone, Bill."

Billy stepped a little closer, being careful not to move too quickly. "You're not thinking of driving are you? Give me the keys, Dad. You're drunk."

Neville ignored him and proceeded down the path, unable to put one foot in front of the other in a straight line.

Billy breathed in and out loudly through his nose, walking confidently up the street this time.

His father stood there, swaying slightly, searching the

bunch of keys in his hands for the right one before moving forwards to the gate. He looked up, seemingly a little surprised to see Billy there in front of him.

"Dad, give me the keys." He held his hand out over the gate and watched his father, his eyes steely and determined despite the fear in his heart.

"Get out of my way, Bill." Nev continued to move forwards, reaching his hand out and grabbing the top of the gate. He pushed, but Billy's grip was stronger and the gate didn't budge. "I'm warning you, Billy. Get the fuck out of my way."

"I'm not letting you drive, Dad. Give me the keys and I'll open the gate. I'll drive you."

Neville grunted and pushed harder, causing Billy's elbow to buckle slightly. He regained control, but in turn raised the bar on his father's drunken rage. His eyes clouded over and he grimaced before swinging his shoulder back and smashing his fist into his son's nose.

"Fuck!" Billy dropped his hand from the top of the gate to grab his blood-covered face, bending double and wincing with the pain that rang like a cymbal around his head.

Neville took the opportunity to push the gate open, but Billy was still adamant. The pent-up anger of years of taking his shit was well and truly loose. He stood up and stepped forwards without another thought, no idea what his next move would be, and grabbed at his dad's arm. Pushing his face into his father's, he spat out the words that were on his tongue. "You're not fucking driving, Dad. Look at you! You're a fucking mess. What is *wrong* with you?"

Neville yanked away but lost his balance and fell into the hedge, flailing to try to steady himself. "Bill, get the fuck

354

away from me. I don't know why you've come back. I told you: you leave, you don't get to come back." He lashed his arm out again, but Billy was on his toes this time and was able to get a hold of it.

"I'm not letting you drive, Dad. I'm not letting you kill yourself. Get a fucking grip and give me the keys."

Whether it was anger at Billy, anger at himself, dormant and unresolved grief for his wife or just the whiskey in his blood, something surged through Neville and gave him the bodily strength he needed to push Billy from him and throw him to the ground.

"I said leave me alone, Bill." He walked away from him towards the van.

Billy got to his feet and ran at his father, attempting to wrestle the keys from him, but Neville had already twisted the key and had his hand on the door handle. There was no way Billy was strong enough to stop him from getting in, so in a moment of panic, he ran around the other side and climbed through the passenger door, throwing himself into the seat and grabbing the seatbelt as the engine roared to life.

There was red mist and the groggy bravado that alcohol brings, and Neville dropped his foot on the accelerator before Billy had time to slam the door shut.

The small back streets of York, lined with row upon row of terraced houses, were not cut out for the weaving and speeding of vehicles. The twenty miles per hour speed limit was more than generous, but the breakneck speed at which the white van hurtled down Elton Terrace went unnoticed by the residents tucked up inside their houses. It went unnoticed by the little old lady who turned the corner to enter the Spar. It went unnoticed by the window cleaner who struggled to reach the top window on number sixty-five and had to climb back down to extend his ladder.

It went unnoticed by Eve who was curled up asleep in her bed, waiting for Billy's return.

The young boy with the blonde hair and freckles stopped in the middle of the pavement to fix the chain on his bike. He lifted his leg over the crossbar and crouched down to see where it had come off.

Reaching under the pedal, his head snapped up sharply at the screech of tires on the road behind him, and he twisted to see what was happening.

The long, continuous beeping of a car horn was quickly followed by the sound of metal crunching against metal, and his mouth dropped open as he watched the silver Mini Cooper skid across the road and spin onto its side as it smashed into the front corner of the white van.

Wide-eyed, the boy slowly got to his feet. "Coooooooool!"

House doors flew open and fraught women flung their hands to their mouths as they took in the wreckage before them.

A voice from one of them eventually cut through the stunned silence. "Someone call an ambulance!"

The boy hooked his chain back on, climbed on his seat and pushed away, never once taking his eyes from the crash.

It was the noise of the sirens that filtered into Billy's consciousness first. The sharp pain in his head followed quickly, and he reached his fingers tentatively to an intense throbbing on the left side. He winced as he realised he could barely lift his arm, the discomfort in his neck and shoulder stopping him. He wasn't sure he wanted to open his eyes as he had little recollection of where he was or who he was with. However, the sound of a door opening next to him and an unfamiliar voice urged him to try. His eyelashes were sticky with blood, and the sunlight that streamed in through the windows burned into his retinas. Opening his mouth to speak, he went to turn his head to work out who it was that was asking him questions, but stopped immediately, the sharp pain a hindrance.

A tall blonde in a green uniform was standing very close to him, her face calm and kind. "Hey there. My name's Jo. Can you hear me?"

He attempted to nod but gave up the idea quickly.

"Okay, good. What's your name, buddy?"

He blinked a couple of times and then opened his mouth to speak. Nothing came out so he coughed to clear his throat "Um, Taylor."

"Okay, Taylor, you've been in a road traffic accident. Can you tell me where it hurts?"

"It's Billy. Sorry. Billy Taylor."

"Okay. Can you tell me if you are hurting anywhere, Billy?"

He tried again to reach up to his neck but it was too painful. "My neck. All up my neck. And my head."

She ducked away. "Harry, neck pain. Come and assist please."

The back doors of the van opened and someone else got in behind him.

"This is Harry. He's one of the fire crew and he's just going to help keep you safe while we check your injuries, okay? Harry, this is Billy."

"Hey, Billy. I'm just going to hold your head still, okay?" Harry placed his hands either side of Billy's face over his ears and waited for Jo to continue.

"I'm just going to get something to keep your neck still and safe. Harry will stay here with you."

"I'm here."

Jo disappeared again and returned a few seconds later with a cervical collar. She fixed it around his neck, double checking the fastenings. It was uncomfortable, and Billy closed his eyes, leaning his body back against the seat. Everything was a whirr of activity around him, but he found it difficult to focus on any one thing. He was aware of commotion and busyness on the road outside the driver's side, but he couldn't see what it was. There was someone else in his peripheral vision wearing a green uniform and there was hurried conversation. He picked out the words laryngeal mask and defib. He wanted to ask questions but he wasn't sure which ones.

His head was fuzzy, and he didn't quite remember why he was here. When the term CPR was mentioned, it sparked something inside of him, but he wasn't sure he even wanted to know.

"I need to do a quick check for any more injuries now. I'm going to run my hands over your body. If it hurts, try to let me know, okay?"

Billy blinked and grimaced in acknowledgement, and Jo gently ran her gloved hands over his skin, starting with his head, gently applying pressure. He winced as she touched the left side of his temple.

"That hurts?"

"Yeah."

"No bleeding, but you're growing a nice egg there." She grinned at him. Her blue eyes sparkled with fun, and Billy smiled back, confused at the juxtaposition hovering in the air.

"Right. Everything else seems in order up here, but you have a lot of dry blood on your face. Does your nose hurt?"

Billy almost laughed. "Yeah. Like a mother fucker." He finished the sentence with his eyes trained on the road in front of the van as the memory returned to him.

He hesitated, his eyes clouding over before he continued. "It's from when my dad smashed his fist into my face because I tried to stop him from drink driving." Saying it out loud like that brought the absurdity of the situation to the surface and he let out an incredulous chuckle. "Where is my dad, anyway?"

Jo's eyes flicked to the fireman in the back "Your dad is being seen to by my colleague, okay, Billy?" She turned to Harry. "Not sure it's hit him yet."

Harry nodded, and Jo turned back to Billy.

Her other colleague appeared at her side and urged her away from the van. He spoke in a low voice that Billy couldn't decipher and then Jo walked away. She came back with a large plastic sheet and climbed in the back next to Harry. Glancing at him, she nodded towards the door. "High mechanism of injury."

Harry nodded and got out of the van, and Jo scooted over behind Billy. All this technical talk was confusing him, and he just wanted to get out and get back to Eve.

"Okay, buddy, we need to get you out of the vehicle as safely and as easily as possible. In a few minutes, the firemen are going to remove the roof of the van using what we call 'the jaws of life'. I am going to hold this plastic sheeting over us both to avoid any loose debris attacking you. It's not very pleasant, but it will be over before you know it."

He wasn't sure why they couldn't just let him get out of the car. He looked up out of the front windscreen and watched as a fire fighter stood pointing a hose at the van.

"He's there in case of any emergencies. Nothing to worry about."

Billy's vision was a little blurry and the woozy feel of sleep washed over him a couple of times. Harry walked towards the car with a contraption resembling a pneumatic drill but with a giant claw on the end, followed by more firemen. A flurry of movement around the van had Billy following the men with his eyes, but Jo continued talking to him and distracted him.

"They're going to cut the A posts, the one near the windscreen, and then the B posts just here." She pointed to the column by the door. "They will do this on both sides and then cut at the back there. The roof will come clean off and we can then get you out safely." As she spoke, the fireman attacked the metal of the car with the jaws. As it bent out of shape, the windows began to smash, bits of glass flying inwards towards them, the noise of them hitting the plastic confusing him even further.

"Can't I just get out now? I need to get out."

"We will have you out in no time. Hang in there."

It didn't take long, and once the roof had been removed, an extrication device was applied to Billy to help splint his spinal column. The other man dressed in green arrived at the side of Billy, along with two firemen, and slid a spinal board behind him. Jo got out of the back of the van and helped to slide Billy up the board and out onto a stretcher.

"Good job, buddy. We'll get you in the ambulance and

then I'll double check for other injuries, okay?"

Billy still wasn't saying much. He couldn't understand what all the fuss was about.

Once in the ambulance, the extrication device was removed, and Jo cut off Billy's clothes.

"Whoa, whoa, whoa… any need for this? I just need to get home and sorted. My girlfriend is waiting for me."

"Try to lie still, Billy. I just need to do another check for any injuries now that you're more easily accessible."

After a thorough check, she was satisfied that there was nothing more to attend to. She took his pulse and blood pressure. A bright light was shone into his eyes and his respiratory rate was checked.

"GCS is 12."

The other green clad bloke nodded. "Yeah, thought it might be a bit low. He's not quite with it, is he?" He handed a clipboard to Jo and she scribbled something on it.

"Okay, we're good."

The hospital bed was uncomfortable, and as Billy lay flat on it, forcing himself to stay still, he found it hard to concentrate on what Dobbo was saying. The events leading up to the crash were trickling back into his memory now and the reality of the situation had caught up with him.

Dobbo was pacing the floor, his hand on the back of his neck as he hissed into the phone at whoever he was cross with. Inside, Billy's body felt hollow. It was as if someone had sliced him open, removed every organ, every blood vessel and nerve and then sewn him back up again. For a moment, he was actually convinced that that was what had happened. There was no feeling there, just a dull numbness.

He didn't dare close his eyes in case he saw, for the

hundredth time, the Mini come hurtling towards them in slow motion, the horror on the face of the young girl who was at the wheel. The noises still rang in his ears: the crunching, the screeching, the sound of his own voice shouting out, screaming at his father to stop. He'd tried to reach out and turn the wheel, but it had been too late.

He wiggled his toes to check they were still there and forced his mind to return to the present, and followed his friends with his eyes and tried to work out who he was talking to.

His head hurt and he was tired, but sleep wasn't an option. With sleep would come nightmares that he wasn't sure he could handle. Too much fucked up activity in his recent memory would be sure to play out in the most frightening of ways behind his eyelids.

Ending the call, Dobbo came to sit on the chair next to the bed. "Sorry, buddy. That was work. How you feeling?"

"Grand."

He smiled sadly. "I've rung Mum. She's going to come round after she's finished cleaning. She'll bring you some clothes and toiletries and stuff. Have they said how long you have to stay here?"

"For observation. However long that is."

Dobbo nodded. "So, umm. Have you asked them?"

Billy gently shook his head. He didn't dare ask them. In his heart of hearts, he was too fucking scared of his reaction either way. There was no perfect scenario. There was no ending to this that was particularly happy, so he decided to lie there in blissful ignorance for a while longer.

"What about the girl?"

Billy shook his head. "Don't know."

Learning forwards onto his thighs, Dobbo lowered

his head. "What a knobhead. Sorry, pal, but Jesus Christ."

Billy stared ahead, agreeing silently. "Have you rung Eve?"

"I tried, but there was no answer. Left a message."

"She'll be sleeping. I promised her I would be back, and she won't even know I'm not."

"Not meaning to pry or anything, but what's going on with her, mate?"

Billy let out an exasperated sigh. "It's fucking complicated, dude. I…" He squeezed his eyes tight before moving them to look at Dobo. "She has just found out, after thirteen years, that she was sexually abused when she was little, by her uncle." He wasn't sure sharing it was the best idea, but getting it out of his throat was a relief.

"Sh-i-i-t." Dobbo sat up, his eyes wide. "Serious?"

"Yup."

"Jesus, I'm sorry. That's fucked up."

"Yup." He lifted his good arm and scratched the side of his nose. "She needs me and look at me."

Dobson clenched his back teeth. "With all due respect, Bill, you've just been in a car crash. I think she can cope for a couple of days, don't you?"

As Billy opened his mouth to speak, the door to his room opened and two police officers entered with the nurse.

"He needs to rest, so just ten minutes."

The male officer nodded and smiled in thanks, glancing over at Dobbo, who needed no instruction.

He leaned over and took Billy's hand, squeezing it. "I'll catch you a bit later. I'll wait for Mum in the reception area."

The male officer stood at the end of the bed and smiled sympathetically as the female officer sat in the chair next to his bed.

"Hi, Billy."

He nodded and cleared his throat. "Hi."

"I'm Detective Inspector Jackson, and this is my colleague DI Davies. We need to ask you some questions regarding the accident you were in today."

Billy nodded again, his eyes trained on a black smudge on the wall. He was not ready for this. He had hoped he could have another day before he found out so he had time to mentally prepare and practice his reactions. His heartbeat was irregular and his mouth dry.

"Could you describe for us the events leading up to the crash in as much detail as you can remember."

He coughed again, and DI Jackson passed him a plastic cup of lukewarm water, which he sipped on.

"Take your time."

Billy pushed his hands against the mattress to sit up a bit. "I'd gone round to see my dad. We'd not spoken in a few weeks and I wanted to clear the air. Our relationship has always been… antagonistic."

"Go on."

"As I approached the house, he was coming out of the front door and it was very clear to me that he had been drinking. As I walked closer, his intention to get in the van and drive it became evident and I tried to discourage him."

"How did you try to discourage him?"

"I suggested to him that he give me the keys to the van and said that I wouldn't allow him to drive while under the influence."

"Mmhm. And then what happened?" DI Davis scribbled in his notepad.

"He ignored my requests and continued to move

towards the van. I stood in front of the gate to try to stop him from getting past and he punched me." Billy absentmindedly lifted his hand to touch his nose. He coughed again. "Anyway, there was a bit of a tussle, and I ended up on the floor. He got in the van and I just acted on impulse. I got in the car with him. He was speeding. He put his foot down in a twenty zone and it wasn't long after that…" He closed his eyes again, trying to block out the images that were flickering like an old movie in front of him.

"Okay. That's fine, Billy. Thank you."

"Is he dead?" The words rushed out of his mouth without much thought, and he clenched his back teeth at the alien feel of them on his lips.

DI Jackson flicked her eyes up to her colleague who nodded at her. She reached out and took hold of Billy's hand and squeezed it in much the same way that Dobbo had done only minutes earlier.

"I'm sorry, Billy. He was killed on impact."

Billy nodded and waited for it to come. Waited for what he was not sure of, but something was bound to follow.

CHAPTER
twenty eight

Out Of The Dark – Dia Frampton

WAKING UP IN almost darkness, disorientation the only feeling she could put her finger on, Eve sat up and looked around the room. A sliver of fading daylight lay across the end of the bed, indicating that she'd slept all day, comforted in the knowledge that Billy would be back to sit with her.

As her eyes became accustomed to the dark, she realised something wasn't quite right.

It was too quiet.

"Billy?" She felt the bed beside her. The sheets were cold—he hadn't been back. "Billy?" Dropping her feet to the floor, she padded out to the bathroom and peered inside.

It was empty.

Utter panic and desperation filled her up now. She flicked the light on in her bedroom, swallowing the feeling of nausea as she grabbed for her phone. Turning it on, she saw the missed call and the voicemail from Dobbo. Pressing play, she held it to her ear, and squinted against the sound of her heart pounding in her ears to try to hear the message.

The only words she caught at first were 'Billy' and 'accident', and her face crumpled with emotion. "No. No, no, no, no, no…" She pressed play again, dropping her phone from her scrabbling fingers and trying hard to block out the thumping of her heart. She bent to retrieve it and sat down on the edge of the bed, staring at the floor as the message played again.

Hey, Eve, it's Dobo. Listen, I'm at the hospital with Bill. There's been… well there's been an accident. He's okay, so don't panic. He's got to be kept in for observation, but… anyway… just letting you know so you can come down, or whatever. I'll speak to you later. Don't worry. He's fine.

Eve hung up. A new wave of fear swept across her back, and she sat motionless, eyes wide open with a buzzing of hopelessness niggling at her ears.

All of the events from the past fortnight whirled above her head—a murder of black crows, relentless and unforgiving. She couldn't do this alone. She needed to get to the hospital but couldn't bear the thought of being in a place like that with so much misery and hurt.

Why hadn't he come back?

She looked back down at her phone and scrolled to Billy's number. She held it to her ear again and listened to it ring. It clicked to voicemail.

Hi, this is Billy - you know what to do.

She hung up. And then she dialled again.

Hi this is Billy - you know what to do.

She hung up again and stared at the picture of him next to his name.

367

As she looked at it, the phone began to vibrate in her hand and the picture changed to Dobbo. She jumped and dropped the phone again.

Picking it up quickly, she slid her finger across the screen. "Hello?"

"Hi, Eve. It's Dobbo. Bill asked if I'd give you a ring and see if you're okay."

"Where is he?" Her voice came out strained and cracked, and she swallowed in a bid to dissuade the tears.

"Did you not get my voicemail?"

She paused before answering, gathering herself together and remembering the message she had listened to. She took a deep breath. "Yeah… Is he okay?"

"He's fine. Just resting. He's got some neck pain and some bruising, I think, but he will live. He is a tough cookie."

Eve smiled through her distress and nodded. "He is."

"Umm… There's something else. I need to let you know that… well, it was a car accident. When he went to see his dad, he ended up trying to stop him from drink driving. He got in the car with him to try to persuade him to stop, and… That's when it happened, and well, his dad didn't make it. He was killed on impact."

Eve's hand flew to her mouth as she gasped, her eyes wide. There were no words on her tongue, and she sat there, trying to swallow the facts she had just been handed.

"So anyway, I rang to see if you were okay and if you wanted a lift to the hospital. I could come get you. I know it's just round the corner, but…"

Eve nodded, her hand still across her mouth.

"Eve?"

Nothing.

"Hello? Eve?"

She snapped back on. "Sorry, yes. Yes, please." She glanced at the clock on her wall. It was six pm. "I can be ready in about fifteen minutes. Is that okay?"

"Sure. I'll wait outside. See you then."

Eve hung up and sat cross-legged on the bed, unable to move.

It was all fucked up. Every bit of everything was a mess and she wasn't sure how much more heartache she could take. Someone was sitting up there laughing at her and the people she cared for, plotting the next thing to break them all.

Numb and shaking, she pulled on her hoodie and grabbed her phone and keys. She piled her hair on top of her head and made her way downstairs, slipping into her Docs as she passed them. Running the cold tap, she stared out of the kitchen window, her mind racing back just a couple of months to when life was good, simpler, less painful...

How had things gone so wrong, so quickly?

The sound of a car horn jolted her from her thoughts, and she left the house, locking the door behind her.

Sitting silently in the passenger seat as Dobbo drove them to the hospital, she only realised when they got halfway there that she hadn't given thought to the fact she was in a car.

"You okay?" He glanced across at her. He wasn't to let on that he knew, but it was so obvious to him that she had had the life literally scooped out of her. Her skin was pale and her eyes lifeless. The sparkle that always seemed to whip around in the air wherever she was near just wasn't there.

She turned her head slowly and nodded, a sad smile

369

pulling at her lips.

They arrived moments later, the pair of them walked into the ward, Eve nervous with her arms folded across her chest, struggling to keep her cool. It wasn't that the hospital was teeming with people that she felt the need to run from: it was the sense of loss that seemed to ooze from the walls—that smell that got stuck in the back of your throat and told tales of death and disease.

There were waiting rooms that were dotted with couples and families and drunken 'tom-foolers' with dried blood smeared across their broken hands and faces. It wasn't the ideal place to be in, but her heart ached to see Billy, so she pushed on through, eager to hear his voice and feel his skin on hers.

Prepared for the worst, she was pleasantly surprised as they pulled the curtain aside and she saw him awake, with just a neck brace and a bumped head.

"Hey."

Billy turned his head towards her voice. "Hey, baby." He held his hand out and she moved forwards quickly and took it, sitting on the edge of the plastic-backed chair.

"I'll…" Dobbo thumbed behind him. "I'll go grab a coffee. Anyone want anything?"

Eve smiled up at him and shook her head.

"No thanks, buddy. Cheers for bringing her." He looked back at Eve, taking in her complexion and the plethora of emotions that danced a funeral dance in her eyes. "You okay?"

She nodded. "You?"

"Yeah, I'm grand." He smiled and motioned for her to come closer.

She dragged the chair and leaned over, pressing her

cheek to his hand. "Look at us. We are a mess." More tears welled and fell, and she wiped them away quickly.

"Hey, we'll get there."

She sat up and looked him in the eye. "I hope so. I really hope so."

CHAPTER
twenty nine

Peppermint – Say Lou Lou
Blame – Denai Moore

BILLY HAD BEEN out of hospital for a week. He had fallen into a dark hole since his release. The horror of the present had slowly seeped into him, and it was drowning him. The post-mortem had fucked with his mind. The thought of them cutting his father open and seeing his heart—the heart he had not revealed to his own son for years—became a bit of an obsession.

His and Eve's love had become needy and desperate in the days after the crash. It was all-consuming, and they hadn't been able to see through the thickness of it in order to start living again. 'I love you' seemed to be the only sustenance that they'd needed. They'd fed off it, and each time it was whispered or growled or screamed, their bellies felt full and they could carry on.

The pair had been flailing around in their own hurt and grief that fed off the pain of the other like a parasite. During the day, they'd moved almost like zombies through the house, going through the motions of daily life, clinging to one another when one of them remembered and broke down. At night, they'd lain side by side, sometimes with their bodies entwined, sometimes with their backs facing each other as they tried to protect one another from their hurt and pain. They had kissed with a fervent hunger, devouring each other with an urgency that had not been there before. They had made love into the early hours of the mornings, and they had fucked, hard, almost aggressively, falling into each other in a mess of sweat and tears, desperate to feel only each other and block out the noise.

Crouching down, Billy kissed the tips of his fingers, pressing them against the wood of the coffin before standing and shoving his hands in his suit trouser pockets.

"Rest in peace now, Dad." He rolled his eyes at the clichéd saying, but it seemed the most fitting for the moment. Neville had lived his life in turmoil, unable to grapple back and be the man his wife would be proud of. Now he could sleep. Now he was rid of the nightmares and the sadness, and he didn't have to try anymore.

The only other funeral he had ever been to had been his Grandma's. His Grandad on his father's side had died when he was too little to go. Neville had no other family. He'd been an only child. Most of his close family had passed on, and Billy hadn't invited anyone else.

After struggling to find the words he needed, he had sat in front of his mum the day before and watched her face crumple as she absorbed the news that her husband was dead. He'd spared her the finer details, explaining that it was an accident, a simple error in judgment, no one's fault… He hadn't been able to bear to watch her deal with the fact that the man she'd fallen in love with was an abusive drunk. She hadn't needed to know.

He moved forwards and wiped a tear from her cheek.

"It's okay, Mum. You'll wake up tomorrow and you won't even remember I've been here."

He smiled sadly and kissed the top of her head. "I'm going away for a bit, Mum. Got some stuff to sort out. I'll be back before you know it, though, okay?"

But Jenny had gone again.

Walking away from the graveside, Billy stood alone at the cemetery gates, looking back up the hill. His eyes scanned the horizon for some sort of sign, a message—hell, even a thunderbolt—but it didn't come. A weary sigh escaped his lungs as he turned, his head low, and walked back to his car.

Gripping the steering wheel tightly, he rolled his plans around his head for the hundredth time.

He'd lost. He'd lost the fight to hold on and was falling apart internally. If he stayed, life would go on as normal, but he didn't want that. He didn't want to trundle along with everything around him reminding him of what a mess it all was. He needed something new.

Defeated, he rested his forehead on his hands and closed his eyes.

He had no idea how long he'd been there, and it wasn't until the passenger side door opened that he really registered that he hadn't moved.

"Hey."

"Hey, dude. What are you doing here?"

"I figured you might need a bit of support." Dobbo gifted him a can of beer and smiled a sad smile.

Billy took it and pulled at the ring on the top, tipping the cold liquid into his mouth, but he stopped short, shaking his head. "No. I can't. I can't go down this route." He handed it back to Dobbo who nodded with a quiet understanding. He grabbed Billy around the neck and pulled him to him, squeezing gently, conveying all the unspoken words that wouldn't come because of male bravado and trying to stay strong for his buddy.

Billy looked off into the middle distance, his mind a whirr. "Mate, my body is numb, yet every nerve ending stings with such a deep fucking sense of loss that I feel like ripping my skin off."

Dobbo nodded, unsure how to respond, and the pair sat in peaceful silence for a while.

"So, what is next for you, mate? What does the rest of your life have in store for you?"

Billy pursed his lips and flicked his eyes to his friend. "I've been asked to go gigging in London with Eboracum Rain."

A bubble of excitement rose inside of Dobbo as he turned to look at him. "That's awesome."

Billy smiled briefly, but the flexing muscles in his jaw quickly replaced it. "I know, and…"

Dobbo stayed silent, waiting for Billy to finish the sentence that he hoped was already rehearsed and ready to come out.

"I'm going to go."

Filling his cheeks with air and letting it out slowly, trying to disguise the grin that was pulling at his mouth, Dobbo replied. "That, mate, is the best fucking news I have heard in a long fucking time." He clapped him on the back. "It will do you the world of good. You'll have a fucking ball."

"Yeah."

"Wow. What an opportunity."

Billy nodded, dipping his head and allowing the grin to return as the prospect of playing to live crowds for two months continued to sink in.

"I am really looking forward to it."

"Have you told Eve?"

And the smile was gone again. Billy shook his head. "Nope." He popped the 'p' at the end and glanced across at Dobbo, holding his breath.

"Okay, but you're going to tell her, right?"

Billy reached out and curled a tight fist around the steering wheel and squinted off to the hillside before releasing the most painful words he had ever spoken. "I don't want her to come."

Eyes wide, Dobbo raised his brow. "Jesus." He sucked air through his teeth and winced. "Good luck with that then."

Still unsure about his intentions, Billy pursed his lips and nodded. "I can't see her again, mate."

"Huh?"

"I can't see her again. If I look in those eyes again, I won't leave. And I need to leave. I need to get the fuck out of here and get sorted. I've got a packed bag and my guitar in the boot and a wallet full of cash."

"What?" He sat up and turned his body to face Billy.

"I'm leaving today."

"Shit, man."

"Hmmm. I was going to come to see you after this riveting affair." He waved a hand nonchalantly at the window towards the cemetery. "But obviously you're here now. I, umm…" Leaning over Dobbo's legs, he flipped open the glove compartment, pulling out a white envelope. "I need you to go and see her for me. Give her this." He held it out and Dobbo took it from him, fingering the envelope and turning it over in his hands, already dreading the imminent conversation with Eve.

"Sure. Course I will."

"Thanks, bud."

"So, what made you decide?" He studied Billy's face as he waited for his reply.

"To be honest? It was you that kinda sparked off the thought process when you told me she could manage by herself while I was in hospital. It didn't really register until I got out, though. There I was, lying in a hospital bed because of my drunken fucking father—my drunken father who'd shown me no love for nearly five years and who had just killed himself because he wasn't man enough to face his grief and the grief of his son—with a mother who didn't know who the hell I was, grandparents who didn't speak to me for months on end, and nothing much to show for any of it… yet I was still worrying about someone else."

Dobbo nodded. He wanted so much more for his friend and was pleased that he had come to this conclusion by himself, albeit with a little shove. He didn't need to respond. Everything had been said now and it was time to lighten the mood.

"So…" He turned to his best mate and punched his arm playfully. "You're not gonna forget the little people when you're rich and famous, right?"

"Ha! I don't think it's going to be that easy."

"Just remember where you came from, eh? So, are you driving down?"

"No. I'm going to get a train. No point having a car in London. We'll be travelling round in a van together and bunking wherever we can find a space on the floor, I think." His mouth pulled into a smile.

"Sounds immense! What time do you leave?"

Billy scratched the side of his cheek and pressed his head back firmly on the headrest. He flicked his eyes to his friend and raised his eyebrows. "In two hours."

***

IT WAS THE first day Eve had been without Billy since his release. She'd wanted to go with him to his father's funeral, to support him, but also so she was near him, but he had been adamant that it was something he needed to do alone.

Rachel was due back from Japan that afternoon, and Eve was determined to make the place look a bit more like home rather than the morgue that it felt like to her. Pottering around the house, she mindlessly straightened cushions and washed the odd plate and cup that they had left lying around. Without him there, she wasn't sure how life worked. He'd been an unusually long time, and uneasiness was settling in the pit of her stomach.

She'd had some 'Welcome Home' balloons delivered to the house and was deciding where to put them when the doorbell rang.

Walking nervously to it, she opened the door a crack.

"Hey, Eve. Can I come in?"

"Um, sure." Eve's eyes flickered over Dobbo's face, a wave of nausea washing over her as she stood awkwardly, waiting to hear whatever it was that was going to come out of his mouth.

He lifted his arm, rubbing the back of his neck and

squinting at the ceiling.

"Spit it out, Paul." She was not in the mood for games and already knew it wasn't good news.

Dobbo sighed and reached into his back pocket, pulling out the envelope that Billy had handed him not two hours before.

Eve eyed it like it was poison and backed away. "What is it? I don't want it. Take it away with you and leave, please."

"Eve…"

"No. No. I don't want it. You can take it back. Where is he?"

"Eve… I can't…"

Her face contorted and she leaned forward, her voice echoing down the hallway. "Where the fuck is he, Paul?" She moved towards him, shoving past him and slipping into her boots. She spun around and pushed at his chest. "Tell me where he is, or so help me God…"

"He's gone, Eve."

"Gone where?"

Dobbo bowed his head. "He's at the train station."

"Why? Where is he going? Why does he need to get a train?"

"Eve, you gotta let him go."

"I said where. *Where* is he going? Tell me where he is going."

He had never seen this side of her before, venomous and angry. "London. He's going to London." He sighed and bowed his head. She needed to know. "He doesn't want you to go after him, Eve."

Fear.

It was the only thing she could feel now. Flickering back and forth across his face, her eyes begged him to help

379

her, but he just stood there, uncomfortable.

At first, her voice was quiet, pleading. "Paul, please?"

Torn between being loyal and caving because she looked so broken, he shrugged. "I'm sorry, Eve. I really am."

Charged with the need to survive, she switched into fight mode. Leaning forward, she snatched the envelope from his hands and stuffed it her bag as she grabbed it from the floor. She opened the front door and turned to Dobo. "Thanks for nothing."

Balloons still clutched tightly in her hand, she ran.

She ran for her life.

***

"EVE!" DOBBO'S VOICE carried across the station and Eve swiped the back of her hand across her eyes in an attempt to dispel the tears, her heart beating fast and her breathing irregular. She spun towards the sound, the string from the balloons twisting gently around her arm as they moved with her.

Why was he even here? Why had he bothered to follow?

She blinked and breathed in shakily giving Billy's best friend a look that said, 'how could you?' and then turned back around at the last minute, walking towards the barriers to the platforms, flashing her newly purchased ticket at the guard.

The guard nodded, letting her through, and she ran into the hub of the place.

"Eve, wait!"

The large, busy station was buzzing with travellers arriving and leaving, lovers embracing and shoppers rushing to catch the train home. Small children lingered behind mothers with frayed tempers, and a gaggle of teenagers giggled and preened themselves. Eve lifted her head up to the departures board, scanning her squinting eyes quickly across the bright orange lettering.

There were trains departing to every city she could imagine, but she could not find the word she was looking for.

Huddles of families and friends sat relaxed outside the pop-up eateries and coffee houses, their animated chatter that hurt her ears interjected with the faceless voice that announced the departures and arrivals.

The train to London was not mentioned.

Eve's blue light switched on and she twirled around in the empty space she was occupying, looking for something, someone, anything that could tell her what she wanted to find out. Her ears buzzed and her old friends Fear and Anxiety began to tiptoe up her spine.

Eve didn't register that she had dropped to her knees, her hands clawing inside her bag for her phone, the mantra that had picked up pace in the last few minutes playing over and over.

"Please. Please. Please. Please."

She unlocked the home screen, her fingers shaking, and scrolled to find his number. Hitting the green button, she moved the phone to her ear, squeezing her eyes shut tight as she listened to the dial tone.

Dobbo caught her up and stood over her. "Eve, babe, what are you doing?"

She tried to speak, but nothing came out.

He bent his knees and squatted beside her, reaching out to move her hair from her face.

Eve's wide eyes stared at him, questioning him, accusing him.

Hi, this is Billy - you know what to do.

He ducked his head and pinched the bridge of his nose before looking back at her face.

"Eve, he's gone."

She dragged the phone slowly down the side of her face, her eyes still wide, staring at Dobbo and trying to process the information. Her hand shook, and even though she was kneeling, her legs could not support her any longer and her body slipped to the side. She couldn't feel the pain in her knuckles as she gripped tightly to the balloons she'd forgotten she was holding. She couldn't feel the shiver across her bare skin in the cool building. The aching in her feet from running for the first time in months was insignificant compared to the pain that shot through her chest and the breaking of her heart.

Dobbo moved forwards quickly to catch her, her breathing now shallow, the tears falling freely.

"Eve, breathe, babe."

"Eve?" A familiar voice jolted him, and he looked up to see Rachel running across the tiles to where he and Eve sat with pedestrians weaving past, glancing at the spectacle on the floor. Rachel crouched down in front of her and pulled her into a hug, smoothing her hair and rubbing her back. Getting off the train, she had tried to ring Eve but only got the answering machine.

"Shh. Come on, dude. Shh." She kissed the top of Eve's head and flicked her eyes towards Dobbo, who sat motionless, watching the scene. She gave him a tight smile that asked a thousand questions as he watched on sympathetically. She mouthed to him as she continued to calm Eve down. "What. The. Fuck?"

He frowned at her, no idea why she wasn't in the loop

here.

"Excuse me." A station guard had walked over and was about to release a spiel, but Dobbo stood up quickly and faced him, interjecting before he had chance to say anything else. "Sorry, mate. Any chance we can get a glass of water? We'll try and move her over to the benches."

"Umm." The guard looked nervously across the station and coughed into his hand. "Sure. I'll be back in a sec."

Shoving his hands into the back pockets of his jeans, Dobbo turned back around to Rachel, who had removed her coat and wrapped Eve's shoulders in it.

She glanced up at him. "She's gone into shock, I think. She's shivering. What the fucking hell has gone on?"

She'd sent Eve the odd e-mail from Japan but hadn't thought much of it when she hadn't heard back, knowing she was spending Christmas with her mum and Billy.

Dobbo crouched back down next to the girls and rubbed a hand down Eve's back, ignoring the question with no idea how to answer it. "We need to move her from the crowds. That guy is gonna come back with a glass of water and he's gonna want her out of the way."

"Well she can't fucking walk in this state, Dobson."

"Whoa! Okay, stressy. I never suggested that she should. I'll carry her."

Rachel snorted. "Not much chance of that, matey. I'm lucky she's even letting me hold her, never mind you."

He rolled his eyes and shook his head as he bent down and scooped Eve from the floor. He'd promised Billy that he wouldn't let anything happen to her, and he was damn sure he would do everything he could to keep that promise.

CHAPTER
thirty

Couldn't Care Less — The Cardigans

SITTING IN THE back of Dobson's car an hour later, Eve stared blankly out of the window, her finger and thumb rubbing the smooth silver of the heart that hung around her neck. "I don't know how to make myself work without him."

Rachel inhaled deeply, moving Eve's hair from her face and choking back a lump in her throat that was aching for her friend. She squeezed her eyes shut. "You will, dude… I promise. You will."

After a minute or two, Eve moved her hand slowly to her bag that she held tightly, opening it and extracting the envelope. She moved her eyes across her name that was scrawled on the front and, carefully pulling at the seal, she took the note out and unfolded it, the tears she knew would fall already lining up ready to do their thing.

My beautiful girl
You are my heart. You always have been, and I love you. Know

this before you read on.

Life has a funny way of throwing things at you that you think you can't handle. You are living proof of that. Look at you... You are so strong, baby—the strongest person I have ever known—and I know you can do this. You have so much sparkle and so much to give.

I'm not strong like you. I am dealing with some damn heavy shit, too, and I am really struggling. I've never allowed myself to grieve. I've carried the pain of others for so many years, always reliable, always trustworthy, but I am grieving now. For lost love, for lost time... for a father I never really knew and a mother I barely remember knowing. And it's too late. It's too late to fight for any of it because they're gone. I can't get it back, and I don't know how to process that right now. I don't know where I belong or where I fit.

I'm so sorry, baby. I can't stay and help to fix you. I can't carry you and keep you safe because I am on my fucking knees. I am too broken, and I need to find out who I am. I need to search for the other half of Billy Taylor, the one who can give and love completely.

I have been given the opportunity to go gig with a band, so I am off to "do music", just like you said.

But I don't want you to follow my heart, too. I don't want you to try to find me because you won't get better with me around. I hurt too much. I want you to stay and heal, go and build bridges with your mum. Cherish her. She only ever loved you and wanted to protect you.

Finish your degree, and, well, who knows? Somewhere in the middle, our mended hearts might follow each other again.

Go scatter some elephants, baby . . . I'll never forget

I love you,

Billy x

Folding it neatly, she slipped it back inside her bag, the tears of her broken heart rolling freely and silently.

She had known their relationship had become unhealthy, but she wasn't whole without him. Some days she'd wanted to scratch his skin off so she could climb inside him just to get closer—ironic, given the need to get as far away from him as possible in the beginning.

They'd existed, wrapped up in each other's bodies, hoping to discover each other's souls again, and now, he'd slipped out of her reach and she'd been powerless to stop it.

A pain and a piercing screaming rattled around her head that was empty aside from sadness and darkness, and where there had been nothing but love and hope for a better future for her, there was now only fear.

To be continued...

AUTHOR'S
note

Housing Elephants deals with real life issues. If you or anyone you know or love is dealing with grief, loss, mental health issues or alcohol-related problems, I urge you to reach out, either by speaking to a family member, a close friend or colleague, or by accessing the wonderful charities and organisations that are set up to give the kind of support that you or they deserve.

acknowledgements

To H. my editor, friend and bestest knobhead... I'm not sure I need to spell it out, but I appreciate you so, so much. Thank you for everything you have done for this book, and everything
you continue to do. Love you, init.

To Leanne, my formatter... You have the patience of a saint, and I cannot thank you enough for making the inside of my re-branded first book baby so, so beautiful!
You're stuck with me now! Sorry!

To my Nellies... You rock. My reader group, the E.L.Jelephant House, where you all reside is literally my safe place in the crazy world of social media. I have made genuine friendships with so many of you, and if I had space, I would thank you all individually. Thank you for championing me, thank you for pushing me, thank you for wanting my work so badly that you resort to bullying.
I love you all hard! Don't ever leave me!

*To Jo, my childhood friend...*You gave your time for nothing to share your expertise so that the tricky scene I wrote was accurate and life-like. Thank you, my lovely. I love you and I miss you.

*To my mot...*Love you, mate.

*To my boys...*You let me write, never nagging at me for being plugged into my headphones, never begrudging me the time spent working towards my dream.
Ben, you are always my inspiration. You have grown into such a caring, funny and intelligent young man and I am so very proud of you. You make me laugh every day and I am so blessed that you are mine. I love you more than...
Steve, as much as you pretend not to be interested, I know your quiet confidence in my ability to do this. I love that you understood my need to have it completed before you read it—not that you have yet! This had to be something I did for myself, without asking for your help. I love you so very muchly.

*To my Penguin...*Miss you, dude, and love you somethin' fierce.

*And finally, to my readers...*You're the ones who will make this a dream come true for me. Thank you for investing your money and time in my words. I do hope you enjoy it.
Love, ELJ x

MORE FROM
eleanor lloyd-jones

Whispers From The East
www.books2read.com/WFTE

Beauty Of A Monster - Part One: Seduction
www.books2read.com/BOAM

Beauty Of A Monster - Part Two: Redemption
www.books2read.com/BOAM2

Too Good Girl
http://www.books2read.com/TGG

Coming Soon from Eleanor Lloyd-Jones

Scattering Elephants: Book Two in the Follow Your
Heart Duet

We Did It For Love

ABOUT
the author

Eleanor Lloyd-Jones is and always has been a perpetual daydreamer. A mum of one and a full-time primary school teacher, she spins plates and chases her tail in order that she can live out the dream she has had since being a little girl: to write stories.

Like lots of indie authors, her ambition is to hit the big time, make all the lists and have some hot-shot movie producer pick up one of her books and turn it into the next blockbuster so she can write for a living. Until that happens, she is content to type away, bringing her imagination to life in the hopes that the people who read her words get some sort of enjoyment out of them and love her characters as much as she does.

Printed in Great Britain
by Amazon

84161867R00226